A DREAM OF ARMAGEDDON

H.G. WELLS

A DREAM OF ARMAGEDDON

THE COMPLETE SUPERNATURAL TALES

FALL RIVER PRESS

Originally published as
The Man Who Could Work Miracles:
The Supernatural Tales of H.G. Wells
© 2006 by Tartarus Press

This 2009 edition published by Fall River Press

Acknowledgments appear on page 365.

Fall River Press
122 Fifth Avenue
New York, NY 10011

ISBN: 978-1-4351-1583-5

Printed and bound in the United States of America

1 3 5 7 9 10 8 6 4 2

CONTENTS

INTRODUCTION

by Brian Stableford

WITH only a handful of exceptions, H.G. Wells's short stories belong to a particular and limited phase of the evolution of popular fiction, which lasted from 1891 until 1906 or thereabouts, and whose nature and fate Wells was one of the first observers to recognise. By the time he wrote an introduction to the eclectic selection *The Country of the Blind and Other Stories* in 1911—the same year in which he published his final grab-bag of reprints in the U.S. as *The Door in the Wall and Other Stories*—he was already looking back on that phase as a distant prospect, not merely in his own career but in the history of short fiction.

In that introduction Wells described the sudden emergence of a new fleet of markets for short fiction in the 1890s, as a result of the founding of a large number of new magazines of various kinds, with the result that 'no short story of the slightest distinction went for long unrecognised'. There was still a relative abundance of popular magazines in 1911—although their number was soon to be severely trimmed by the Great War—but the nature of the marketplace had shifted considerably. Wells observed that he made his own prolific contributions when 'the sixpenny popular magazines had still to deaden down the conception of what a short story might be to the imaginative limitation of the common reader—and a maximum length of six thousand words'. He knew how fortunate he was to have made his own debut in a period when the magazines were still in their experimental phase, willing to try anything, and how fortunate he also was to have been able to move on once their editors had calculated the lowest common denominator of their audience response—exactly the kind of story guaranteed to please most of the readers most of the time—and had no further need or desire to try anything unusual.

When Wells rewrote his introduction to *The Country of the Blind and Other Stories* as an introduction to the Golden Cockerel Press edition of a revised version of *The Country of the Blind* in 1939 he was in a more jaundiced mood, almost regretful of the fact that he had ever written the imaginative fiction that brought him his first literary success, or of the fact that it had coloured his subsequent reputation to such a great extent. In that revised essay he dismissed most of his early fiction as mere hackwork—'I turned out tale after tale like a baker making fruit tarts'—but again he represented his eventual defection from that field of play as a failure of the marketplace, which had become far too rigid in its notion of what a short story should contain and how it ought to be formulated to be hospitable to the work of a man who had begun 'to write stories to please myself and to satisfy the new and more exacting standards I had admitted to my writing-desk'— by which he meant, of course, stories like 'The Country of the Blind'.

The bulk of the stories in this present collection belong to these two phases of Well's career: the productive phase—which was, in spite of his own subsequent remarks, more an experimental phase than one of mere commercial hackwork—and the stubborn phase, in which he wrote much less but with more personal aims and higher standards of artistry in mind. Because it is a showcase collection of supernatural stories, however, it also includes stories from two other phases in his career, which would be impossible to illustrate so well in a collection of any other sort: the phase in which he first set out to write short fiction, some years before he was able to sell such work, and the belated phase in which he sometimes used the short story format almost as a despairing gesture, to express some frustrating idea that he needed to get off his chest.

☙

The two stories that Wells published in the November-December 1888 and December 1888-January 1889 issues of *The Science Schools Journal*, 'The Devotee of Art' and 'Walcote', are quite different from anything else he wrote, and show markedly different influences and intentions. Although Wells had founded the journal in question, he was no longer its editor by then. The contributions he had made to the magazine while he was in sole charge had all been speculative articles, save for the aborted serial 'The Chronic Argonauts', which had not yet succeeded in adapting its expository essay on the possible future of life on Earth to a suitable fictional frame-narrative. For Wells, at that time, there was still an unbridgeable gulf between science and fiction, even though the principal literary model for both 'The Devotee of Art' and 'Walcote' is clearly Edgar Allan Poe, who had made numerous experiments of his own in trying to bridge that gap.

These two early stories are florid moral tales, which focus intently on the inner workings of guilt, using fanciful devices to externalise the interior pressures of conscience—although each story stops one significant step short of taking that externalising process to the point of an actual supernatural manifestation, both making use of conventional narrative get-out-of-jail-free cards that no longer work to their advantage. What is remarkable about the stories, in long retrospect, is their stylistic decoration: their conscientious deployment of decadent flourishes and motifs.

'The Devotee of Art' goes so far as to suggest that its hallucinating protagonist might have overdosed on Swinburne—a poet conspicuous by his absence from the long list of contemporary poets Wells claimed in his 1934 autobiography to have read enthusiastically in 1887-88, while dabbling in versification himself. The two versions of the introduction cited previously both admit that the new magazines that fascinated him most in the 1890s were not those to which he made his own most substantial contributions but W.E. Henley's *National Observer*—regarded as a haven of English decadent style before Henley abruptly distanced himself from the term the day after Oscar Wilde's conviction—and John Lane's *Yellow Book*. Wells always spoke kindly, too, of Frank Harris—another editor of the same stripe—who was the first to pay him real money for an article in the *Fortnightly Review*. He also let slip in his autobiography that his first attempt at a novel was a lurid melodrama akin to Eugene Sue's *The Mysteries of Paris*, which suggests that he was aware of the French tradition of popular fiction that had likewise taken Poe to its bosom.

Wells' early exploits as a professional writer for pay were, however, far from Poesque; they consisted of contributions to the queries columns of *Tit-Bits, Answers* and *Pearson's Weekly*, which paid half a crown a time—double if one could pull off the trick of successfully submitting a printworthy question to which one then supplied the answer. He moved on from that to writing articles of the same speculative sort that he had published in his own issues of *The*

Science Schools Journal, mostly for *The Pall Mall Budget*, and actually had to be cajoled by the editor to begin contributing short stories to that periodical. He began with anecdotal pieces and mildly offbeat crime stories, those being the common currency of the period, but soon moved on to exploit the same kinds of ideas that he was using in his articles, albeit less adventurously a first.

'The Flowering of the Strange Orchid'—published nearly six years after 'Walcote'—is one of several nineteenth-century tales of human encounters with a bloodthirsty plant, although it became the new prototype for many subsequent endeavours in that vein. 'The Lord of the Dynamos', which followed hot on the heels of 'The Flowering of the Strange Orchid' in *The Pall Mall Budget*, is more striking in its novelty, and is one of the earliest stories that invites consideration as a thoroughly *Wellsian* piece of work. The stylistic affectations and standardised narrative apparatus of his earlier works have been abandoned here; he is now striving to be distinctive in his use of an idea, and the 'supernatural' component of the story remains internalised, giving rise to action via the workings of exotic psychology rather than manifesting itself in any paranormal fashion.

At this point in his career, Wells might conceivably have given up on supernatural fiction entirely, preferring to draw his monsters from the fringes of the science-fictional imagination or locating them within abnormal psychology, in a thoroughly modern manner. He did not do so, however. Significantly, for much of his career, he insisted on lumping together his scientific romances with supernatural novels in lists of his previous publications under the rubric 'Fantastic and Imaginative Romances'—but this is not to say that he made no distinction between works like *The Time Machine* and *The First Men in the Moon* on the one hand and *The Wonderful Visit* and *The Sea Lady* on the other. He chose to emphasise the similarities rather than the differences because he recognised that all imaginative fiction relied on facilitating devices of dubious rational plausibility. He knew full well that the time machine and Cavorite were arbitrary inventions, mere narrative devices used as plot-levers much as an angel or a mermaid might be employed—but he did not use such levers to the same narrative ends, and in the short supernatural fiction he produced in the late 1890s one can see him exploring, with considerable enterprise, exactly what kind of psychological plausibility supernatural motifs might still have, even in a world where they could no longer be taken seriously.

☙

There is an obvious relationship between 'The Temptation of Harringay' and 'The Devotee of Art', not merely in its theme but in its continuation of beginnings made by Poe, but its anti-hero is certainly not steeped in Swinburne. The story is a non-stereotypical *conte cruel*, cleverly sharpened by the simultaneous evocation of comedy and horror—whose sum, in this case and many subsequent ones, is a particular kind of black irony tinged with contempt as well as flippancy. Although the proportions of that mix were varied in his later works in the same vein, its basic components remained much the same, and when he deployed them skilfully the recipe always produced that distinctive Wellsian taste.

'The Moth' and 'Pollock and the Porroh Man' are delusional fantasies of a very similar stripe to 'The Temptation of Harringay', stressing the element of psychological horror, but 'Under the Knife' adds a significant extra twist. The story first extrapolates what sets out to be a conventional posthumous fantasy into a cosmic vision reminiscent of Poe's 'Mesmeric Revelation' and then refuses point-blank to dissolve the grandeur of that vision in the acid-bath of *conte cruel* irony, preferring a more uplifting note of closure.

The trajectory tested in 'Under the Knife' was followed again, albeit in a more sober and restrained fashion, in 'The Plattner Story'— of which Wells thought highly enough to select it as the title-story of his second collection. Although the story makes use of a calculated ambiguity that has become almost as clichéd as the literary dream, explicitly informing the reader that the experience described might be no more than a hallucination while simultaneously providing 'objective' evidence that *something* very odd occurred, the effect of the story is not at all dependent on that framing contrivance; here, as in his early scientific romances, Wells is moving from the cultivation of narrative effect for its own sake into the alluring realm of the *conte philosophique*.

Like Voltaire, the pioneer of that kind of short story, Wells was to find supernatural apparatus very convenient in providing facilitating devices for his carefully-guided flights of fancy, but he was also to make much more prolific and productive use of his own recipe for the manufacture of *contes cruels*. 'The Red Room' and 'The Story of the

Late Mr Elvesham' both re-examine classic supernatural story motifs in this hybrid fashion, while 'The Apple' exaggerates the components of contempt and flippancy in producing a kind of inversion of 'Under the Knife', in which the opportunity of visionary enlightenment is ironically refused—a motif that was to recur in Wells's subsequent work with increasing frequency and intensity as his frustration with the unwillingness of his fellow men to share his own visions of future possibility and necessity increased inexorably.

'The Crystal Egg' returned to visionary fantasy of a relatively modest sort, preferring a science-fictional resolution in order to lend authority to the visionary revelation, which is one of several contrasted accounts he gave, in various formats, of life on Mars. 'The Presence by the Fire' similarly develops the notion of an exotic optical effect, but is unusually sentimental—at least by Wells's unusually exacting standards —in allowing the delusion to bring a measure of consolation along with its bitter irony. Wells was by no means incapable of sentimentality, of course—his nostalgic social comedies, such as *Kipps* and *The History of Mr Polly*, are abundantly supplied with it—but it is something he usually confined to the sphere of the depressingly quotidian. There is, however, a similar leavening of sentimentality in the story in which Wells first took his enterprising combination of the *conte philosophique* and his own brand of the *conte cruel* to a new and magnificent extreme: 'The Man Who Could Work Miracles'.

'The Man Who Could Work Miracles' is an archetypal item of Wellsiana, and a key example of the magnificent things that could be done with the short story in this hectic phase of its evolution. The combination of ironic comedy and visionary extravagance is here allowed free rein, unconstrained by any excessively-dutiful suggestion that it might all have been a dream. The 'what if. . . ?' component of the story is allowed to accelerate uninhibitedly to its perversely logical end-point, and the closure of the story is achieved without the deflationary effect that is a customary, if not compulsory, element of the *conte cruel* framework. It was, however, almost the last endeavour of its kind; it may well have been the writing of this *tour de force* that convinced Wells that he ought to give up trying to adapt his ambitions to the increasingly narrow demands of the magazine marketplace, whose gatekeepers were already becoming rather pusillanimous, even though the formula of the magazine story would not be set in mundane stone for a few years yet.

The vast majority of the *contes philosophiques* that he produced thereafter were planned and executed as novels; although they were often less than wholly satisfactory in that kind of framework, they were easier to publish. The modern reader might assume that they were also more lucrative, but that is not necessarily so; writers of the 1920s who did adapt their fiction to the formularistic requirements of advertising-supported 'slick magazines', or even to the equally-formularistic requirements of U.S. pulps, could often make far more money from short fiction than books. Wells made the bulk of his own income after the turn of the century from journalism rather than books, and his quasi-novelistic *contes philosophiques* were probably the least successful of his publications in volume form.

ભ

'The Stolen Body'—which might well have been written before 'The Man Who Could Work Miracles', although it reached print slightly later—was the last of Wells's conventional *contes cruels*. There was something of a gap before his next supernatural stories, 'A Vision of Judgment' and 'A Dream of Armageddon', which were written to a very different prospectus. These mocking religious fantasies, anticipate the 'sarcastic fantasies' he produced in some profusion in his later years, when the component of scathing contempt came very much to the fore in his narrative strategy, sometimes to the unfortunate exclusion of other literary values. Although there is an element of religious satire in 'The Man Who Could Work Miracles', it is not unduly brutal, but these two stories revel in their own inability to take themselves seriously in any but a jeering fashion. Wells was by no means done with earnest *contes philosophiques*, however; 'The New Accelerator' is one of his purest, well within the margin of science fiction in spite of the supernatural nature of its facilitating device.

'The Inexperienced Ghost' is a slighter story than most of Wells's *contes philosophiques*, and probably owes much of its popularity to the abrupt twist in its tail, but it also has an unusual charm by virtue of its oddly subdued and plaintive tone. Like 'The Red Room', it is a calculated revisitation of a classic theme, but in a very different mood. That quirkily reflective mood is reproduced to very similar effect in 'Mr Skelmersdale in Fairyland'—a story that would not benefit in the least from a climactic twist. 'The Truth About Pyecraft' retains it too;

although it probably does not seem to most readers to be revisiting familiar turf, it is not impossible that Wells had read R.D. Blackmore's *Tommy Upmore*, and was reassessing the theme of that uncommonly annoying fantasy novel from his own ideological perspective. 'The Magic Shop' is perhaps the most charming of this little subset of stories, because its nostalgic component seems so neatly appropriate; like 'The Inexperienced Ghost', it is often reprinted as a children's story

Another manifest change of literary gear separates 'The Magic Shop' from 'The Country of the Blind', the latter being a wholehearted excursion into allegory. It is probably more self-revealing than Wells knew when he first wrote it, although he had undoubtedly become hyperconscious of its personal significance when he rewrote it for the Golden Cockerel Press edition—a version that almost no one prefers to the original, whose *conte cruel* ending is far the more appropriate of the two variants. Like 'The Man Who Could Work Miracles', 'The Country of the Blind' is a masterpiece, which conjoins several threads in Wells's work in an unexpected but very satisfying fashion. Although it is a quintessential study in the anatomy of frustration, very different in ambition and direction from the four supernatural stories that preceded it, it does benefit from the curious kind of plaintiveness that the stories in that subset had explored and developed. It could easily have been an angrier and more brutal story than it is, but the deftness of its touch adds considerably to its effect.

Wells was not done with that curious plaintiveness, for he had yet to bring its into its clearest focus by making it the primary subject-matter of a story. He did that to quietly heart-rending effect in 'The Door in the Wall', a story that remains a personal favourite of many readers in whom its allegory strikes an emotional chord. It is a story that Wells could only have written at a relatively late stage in his career as a short story writer, redolent with a sense of farewell—indeed, one might more easily believe that he had written it a good deal later in his career as a whole, when he really was past the prime of his ambition and achievement. It can be regarded as his *adieu* to the short story form; he did not publish another for three years and all his work thereafter is by way of casual addenda. Several later items were included in *The Door in the Wall and Other Stories*, but they are all conscientiously mannered, stridently emphasising their own artificiality; they included the mock-allegorical items 'The Beautiful Suit', 'The Story of the Last Trump' and 'The Pearl of Love'.

'The Story of the Last Trump'—which returned to the same sarcastic vein as 'A Vision of Judgment' and 'A Dream of Armageddon' —was not published in a magazine, but as an admittedly-eccentric inclusion in the recklessly self-indulgent 'novel' *Boon*, from which the similarly mock-allegorical 'The Wild Asses of the Devil' is also taken. Wells noted in his introduction to the Golden Cockerel *Country of the Blind* that an American editor had rejected 'The Pearl of Love' with the comment that he had 'never seen such a story'—which Wells presumably took as a compliment, although it might be held to establish the narrowness of the editor's education. The story is, in fact, similar in style, tone and import to many of the exotic vignettes produced by conscientious members of the French Decadent Movement, but in 1925 it was a blatantly anachronistic presence in *The Strand Magazine*, where its appearance was a testament to Wells' reputation rather than editorial preference.

'The Queer Story of Brownlow's Newspaper' is not actually that odd, viewed as a dramatisation of the frustration of which Wells was then complaining on a regular basis, but its appearance in *The Strand* does qualify as a break in that periodical's editorial policy, which had become even more unadventurous by 1932. 'Answer to Prayer' was an even odder presence in the *New Statesman*, and its off-hand alloy of irony and contempt does little credit to its author's former artistry, although it is very similar in its outlook and manner to the longer sarcastic fantasies that he produce in some profusion in its wake.

ᘒ

There is a sense in which Wells's supernatural fiction, seen in sum, is unlikely to seem central to the tradition to the *aficionado* of such fiction, by virtue of its obvious reluctance to take supernatural motifs seriously *in themselves*. He does, however, use such devices to very serious purposes as well as playfully—and, as in his pioneering science fiction, it is the deft manner in which he often combines the serious and the playful that gives his work a distinctive quality and a keen edge. He was one of the most significant descendants of Voltaire in his recruitment of supernatural devices to the services of the *conte philosophique*, but the fact that he wrote most of his fiction in a professional spirit, orientated towards a particular marketplace, encouraged him to give it a smooth frankness that few other modern neo-Voltaireans were able to deploy.

Although Wells's Voltairean ambitions eventually left him high and dry when the level of the marketplace sank into stagnancy, the necessity of making his work marketable while the popular magazines were still in their experimental phase allowed him to build bridges of a kind whose construction became much more difficult thereafter for some four decades. It was not until the 1950s that popular market space was permanently reopened to deft combinations of the *conte cruel* and the *conte philosophique*, often leavened with a joyous flippancy and a curious plaintiveness not dissimilar to Wells's, in such venues as *The Magazine of Fantasy and Science Fiction*.

Work of this general sort is much more familiar to us nowadays, numerous writers having fallen into the habit of repeatedly crossing the borders between supernatural fiction and science fiction, with healthy synergistic effects, in the second half of the twentieth century —notable examples include Fritz Leiber, L. Sprague de Camp, Poul Anderson and James Morrow. All those writers, and many others, have carried forward conscientiously-variegated 'Wellsian' projects with renewed energy and considerable skill, but their inter-generic work has been historically disconnected from its foundations by the intervention of stringently stereotyped patterns of short fiction in the first half of the twentieth century. This showcase collection of Wells's supernatural fiction will permit its readers to discern the broad extent to which modern philosophical fantasy rests on precedents laid by Wells, and will allow his landmark works in that vein—which all literate people ought to have read at least once—to be set within a more complex web of steadily-evolving work.

THE DEVOTEE OF ART*

ALEC had heard his wife playing, and had thrown down his brushes and come to the chair beside the old-fashioned square piano. It was a wide, velvet-covered arm-chair, in which he had perforce to clasp his hands behind his head and lounge luxuriously if he meant to sit in it at all—a chair not easily to be sat in without perfect easiness, a chair with the embrace of Morpheus and the inspiration of the herb Papaver.

Isabel was playing very sweetly; she played by feeling as well as touch; something of Wagner's it was, something as uncertain and vari-able, and as invariably attractive as life itself. To listen—in that arm-chair—was like hearing the Sirens; existence became—'spiritualised,' the word is—suddenly emancipated from all necessary cares and courses.

Alec had been tormenting his brain all day with the expression of a curiously obdurate face, feeling an idea growing frayed and colour-less, like a captured butterfly, as he attempted to fix what beauty it had for the common eye; and the escape from technique was delicious. He slipped away from realities gladly, and wandered—no longer mortal man, but immortal soul again—in the realms of the imagination, deal-ing with realities boldly as became a deathless spirit. He had been working all day to develop his conception of a knightly vigil; and as Isabel played andante, the vision the music inspired him with was full of violet shadows in mysterious temples, solitary pink flames before ghostly altars, tenebrous gleamings, white robed figures faintly seen, prayer and awe—all very vague indeed, but all exceedingly beautiful. Presently, however, her white hands passed into swift allegro and his fancies grew insensibly more animated. Into his shadowy dim aisles processions came marching, torchlight banished the dimness and blazed paler into day, figures flowed in more and more, more and more the scene grew crowded, dignified priests and warriors grew

* See later revised version of this story, 'The Temptation of Harringay'.

1

more numerous, younger, more active, swarming and overflowing until temples, altars, processions, all order and stability vanished in a mazy dance of exultant figures, knights and dames, shepherds and shepherd-esses, clowns, grotesques, Punchinellos, corphyrées, humanity, finally danced under by a whirl of ideal creations, imps, gnomes, fairies, satyrs, hamadryads, harpies, and oreads. Faster and faster they danced in intricate kaleidoscopic figures. Suddenly through them all, like the news of a death in a ball-room, passed a shudder, a jar,—blackness rapt them away!—the music had stopped.

'Alec,' said Isabel, 'you are going to sleep; you distinctly snored.'

'My dear girl! nothing could have been further from my thoughts. I was just shutting my eyes to enjoy the music, and thinking over a little problem in composition.' He felt quite hurt.

Isabel turned back to the piano, and Alec, to avoid a repetition of this unjust misconception—she was always thinking him sleepy or unwell when reverie engaged him—opened his eyes as wide as possible and fixed them unblinkingly on her face.

'My dear, Alec, don't look like that! Are you ill? Or is there any-thing wrong with my hair?'

Isabel had curly dark brown hair, that dark brown which gleams golden in a slanting light. It was a little out (so Isabel called it) that night, and there were ever so many little misty gold curves and wreaths fading away round her head—the amber-shaded lamp beside her gave her quite a halo of them.

'Only Sylphs, dear Belinda,' said Alec, lazily, suppressing some annoyance. 'Does my look disturb you?'

Isabel considered as she went on playing. 'I don't want you to stare like a hairdresser's wig block,' she said judicially; 'but you may *look* at me if you like.'

So Alec went on looking, with greatly subdued violence, however, at the glory-surrounded head and the shadowed face.

'It was a sweet face,' Alec meditated, 'soft lined, tender-looking; one of those pale faces with dark eyes that are not perhaps beautiful but infinitely capable of beautiful expressions, a face never wearisome while there is life, and yet—.' Alec loved his wife very greatly—more by far than he loved himself or any other loveable being, and yet—. There was this little 'and yet—,' this one fatal objection, very much present in Alec's mind just then, suggested by the slight vulgarity of those few words of his wife to begin with, and fostered perhaps by the subdued discontent of the air that now prevailed in the music: Isabel, he thought, was a force in life antagonistic to art.

Alec was an artist not only by choice of *metir,* but of spiritual compulsion. So he fancied, and just then was thinking that his supreme love was not to be found in that warmly illuminated room, but in the dim-lit studio beyond; that for one wedded to eternal Art, marriage was a sad mistake, even, indeed, a sort of bigamy. He had been reading, as the omniscient reader will observe, that child of fancy, Algernon Swinburne; and that and Isabel's pathetic transitions from phantasies to snores, and from sylph-surrounded heads to hairdressers' wig blocks, and the melancholy music—it was really melancholy now—all worked together. It was, in fact, one of those painful moments of domestic dissatisfaction not uncommon to recently-married young men who are moderately clever and immoderately ambitious—especially after days passed in badly arranged and unsuccessful work. The theory of the wife being an earthly clog is so soothing to self love. *Ars longa vita brevis,* he thought, not a new or original idea, but one remembered from copybook learning; and here he, the artist, was actually making his *vita brevior* by becoming domesticated! Among other equally poignant reminders, Milton's words, 'and that one talent which is death to hide,' came into his mind. Death! the loss of immortality! were the appointed moments of probation indeed gliding inevitably by? Perish the thought! At that moment he seemed to himself—the music and the easy chair inspiring another Merlin in the spell of another Vivien; he, the potential creator of spell-beautiful paintings, spending his moments, his hours, pleasing and being pleased by a wife who compared *him* to a hairdresser's wigblock.

It was his duty to his supreme mistress, Art, not to permit this a moment longer. He would return to his proper sphere. His act was swifter than his resolution, although that supervened very suddenly on his wandering discontents.

He did not venture to look round at Isabel as he rose and walked straight into his studio, but as he closed the door he heard that the music ceased abruptly and that her dress rustled.

He lit the white-burning Solar lamp and turned it towards his picture.

Just then he heard the door behind him creak, and turning, saw it pushed open very softly, and Isabel, her face full of solicitude, appear looking in. Probably she fancied he was ill. When, however, his sudden

3

asperity of expression became evident, she disappeared, the door closing noiselessly.

It was an Italian model he had been troubled about. The fellow had fine white features, mobile lips, and liquid eyes; he was to be the knight keeping vigil. When Alec had first seen him he had been struck merely by the possibilities of looking impassioned which this young man possessed. He was fit to go into a picture quite unmodified, 'Kneel. Look devout,' he would have to say, paint him forthwith, and the thing would be done. But that day as he had worked at his knight's features he had been surprised and annoyed to find a curious phenomenon appearing through his efforts. Try as he would, copy with never so much painful accuracy the adolescent countenance before him, a curious sinister expression *would* come somehow upon the canvas, a look of age, and instead of devotion, furtive ridicule. He could not understand it—had been glad to leave patching it to hear his wife's playing. Now, this evening, disregarding subtleties of tint, he would have another try, wrestle with and overcome this difficulty.

'Some little inaccuracy does it,' he said; 'eyebrows probably too oblique,'—therewith turning the white light full upon his work and taking up palette and brushes.

The face on the canvas certainly seemed animated by a spirit of its own. Where the expression of diablerie came in he found impossible to discover. Experiment was necessary. The eyebrows—it could scarcely be the eyebrows? But he altered them. No, that was no better; in fact, if anything, a trifle more satanic. The corner of the mouth? Pah! more than ever a Mephistophilesian leer—and now, re-touched, it is ominously grim. The eye then? Catastrophe! he had filled his brush with vermilion instead of brown, and yet he had felt sure it was brown! The eye seemed now to have rolled in its socket, glowing on him an eye of fire. In a flash of passion he struck the brush full of bright red athwart the picture; and then a very curious thing, a very strange thing indeed, occurred—if it *did* occur.

The diabolified Italian before him shut both his eyes, pursed his mouth, and wiped the colour off his face with his hand!

Then the *red eye* opened again and the face smiled. 'That was rather hasty of you,' it said.

Curiously enough, Alec did not feel frightened or very much astonished. Perhaps he was too much exasperated. 'Why do you keep moving about then,' he said, 'making faces and all that, sneering and squinting while I am painting you?'

'I don't,' said the picture.

'You *do,*' said Alec.

'It's yourself,' said the picture.

'It's *not* myself,' said Alec.

'It *is* yourself,' said the picture. 'No! don't go hitting me with paint again, because it's true. You have been trying to *fluke* an expression on my face all day. Really you haven't an idea what your picture ought to look like.'

'I have,' said Alec.

'You have *not,*' contradicted the picture; 'you *never* have with your pictures. You always start with the vaguest presentiment of what you are going to do; it is to be something beautiful—you are sure of that—and devout, perhaps, or tragic; but beyond that it is all experiment and chance. My dear fellow! you don't surely think you can paint a picture like that?'

Alec felt there was a lot of truth in all this. 'What am I to do then?'

'Get an inspiration.'

'But I thought this was an inspiration.'

'Inspiration,' sneered the sardonic figure; 'a fancy that came from your seeing an organ-grinder looking up at a window! Vigil! ha, ha!'

Alec groaned. 'Too true! I am married. The days of inspiration are past. Oh, to undo it! I would give anything in life for a return of inspiration, for a release from the humdrum life of small domesticities that is beginning. I—who would have given my soul to art!'

'As you wish,' said the figure, and then everything was still.

'Eh!' cried Alec, suddenly startled out of his cool acceptance of this phenomenon by a swift, uncomfortable realisation.

'Did you speak?' he said, after a pause.

'I say—Vezetti—*or*—whoever you are, did you say anything?'

In the stillness he could hear his own heart beating. The picture was motionless and voiceless, but the *red eye* glowed like a coal.

Very slowly he approached, and passed his hand over the paint. Paint, sure enough—unsophisticated paint. He must have been dreaming; he had read plenty of scientific matter about hallucinations and so forth, and so he was not too horribly frightened; still—. He felt the red eye, but that was perfectly cool.

'Do you want to say anything more?' asked Alec, deliberately jumbling together all the colours on his palette; 'because, if not—'

Dab, dab, dab, he proceeded to paint out this disagreeably outspoken creation as quickly as he could. He had some difficulty in getting out the red eye; it seemed to glow through the coatings he laid over it. At last, however, with what seemed like a quietly ironical wink, it disappeared.

Smear, smudge, wriggle, every stroke of the obnoxious figure was presently hidden. With a feeling of relief Alec drew back from the canvas. 'I am a superstitious fellow,' he was thinking dubiously, as he surveyed the wreck, when suddenly some lines in his aimless smearing caught his eye. 'By Jove!' he exclaimed, 'there's an idea there!' He framed his eyes with his hands.

He heard a light tapping at the door. It was his wife. Presently the door opened, but he did not turn towards her. 'Alec,' she said, 'do you know the time?' She received no answer. 'It is nearly midnight, Alec.' Still no answer. 'Are you going to paint all night, Alec?'

'Oh! yes! yes!' he answered, without turning, in a tone that made it almost a curse; and when with a faint twinge of compunction he looked round, she had gone away.

It was really a splendid idea; splendid idea is not enough; it was almost as if a divine revelation had come to Alec. The curves above suggested the intersecting arching of the roof; that smear below, the knight keeping vigil; and between, that white space, what he had been feeling for all along, a group, the watching spirits of Chivalry, Generosity, Purity, and Religion. Beautiful in form and colour, definite as bodily sight, the conception had come to him. In another minute he was frantically preparing colours. Morning should see the work under way.

He was working feverishly in the dead of night when his wife's finger-nails tapped at his studio door again. As he stepped back to get a view of his work he saw her standing in her white nightdress in the doorway. 'Alec,' she said, 'it is four o'clock. You will make yourself ill.'

'Go away,' Alec answered roughly, and as her footsteps slipped along the passage he went to the door and, slamming, locked it. He thought he heard her cry, but just then his eye caught the growing picture and he forgot everything else.

6

When the pale daylight came streaming into the room to show the yellow in his Solar lamp, Alec was still working in frantic haste. The great masses of the picture were blocked in; already it was beautiful.

What was that? A rapping at the door. 'Come in.' The door is locked however. With his eyes on his picture he opens it, and hears the voice of Lizzie, the little serving maid.

'Oh, if you please, sir, missus sent me to say as she's ill, and will you come to see her.'

'Ill?' said Alec, walking up to the picture and touching in some purple.

'She slipped upon the stairs, sir, last night, and her side and back are just dreffle painful this morning, sir.'

'This moonlit window is supreme,' said Alec, absently painting. 'Ah—Lizzie!'

'Yessir.'

'Fetch me some coffee and bread and butter;' and quite forgetful of his wife's illness—news, indeed, that he imperfectly heard—he goes on with his great idea of expressing the profound stillness round the watching knight by metameric vertical praying figures in the windows and on the monuments. It was a real, an undeniable inspiration which had come to him at last. Previously he thought his idea had been as spiritless almost as that extraordinary painting of the same subject saved up for an ill-starred posterity in the Chantrey Room, South Kensington. Now, in richness of accessories and colour it was worthy of Titian; in harmony of line, of Leighton or Raphael. This idea was the morning star of his fame. Work, work, work, a fortnight, perhaps, or three weeks, and then—the dawn of immortality!

The hours seemed to fly by as the masterpiece grew slowly into beauty. As it grew, all possibilities of fatigue seemed to pass away from him—he felt neither hunger nor thirst. As it grew, it entranced him more and more; fainter and fainter outward impressions came to him. Some indistinct memories of various people interrupting him, saying stupid irrelevant things about his wife being ill and what not, of the lamp being lit again, and presently going out amid a stream of red sparks up the chimney, of his having to rave the house down to get it refilled, various people trying insanely to quiet him, of the clock having stopped, and of sleeping by snatches in his clothes at the foot of the easel. But all these impressions were faint and intermingled, more like the swift imperfections of a dream than real occurrences. The one consequent idea, the one grand organic growth, was the Great Picture. Ever more beautiful, nearer and nearer to perfection it grew.

It was sublime, this flawless creating under his inspired fingers. Days slipped by unheeded; thrice the Solar lamp had flickered out. Alec's life would have been altogether supreme had it not been for the faint but persistent intimations of evil to his wife, and for the reminiscences of the figure with the *red eye* that came to disturb his snatches of slumber. These things imported a vague uneasiness into the ecstatic dream of pure art he was living.

'Your wife is dangerously ill; her fall has injured her internally. She may be dying.'

'Eh! What! Is it you?'

It was his wife's mother, and behind her the doctor. They were looking at him with a peculiar dread in their eyes. But he did not mind that. Everyone had been odd these last few days.

'She is dying,' the Doctor said, solemnly.

'Dying is she? Who did you say?' He went up to the picture again, touching it fondly.

'Your wife.'

'My wife—Doctor! what's the day of the month?'

'The Vigil. Don't go away, Doctor, without seeing my picture. What did you say the date?'

'Eh! Then there's—yes, just time for the Academy!'

Presently he was standing on the landing bawling, 'Lizzie!'

'In the name of heaven, man, be quiet! Do you want to commit murder?'

'Murder! Nonsense! I want a cab. The Vigil is finished!'

The precious picture! He must carry the canvas down in his own arms. How hushed the house was. The two servants stood in the background in the hall with a look of profound awe on their faces. The triumph of accomplishment is already beginning. Evidently they know *now* that he is a genius. All the world will know that soon.

As he enters the cab the Doctor appears at the door with a white face, comes down the steps and clutches his arm, saying something.

'You idiot! Leave go my arm, will you?'

Then the cab is rumbling on its way to Burlington House. Alec, with the picture on his knees, regards it lovingly.

It is very beautiful, but the light is dim. Presently it seems as if— yes, the light is shimmering through; the oiled canvas is growing transparent. It is really very strange; indeed, it is disagreeable. The work he has painted over shows; all the elemental smears and smudges are there. Then beneath that, the *thing* that those smears and smudges were to hide, *that* begins to grow perceptible. First, a red glimmer, then a faint outline. The sinister face, the ardent eye, become every moment more emphatic, seeming to have burnt out all the beauty he has worked for. Yes! it is the diabolical figure with the *red eye*, grinning exultantly; then, with a laugh, speaking:

'You see I am still here.'

'Who—what?' gasps Alec, and then, with lower jaw dropping, is silent.

'You are consecrated to art now. My friend, did you catch what the Doctor said to you?'

Smash!

All is indistinct for a little while after this; there is even a slight confusion about his identity. He sees himself lying with a crushed hand among the wreck of the cab, which has collided with a timber wagon. He can feel the pain and tingling of the wound, notices the great picture smashed hopelessly beside him, a gaping hole knocked through it, simulating curiously the shape of that weird red-eyed figure, and then the thought comes into his mind, *where is he?*

Then it is a hospital ward. The transition is abrupt; probably he has fainted. 'His hand is to be amputated,' one hard-featured nurse tells another in his hearing.

Hand and work gone together—the *ignis fatuus* of immortality has vanished. Bitterness and sorrow come upon him, and the need of refuge and comfort. With a great yearning, his thoughts rush back to his wife, her gentle touch, her tender eyes, her soothing voice. A frightful pang goes through him—the Doctor's words come to his mind 'In the name of decency come back—she is dead.' The nympholept is disenchanted. What has he cast away for the phantasm of praise? Then the full comprehension of his acts appears in all its hideousness. Oh, the vileness, the folly, the mad ingratitude of it! What could have impelled him, what demon possessed him?

'You were inspired.'

He turns his head. Beside the bed with folded arms and grimly smiling face, stands his creation, the red-eyed man.

He would scream, but he can find no voice; would spring away out of the bed, but motion is denied him.

'You wished to be inspired. Art and the domestic virtues jarred together. Your wife is dead; she had to die when you gave your soul to art.'

'Gave my soul to art?'

'Yes. Ha, hah! It is a pity your hand is smashed.'

And suddenly the red-eyed man had sat down on Alec's body and was glaring with his one fiery orb into his face. 'What did you make *me* for?' His breath was sulphurous, it made Alec's nostrils and mouth burn; and the arm too grew terribly painful again, as though a thousand red-hot needles were probing it.

'Oh, my wife! I am dying.'

'Don't call your wife; you are mine,' hissed the fiend close to his face.

'Listen!' he continued, with cruel deliberation. 'When a painter paints a form without a soul to it, without, that is, a clear intention expressed by it; when he paints aimlessly and recklessly in the hope of some spirit coming into it by accident—*sometimes a spirit comes.* I came so to yours, and you know the bargain I struck with you.'

It was horrible. The demon was as heavy as lead, and his breath burnt Alec's nostrils. But the most bitter of all the terrible things he was suffering, more bitter even than his fear and agony for himself, was his remorse for his wife. Sacrificed for art—what was art compared with her loving, protean sweetness? His short married life with her, a thousand things that he had forgotten, came rushing back to his memory with the bitter hopelessness of the Peri's glimpse of heaven.

'My wife,' he cried, 'my wife!'

The demon bent closely over him, hoarsely whispering, 'Gone, gone.' Then he stretched out something black over his eyes—a cloak, or was it a wing?

All was as black as futurity. A sense then of sinking swiftly down through a black, bottomless void. Could he be dying—or dead? It seemed as if he was being sucked down an infinite black funnel, an eternal maelstrom. Was there no hope? Suddenly through the awful silent space sounded his wife's voice—

'Alec!'

He looked up. She stood a measureless distance above, clothed in radiant light, looking down with infinite compassion and forgiveness upon him. He stretched out his arms, and would have cried to her, but his voice would not come to him. Then into his mind came the thought of that great gulf which separates those who have despised love from joy and beauty for ever.

Down, down, down.

'Alec!'

'Alec, wake up!'

He was sitting in the old velvet-covered arm-chair beside the piano, and his wife was bending over him. He blinked like an owl. Then he realised that he had pins and needles in his left arm. 'Have I been to sleep?' he asked.

'Yes, of course. When I saw you going to sleep again, I knew it was no good trying to prevent you, so I left off playing and went away. I should have thought, though, that Lizzie, dropping the tray downstairs, would have been sufficient to wake you.

'That,' said Alec, rubbing his eyes as he rose from the old arm-chair's embrace; 'why, that must have been the cab accident!'

'You are very affectionate tonight,' his wife said presently, as they went downstairs together.

'I am repenting, dearest, of a sin against you, of letting an idle dream come between us.'

And thereupon he was 'very affectionate' again.

WALCOTE

IT WAS Christmas Eve at Walcote. Most of the long saloon was in deep shadow, only here and there faint glimmers of reflected light showed where tables and vases and chairs and lounges were placed. A low screen stood before the wide fireplace. Ever and again the ruddy flicker from the spitting logs would leap and beckon over this, calling into visible existence a spectral faint room, the tall white caryatides of the great entrance, the bronze Satan that stood by the grand piano. As the unsteady shadows moved it seemed as if this latter figure stirred, waving its upraised arm, and as if the satyr caryatides smiled. A clock that ticked invisible in the dense obscurity above the mantel struck, in deep insistent tones, eleven. As the chime died away, the flickering flames sank behind the screen, a swift darkness swallowed the indistinct red room, the stirring Satan, the leering portals vanished in the black.

There was a stirring in a distant corner, a rustling noise, a sharp click, a faint clinking like the moving of a chain. Then all was silent, save the hissing and bubbling of the sap in the fire. One of the logs began a thin singing that speedily died away like the whistling of a frightened lad before the ominous stillness of the dark.

'Sss,' suddenly sounded in the corner—an echo of the fire.

'Sss.' 'Oh Edwin!'

The red tongues of fire leaped nervously up again. Dim and indistinct in one corner was a bird-like form on a perch, a gilt chain glittering faintly. The bronze nodded, the colossal distortion of its shadow on the wall crouched and leaped, the satyrs leered and blinked. The clock snapped up the seconds with grim destructive emphasis. Then unsteady footsteps could be heard without.

The thinnest golden line shone under the great door. The door swung open wide; two footmen appearing bearing silver candlesticks, other figures showing behind them.

As the light poured into the room and revealed all its elegances of silk and velvet and white and gold, it was as if the satyrs, ceasing to leer, grew breathless and motionless, as though the raised hand of Satan halted in anticipation. The beating of the clock was no longer audible, it seemed to be hushed in expectation. A figure of old Time, swaying his scythe, a remorseless, deliberate, a dreadful representation of the inevitable became visible above it. Everything was now real, distinct, and brilliant. On a fantastic perch in the corner a grey parrot blinked in the brightness.

The footmen advanced together, deposited the candles on a small round table, removed the screen, and drew the polished table nearer the fire. Three richly-dressed gentlemen followed.

'This is ever so much the best room, Edwin,' said one of these sauntering in with his hands in his pockets. He was a fair complexioned, ruddy-faced youth, splendidly attired in cherry-coloured satin and noble lace. He addressed his remark to one older, taller, darker, but as resplendent as himself. 'I don't see, cousin, why you should object to come here,' he continued, 'I think—'

'It doesn't matter now, Claude,' said the one he had addressed as cousin, recent annoyance and present discomfort very evident in his voice. 'A passing fancy struck me. It's all right now—all right now we are here. Vitzelley, where will you sit?'

'Vitzelley,' exclaimed the younger at the same moment, 'have you noticed our parrot before?—curious bird—dumb with grief ever since the—the apotheosis of cousin Harry.'

Vitzelley hesitated between them and answered both. 'There. No.' He was a small-eyed, keen-faced man, much older and far more soberly clad than his two companions.

'Yes,' repeated Claude, 'dumb with grief. Polly! pretty Polly,' approaching it. 'No answer, you see, Vitzelley.'

The parrot raised one claw and stretched its fleshy digits, clicked its beak, and inclined its head to his finger.

'Poll, scratchy Poll. I suppose, Vitzelley, you have heard some hundred and fifty variations of our family mystery. All sorts of lies are flying about.'

'The cards are ready, Claude,' said Edwin in a warning voice, as the footmen, completing their arrangements, quietly vanished: 'Come and sit down.'

13

Vitzelley glanced from one to the other. He took the first pack in his hand and ran his fingers over the edges. 'The old game, of course,' he said to Edwin.

Claude came and sat down, thrusting his chair back to display the embroidery of his vest. 'Pass that decanter, Vitzelley,' he said. 'My cards these? Ah! Fortuna, Fortuna!'

'Vitzelley is too polite to get interested about Sir Harry,' he went on presently, pouring from the decanter as he spoke: 'before us—that is.'

'I wish you would cut,' said his cousin.

Vitzelley took the cards to deal. Then with a quiet glance at Edwin, 'I have heard very little of your affair. Sir Harry thought fit to disappear because—because he had been playing cards?'

Edwin bowed his head assentingly. 'It is the only explanation possibly suggesting itself. We are waiting, Claude,' he said, nervously, as if desirous of changing the subject.

'That's stuff,' ejaculated Claude, playing. '*I* know more than that. You *know* more than that. Sir Harry never played.'

This flat contradiction caused Edwin to turn white, and glance with sharp malevolence at his cousin. It seemed to nettle him excessively. 'You know very little about it, Claude,' he retorted.

'I know Sir Harry never played cards.'

'To my knowledge he did. Confound it!'—he had played the wrong card. 'Well, well! I wish, Claude, you could avoid trying to begin a wrangle at cards.'

'Who wants to wrangle?—not me! Sir Harry never played.'

An uncomfortable silence followed. The game going on without a monosyllable being spoken. Then Claude drank, sucked his lips and turned to Vitzelley. 'No, Vitzelley, the disappearance of Sir Harry was no bolt from his debts of honour. We are an honourable family still. I believe—.' The young man's face assumed an exceedingly sapient and confidential expression. An anxious look came into Edwin's eyes— 'there was a lady in the case.'

A crimson flush swept over Edwin's forehead, but he looked relieved. 'Another pack, Vitzelley. Filthy luck, then, for me. It's the port. My head is as muddled and crowded as—as—'

'As a rotting corpse,' supplied Claude, compensating himself for the recent passage of arms.

14

Another grim pause supervened, Edwin manifesting much disturbance.

'I never rightly heard the particulars of this affair,' said Vitzelley, sweeping in the stakes he had just won, and seeing out of his narrow eyes, with considerable approval, the increasing distraction of one cousin and the intoxication of the other. 'Was there anything odd?'

'No, delightfully simple, all of it,' answered Claude. 'Just pass the decanter. Thanks. Two significant facts; one Sir Harry was; two he is not. Incidentally, the day he vanished that parrot was struck dumb. That is all. You saw your brother last, by-the-bye, Edwin. Tell us all about it.'

Edwin was white, and he was now playing wildly. 'The cards are bewitched tonight,' he said, between his teeth. He ignored Claude's words entirely.

'By Jove, Edwin!' burst out the irrepressible Claude; 'why, it must be just a year tonight! Vitzelley, this is the twenty-fourth of December. Christmas Eve? of course, yes. This is the anniversary of that last appearance. Vitzelley, don't ghosts—'

'I wish you would stop this sort of thing, Claude. It distracts one from the play.' Edwin certainly looked most strangely uncomfortable.

'My dear fellow! most valuable thought of mine—to you—this anniversary idea. When the year is up, you can take out—what is it?— letters of administration.'

Edwin was drumming with his strong white hand on the table, and pretending to examine the lace at his wrist. 'You are stopping the game, Claude.'

'This, Edwin,' presently resumed Claude, assuming great confidence with Vitzelley, 'is a sly old dog, Vitz. You, you're a sly old dog, too, to pull in like you *are* doing. That's by the way. Well, this Edwin always pretends to get huffy, get his feelings hurt, when we fall a talking about this disappearance. Really he profits up to the hilt. You must know Sir Harry was going to marry; happy girl, happy day, all fixed. If he had married and got a little boy, poor old Eddy—out in the cold for ever. *Now*, he's as good as baronet—will be baronet I suppose after awhile. Eh?'

'Did you really see him last?' asked Vitzelley, with a penetrating look at Edwin.

Edwin moistened his dry lips and looked straight into his face. He seemed watching his words as he spoke. 'On Christmas Eve, last year, I left my brother here in this room, sitting before this fire, about eleven. About—about this time—it must have been—' His eye fell instinctively on the clock. 'The footman who sleeps in the pantry below heard a bumping above and the parrot chattering. I—I was already in bed, and heard nothing at all. The next morning Sir Harry had vanished. Everything had been put straight—in fact, I mean, nothing had been disturbed apparently in this room or anywhere. Since then—'

'Viz, my lad, pass the bottle. It must have been the devil,' said Claude. 'Apotheosis.'

'The thing has been no joke to me,' complained Edwin, breathing more freely, as Vitzelley turned his attention to the cards again. 'The disappearance'

'Four minutes to twelve,' interrupted Claude, 'and Saturday. Vitzelley, if we play till Sunday we see the devil, don't we? I wonder if he's like our Satan here. Perhaps he'll bring Sir Harry back.'

'*Do*, in heaven's name, stop that,' cried Edwin, nervous now to savageness. 'You know how his disappearance has weighed on my mind; how I would give my soul to have Sir Harry, or Sir Harry's body, discovered—'

'*Oh, Edwin!*'

Edwin became livid. 'What was that? Did you speak, Vitzelley? Did you hear anything?'

Vitzelley was looking a little startled. 'I did not speak. I thought I heard something.'

'I didn't,' said Claude. 'Vitzelley, it's two to twelve. What happens at midnight if we keep on playing cards?'

'The red cards turn black, and the black blood red,' said Vitzelley, drily; 'and the picture cards make faces at you. That is all. Nothing very dreadful. What's the matter with you, Walcote; why don't you deal?'

'What are you glowering at in the candle flame?' cried Claude. 'One would think it was burning blue. Don't be alarmed. It wants one minute to midnight yet.'

Edwin answered with a peculiar quiver and gasping. 'I—It's nothing, nothing. Fancy. I am always fancying—. *You* can't see anything, can you? Pah, how the thing jumps and struggles! not dead yet. Will it ever be quiet? The flame, I mean.'

His face was ghastly, a sickly dew was glistening on his forehead. He made a peculiar clutching motion at the candle, then looked with startled fearful scrutiny at Vitzelley, put his hand to his forehead and then on the cards.

'The candle only flickers because it wants snuffing. There is a purple glow at the neck—wick I mean—and—'

One. Two. Three. Four. Five. Six. Slowly and solemnly the deep-voiced clock struck *Twelve*.

As the vibration of the last stroke died away, Edwin with a loud expression of disgust flung down his cards. 'The face,' he said. 'The face—with the black tongue out! The cards, the Knaves and Kings, white faces and purple necks. What a maniac I was to come here—this room—tonight! Bah! You fools! It's a joke! What are you fools staring at?'

Neither answered a word. Vitzelley had suddenly folded his arms and leaned over the table towards him. Claude had swiftly snatched up his cards, glanced at them fearfully, and then with a slightly relieved face turned to Edwin.

A stillness, and then a low, unearthly, pervading voice sounding through it, going searchingly through all the space around them, an agonised choking voice.

'*Oh, Edwin! oh, my mother! spare me, spare me! oh!*'—ending in a prolonged sobbing groan.

Claude's hair rose on end. Vitzelley moved not, spoke never a word. With fingers crushing the cards in his hand, with head bowed down, distorted mouth and blinking eyes, Edwin sat, as though awaiting the stroke of doom.

The clock ticked on exultantly in the horrible stillness. The bronze Satan stood expectant behind them, the satyrs stared across the room in suppressed excitement. The shadow of Satan's uplifted arm hung terrible above the crouching shadow of Edwin. The parrot shifted on his perch and clanked its chain. A card fell audibly on the floor. Then they heard an aerial voice, that made them involuntarily glance at his cadaverous face.

'*Ah! . . . the priest's hole in the turret!*'

It was Edwin's voice, but he had not spoken.

Another terrible hiatus in sound, a minute—or an hour. Then a dawning light of comprehension shone in Edwin's eyes. He started up furious, his chair reeling over with a crash, and made three strides towards the parrot. The bird gave an eldritch shriek and flapped open its wide grey wings. Then Vitzelley had gripped Edwin's arm and they stood confronting.

'Fate,' said Vitzelley. 'You must submit. We know—enough.'

A pause and then an intense whisper. 'Yes, I killed him—here—last Christmas Eve. Fool that I was to come here, this night of all! We drank and quarrelled. He had stood in my way to wealth, and his wealth had won my Annie from me. He taunted me. How I hated him then! I struck him suddenly with the poker, felled him, leaped on him, strangled him. There is a secret chamber in the disused turret where once the priests were hidden. Only he and I knew. He is there, rat eaten, mummified . . .

'Vitzelley, leave my arm for a moment.'

He turned and faced them both.

Suddenly his rapier glittered in the light. It flashed, and the parrot toppled over and hung headless by its chain, flashed again and he was staggering, falling forward, to roll over and sigh, and lie motionless before them—to love, hate, and sin nevermore. At his feet lay the head of the parrot, the fleshy tongue still faintly quivering.

The candles flickered as if with a passing breath, the shadowy Satan moved strangely on the wall. Over the marble mantel old Time swayed his scythe grim and restless, hewing out irrevocable things.

THE FLOWERING OF THE
STRANGE ORCHID

THE buying of orchids always has in it a certain speculative flavour. You have before you the brown shrivelled lump of tissue, and for the rest you must trust your judgment, or the auctioneer, or your good luck, as your taste may incline. The plant may be moribund or dead, or it may be just a respectable purchase, fair value for your money, or perhaps—for the thing has happened again and again—there slowly unfolds before the delighted eyes of the happy purchaser, day after day, some new variety, some novel richness, a strange twist of the labellum, or some subtler colouration or unexpected mimicry. Pride, beauty, and profit blossom together on one delicate green spike, and, it may be, even immortality. For the new miracle of Nature may stand in need of a new specific name, and what so convenient as that of its discoverer? 'Johnsmithia'! There have been worse names.

It was perhaps the hope of some such happy discovery that made Winter-Wedderburn such a frequent attendant at these sales—that hope, and also, maybe, the fact that he had nothing else of the slightest interest to do in the world. He was a shy, lonely, rather ineffectual man, provided with just enough income to keep off the spur of necessity, and not enough nervous energy to make him seek any exacting employment. He might have collected stamps or coins, or translated Horace, or bound books, or invented new species of diatoms. But, as it happened, he grew orchids, and had one ambitious little hot-house.

'I have a fancy,' he said over his coffee, 'that something is going to happen to me today.' He spoke—as he moved and thought—slowly.

'Oh, don't say *that*!' said his housekeeper—who was also his remote cousin. For 'something happening' was a euphemism that meant only one thing to her.

'You misunderstand me. I mean nothing unpleasant . . . though what I do mean I scarcely know.

'Today,' he continued, after a pause, 'Peters' are going to sell a batch of plants from the Andamans and the Indies. I shall go up and see what they have. It may be I shall buy something good, unawares. That may be it.'

He passed his cup for his second cupful of coffee.

'Are those the things collected by that poor young fellow you told me of the other day?' asked his cousin as she filled his cup.

'Yes,' he said, and became meditative over a piece of toast.

'Nothing ever does happen to me,' he remarked presently, beginning to think aloud. 'I wonder why? Things enough happen to other people. There is Harvey. Only the other week—on Monday he picked up sixpence, on Wednesday his chicks all had the staggers, on Friday his cousin came home from Australia, and on Saturday he broke his ankle. What a whirl of excitement!—compared to me.'

'I think I would rather be without so much excitement,' said his housekeeper. 'It can't be good for you.'

'I suppose it's troublesome. Still . . . you see, nothing ever happens to me. When I was a little boy I never had accidents. I never fell in love as I grew up. Never married. . . . I wonder how it feels to have something happen to you, something really remarkable.

'That orchid-collector was only thirty-six—twenty years younger than myself—when he died. And he had been married twice and divorced once; he had had malarial fever tour times, and once he broke his thigh. He killed a Malay once, and once he was wounded by a poisoned dart. And in the end he was killed by jungle-leeches. It must have all been very troublesome, but then it must have been very interesting, you know—except, perhaps, the leeches.'

'I am sure it was not good for him,' said the lady, with conviction.

'Perhaps not.' And then Wedderburn looked at his watch. 'Twenty-three minutes past eight. I am going up by the quarter-to-twelve train, so that there is plenty of time. I think I shall wear my alpaca jacket—it is quite warm enough—and my grey felt hat and brown shoes. I suppose—'

He glanced out of the window at the serene sky and sunlit garden, and then nervously at his cousin's face.

'I think you had better take an umbrella if you are going to London,' she said in a voice that admitted of no denial. 'There's all between here and the station coming back.'

When he returned he was in a state of mild excitement. He had made a purchase. It was rare that he could make up his mind quickly enough to buy, but this time he had done so.

'There are Vandas,' he said, 'and a Dendrobe and some Palaeonophis.' He surveyed his purchases lovingly as he consumed his soup. They were laid out on the spotless tablecloth before him, and he was telling his cousin all about them as he slowly meandered through his dinner. It was his custom to live all his visits to London over again in the evening for her and his own entertainment.

'I knew something would happen today. And I have bought all these. Some of them—some of them—I feel sure, do you know, that some of them will be remarkable. I don't know how it is, but I feel just as sure as if some one had told me that some of these will turn out remarkable.

'That one'—he pointed to a shrivelled rhizome—'was not identified. It may be a Palaeonophis—or it may not. It may be a new species, or even a new genus. And it was the last that poor Batten ever collected.'

'I don't like the look of it,' said his housekeeper. 'It's such an ugly shape.'

'To me it scarcely seems to have a shape.'

'I don't like those things that stick out,' said his housekeeper.

'It shall be put away in a pot tomorrow.'

'It looks,' said the housekeeper, 'like a spider shamming dead.'

Wedderburn smiled and surveyed the root with his head on one side. 'It is certainly not a pretty lump of stuff. But you can never judge of these things from their dry appearance. It may turn out to be a very beautiful orchid indeed. How busy I shall be tomorrow! I must see to-night just exactly what to do with these things, and tomorrow I shall set to work.

'They found poor Batten lying dead, or dying, in a mangrove swamp—I forget which,' he began again presently, 'with one of these very orchids crushed up under his body. He had been unwell for some days with some kind of native fever, and I suppose he fainted. These mangrove swamps are very unwholesome. Every drop of blood, they say, was taken out of him by the jungle-leeches. It may be that very plant that cost him his life to obtain.'

'I think none the better of it for that.'

'Men must work though women may weep,' said Wedderburn with profound gravity.

'Fancy dying away from every comfort in a nasty swamp! Fancy being ill of fever with nothing to take but chlorodyne and quinine—if men were left to themselves they would live on chlorodyne and quinine—and no one round you but horrible natives! They say the Andaman islanders are most disgusting wretches—and, anyhow, they can scarcely make good nurses, not having the necessary training. And just for people in England to have orchids!'

'I don't suppose it was comfortable, but some men seem to enjoy that kind of thing,' said Wedderburn. 'Anyhow, the natives of his party were sufficiently civilised to take care of all his collection until his colleague, who was an ornithologist, came back again from the interior; though they could not tell the species of the orchid and had let it wither. And it makes these things more interesting.'

'It makes them disgusting. I should be afraid of some of the malaria clinging to them. And just think, there has been a dead body lying across that ugly thing! I never thought of that before. There! I declare I cannot eat another mouthful of dinner.'

'I will take them off the table if you like, and put them in the window-seat. I can see them just as well there.'

The next few days he was indeed singularly busy in his steamy little hot-house, fussing about with charcoal, lumps of teak, moss, and all the other mysteries of the orchid cultivator. He considered he was having a wonderfully eventful time. In the evening he would talk about these new orchids to his friends, and over and over again he reverted to his expectation of something strange.

Several of the Vandas and the Dendrobrium died under his care, but presently the strange orchid began to show signs of life. He was delighted and took his housekeeper right away from jam-making to see it at once, directly he made the discovery.

'That is a bud,' he said, 'and presently there will be a lot of leaves there, and those little things coming out here are aerial rootlets.'

'They look to me like little white fingers poking out of the brown,' said his housekeeper. 'I don't like them.'

'Why not?'

'I don't know. They look like fingers trying to get at you. I can't help my likes and dislikes.'

'I don't know for certain, but I don't *think* there are any orchids I know that have aerial rootlets quite like that. It may be my fancy, of course. You see they are a little flattened at the ends.'

'I don't like 'em,' said his housekeeper, suddenly shivering and turning away. 'I know it's very silly of me—and I'm very sorry, particularly as you like the thing so much. But I can't help thinking of that corpse.'

'But it may not be that particular plant. That was merely a guess of mine.'

His housekeeper shrugged her shoulders. 'Anyhow I don't like it,' she said.

Wedderburn felt a little hurt at her dislike to the plant. But that did not prevent his talking to her about orchids generally, and this orchid in particular, whenever he felt inclined.

'There are such queer things about orchids,' he said one day; 'such possibilities of surprises. You know, Darwin studied their fertilisation, and showed that the whole structure of an ordinary orchid-flower was contrived in order that moths might carry the pollen from plant to plant. Well, it seems that there are lots of orchids known the flower of which cannot possibly be used for fertilisation in that way. Some of the Cypripediums, for instance; there are no insects known that can possibly fertilise them, and some of them have never been found with seed.'

'But how do they form new plants?'

'By runners and tubers, and that kind of outgrowth. That is easily explained. The puzzle is, what are the flowers for?

'Very likely,' he added, '*my* orchid may be something extraordinary in that way. If so I shall study it. I have often thought of making researches as Darwin did. But hitherto I have not found the time, or something else has happened to prevent it. The leaves are beginning, to unfold now. I do wish you would come and see them!'

But she said that the orchid-house was so hot it gave her the headache. She had seen the plant once again, and the aerial rootlets, which were now some of them more than a foot long, had unfortunately reminded her of tentacles reaching out after something; and they got into her dreams, growing after her with incredible rapidity. So that she had settled to her entire satisfaction that she would not see that plant again, and Wedderburn had to admire its leaves alone. They were of the ordinary broad form, and a deep glossy green, with splashes and dots of deep red towards the base. He knew of no other leaves quite like them. The plant was placed on a low bench near the thermometer, and close by was a simple arrangement by which a tap dripped on the hot-water pipes and kept the air steamy. And he spent his afternoons now with some regularity meditating on the approaching flowering of this strange plant.

And at last the great thing happened. Directly he entered the little glass house he knew that the spike had burst out, although his great *Palaeonophis Lowii* hid the corner where his new darling stood. There was a new odour in the air, a rich, intensely sweet scent, that overpowered every other in that crowded, steaming little greenhouse.

Directly he noticed this he hurried down to the strange orchid. And, behold! the trailing green spikes bore now three great splashes of blossom, from which this overpowering sweetness proceeded. He stopped before them in an ecstasy of admiration.

The flowers were white, with streaks of golden orange upon the petals; the heavy labellum was coiled into an intricate projection, and a wonderful bluish purple mingled there with the gold. He could see at once that the genus was altogether a new one. And the insufferable scent! How hot the place was! The blossoms swam before his eyes.

He would see if the temperature was right. He made a step towards the thermometer. Suddenly everything appeared unsteady. The bricks on the floor were dancing up and down. Then the white blossoms, the green leaves behind them, the whole greenhouse, seemed to sweep sideways, and then in a curve upward.

ଔ

At half-past four his cousin made the tea, according to their invariable custom. But Wedderburn did not come in for his tea.

'He is worshipping that horrid orchid,' she told herself, and waited ten minutes. 'His watch must have stopped. I will go and call him.'

She went straight to the hot-house, and, opening the door, called his name. There was no reply. She noticed that the air was very close, and loaded with an intense perfume. Then she saw something lying on the bricks between the hot-water pipes.

For a minute, perhaps, she stood motionless.

He was lying, face upward, at the foot of the strange orchid. The tentacle-like aerial rootlets no longer swayed freely in the air, but were crowded together, a tangle of grey ropes, and stretched tight with their ends closely applied to his chin and neck and hands.

She did not understand. Then she saw from under one of the exultant tentacles upon his cheek there trickled a little thread of blood.

With an inarticulate cry she ran towards him, and tried to pull him away from the leech-like suckers. She snapped two of these tentacles, and their sap dripped red.

Then the overpowering scent of the blossom began to make her head reel. How they clung to him! She tore at the tough ropes, and he and the white inflorescence swam about her. She felt she was fainting, knew she must not. She left him and hastily opened the nearest door, and, after she had panted for a moment in the fresh air, she had a brilliant inspiration. She caught up a flower-pot and smashed in the windows at the end of the greenhouse. Then she re-entered. She tugged now with renewed strength at Wedderburn's motionless body, and brought the strange orchid crashing to the floor. It still clung with the grimmest tenacity to its victim. In a frenzy, she lugged it and him into the open air.

Then she thought of tearing through the sucker rootlets one by one, and in another minute she had released him and was dragging him away from the horror.

He was white and bleeding from a dozen circular patches.

The odd-job man was coming up the garden, amazed at the smashing of glass, and saw her emerge, hauling the inanimate body with red-stained hands. For a moment he thought impossible things.

'Bring some water!' she cried, and her voice dispelled his fancies. When, with unnatural alacrity, he returned with the water, he found her weeping with excitement, and with Wedderburn's head upon her knee, wiping the blood from his face.

'What's the matter?' said Wedderburn, opening his eyes feebly, and closing them again at once.

'Go and tell Annie to come out here to me, and then go for Doctor Haddon at once,' she said to the odd-job man so soon as he brought the water; and added, seeing he hesitated, 'I will tell you all about it, when you come back.'

Presently Wedderburn opened his eyes again, and, seeing that he was troubled by the puzzle of his position, she explained to him, 'You fainted in the hot-house.'

'And the orchid?'

'I will see to that,' she said.

Wedderburn had lost a good deal of blood, but beyond that he had suffered no very great injury. They gave him brandy mixed with some pink extract of meat, and carried him upstairs to bed. His house-keeper told her incredible story in fragments to Dr Haddon. 'Come to the orchid-house and see,' she said.

The cold outer air was blowing in through the open door, and the sickly perfume was almost dispelled. Most of the torn aerial rootlets lay already withered amidst a number of dark stains upon the bricks. The stem of the inflorescence was broken by the fall of the plant, and the flowers were growing limp and brown at the edges of the petals. The doctor stooped towards it, then saw that one of the aerial rootlets still stirred feebly, and hesitated.

The next morning the strange orchid still lay there, black now and putrescent. The door banged intermittently in the morning breeze, and all the array of Wedderburn's orchids was shrivelled and prostrate. But Wedderburn himself was bright and garrulous upstairs in the glory of his strange adventure.

THE LORD OF THE DYNAMOS

THE chief attendant of the three dynamos that buzzed and rattled at Camberwell and kept the electric railway going, came out of Yorkshire, and his name was James Holroyd. He was a practical electrician but fond of whisky, a heavy, red-haired brute with irregular teeth. He doubted the existence of the Deity but accepted Carnot's cycle, and he had read Shakespeare and found him weak in chemistry. His helper came out of the mysterious East, and his name was Azuma-zi. But Holroyd called him Pooh-bah. Holroyd liked a nigger help because he would stand kicking—a habit with Holroyd—and did not pry into the machinery and try to learn the ways of it. Certain odd possibilities of the negro mind brought into abrupt contact with the crown of our civilisation Holroyd never fully realised, though just at the end he got some inkling of them.

To define Azuma-zi was beyond ethnology. He was, perhaps, more negroid than anything else, though his hair was curly rather than frizzy, and his nose had a bridge. Moreover, his skin was brown rather than black, and the whites of his eyes were yellow. His broad cheekbones and narrow chin gave his face something of the viperine V. His head, too, was broad behind, and low and narrow at the forehead, as if his brain had been twisted round in the reverse way to a European's. He was short of stature and still shorter of English. In conversation he made numerous odd noises of no known marketable value, and his infrequent words were carved and wrought into heraldic grotesqueness. Holroyd tried to elucidate his religious beliefs, and—especially after whisky—lectured to him against superstition and missionaries. Azuma-zi, however, shirked the discussion of his gods, even though he was kicked for it.

Azuma-zi had come, clad in white but insufficient raiment, out of the stoke-hole of the *Lord Clive,* from the Straits Settlements and beyond, into London. He had heard even in his youth of the greatness and riches of London, where all the women are white and fair and even the beggars in the streets are white; and he had arrived, with newly-earned gold coins in his pocket, to worship at the shrine of civilisation. The day of his landing was a dismal one; the sky was dun, and a windworried drizzle filtered down to the greasy streets, but he plunged boldly into the delights of Shadwell, and was presently cast up, shattered in health, civilised in costume, penniless, and, except in matters of the direst necessity, practically a dumb animal, to toil for James Holroyd, and to be bullied by him in the dynamo shed at Camberwell. And to James Holroyd bullying was a labour of love.

There were three dynamos with their engines at Camberwell. The two that have been there since the beginning are small machines; the larger one was new. The smaller machines made a reasonable noise; their straps hummed over the drums, every now and then the brushes buzzed and fizzled, and the air churned steadily, whoa! whoo! whoo! between their poles. One was loose in its foundations and kept the shed vibrating. But the big dynamo drowned these little noises altogether with the sustained drone of its iron core, which somehow set part of the ironwork humming. The place made the visitor's head reel with the throb, throb, throb of the engines, the rotation of the big wheels, the spinning ballvalves, the occasional spittings of the steam, and over all the deep, unceasing, surging note of the big dynamo. This last noise was from an engineering point of view a defect, but Azuma-zi accounted it unto the monster for mightiness and pride.

If it were possible we would have the noises of that shed always about the reader as he reads, we would tell all our story to such an accompaniment. It was a steady stream of din, from which the ear picked out first one thread and then another; there was the intermittent snorting, panting, and seething of the steam-engines, the suck and thud of their pistons, the dull beat on the air as the spokes of the great driving wheels came round, a note the leather straps made as they ran tighter and looser, and a fretful tumult from the dynamos; and, over all, sometimes inaudible, as the ear tired of it, and then creeping back upon the senses again, was this trombone note of the big machine. The floor never felt steady and quiet beneath one's feet, but quivered and jarred. It was a confusing, unsteady place, and enough to send any one's thoughts jerking into odd zigzags. And for three months, while the big strike of the engineers was in progress, Holroyd who was a blackleg, and Azuma-zi who was a mere black, were never out of the stir and eddy of it, but slept and fed in the little wooden shanty between the shed and the gates.

Holroyd delivered a theological lecture on the text of his big machine soon after Azuma-zi came. He had to shout to be heard in the din. 'Look at that,' said Holroyd; 'where's your 'eathen idol to match 'im?' And Azuma-zi looked. For a moment Holroyd was inaudible, and then Azuma-zi heard: 'Kill a hundred men. Twelve per cent on the ordinary shares,' said Holroyd, 'and that's something like a Gord.'

Holroyd was proud of his big dynamo, and expatiated upon its size and power to Azuma-zi until heaven knows what odd currents of thought that the incessant whirling and shindy set up within the curly black cranium. He would explain in the most graphic manner the dozen or so ways in which a man might be killed by it, and once he gave Azuma-zi a shock as a sample of its quality. After that, in the breathing times of his labour—it was heavy labour, being not only his own, but most of Holroyd's—Azuma-zi would sit and watch the big machine. Now and then the brushes would sparkle and spit blue flashes, at which Holroyd would swear, but all the rest was as smooth and rhythmic as breathing. The band ran shouting over the shaft, and ever behind one as one watched was the complacent thud of the piston. So it lived all day in this big airy shed, with him and Holroyd to wait upon it; not prisoned up and slaving to drive a ship as the other engines he knew—mere captive devils of the British Solomon—had been, but a machine enthroned. Those two smaller dynamos Azuma-zi by force of contrast despised; the large one he privately christened the Lord of the Dynamos. They were fretful and irregular, but the big dynamo was steady. How great it was! How serene and easy in its working! Greater and calmer even than the Buddhas he had seen at Rangoon, and yet not motionless, but living! The great black coils spun, spun, spun, the rings ran round under the brushes, and the deep note of its coil steadied the whole. It affected Azuma-zi queerly.

Azuma-zi was not fond of labour. He would sit about and watch the Lord of the Dynamos while Holroyd went away to persuade the yard porter to get whisky, although his proper place was not in the dynamo shed but behind the engines, and, moreover, if Holroyd caught him skulking he got hit for it with a rod of stout copper wire. He would go and stand close to the colossus, and look up at the great leather band running overhead. There was a black patch on the band that came round, and it pleased him somehow among all the clatter to watch this return again and again. Odd thoughts spun with the whirl of it. Scientific people tell us that savages give souls to rocks and trees—and a machine is a thousand times more alive than a rock or a tree. And Azuma-zi was practically a savage still; the veneer of civilisation lay no deeper than his slop suit, his bruises, and the coal grime on his face and hands. His father before him had worshipped a meteoric stone; kindred blood, it may be, had splashed the broad wheels of juggernaut.

He took every opportunity Holroyd gave him of touching and handling the great dynamo that was fascinating him. He polished and cleaned it until the metal parts were blinding in the sun. He felt a mysterious sense of service in doing this. He would go up to it and touch its spinning coils gently. The gods he had worshipped were all far away. The people in London hid their gods.

At last his dim feelings grew more distinct and took shape in thoughts, and at last in acts. When he came into the roaring shed one morning he salaamed to the Lord of the Dynamos, and then, when Holroyd was away, he went and whispered to the thundering machine that he was its servant, and prayed it to have pity on him and save him from Holroyd. As he did so a rare gleam of light came in through the open archway of the throbbing machine-shed, and the Lord of the Dynamos, as he whirled and roared, was radiant with pale gold. Then Azuma-zi knew that his service was acceptable to his Lord. After that he did not feel so lonely as he had done, and he had indeed been very much alone in London. Even when his work-time was over, which was rare, he loitered about the shed.

The next time Holroyd maltreated him, Azuma-zi went presently to the Lord of the Dynamos and whispered, 'Thou seest, O my Lord!' and the angry whirr of the machinery seemed to answer him. Thereafter it appeared to him that whenever Holroyd came into the shed a different note mingled with the sounds of the dynamo. 'My Lord bides his time,' said Azuma-zi to himself. 'The iniquity of the fool is not yet ripe.' And he waited and watched for the reckoning. One day there was evidence of short circuiting, and Holroyd, making an unwary examination—it was in the afternoon—got a rather severe shock. Azuma-zi from behind the engine saw him jump off and curse at the peccant coil.

'He is warned,' said Azuma-zi to himself. 'Surely my Lord is very patient.'

Holroyd had at first initiated his 'nigger' into such elementary conceptions of the dynamo's working as would enable him to take temporary charge of the shed in his absence. But when he noticed the manner in which Azuma-zi hung about the monster he became suspicious. He dimly perceived his assistant was 'up to something,' and connecting him with the anointing of the coils with oil that had rotted the varnish in one place, he issued an edict, shouted above the confusion of the machinery, 'Don't 'ee go nigh that big dynamo any more, Pooh-bah, or a'll take thy skin off!' Besides, if it pleased Azuma-zi to be near the big machine, it was plain sense and decency to keep him away from it.

Azuma-zi obeyed at the time, but later he was caught bowing before the Lord of the Dynamos. At which Holroyd twisted his arm and kicked him as he turned to go away. As Azuma-zi presently stood behind the engine and glared at the back of the hated Holroyd, the noises of the machinery took a new rhythm and sounded like four words in his native tongue.

It is hard to say exactly what madness is. I fancy Azuma-zi was mad. The incessant din and whirl of the dynamo shed may have churned up his little store of knowledge and big store of superstitious fancy, at last, into something akin to frenzy. At any rate, when the idea of making Holroyd a sacrifice to the Dynamo Fetich was thus suggested to him, it filled him with a strange tumult of exultant emotion.

That night the two men and their black shadows were alone in the shed together. The shed was lit with one big arc-light and winked and flickered purple. The shadows lay black behind the dynamos, the ball governors of the engines whirled from light to darkness, and their pistons beat loud and steadily. The world outside seen through the open end of the shed seemed incredibly dim and remote. It seemed absolutely silent, too, since the riot of the machinery drowned every external sound. Far away was the black fence of the yard with grey shadowy houses behind, and above was the deep blue sky and the pale little stars. Azuma-zi suddenly walked across the centre of the shed above which the leather bands were running, and went into the shadow of the big dynamo. Holroyd heard a click, and the spin of the armature changed.

'What are you dewin' with that switch?' he bawled in surprise. 'Han't I told you—'

Then he saw the set expression of Azuma-zi's eyes as the Asiatic came out of the shadow towards him.

In another moment the two men were grappling fiercely in front of the great dynamo.

'You coffee-headed fool!' gasped Holroyd, with a brown hand at his throat. 'Keep off those contact rings.' In another moment he was tripped and reeling back upon the Lord of the Dynamos. He instinctively loosened his grip upon his antagonist to save himself from the machine.

The messenger, sent in furious haste from the station to find out what had happened in the dynamo shed, met Azuma-zi at the porter's lodge by the gate. Azuma-zi tried to explain something, but the messenger could make nothing of the black's incoherent English, and hurried on to the shed. The machines were all noisily at work, and nothing seemed to be disarranged. There was, however, a queer smell of singed hair. Then he saw an odd-looking crumpled mass clinging to the front of the big dynamo, and, approaching, recognised the distorted remains of Holroyd.

The man stared and hesitated a moment. Then he saw the face, and shut his eyes convulsively. He turned on his heel before he opened them, so that he should not see Holroyd again, and went out of the shed to get advice and help.

When Azuma-zi saw Holroyd die in the grip of the Great Dynamo he had been a little scared about the consequences of his act. Yet he felt strangely elated, and knew that the favour of the Lord Dynamo was upon him. His plan was already settled when he met the man coming from the station, and the scientific manager who speedily arrived on the scene jumped at the obvious conclusion of suicide. This expert scarcely noticed Azuma-zi, except to ask a few questions. Did he see Holroyd kill himself? Azuma-zi explained he had been out of sight at the engine furnace until he heard a difference in the noise from the dynamo. It was not a difficult examination, being untinctured by suspicion.

The distorted remains of Holroyd, which the electrician removed from the machine, were hastily covered by the porter with a coffee-stained tablecloth. Somebody, by a happy inspiration, fetched a medical man. The expert was chiefly anxious to get the machine at work again, for seven or eight trains had stopped midway in the stuffy tunnels of the electric railway. Azuma-zi, answering or misunderstanding the questions of the people who had by authority or impudence come into the shed, was presently sent back to the stoke-hole by the scientific manager. Of course a crowd collected outside the gates of the yard—a, crowd, for no known reason, always hovers for a day or two near the scene of a sudden death in London—two or three reporters percolated somehow into the engine shed, and one even got to Azuma-zi; but the scientific expert cleared them out again, being himself an amateur journalist.

Presently the body was carried away, and public interest departed with it. Azuma-zi remained very quietly at his furnace, seeing over and over again in the coals a figure that wriggled violently and became still. An hour after the murder, to anyone coming into the shed things would have looked exactly as if nothing remarkable had ever happened there. Peeping presently from his engine-room the black saw the Lord Dynamo spin and whirl beside his little brothers, and the driving-wheels were beating round and the steam in the pistons went thud, thud, exactly as it had been earlier in the evening. After all, from the mechanical point of view it had been a most insignificant incident—the mere temporary deflection of a current. But now the slender form and slender shadow of the scientific manager replaced the sturdy outline of Holroyd travelling up and down the lane of light upon the vibrating floor under the straps between the engines and the dynamos.

'Have I not served my Lord?' said Azuma-zi inaudibly from his shadow, and the note of the great dynamo rang out full and clear. As he looked at the big whirling mechanism the strange fascination of it that had been a little in abeyance since Holroyd's death resumed its sway.

Never had Azuma-zi seen a man killed so swiftly and pitilessly. The big humming machine had slain its victim without wavering for a second from its steady beating. It was indeed a mighty god.

The unconscious scientific manager stood with his back to him, scribbling on a piece of paper. His shadow lay at the foot of the monster.

Was the Lord Dynamo still hungry? His servant was ready.

Azuma-zi made a stealthy step forward; then stopped. The scientific manager suddenly ceased his writing, walked down the shed to the endmost of the dynamos, and began to examine the brushes.

Azuma-zi hesitated, and then slipped across noiselessly into the shadow by the switch. There he waited. Presently the manager's foot-

33

steps could be heard returning. He stopped in his old position, unconscious of the stoker crouching ten feet away from him. Then the big dynamo suddenly fizzled, and in another moment Azuma-zi had sprung out of the darkness upon him.

The scientific manager was gripped round the body and swung towards the big dynamo. Kicking with his knee and forcing his antagonist's head down with his hands, he loosened the grip on his waist and swung round away from the machine. Then the black grasped him again, putting a curly head against his chest, and they swayed and panted as it seemed for an age or so. Then the scientific manager was impelled to catch a black ear in his teeth and bite furiously. The black yelled hideously.

They rolled over on the floor, and the black, who had apparently slipped from the vice of the teeth or parted with some ear—the scientific manager wondered which at the time—tried to throttle him. The scientific manager was making some ineffectual efforts to claw something with his hands and to kick, when the welcome sound of quick footsteps sounded on the floor. The next moment Azuma-zi had left him and darted towards the big dynamo. There was a splutter amid the roar.

The officer of the company who had entered stood staring as Azuma-zi caught the naked terminals in his hands, gave one horrible convulsion, and then hung motionless from the machine, his face violently distorted.

'I'm jolly glad you came in when you did,' said the scientific manager, still sitting on the floor.

He looked at the still quivering figure. 'It is not a nice death to die, apparently—but it is quick.'

The official was still staring at the body. He was a man of slow apprehension.

There was a pause.

The scientific manager got up on his feet rather awkwardly, He ran his fingers along his collar thoughtfully, and moved his head to and fro several times.

'Poor Holroyd! I see now.' Then almost mechanically he went towards the switch in the shadow and turned the current into the railway circuit again. As he did so the singed body loosened its grip upon the machine and fell forward on its face. The core of the dynamo roared out loud and clear, and the armature beat the air.

So ended prematurely the worship of the Dynamo Deity, perhaps the most short-lived of all religions. Yet withal it could at least boast a Martyrdom and a Human Sacrifice.

THE TEMPTATION OF HARRINGAY*

IT IS quite impossible to say whether this thing really happened. It depends entirely on the word of R.M. Harringay, who is an artist.

Following his version of the affair, the narrative deposes that Harringay went into his studio about ten o'clock to see what he could make of the head that he had been working at the day before. The head in question was that of an Italian organ-grinder, and Harringay thought—but was not quite sure—that the title would be the 'Vigil'. So far he is frank, and his narrative bears the stamp of truth. He had seen the man expectant for pennies, and with a promptness that suggested genius, had had him in at once.

'Kneel. Look up at that bracket,' said Harringay. 'As if you expected pennies.

'Don't *grin*!' said Harringay. 'I don't want to paint your gums. Look as though you were unhappy.'

Now, after a night's rest, the picture proved decidedly unsatisfactory. 'It's good work,' said Harringay. 'That little bit in the neck. . . . But.'

He walked about the studio and looked at the thing from this point and from that. Then he said a wicked word. In the original the word is given.

'Painting,' he says he said. 'Just a painting of an organ-grinder—a mere portrait. If it was a live organ-grinder I wouldn't mind. But somehow I never make things alive. I wonder if my imagination is wrong.' This, too, has a truthful air. His imagination *is* wrong.

'That creative touch! To take canvas and pigment and make a man—as Adam was made of red ochre! But this thing! If you met it walking about the streets you would know it was only a studio production. The little boys would tell it to "Garnome and git frimed." Some little touch. . . . Well—it won't do as it is.'

* See earlier version of this story, 'The Devotee of Art'.

He went to the blinds and began to pull them down. They were made of blue holland with the rollers at the bottom of the window, so that you pull them down to get more light. He gathered his palette, brushes, and mahlstick from his table. Then he turned to the picture and put a speck of brown in the corner of the mouth; and shifted his attention thence to the pupil of the eye. Then he decided that the chin was a trifle too impassive for a vigil.

Presently he put down his impedimenta, and lighting a pipe surveyed the progress of his work. 'I'm hanged if the thing isn't sneering at me,' said Harringay, and he still believes it sneered.

The animation of the figure had certainly increased, but scarcely in the direction he wished. There was no mistake about the sneer. 'Vigil of the Unbeliever,' said Harringay. 'Rather subtle and clever that! But the left eyebrow isn't cynical enough.'

He went and dabbed at the eyebrow, and added a little to the lobe of the ear to suggest materialism. Further consideration ensued. 'Vigil's off, I'm afraid,' said Harringay. 'Why not Mephistopheles? But that's a bit *too* common. 'A Friend of the Doge'—not so seedy. The armour won't do, though. Too Camelot. How about a scarlet robe and call him 'One of the Sacred College'? Humour in that, and an appreciation of Middle Italian History.'

'There's always Benvenuto Cellini,' said Harringay; 'with a clever suggestion of a gold cup in one corner. But that would scarcely suit the complexion.'

He describes himself as babbling in this way in order to keep down an unaccountably unpleasant sensation of fear. The thing was certainly acquiring anything but a pleasing expression. Yet it was as certainly becoming far more of a living thing than it had been—if a sinister one—far more alive than anything he had ever painted before. 'Call it "Portrait of a Gentleman," ' said Harringay; 'A Certain Gentleman.'

'Won't do,' said Harringay, still keeping up his courage. 'Kind of thing they call Bad Taste. That sneer will have to come out. That gone, and a little more fire in the eye—never noticed how warm his eye was before—and he might do for—? What price Passionate Pilgrim? But that devilish face won't do—*this* side of the Channel.

'Some little inaccuracy does it,' he said; 'eyebrows probably too oblique'—therewith pulling the blind lower to get a better light, and resuming palette and brushes.

The face on the canvas seemed animated by a spirit of its own. Where the expression of diablerie came in he found impossible to discover. Experiment was necessary. The eyebrows—it could scarcely be the eyebrows? But he altered them. No, that was no better; in fact, if anything, a trifle more satanic. The corner of the mouth? Pah! more than ever a leer—and now, retouched, it was ominously grim. The eye, then? Catastrophe! he had filled his brush with vermilion instead of brown, and yet he had felt sure it was, brown! The eye seemed now to have rolled in its socket, and was glaring at him an eye of fire. In a flash of passion, possibly with something of the courage of panic, he struck the brush full of bright red athwart the picture; and then a very curious thing, a very strange thing indeed, occurred—if it *did* occur.

The diabolified Italian before him shut both his eyes, pursed his mouth, and wiped the colour off his face with his hand.

Then the *red eye* opened again, with a sound like the opening of lips, and the face smiled. 'That was rather hasty of you,' said the picture.

Harringay states that, now that the worst had happened, his self-possession returned. He had a saving persuasion that devils were reasonable creatures.

'Why do you keep moving about then,' he said, 'making faces and all that—sneering and squinting, while I am painting you?'

'I don't,' said the picture.

'You *do*,' said Harringay.

'It's yourself,' said the picture.

'It's *not* myself,' said Harringay.

'It *is* yourself,' said the picture. 'No! don't go hitting me with paint again, because it's true. You have been trying to fluke an expression on my face all the morning. Really, you haven't an idea what your picture ought to look like.'

'I have,' said Harringay.

'You have *not*,' said the picture: 'You *never* have with your pictures. You always start with the vaguest presentiment of what you are going to do; it is to be something beautiful—you are sure of that—and devout, perhaps, or tragic; but beyond that it is all experiment and chance. My dear fellow! you don't think you can paint a, picture like that?'

Now it must be remembered that for what follows we have only Harringay's word.

'I shall paint a picture exactly as I like,' said Harringay, calmly.

This seemed to disconcert the picture a little. 'You can't paint a picture without an inspiration,' it remarked.

'But I *had* an inspiration—for this.'

'Inspiration!' sneered the sardonic figure; 'a fancy that came from your seeing an organ-grinder looking up at a window! Vigil! Ha, ha! You just started painting on the chance of something coming—that's what you did. And when I saw you at it I came. I want a talk with you!

'Art, with you,' said the picture—'it's a poor business. You potter. I don't know how it is, but you don't seem able to throw your soul into it. You know too much. It hampers you. In the midst of your enthusiasms you ask yourself whether something like this has not been done before. And . . .'

'Look here,' said Harringay, who had expected something better than criticism from the devil. 'Are you, going to talk studio to me? He filled his number twelve hoghair with red paint.

'The true artist,' said the picture, 'is always an ignorant man. An artist who theorises about his work is no longer artist but critic. Wagner . . . I say!—What's that red paint for?'

'I'm going to paint you out,' said Harringay. 'I don't want to hear all that Tommy Rot. If you think just because I'm an artist by trade I'm going to talk studio to you, you make a precious mistake.'

'One minute,' said the picture, evidently alarmed. 'I want to make you an offer—a genuine offer. It's right what I'm saying. You lack inspirations. Well. No doubt you've heard of the Cathedral of Cologne, and the Devil's Bridge, and—'

'Rubbish,' said Harringay. 'Do you think I want to go to perdition simply for the pleasure of painting a good picture, and getting it slated. Take that.'

His blood was up. His danger only nerved him to action, so he says. So he planted a dab of vermilion in his creature's mouth. The Italian spluttered and tried to wipe it off—evidently horribly surprised. And then—according to Harringay—there began a very remarkable struggle, Harringay splashing away with the red paint, and the picture wriggling about and wiping it off as fast as he put it on. '*Two* master-pieces,' said the demon. 'Two indubitable masterpieces for a Chelsea artist's soul. It's a bargain?' Harringay replied with the paint brush.

For a few minutes nothing could be heard but the brush going and the spluttering and ejaculations of the Italian. A lot of the strokes he caught on his arm and hand, though Harringay got over his guard often enough. Presently the paint on the palette gave out and the two antagonists stood breathless, regarding each other. The picture was so smeared with red that it looked as if it had been rolling about a slaughterhouse, and it was painfully out of breath and very uncomfortable with the wet paint trickling down its neck. Still, the first round was in its favour on the whole. 'Think,' it said, sticking pluckily to its point, 'two supreme masterpieces—in different styles. Each equivalent to the Cathedral . . .'

'*I* know,' said Harringay, and rushed out of the studio and along the passage towards his wife's boudoir.

In another minute he was back with a large tin of enamel—Hedge Sparrow's Egg Tint, it was, and a brush. At the sight of that the artistic devil with the red eye began to scream. '*Three* masterpieces—culminating masterpieces.'

Harringay delivered cut two across the demon, and followed with a thrust in the eye. There was an indistinct rumbling. '*Four* masterpieces,' and a spitting sound.

But Harringay had the upper hand now and meant to keep it. With rapid, bold strokes he continued to paint over the writhing canvas, until at last it was a uniform field of shining Hedge Sparrow tint. Once the mouth reappeared and got as far as '*Five* master—' before he filled it with enamel; and near the end the red eye opened and glared at him indignantly. But at last nothing remained save a gleaming panel of drying enamel. For a little while a faint stirring beneath the surface puckered it slightly here and there, but presently even that died away and the thing was perfectly still.

Then Harringay—according to Harringay's account—lit his pipe and sat down and stared at the enamelled canvas, and tried to make out clearly what had happened. Then he walked round behind it, to see if the back of it was at all remarkable. Then it was he began to regret he had not photographed the Devil before he painted him out.

This is Harringay's story—not mine. He supports it by a small canvas (24 by 20) enamelled a pale green, and by violent asseverations. It is also true that he never has produced a masterpiece, and in the opinion of his intimate friends probably never will.

THE MOTH

PROBABLY you have heard of Hapley—not W.T. Hapley, the son, but the celebrated Hapley, the Hapley of *Periplaneta Hapliia,* Hapley the entomologist.

If so you know at least of the great feud between Hapley and Professor Pawkins, though certain of its consequences may be new to you. For those who have not, a word or two of explanation is necessary, which the idle reader may go over with a glancing eye if his indolence so incline him.

It is amazing how very widely diffused is the ignorance of such really important matters as this Hapley-Pawkins feud. Those epoch-making controversies, again, that have convulsed the Geological Society are, I verily believe, almost entirely unknown outside the fellowship of that body. I have heard men of fair general education even refer to the great scenes at these meetings as vestry-meeting squabbles. Yet the great hate of the English and Scotch geologists has lasted now half a century, and has 'left deep and abundant marks upon the body of the science'. And this Hapley-Pawkins business, 'though perhaps a more personal affair, stirred passions as profound, if not profounder. Your common man has no conception of the zeal that animates a scientific investigator, the fury of contradiction you can arouse in him. It is the *odium theologicum* in a new form. There are men, for instance, who would gladly burn Sir Ray Lankester at Smithfield for his treatment of the Mollusca in the *Encyclopaedia.* That fantastic extension of the Cephalopods to cover the Pteropods. . . . But I wander from Hapley and Pawkins.

It began years and years ago with a revision of the Microlepidoptera (whatever these may be) by Pawkins, in which he extinguished a new species created by Hapley. Hapley, who was always quarrelsome, replied by a stinging impeachment of the entire classification of

41

Pawkins.[1] Pawkins in his 'Rejoinder'[2] suggested that Hapley's microscope was as defective as his power of observation, and called him an 'irresponsible meddler'—Hapley was not a professor at that time. Hapley in his retort,[3] spoke of 'blundering collectors,' and described, as if inadvertently, Pawkins's revision as a 'miracle of ineptitude'. It was war to the knife. However, it would scarcely interest the reader to detail how these two great men quarrelled, and how the split between them widened until from the Microlepidoptera they were at war upon every open question in entomology. There were memorable occasions. At times the Royal Entomological Society meetings resembled nothing so much as the Chamber of Deputies. On the whole, I fancy Pawkins was nearer the truth than Hapley. But Hapley was skilful with his rhetoric, had a turn for ridicule rare in a scientific man, was endowed with vast energy, and had a fine sense of injury in the matter of the extinguished species; while Pawkins was a man of dull presence, prosy of speech, in shape not unlike a water-barrel, over-conscientious with testimonials, and suspected of jobbing museum appointments. So the young men gathered round Hapley and applauded him. It was a long struggle, vicious from the beginning and growing at last to pitiless antagonism. The successive turns of fortune, now an advantage to one side and now to another—now Hapley tormented by some success of Pawkins, and now Pawkins outshone by Hapley, belong rather to the history of entomology than to this story.

But in 1891 Pawkins, whose health had been bad for some time, published some work upon the 'mesoblast' of the Death's-Head Moth. What the mesoblast of the Death's-Head Moth may be does not matter a rap in this story. But the work was far below his usual standard, and gave Hapley an opening he had coveted for years. He must have worked night and day to make the most of his advantage.

In an elaborate critique he rent Pawkins to tatters—one can fancy the man's disordered black hair, and his queer dark eyes flashing as he went for his antagonist—and Pawkins made a reply, halting, ineffectual, with painful gaps of silence, and yet malignant. There was no mistaking his will to wound Hapley, nor his incapacity to do it. But

---

[1] 'Remarks on a Recent Revision of Microlepidoptera', *Quart. Journ. Entomological Soc.*, 1863
[2] 'Rejoinder to Vertain Remarks', etc, *Ibid*. 1864
[3] 'Further Remarks', etc. *Ibid*

few of those who heard him—I was absent from that meeting—realised how ill the man was.

Hapley got his opponent down, and meant to finish him. He followed with a brutal attack upon Pawkins, in the form of a paper upon the development of moths in general, a paper showing evidence of an extraordinary amount of labour, couched in a violently controversial tone. Violent as it was, an editorial note witnesses that it was modified. It must have covered Pawkins with shame and confusion of face. It left no loophole; it was murderous in argument, and utterly contemptuous in tone; an awful thing for the declining years of a man's career.

The world of entomologists waited breathlessly for the rejoinder from Pawkins. He would try one, for Pawkins had always been game. But when it came it surprised them. For the rejoinder of Pawkins was to catch influenza, proceed to pneumonia, and die.

It was perhaps as effectual a reply as he could make under the circumstances, and largely turned the current of feeling against Hapley. The very people who had most gleefully cheered on those gladiators became serious at the consequence. There could be no reasonable doubt the fret of the defeat had contributed to the death of Pawkins. There was a limit even to scientific controversy, said serious people. Another crushing attack was already in the press and appeared on the day before the funeral. I don't think Hapley exerted himself to stop it. People remembered how Hapley had hounded down his rival and forgot that rival's defects. Scathing satire reads ill over fresh mould. The thing provoked comment in the daily papers. It was that made me think you had probably heard of Hapley and this controversy. But, as I have already remarked, scientific workers live very much in a world of their own; half the people, I dare say, who go along Piccadilly to the Academy every year could not tell you where the learned societies abide. Many even think that research is a kind of happy-family cage in which all kinds of men lie down together in peace.

In his private thoughts Hapley could not forgive Pawkins for dying. In the first place, it was a mean dodge to escape the absolute pulverisation Hapley had in hand for him, and in the second, it left Hapley's mind with a queer gap in it. For twenty years he had worked hard, sometimes far into the night, and seven days a week, with microscope, scalpel, collecting-net, and pen, and almost entirely with reference to Pawkins. The European reputation he had won had come as an incident in that great antipathy. He had gradually worked up to a climax in this last controversy. It had killed Pawkins, but it had also thrown Hapley out of gear, so to speak, and his doctor advised him to give up work for a time, and rest. So Hapley went down into a quiet village in Kent, and thought day and night of Pawkins and good things it was now impossible to say about him.

At last Hapley began to realise in what direction the preoccupation tended. He determined to make a fight for it, and started by trying to read novels. But he could not get his mind off Pawkins, white in the face and making his last speech—every sentence a beautiful opening for Hapley. He turned to fiction—and found it had no grip on him. He read the *Island Nights' Entertainments* until his 'sense of causation' was shocked beyond endurance by the Bottle Imp. Then he went to Kipling, and found he 'proved nothing' besides being irreverent and vulgar. These scientific people have their limitations. Then unhappily he tried Besant's *Inner House,* and the opening chapter set his mind upon learned societies and Pawkins at once.

So Hapley turned to chess, and found it a little more soothing. He soon mastered the moves and the chief gambits and commoner closing positions, and began to beat the Vicar. But then the cylindrical contours of the opposite king began to resemble Pawkins standing up and gasping ineffectually against checkmate, and Hapley decided to give up chess.

Perhaps the study of some new branch of science would after all be better diversion. The best rest is change of occupation. Hapley determined to plunge at diatoms, and had one of his smaller microscopes and Halibut's monograph sent down from London. He thought that perhaps if he could get up a vigorous quarrel with Halibut, he might be able to begin life afresh and forget Pawkins. And very soon he was hard at work in his habitual strenuous fashion at these microscopic denizens of the wayside pool.

It was on the third day of the diatoms that Hapley became aware of a novel addition to the local fauna. He was working late at the microscope, and the only light in the room was the brilliant little lamp with the special form of green shade. Like all experienced microscopists, he kept both eyes open. It is the only way to avoid excessive fatigue. One eye was over the instrument, and bright and distinct before that was the circular field of the microscope, across which a brown diatom was slowly moving. With the other eye Hapley saw, as it were, without seeing. He was only dimly conscious of the brass side of the instrument, the illuminated part of the tablecloth, a sheet of note-paper, the foot of the lamp, and the darkened room beyond.

Suddenly his attention drifted from one eye to the other. The tablecloth was of the material called tapestry by shopmen, and rather brightly coloured. The pattern was in gold, with a small amount of crimson and pale blue upon a greyish ground. At one point the pattern seemed displaced, and there was a vibrating movement of the colours at this point.

Hapley suddenly moved his head back and looked with both eyes. His mouth fell open with astonishment.

It was a large moth or butterfly; its wings spread in butterfly fashion!

It was strange it should be in the room at all, for the windows were closed. Strange that it should not have attracted his attention when fluttering to its present position. Strange that it should match the tablecloth. Stranger far that to him, Hapley, the great entomologist, it was altogether unknown. There was no delusion. It was crawling slowly towards the foot of the lamp.

'New Genus, by heavens! And in England!' said Hapley, staring.

Then he suddenly thought of Pawkins. Nothing would have mad-dened Pawkins more. . . . And Pawkins was dead!

Something about the head and body of the insect became singu-larly suggestive of Pawkins, just as the chess king had been.

'Confound Pawkins!' said Hapley. 'But I must catch this.' And looking round him for some means of capturing the moth, he rose slowly out of his chair. Suddenly the insect rose, struck the edge of the lamp-shade—Hapley heard the 'ping'—and vanished into the shadow.

In a moment Hapley had whipped off the shade, so that the whole room was illuminated. The thing had disappeared, but soon his practised eye detected it upon the wall-paper near the door. He went towards it, poising the lamp-shade for capture. Before he was within striking distance, however, it had risen and was fluttering round the room. After the fashion of its kind, it flew with sudden starts and turns, seeming to vanish here and reappear there. Once Hapley struck, and missed; then again.

The third time he hit his microscope. The instrument swayed, struck and overturned the lamp, and fell noisily upon the floor. The lamp turned over on the table and, very luckily, went out. Hapley was left in the dark. With a start he felt the strange moth blunder into his face.

It was maddening. He had no lights. If he opened the door of the room the thing would get away. In the darkness he saw Pawkins quite distinctly laughing at him. Pawkins had ever an oily laugh. He swore furiously and stamped his foot on the floor.

There was a timid rapping at the door.

Then it opened, perhaps a foot, and very slowly. The alarmed face of the landlady appeared behind a pink candle flame; she wore a night-cap over her grey hair and had some purple garment over her shoulders. 'What *was* that fearful smash?' she said. 'Has anything—' The strange moth appeared fluttering about the chink of the door. 'Shut that door!' said Hapley, and suddenly rushed at her.

The door slammed hastily. Hapley was left alone in the dark. Then in the pause he heard his landlady scuttle upstairs, lock her door, and drag something heavy across the room and put against it.

It became evident to Hapley that his conduct and appearance had been strange and alarming. Confound the moth! And Pawkins! However, it was a pity to lose the moth now. He felt his way into the hall and found the matches, after sending his hat down upon the floor with a noise like a drum. With the lighted candle he returned to the sitting-room. No moth was to be seen. Yet once for a moment it seemed that the thing was fluttering round his head. Hapley very suddenly decided to give up the moth and go to bed. But he was excited. All night long his sleep was broken by dreams of the moth, Pawkins, and his land-lady. Twice in the night he turned out and soused his head in cold water.

One thing was very clear to him. His landlady could not possibly understand about the strange moth, especially as he had failed to catch it. No one but an entomologist would understand quite how he felt. She was probably frightened at his behaviour, and yet he failed to see how he could explain it. He decided to say nothing further about the events of last night. After breakfast he saw her in her garden, and decided to go out and talk to reassure her. He talked to her about beans and potatoes, bees, caterpillars, and the price of fruit. She replied in her usual manner, but she looked at him a little suspiciously, and kept walking as he walked, so that there was always a bed of flow-ers, or a row of beans, or something of the sort, between them. After a while he began to feel singularly irritated at this, and, to conceal his vexation, went indoors and presently went out for a walk.

The moth, or butterfly, trailing an odd flavour of Pawkins with it, kept coming into that walk though he did his best to keep his mind off it. Once he saw it quite distinctly, with its wings flattened out, upon the old stone wall that runs along the west edge of the park, but going up to it he found it was only two lumps of grey and yellow lichen. 'This,' said Hapley, 'is the reverse of mimicry. Instead of a butterfly looking like a stone, here is a stone looking like a butterfly!' Once something hovered and fluttered round his head, but by an effort of will he drove that impression out of his mind again.

In the afternoon Hapley called upon the Vicar, and argued with him upon theological questions. They sat in the little arbour covered with brier, and smoked as they wrangled. 'Look at that moth!' said Hapley, suddenly, pointing to the edge of the wooden table.

'Where?' said the Vicar.

'You don't see a moth on the edge of the table there?' said Hapley.

'Certainly not,' said the Vicar.

Hapley was thunderstruck. He gasped. The Vicar was staring at him. Clearly the man saw nothing. 'The eye of faith is no better than the eye of science,' said Hapley awkwardly.

'I don't see your point,' said the Vicar, thinking it was part of the argument.

That night Hapley found the moth crawling over his counterpane. He sat on the edge of the bed in his shirt-sleeves and reasoned with himself. Was it pure hallucination? He knew he was slipping, and he battled for his sanity with the same silent energy he had formerly displayed against Pawkins. So persistent is mental habit that he felt as if it were still a struggle with Pawkins. He was well versed in psychology. He knew that such visual illusions do come as a result of mental strain. But the point was, he did not only *see* the moth, he had heard it when it touched the edge of the lamp-shade and afterwards when it hit against the wall, and he had felt it strike his face in the dark.

He looked at it. It was not at all dream-like but perfectly clear and solid-looking in the candle-light. He saw the hairy body and the short feathery antennae, the jointed legs, even a place where the down was rubbed from the wing. He suddenly felt angry with himself for being afraid of a little insect.

His landlady had got the servant to sleep with her that night, because she was afraid to be alone. In addition she had locked the door and put the chest of drawers against it. They listened and talked in whispers after they had gone to bed, but nothing occurred to alarm them. About eleven they had ventured to put the candle out and had both dozed off to sleep. They woke with a start, and sat up in bed, listening in the darkness.

Then they heard slippered feet going to and fro in Hapley's room. A chair was overturned and there was a violent dab at the wall. Then a china mantel ornament smashed upon the fender. Suddenly the door of the room opened, and they heard him upon the landing. They clung to one another, listening. He seemed to be dancing upon the staircase. Now he would go down three or four steps quickly, then up again, then hurry down into the hall. They heard the umbrella-stand go over, and the fanlight break. Then the bolt shot and the chain rattled. He was opening the door.

They hurried to the window. It was a dim grey night; an almost unbroken sheet of watery cloud was sweeping across the moon, and the hedge and trees in front of the house were black against the pale roadway. They saw Hapley, looking like a ghost in his shirt and white trousers, running to and fro in the road and beating the air. Now he would stop, now he would dart very rapidly at something invisible, now he would move upon it with stealthy strides. At last he went out of sight up the road towards the down. Then while they argued who should go down and lock the door, he returned. He was walking very fast, and he came straight into the house, closed the door carefully, and went quietly up to his bedroom. Then everything was silent.

'Mrs Colville,' said Hapley, calling down the staircase next morning, 'I hope I did not alarm you last night.'

'You may well ask that!' said Mrs Colville.

'The fact is, I am a sleep-walker, and the last two nights I have been without my sleeping mixture. There is nothing to be alarmed about, really. I am sorry I made such an ass of myself. I will go over the down to Shoreham, and get some stuff to make me sleep soundly. I ought to have done that yesterday.'

But half-way over the down, by the chalk pits, the moth came upon Hapley again. He went on, trying to keep his mind upon chess problems, but it was no good. The thing fluttered into his face, and he struck at it with his hat in self-defence. Then rage, the old rage—the rage he had so often felt against Pawkins—came upon him again. He went on, leaping and striking at the eddying insect. Suddenly he trod on nothing, and fell headlong.

There was a gap in his sensations, and Hapley found himself sitting on the heap of flints in front of the opening of the chalkpits, with a leg twisted back under him. The strange moth was still fluttering round his head. He struck at it with his hand, and turning his head saw two men approaching him. One was the village doctor. It occurred to Hapley that this was lucky. Then it came into his mind with extraordinary vividness, that no one would ever be able to see the strange moth except himself, and that it behoved him to keep silent about it.

Late that night, however, after his broken leg was set, he was feverish and forgot his self-restraint. He was lying flat on his bed, and he began to run his eyes round the room to see if the moth was still about. He tried not to do this, but it was no good. He soon caught sight of the thing resting close to his hand, by the night-light, on the green tablecloth. The wings quivered. With a sudden wave of anger he smote at it with his fist, and the nurse woke up with a shriek. He had missed it.

'That moth!' he said; and then: 'It was fancy. Nothing!'

All the time he could see quite clearly the insect going round the cornice and darting across the room, and he could also see that the nurse saw nothing of it and looked at him strangely. He must keep himself in hand. He knew he was a lost man if he did not keep himself in hand. But as the night waned the fever grew upon him, and the very dread he had of seeing the moth made him see it. About five, just as the dawn was grey, he tried to get out of bed and catch it, though his leg was afire with pain. The nurse had to struggle with him.

On account of this, they tied him down to the bed. At this the moth grew bolder, and once he felt it settle in his hair. Then, because he struck out violently with his arms, they tied these also. At this the moth came and crawled over his face, and Hapley wept, swore, screamed, prayed for them to take it off him, unavailingly.

The doctor was a blockhead, a just-qualified general practitioner, and quite ignorant of mental science. He simply said there was no moth. Had he possessed the wit he might still perhaps have saved Hapley from his fate by entering into his delusion, and covering his face with gauze as he prayed might be done. But, as I say, the doctor was a blockhead; and until the leg was healed Hapley was kept tied to

49

his bed, with the imaginary moth crawling over him. It never left him while he was awake and it grew to a monster in his dreams. While he was awake he longed for sleep, and from sleep he awoke screaming.

So now Hapley is spending the remainder of his days in a padded room, worried by a moth that no one else can see. The asylum doctor calls it hallucination; but Hapley, when he is in his easier mood and can talk, says it is the ghost of Pawkins, and consequently a unique specimen and well worth the trouble of catching.

POLLOCK AND THE PORROH MAN

IT WAS in a swampy village on the lagoon river behind the Turner Peninsula that Pollock's first encounter with the Porroh man occurred. The women of that country are famous for their good looks—they are Gallinas with a dash of European blood that dates from the days of Vasco de Gama and the English slave-traders, and the Porroh man, too, was possibly inspired by a faint Caucasian taint in his composition. (It's a curious thing to think that some of us may have distant cousins eating men on Sherboro Island or raiding with the Sofas.) At any rate, the Porroh man stabbed the woman to the heart as though he had been a mere low-class Italian, and very narrowly missed Pollock. But Pollock, using his revolver to parry the lightning stab which was aimed at his deltoid muscle, sent the iron dagger flying, and, firing, hit the man in the hand.

He fired again and missed, knocking a sudden window out of the wall of the hut. The Porroh man stooped in the doorway, glancing under his arm at Pollock. Pollock caught a glimpse of his inverted face in the sunlight, and then the Englishman was alone, sick and trembling with the excitement of the affair, in the twilight of the place. It had all happened in less time than it takes to read about it.

The woman was quite dead, and having ascertained this, Pollock went to the entrance of the hut and looked out. Things outside were dazzling bright. Half a dozen of the porters of the expedition were standing up in a group near the green huts they occupied, and staring towards him, wondering what the shots might signify. Behind the little group of men was the broad stretch of black fetid mud by the river, a green carpet of rafts of papyrus and water-grass, and then the leaden water. The mangroves beyond the stream loomed indistinctly through the blue haze. There were no signs of excitement in the squat village, whose fence was just visible above the cane-grass.

51

Pollock came out of the hut cautiously and walked towards the river, looking over his shoulder at intervals. But the Porroh man had vanished. Pollock clutched his revolver nervously in his hand.

One of his men came to meet him, and as he came, pointed to the bushes behind the hut in which the Porroh man had disappeared. Pollock had an irritating persuasion of having made an absolute fool of himself; he felt bitter, savage, at the turn things had taken. At the same time, he would have to tell Waterhouse—the moral, exemplary, cautious Waterhouse who would inevitably take the matter seriously. Pollock cursed bitterly at his luck, at Waterhouse, and especially at the West Coast of Africa. He felt consummately sick of the expedition. And in the back of his mind all the time was a speculative doubt where precisely within the visible horizon the Porroh man might be.

It is perhaps rather shocking, but he was not at all upset by the murder that had just happened. He had seen so much brutality during the last three months, so many dead women, burnt huts, drying skeletons, up the Kittam River in the wake of the Sofa cavalry, that his senses were blunted. What disturbed him was the persuasion that this business was only beginning.

He swore savagely at the black, who ventured to ask a question, and went on into the tent under the orange-trees where Waterhouse was lying, feeling exasperatingly like a boy going into the headmaster's study.

Waterhouse was still sleeping off the effects of his last dose of chlorodyne, and Pollock sat down on a packing-case beside him, and, lighting his pipe, waited for him to wake. About him were scattered the pots and weapons Waterhouse had collected from the Mendi people, and which he had been repacking for the canoe voyage to Sulyma.

Presently Waterhouse woke up, and after judicial stretching decided he was all right again. Pollock got him some tea. Over the tea the incidents of the afternoon were described by Pollock, after some preliminary beating about the bush. Waterhouse took the matter even more seriously than Pollock had anticipated. He did not simply disapprove, he scolded, he insulted.

'You're one of those infernal fools who think a black man isn't a human being,' he said. 'I can't be ill a day without you must get into some dirty scrape or other. This is the third time in a month that you have come crossways-on with a native, and this time you're in for it with a vengeance. Porroh, too! They're down upon you enough as it is, about that idol you wrote your silly name on. And they're the most vindictive devils on earth! You make a man ashamed of civilisation. To think you come of a decent family! If ever I cumber myself with a vicious, stupid young lout like you again—'

'Steady on, now,' snarled Pollock, in the tone that always exasperated Waterhouse; 'steady on.'

At that Waterhouse became speechless. He jumped to his, feet.

'Look here, Pollock,' he said, after a struggle to control his, breath. 'You must go home. I won't have you any longer. I'm ill enough as it is through you—'

'Keep your hair on,' said Pollock, staring in front of him. 'I'm ready enough to go.'

Waterhouse became calmer again. He sat down on the camp-stool. 'Very well,' he said. 'I don't want a row, Pollock, you know, but it's confoundedly annoying to have one's plans put out by this kind of thing. I'll come to Sulyma with you, and see you safe aboard—'

'You needn't,' said Pollock. 'I can go alone. From here.'

'Not far,' said Waterhouse. 'You don't understand this Porroh business.'

'How should *I* know she belonged to a Porroh man?' said Pollock bitterly.

'Well, she did,' said Waterhouse; 'and you can't undo the thing. Go alone, indeed! I wonder what they'd do to you. You don't seem to understand that this Porroh hokeypokey rules this country, is its law, religion, constitution, medicine, magic. . . . They appoint the chiefs. The Inquisition, at its best, couldn't hold a candle to these chaps. He will probably set Awajale, the chief here, on to us. It's lucky our porters are Mendis. We shall have to shift this little settlement of ours. . . . Confound you, Pollock! And, of course, you must go and miss him.'

He thought, and his thoughts seemed disagreeable. Presently he stood up and took his rifle. 'I'd keep close for a bit, if I were you,' he said over his shoulder as he went out. 'I'm going out to see what I can find out about it.'

Pollock remained sitting in the tent, meditating. 'I was meant for a civilised life,' he said to himself regretfully, as he filled his pipe. 'The sooner I get back to London or Paris the better for me.'

His eye fell on the sealed case in which Waterhouse had put the featherless poisoned arrows they had bought in the Mendi country. 'I wish I had hit the beggar somewhere vital,' said Pollock viciously.

Waterhouse came back after a long interval. He was not communicative, though Pollock asked him questions enough. The Porroh man, it seems, was a prominent member of that mystical society. The village was interested, but not threatening. No doubt the witch-doctor had gone into the bush. He was a great witch-doctor. 'Of course, he's up to something,' said Waterhouse, and became silent.

'But what can he do?' asked Pollock, unheeded.

'I must get you out of this. There's something brewing, or things would not be so quiet,' said Waterhouse, after a gap of silence. Pollock wanted to know what the brew might be. 'Dancing in a circle of skulls,' said Waterhouse; 'brewing a stink in a copper pot.' Pollock wanted particulars. Waterhouse was vague, Pollock pressing. At last Waterhouse lost his temper. How the devil should *I* know?' he said to Pollock's twentieth inquiry what the Porroh man would do. 'He tried to kill you off-hand in the hut. *Now*, I fancy he will try something more elaborate. But you'll see fast enough. I don't want to help unnerve you. It's probably all nonsense.'

That night, as they were sitting at their fire, Pollock again tried to draw Waterhouse out on the subject of Porroh methods. 'Better get to sleep,' said Waterhouse, when Pollock's bent became apparent; 'we start early tomorrow. You may want all your nerve about you.'

'But what line will he take?'

'Can't say. They're versatile people. They know a lot of rum dodges. You'd better get that copper-devil, Shakespear, to talk.'

There was a flash and a heavy bang out of the darkness behind the huts, and a clay bullet came whistling close to Pollock's head. This, at least, was crude enough. The blacks and half-breeds sitting and yarning round their own fire jumped up, and someone fired into the dark.

'Better go into one of the huts,' said Waterhouse quietly, still sitting unmoved.

Pollock stood up by the fire and drew his revolver. Fighting, at least, he was not afraid of. But a man in the dark is in the best of armour. Realising the wisdom of Waterhouse's advice, Pollock went into the tent and lay down there.

What little sleep he had was disturbed by dreams, variegated dreams, but chiefly of the Porroh man's face, upside down, as he went out of the hut, and looked up under his arm. It was odd that this transitory impression should have stuck so firmly in Pollock's memory. Moreover, he was troubled by queer pains in his limbs.

In the white haze of the early morning, as they were loading the canoes, a barbed arrow suddenly appeared quivering in the ground close to Pollock's foot. The boys made a perfunctory effort to clear out the thicket, but it led to no capture.

After these two occurrences, there was a disposition on the part of the expedition to leave Pollock to himself, and Pollock became, for the first time in his life, anxious to mingle with blacks. Waterhouse took one canoe, and Pollock, in spite of a friendly desire to chat with Waterhouse, had to take the other. He was left all alone in the front part of the canoe, and he had the greatest trouble to make the men—who did not love him—keep to the middle of the river, a clear hundred yards or more from either shore. However, he made Shakespear, the Freetown half-breed, come up to his own end of the canoe and tell him about Porroh, which Shakespear, failing in his attempts to leave Pollock alone, presently did with considerable freedom and gusto.

The day passed. The canoe glided swiftly along the ribbon of lagoon water, between the drift of water-figs, fallen trees, papyrus, and palm-wine palms, and with the dark mangrove swamp to the left, through which one could hear now and then the roar of the Atlantic surf. Shakespear told in his soft, blurred English of how the Porroh could cast spells; how men withered up under their malice; how they could send dreams and devils; how they tormented and killed the sons of Ijibu; how they kidnapped a white trader from Sulyma who had maltreated one of the sect, and how his body looked when it was found. And Pollock after each narrative cursed under his breath at the want of missionary enterprise that allowed such things to be, and at the inert British Government that ruled over this dark heathendom of Sierra Leone. In the evening they came to the Kasi Lake, and sent a score of crocodiles lumbering off the island on which the expedition camped for the night.

The next day they reached Sulyma, and smelt the sea breeze, but Pollock had to put up there for five days before he would go on to Freetown. Waterhouse, considering him to be comparatively safe here, and within the pale of Freetown influence, left him and went back with the expedition to Gbemma, and Pollock became very friendly with

Perera, the only resident white trader at Sulyma—so friendly, indeed, that he went about with him everywhere. Perera was a little Portuguese Jew, who had lived in England, and he appreciated the Englishman's friendliness as a great compliment.

For two days nothing happened out of the ordinary; for the most part Pollock and Perera played nap—the only game they had in common—and Pollock got into debt. Then, on the second evening, Pollock had a disagreeable intimation of the arrival of the Porroh man in Sulyma by getting a flesh-wound in the shoulder from a lump of filed iron. It was a long shot, and the missile had nearly spent its force when it hit him. Still it conveyed its message plainly enough. Pollock sat up in his hammock, revolver in hand, all that night, and next morning confided, to some extent, in the Anglo-Portuguese.

Perera took the matter seriously. He knew the local customs pretty thoroughly. 'It is a personal question, you must know. It is revenge. And of course he is hurried by your leaving de country. None of de natives or half-breeds will interfere wid him very much—unless you make it wort deir while. If you come upon him suddenly, you might shoot him. But den he might shoot you.

'Den dere's dis—infernal magic,' said Perera. 'Of course, I don't believe in it—superstition—but still it's not nice to tink dat wherever you are, dere is a black man, who spends a moonlight night now and den a-dancing about a fire to send you bad dreams. . . . Had any bad dreams?'

'Rather,' said Pollock. 'I keep on seeing the beggar's head upside down grinning at me and showing all his teeth as he did in the hut, and coming close up to me, and then going ever so far off, and coming back. It's nothing to be afraid of, but somehow it simply paralyses me with terror in my sleep. Queer things—dreams. I know it's a dream all the time, and I can't wake up from it.'

'It's probably only fancy,' said Perera. 'Den my niggers say Porroh men can send snakes. Seen any snakes lately?'

'Only one. I killed him this morning, on the floor near my hammock. Almost trod on him as I got up.'

'*Ah!*' said Perera, and then, reassuringly, 'Of course it is a—coincidence. Still I would keep my eyes open. Den dere's pains in de bones.'

'I thought they were due to miasma,' said Pollock.

'Probably dey are. When did dey begin?'

Then Pollock remembered that he first noticed them the night after the fight in the hut. 'It's my opinion he don't want to kill you,' said Perera—'at least not yet. I've heard deir idea is to scare and worry a man wid deir spells, and narrow misses, and rheumatic pains, and bad dreams, and all dat, until he's sick of life. Of course, it's all talk, you know. You mustn't worry about it. . . . But I wonder what he'll be up to next.'

'I shall have to be up to something first,' said Pollock, staring gloomily at the greasy cards that Perera was putting on the table. 'It don't suit my dignity to be followed about, and shot at, and blighted in this way. I wonder if Porroh hokeypokey upsets your luck at cards.'

He looked at Perera suspiciously.

'Very likely it does,' said Perera warmly, shuffling. 'Dey are wonderful people.'

That afternoon Pollock killed two snakes in his hammock, and there was also an extraordinary increase in the number of red ants that swarmed over the place; and these annoyances put him in a fit temper to talk over business with a certain Mendi rough he had interviewed before. The Mendi rough showed Pollock a little iron dagger, and demonstrated where one struck in the neck, in a way that made Pollock shiver, and in return for certain considerations Pollock promised him a double-barrelled gun with an ornamental lock.

In the evening, as Pollock and Perera were playing cards, the Mendi rough came in through the doorway, carrying something in a blood-soaked piece of native cloth.

'Not here!' said Pollock very hurriedly. 'Not here!'

But he was not quick enough to prevent the man, who was anxious to get to Pollock's side of the bargain, from opening the cloth and throwing the head of the Porroh man upon the table. It bounded from there on to the floor, leaving a red trail on the cards, and rolled into a corner, where it came to rest upside down, but glaring hard at Pollock.

Perera jumped up as the thing fell among the cards, and began in his excitement to gabble in Portuguese. The Mendi was bowing, with the red cloth in his hand. 'De gun!' he cried. Pollock stared back at the head in the corner. It bore exactly the expression it had in his dreams. Something seemed to snap in his own brain as he looked at it.

Then Perera found his English again.

'You got him killed?' he said. 'You did not kill him yourself?'

'Why should I?' said Pollock.

'But he will not be able to take it off now!'

'Take *what* off?' said Pollock.

'And all dese cards are spoiled!'

'*What* do you mean by taking off?' said Pollock,

'You must send me a new pack from Freetown. You can buy dem dere,'

'But—"take it off"?'

'It is only superstition. I forgot. De niggers say dat if de witches— he was a witch—But it is rubbish. . . . You must make de Porroh man take it off, or kill him yourself. . . . It is very silly.'

Pollock swore under his breath, still staring hard at the head in the corner.

'I can't stand that glare,' he said. Then suddenly he rushed at the thing and kicked it. It rolled some yards or so, and came to rest in the same position as before, upside down, and looking at him.

'He is ugly,' said the Anglo-Portuguese, 'Very ugly. Dey do it on deir faces with little knives.'

Pollock would have kicked the head again, but the Mendi man touched him on the arm. 'De gun?' he said, looking nervously at the head.

'Two—if you will take that beastly thing away,' said Pollock.

The Mendi shook his head, and intimated that he only wanted one gun now due to him, and for which he would be obliged. Pollock found neither cajolery nor bullying any good with him. Perera had a gun to sell (at a profit of three hundred per cent), and with that the man presently departed. Then Pollock's eyes, against his will, were recalled to the thing on the floor.

'It is funny dat his head keeps upside down,' said Perera, with an uneasy laugh. 'His brains must be heavy, like de weight in de little images one sees dat keep always upright wid lead in dem. You will take him wiv you when you go presently. You might take him now. De cards are all spoilt. Dere is a man sell dem in Freetown. De room is in a filthy mess as it is. You should have killed him yourself.'

Pollock pulled himself together, and went and picked up the head. He would hang it up by the lamp-hook in the middle of the ceiling of his room, and dig a grave for it at once. He was under the impression that he hung it up by the hair, but that must have been wrong, for when he returned for it, it was hanging by the neck upside down.

He buried it before sunset on the north side of the shed he occupied, so that he should not have to pass the grave after dark when he was returning from Perera's. He killed two snakes before he went to sleep. In the darkest part of the night he awoke with a start, and heard a pattering sound and something scraping on the floor. He sat up noiselessly, and felt under his pillow for his revolver. A mumbling growl followed, and Pollock fired at the sound. There was a yelp, and something dark passed for a moment across the hazy blue of the doorway. 'A dog!' said Pollock, lying down again.

In the early dawn he awoke again with a peculiar sense of unrest. The vague pain in his bones had returned. For some time he lay watching the red ants that were swarming over the ceiling, and then, as the light grew brighter, he looked over the edge of his hammock and saw something dark on the floor. He gave such a violent start that the hammock overset and flung him out.

He found himself lying, perhaps, a yard away from the head of the Porroh man, It had been disinterred by the dog, and the nose was grievously battered. Ants and flies swarmed over it. By an odd coincidence, it was still upside down, and with the same diabolical expression in the inverted eyes.

Pollock sat paralysed, and stared at the horror for some time. Then he got up and walked round it—giving it a wide berth—and out of the shed. The clear light of the sunrise, the living stir of vegetation before the breath of the dying landbreeze, and the empty grave with the marks of the dog's paws, lightened the weight upon his mind a little.

He told Perera of the business as though it was a jest—a jest to be told with white lips. 'You should not have frighten de dog,' said Perera, with poorly simulated hilarity.

The next two days, until the steamer came, were spent by Pollock in making a more effectual disposition of his possession. Overcoming his aversion to handling the thing, he went down to the river mouth and threw it into the sea-water, but by some miracle it escaped the crocodiles, and was cast up by the tide on the mud a little way up the river, to be found by an intelligent Arab half-breed, and offered for sale to Pollock and Perera as a curiosity, just on the edge of night. The native hung about in the brief twilight, making lower and lower offers, and at last, getting scared in some way by the evident dread these wise white men had for the thing, went off, and, passing Pollock's shed, threw his burden in there for Pollock to discover in the morning.

At this Pollock got into a kind of frenzy. He would burn the thing. He went out straightway into the dawn, and had constructed a big pyre of brushwood before the heat of the day, He was interrupted by the hooter of the little paddle steamer from Monrovia to Bathurst, which was coming through the gap in the bar. 'Thank Heaven!' said Pollock, with infinite piety, when the meaning of the sound dawned upon him. With trembling hands he lit his pile of wood hastily, threw the head upon it and went away to pack his Portmanteau and make his adieux to Perera.

That afternoon, with a sense of infinite relief, Pollock watched the flat swampy foreshore of Sulyma grow small in the distance. The gap in the long line of white surge became narrower and narrower. It seemed to be closing in and cutting him off from his trouble. The feeling of dread and worry began to slip from him bit by bit. At Sulyma belief in Porroh malignity and Porroh magic had been in the air, his sense of Porroh had been vast, pervading, threatening, dreadful. Now manifestly the domain of Porroh was only a little place, a little black band between the sea and the blue cloudy Mendi uplands.

'Goodbye, Porroh!' said Pollock. 'Goodbye—certainly not *au revoir.*'

The captain of the steamer came and leant over the rail beside him, and wished him good-evening, and spat at the froth of the wake in token of friendly ease.

'I picked up a rummy curio on the beach this go,' said the captain. 'It's a thing I never saw done this side of Indy before.'

'What might that be' said Pollock.

'Pickled 'ed,' said the captain.

'*What!*' said Pollock.

' 'Ed—smoked. 'Ed of one of these Porroh chaps, all ornamented with knife-cuts. Why! What's up? Nothing? I shouldn't have took you for a nervous chap. Green in the face. By gosh! you're a bad sailor. All right, eh? Lord, how funny you went! . . . Well, this 'ed I was telling you of is a bit rum in a way. I've got it, along with some snakes, in a jar of spirit in my cabin what I keeps for such curios, and I'm hanged if it don't float tipsy down. Hullo!'

Pollock had given an incoherent cry, and had his hands in his hair. He ran towards the paddle-boxes with a half-formed idea of jumping into the sea, and then he realised his position and turned back towards the captain.

'Here!' said the captain. 'Jack Philips, just keep him off me! Stand off! No nearer, mister! What's the matter with you? Are you mad?'

Pollock put his hand to his head. It was no good explaining.

'I believe I am pretty nearly mad at times,' he said. 'It's a pain I have here. Comes suddenly. You'll excuse me, I hope.'

He was white and in a perspiration. He saw suddenly very clearly all the danger he ran of having his sanity doubted. He forced himself to restore the captain's confidence, by answering his sympathetic inquiries, noting his suggestions, even trying a spoonful of neat brandy in his cheek, and, that matter settled, asking a number of questions about the captain's private trade in curiosities. The captain described the head in detail. All the while Pollock was struggling to keep under a preposterous persuasion that the ship was as transparent as glass, and that he could distinctly see the inverted face looking at him from the cabin beneath his feet.

Pollock had a worse time almost on the steamer than he had at Sulyma. All day he had to control himself in spite of his intense perception of the imminent presence of that horrible head that was over-shadowing his mind. At night his old nightmare returned, until, with a violent effort, he would force himself awake, rigid with the horror of it, and with the ghost of a hoarse scream in his throat.

He left the actual head behind at Bathurst, where he changed ship for Teneriffe, but not his dreams nor the dull ache in his bones. At Teneriffe Pollock transferred to a Cape liner, but the head followed him. He gambled, he tried chess, he even read books, but he knew the danger of drink. Yet whenever a round black shadow, a round black object came into his range, there he looked for the head, and—saw it. He knew clearly enough that his imagination was growing traitor to him, and yet at times it seemed the ship he sailed in, his fellow-passengers, the sailors, the wide sea, was all part of a filmy phantasmagoria that hung, scarcely veiling it, between him and a horrible real world. Then the Porroh man, thrusting his diabolical face through that curtain, was the one real and undeniable thing. At that he would get up and touch things, taste something, gnaw something, burn his hand with a match, or run a needle into himself.

61

So, struggling grimly and silently with his excited imagination, Pollock reached England. He landed at Southampton, and went on straight from Waterloo to his banker's in Cornhill in a cab. There he transacted some business with the manager in a private room, and all the while the head hung like an ornament under the black marble mantel and dripped upon the fender. He could hear the drops fall, and see the red on the fender.

'A pretty fern,' said the manager, following his eyes. 'But it makes the fender rusty.'

'Very,' said Pollock; 'a *very* pretty fern. And that reminds me. Can you recommend me a physician for mind troubles? I've got a little— what is it?—hallucination.'

The head laughed savagely, wildly. Pollock was surprised the manager did not notice it. But the manager only stared at his face.

With the address of a doctor, Pollock presently emerged in Cornhill. There was no cab in sight, and so he went on down to the western end of the street, and essayed the crossing opposite the Mansion House. The crossing is hardly easy even for the expert Londoner; cabs, vans, carriages, mail-carts, omnibuses go by in one incessant stream; to any one fresh from the malarious solitudes of Sierre Leone it is a boiling, maddening confusion. But when an inverted head suddenly comes bouncing, like an indiarubber ball, between your legs, leaving distinct smears of blood every time it touches the ground you can scarcely hope to avoid an accident. Pollock lifted his feet convulsively to avoid it, and then kicked at the thing furiously. Then something hit him violently in the back, and a hot pain ran up his arm.

He had been hit by the pole of an omnibus, and three of the fingers of his left hand smashed by the hoof of one of the horses—the very fingers, as it happened, that he shot from the Porroh man. They pulled him out from between the horses' legs, and found the address of the physician in his crushed hand.

For a couple of days Pollock's sensations were full of the sweet, pungent smell of chloroform, of painful operations that caused him no pain, of lying still and being given food and drink. Then he had a slight fever, and was very thirsty, and his old nightmare came back. It was only when it returned that he noticed it had left him for a day.

'If my skull had been smashed instead of my fingers, it might have gone altogether,' said Pollock, staring thoughtfully at the dark cushion that had taken on for the time the shape of the head.

Pollock at the first opportunity told the physician of his mind trouble. He knew clearly that he must go mad unless something should intervene to save him. He explained that he had witnessed a decapitation in Dahomey, and was haunted by one of the heads. Naturally, he did not care to state the actual facts. The physician looked grave.

Presently he spoke hesitatingly. 'As a child, did you get very much religious training?'

'Very little,' said Pollock.

A shade passed over the physician's face. 'I don't know if you have heard of the miraculous cures—it may be, of course, they are not miraculous—at Lourdes.'

'Faith-healing will hardly suit me, I am afraid,' said Pollock, with his eye on the dark cushion.

The head distorted its scarred features in an abominable grimace. The physician went upon a new track. 'It's all imagination,' he said, speaking with sudden briskness. 'A fair case for faith-healing, anyhow. Your nervous system has run down, you're in that twilight state of health when the bogles come easiest. The strong impression was too much for you. I must make you up a little mixture that will strengthen your nervous system—especially your brain. And you must take exercise.'

'I'm no good for faith-healing,' said Pollock.

'And therefore we must restore tone. Go in search of stimulating air—Scotland, Norway, the Alps—'

'Jericho, if you like,' said Pollock—' where Naaman went.'

However, so soon as his fingers would let him, Pollock made a gallant attempt to follow out the doctor's suggestion. It was now November. He tried football, but to Pollock the game consisted in kicking a furious inverted head about a field. He was no good at the game. He kicked blindly, with a kind of horror, and when they put him back into goal, and the ball came swooping down upon him, he suddenly yelled and got out of its way. The discreditable stories that had driven him from England to wander in the tropics shut him off from any but men's society, and now his increasingly strange behaviour made even his man friends avoid him. The thing was no longer a thing of the eye merely; it gibbered at him, spoke to him. A horrible fear came upon him that presently, when he took hold of the apparition, it would no longer become some mere article of furniture, but would feel like a real dissevered head. Alone, he would curse at the thing, defy it, entreat it; once or twice, in spite of his grim self-control, he addressed it in the presence of others. He felt the growing suspicion in the eyes of the people that watched him—his landlady, the servant, his man.

One day early in December his cousin Arnold—his next of kin—came to see him and draw him out, and watch his sunken yellow face with narrow eager eyes. And it seemed to Pollack that the hat his cousin carried in his hand was no hat at all, but a Gorgon head that glared at him upside down, and fought with its eyes against his reason. However, he was still resolute to see the matter out. He got a bicycle, and, riding over the frosty road from Wandsworth to Kingston, found the thing rolling along at his side, and leaving a dark trail behind it. He set his teeth and rode faster. Then suddenly, as he came down the hill towards Richmond Park, the apparition rolled in front of him and under his wheel, so quickly that he had no time for thought, and, turning quickly to avoid it, was flung violently against a heap of stones and broke his left wrist.

The end came on Christmas morning. All night he had been in a fever, the bandages encircling his wrist like a band of fire, his dreams more vivid and terrible than ever. In the cold, colourless, uncertain light that came before the sunrise, he sat up in his bed, and saw the head upon the bracket in the place of the bronze jar that had stood there overnight.

'I know that is a bronze jar,' he said, with a chill doubt at his heart. Presently the doubt was irresistible. He got out of bed slowly, shivering, and advanced to the jar with his hand raised. Surely he would see now his imagination had deceived him, recognise the distinctive sheen of bronze. At last, after an age of hesitation, his fingers came down on the patterned cheek of the head. He withdrew them spasmodically. The last stage was reached. His sense of touch had betrayed him.

Trembling, stumbling against the bed, kicking against his shoes with his bare feet, a dark confusion eddying round him, he groped his way to the dressing-table, took his razor from the drawer, and sat down on the bed with this in his hand. In the looking-glass he saw his own face, colourless, haggard, full of the ultimate bitterness of despair.

He beheld in swift succession the incidents in the brief tale of his experience. His wretched home, his still more wretched schooldays, the years of vicious life he had led since then, one act of selfish dishonour leading to another; it was all clear and pitiless now, all its squalid folly, in the cold light of the dawn. He came to the hut, to the fight with the Porroh man, to the retreat down the river to Sulyma, to the Mendi assassin and his red parcel, to his frantic endeavours to destroy the head, to the growth of his hallucination. It was a hallucination! He *knew* it was. A hallucination merely. For a moment he snatched at hope. He looked away from the glass, and on the bracket the inverted head grinned and grimaced at him. . . . With the stiff fingers of his bandaged hand he felt at his neck for the throb of his arteries. The morning was very cold, the steel blade felt like ice.

UNDER THE KNIFE

WHAT if I die under it?' The thought recurred again and again as I walked home from Haddon's. It was a purely personal question. I was spared the deep anxieties of a married man, and I knew there were, few of my intimate friends but would find my death troublesome chiefly on account of their duty of regret. I was surprised indeed and perhaps a little humiliated, as I turned the matter over, to think how few could possibly exceed the conventional requirement. Things came before me stripped of glamour, in a clear dry light, during that walk from Haddon's house over Primrose Hill. There were the friends of my youth; I perceived now that our affection was a tradition which we foregathered rather laboriously to maintain. There were the rivals and helpers of my later career: I suppose I had been cold-blooded or undemonstrative—one perhaps implies the other. It may be that even the capacity for friendship is a question of physique. There had been a time in my own life when I had grieved bitterly enough at the loss of a friend; but as I walked home that afternoon the emotional side of my imagination was dormant. I could not pity myself, nor feel sorry for my friends, nor conceive of them as grieving for me.

I was interested in this deadness of my emotional nature—no doubt a concomitant of my stagnating physiology; and my thoughts wandered off along the line it suggested. Once before, in my hot youth, I had suffered a sudden loss of blood and had been within an ace of death. I remembered now that my affections as well as my passions had drained out of me, leaving scarcely anything but a tranquil resignation, a dreg of self-pity. It had been weeks before the old ambitions, and tendernesses, and all the complex moral interplay of a man, had reasserted themselves. Now again I was bloodless; had been feeling down for a week or more. I was not even hungry. It occurred to me that the real meaning of this numbness might be a gradual slipping away from the pleasure-pain guidance of the animal man. It has been proven, I take it, as thoroughly as anything can be proven in this world, that the higher emotions, the moral feelings, even the subtle tendernesses of love, are evolved from the elemental desires and fears of the simple animal: they are the harness in which man's mental freedom goes. And it may be that, as death overshadows us, as our possibility of acting diminishes, this complex growth of balanced impulse, propensity, and aversion whose interplay inspires our acts, goes with it. Leaving what?

I was suddenly brought back to reality by an imminent collision with a butcher-boy's tray. I found that I was crossing the bridge over the Regent's Park Canal which runs parallel with that in the Zoological Gardens. The boy in blue had been looking over his shoulder at a black barge advancing slowly, towed by a gaunt white horse. In the Gardens a nurse was leading three happy little children over the bridge. The trees were bright green; the spring hopefulness was still unstained by the dusts of summer; the sky in the water was bright and clear, but broken by long waves, by quivering bands of black, as the barge drove through. The breeze was stirring; but it did not stir me as the spring breeze used to do.

Was this dullness of feeling in itself an anticipation? It was curious that I could reason and follow out a network of suggestion as clearly as ever: so, at least, it seemed to me. It was calmness rather than dullness that was coming upon me. Was there any ground for the belief in the presentiment of death? Did a man near to death begin instinctively to withdraw himself from the meshes of matter and sense, even before, the cold hand was laid upon his? I felt strangely isolated—isolated without regret—from the life and existence about me. The children playing in the sun and gathering strength and experience for the business of life, the park-keeper gossiping with a nursemaid, the nursing mother, the young couple intent upon each other as they passed me, the trees by the wayside spreading new pleading leaves to the sunlight, the stir in their branches—I had been part of it all, but I had nearly done with it now.

Some way down the Broad Walk I perceived that I was tired, and that my feet were heavy. It was hot that afternoon, and I turned aside and sat down on one of the green chairs that line the way. In a minute I had dozed into a dream, and the tide of my thoughts washed up a vision of the resurrection. I was still sitting in the chair, but I thought myself actually dead, withered, tattered, dried, one eye (I saw) pecked out by birds. 'Awake!' cried a voice; and incontinently the dust of the path and the mould under the grass became insurgent. I had never before thought of Regent's Park as a cemetery, but now through the trees, stretching as far as eye could see, I beheld a flat plain of writhing graves and heeling tombstones. There seemed to be some trouble: the rising dead appeared to stifle as they struggled upward, they bled in their struggles, the red flesh was tattered away from the white bones. 'Awake!' cried a voice; but I determined I would not rise to such horrors. 'Awake!' They would not let me alone. 'Wike up!' said an angry voice. A cockney angel! The man who sells the tickets was shaking me, demanding my penny.

I paid my penny, pocketed my ticket, yawned, stretched my legs, and, feeling now rather less torpid, got up and walked on towards Langham Place. I speedily lost myself again in a shifting maze of thoughts about death. Going across Marylebone Road into that crescent at the end of Langham Place, I had the narrowest escape from the shaft of a cab, and went on my way with a palpitating heart and a bruised shoulder. It struck me that it would have been curious if my meditations on my death on the morrow had led to my death that day.

But I will not weary you with more of my experiences that day and the next. I knew more and more certainly that I should die under the operation; at times I think I was inclined to pose to myself. At home I found everything prepared; my room cleared of needless objects and hung with white sheets; a nurse installed and already at loggerheads with my housekeeper. They wanted me to go to bed early, and after a little resistance I obeyed.

In the morning I was very indolent, and though I read my newspapers and the letters that came by the first post, I did not find them very interesting. There was a friendly note from Addison, my old school friend, calling my attention to two discrepancies and a printer's error in my new book, with one from Langridge venting some vexation over Minton. The rest were business communications. I had a cup of tea but nothing to eat. The glow of pain at my side seemed more massive. I knew it was pain, and yet, if you can understand, I did not find it very painful. I had been awake and hot and thirsty in the night, but in the morning had felt comfortable. In the night-time I had lain thinking of things that were past; in the morning I dozed over the question of immortality. Haddon came, punctual to the minute, with a neat black bag; and Mowbray soon followed. Their arrival stirred me up a little. I began to take a more personal interest in the proceedings. Haddon moved the little octagonal table close to the bedside, and, with his broad black back to me, began taking things out of his bag. I heard the light click of steel upon steel. My imagination, I found, was not altogether stagnant. 'Will you hurt me much?' I said in an off-hand tone.

'Not a bit,' Haddon answered over his shoulder. 'We shall chloroform you. Your heart's as sound as a bell.' And as he spoke, I had a whiff of the pungent sweetness of the anaesthetic.

They stretched me out, with a convenient exposure of my side, and, almost before I realised what was happening, the chloroform was being administered. It stings the nostrils, and there is a suffocating sensation, at first. I knew I should die—that this was the end of consciousness for me. And suddenly I felt that I was not prepared for death: I had a vague sense of a duty overlooked—I knew not what. What was it I had not done? I could think of nothing more to do, nothing desirable left in life; and yet I had the strangest disinclination for death. And the physical sensation was painfully oppressive. Of course the doctors did not know they were going to kill me. Possibly I struggled. Then I fell motionless, and a great silence, a monstrous silence, and an impenetrable blackness came upon me.

There must have been an interval of absolute unconsciousness, seconds or minutes. Then, with a chilly, unemotional clearness, I perceived that I was not yet dead. I was still in my body; but all the multitudinous sensations that come sweeping from it to make up the background of consciousness had gone, leaving me free of it all. No, not free of it all; for as yet something still held me to the poor stark flesh upon the bed—held me, yet not so closely that I did not feel myself external to it, independent of it, straining away from it. I do not think I saw, I do not think I heard; but I perceived all that was going on, and it was as if I both heard and saw. Haddon was bending over me, Mowbray behind me; the scalpel—it was a large scalpel—was cutting my flesh at the side under the flying ribs. It was interesting to see myself cut like cheese, without a pang, without even a qualm. The interest was much of a quality with that one might feel in a game of chess between strangers. Haddon's face was firm and his hand steady; but I was surprised to perceive (*how* I know not) that he was feeling the gravest doubt as to his own wisdom in the conduct of the operation.

Mowbray's thoughts, too, I could see. He was thinking that Haddon's manner showed too much of the specialist. New suggestions came up like bubbles through a stream of frothing meditation, and burst one after another in the little bright spot of his consciousness. He could not help noticing and admiring Haddon's swift dexterity, in spite of his envious quality and his disposition to detract. I saw my liver exposed. I was puzzled at my own condition. I did not feel that I was dead, but I was different in some way from my living self. The grey depression that had weighed on me for a year or more and coloured all my thoughts, was gone. I perceived and thought without any emotional tint at all. I wondered if every one perceived things in this way under chloroform, and forgot it again when he came out of it. It would be inconvenient to look into some heads, and not forget.

Although I did not think that I was dead, I still perceived quite clearly that I was soon to die. This brought me back to the consideration of Haddon's proceedings. I looked into his mind, and saw that he was afraid of cutting a branch of the portal vein. My attention was distracted from details by the curious changes going on in his mind. His consciousness was like the quivering little spot of light which is thrown by the mirror of a galvanometer. His thoughts ran under it like a stream, some through the focus bright and distinct, some shadowy in the half-light of the edge. Just now the little glow was steady; but the least movement on Mowbray's part, the slightest sound from outside, even a faint difference in the slow movement of the living flesh he was cutting, set the light-spot shivering and spinning. A new sense-impression came rushing up through the flow of thoughts, and lo! the light-spot jerked away towards it, swifter than a frightened fish. It was wonderful to think that upon that unstable, fitful thing depended all the complex motions of the man; that for the next five minutes, therefore, my life hung upon its movements. And he was growing more and more nervous in his work. It was as if a little picture of a cut vein grew brighter, and struggled to oust from his brain another picture of a cut falling short of the mark. He was afraid: his dread of cutting too little was battling with his dread of cutting too far.

Then, suddenly, like an escape of water from under a lockgate, a great uprush of horrible realisation set all his thoughts swirling, and simultaneously I perceived that the vein was cut. He started back with a hoarse exclamation, and I saw the brown-purple blood gather in a swift bead, and run rickling. He was horrified. He pitched the red-stained scalpel on to the octagonal table; and instantly both doctors flung themselves upon me, making hasty and ill-conceived efforts to remedy the disaster. 'Ice!' said Mowbray, gasping. But I knew that I was killed, though my body still clung to me.

I will not describe their belated endeavours to save me, though I perceived every detail. My perceptions were sharper and swifter than they had ever been in life; my thoughts rushed through my mind with incredible swiftness, but with perfect definition. I can only compare their crowded clarity to the effects of a reasonable dose of opium. In a moment it would all be over, and I should be free. I knew I was immortal, but what would happen I did not know. Should I drift off presently, like a puff of smoke from a gun, in some kind of half-material body, an attenuated version of my material self? Should I find myself suddenly among the innumerable hosts of the dead, and know the world about me for the phantasmagoria it had always seemed? Should I drift to some spiritualistic seance, and there make foolish, incomprehensible attempts to affect a purblind medium? It was a state of unemotional curiosity, of colourless expectation. And then I realised a growing stress upon me, a feeling as though some huge human magnet was drawing me upward out of my body. The stress grew and grew. I seemed an atom for which monstrous forces were fighting. For one brief, terrible moment sensation came back to me. That feeling of falling headlong which comes in nightmares, that feeling a thousand times intensified, that and a black horror swept across my thoughts in a torrent. Then the two doctors, the naked body with its cut side, the little room, swept away from under me and vanished as a speck of foam vanishes down an eddy.

I was in mid-air. Far below was the West End of London, receding rapidly—for I seemed to be flying swiftly upward—and, as it receded, passing westward, like a panorama. I could see, through the faint haze of smoke, the innumerable roofs chimney-set, the narrow roadways stippled with people and conveyances, the little specks of squares, and the church steeples like thorns sticking out of the fabric. But it spun away as the earth rotated on its axis, and in a few seconds (as it seemed) I was over the scattered clumps of town about Ealing, the little Thames a thread of blue to the south, and the Chiltern Hills and the North Downs coming up like the rim of a basin, far away and faint with haze. Up I rushed. And at first I had not the faintest conception what this headlong rush upward could mean.

Every moment the circle of scenery beneath me grew wider and wider, and the details of town and field, of hill and valley, got more and more hazy and pale and indistinct, a luminous grey was mingled more and more with the blue of the hills and the green of the open meadows; and a little patch of cloud, low and far to the west, shone ever more dazzlingly white. Above, as the veil of atmosphere between myself and outer space grew thinner, the sky, which had been a fair springtime blue at first, grew deeper and richer in colour, passing steadily through the intervening shades until presently it was as dark as the blue sky of midnight, and presently as black as the blackness of a frosty starlight, and at last as black as no blackness I had ever beheld. And first one star and then many, and at last an innumerable host broke out upon the sky: more stars than any one has ever seen from the face of the earth. For the blueness of the sky is the light of the sun and stars sifted and spread abroad blindingly: there is diffused light even in the darkest skies of winter, and we do not see the stars by day only because of the dazzling irradiation of the sun. But now I saw things—I know not how; assuredly with no mortal eyes—and that defect of bedazzlement blinded me no longer. The sun was incredibly strange and wonderful. The body of it was a disc of blinding white light: not yellowish as it seems to those who live upon the earth, but livid white, all streaked with scarlet streaks and rimmed about with a fringe of writhing tongues of red fire. And, shooting half-way across the heavens from either side of it, and brighter than the Milky Way, were two pinions of silver-white, making it look more like than those winged globes I have seen in Egyptian sculpture than anything else I can remember upon earth. These I knew for the solar corona, though I had never seen anything of it but a picture during the days of my earthly life.

When my attention came back to the earth again, I saw that it had fallen very far away from me. Field and town were long since indistinguishable, and all the varied hues of the country were merging into a uniform bright grey, broken only by the brilliant white of the clouds that lay scattered in flocculent masses over Ireland and the west of England. For now I could see the outlines of the north of France and Ireland, and all this island of Britain save where Scotland passed over the horizon to the north, or where the coast was blurred or obliterated by cloud. The sea was a dull grey, and darker than the land; and the whole panorama was rotating slowly towards the east.

All this had happened so swiftly that, until I was some thousand miles or so from the earth, I had no thought for myself. But now I perceived I had neither hands nor feet, neither parts nor organs, and that I felt neither alarm nor pain. All about me I perceived that the vacancy (for I had already left the air behind) was cold beyond the imagination of man; but it troubled me not. The sun's rays shot through the void, powerless to light or heat until they should strike on matter in their course. I saw things with a serene self-forgetfulness, even as if I were God. And down below there, rushing away from me—countless miles in a second—where a little dark spot on the grey marked the position of London, two doctors were struggling to restore life to the poor hacked and outworn shell I had abandoned. I felt then such release, such serenity as I can compare to no mortal delight I have ever known.

It was only after I had perceived all these things that the meaning of that headlong rush of the earth grew into comprehension. Yet it was so simple, so obvious, that I was amazed at my never anticipating the thing that was happening to me. I had suddenly been cut adrift from matter: all that was material of me was there upon earth, whirling away through space, held to the earth by gravitation, partaking of the earth's inertia, moving in its wreath of epicycles round the sun, and with the sun and the planets on their vast march through space. But the immaterial has no inertia, feels nothing of the pull of matter for matter: where it parts from its garment of flesh, there it remains (so far as space concerns it any longer) immovable in space. I was not leaving the earth: the earth was leaving me, and not only the earth, but the whole solar system was streaming past. And about me in space, invisible to me, scattered in the wake of the earth upon its journey, there must be an innumerable multitude of souls, stripped like myself of the material, stripped like myself of the passions of the individual and the generous emotions of the gregarious brute, naked intelligences, things of newborn wonder and thought, marvelling at the strange release that had suddenly come on them!

As I receded faster and faster from the strange white sun in the black heavens, and from the broad and shining earth upon which my being had begun, I seemed to grow, in some incredible manner, vast: vast as regards this world I had left, vast as regards the moments and periods of a human life. Very soon I saw the full circle of the earth, slightly gibbous, like the moon when she nears her full, but very large;

and the silvery shape of America was now in the noonday blaze wherein (as it seemed) little England had been basking but a few minutes ago. At first the earth was large and shone in the heavens, filling a great part of them; but every moment she grew smaller and more distant. As she shrunk, the broad moon in its third quarter crept into view over the rim of her disc. I looked for the constellations. Only that part of Aries directly behind the sun, and the Lion, which the earth covered, were hidden. I recognised the tortuous, tattered band of the Milky Way, with Vega very bright between sun and earth; and Sirius and Orion shone splendid against the unfathomable blackness in the opposite quarter of the heavens. The Pole Star was overhead, and the Great Bear hung over the circle of the earth. And away beneath and beyond the shining corona of the sun were strange groupings of stars I had never seen in my life—notably, a dagger-shaped group that I knew for the Southern Cross. All these were no larger than when they had shone on earth; but the little stars that one scarcely sees shone now against the setting of black vacancy as brightly as the first-magnitudes had done, while the larger worlds were points of indescribable glory and colour. Aldebaran was a spot of blood-red fire, and Sirius condensed to one point the light of a world of sapphires. And they shone steadily: they did not scintillate, they were calmly glorious. My impressions had an adamantine hardness and brightness: there was no blurring softness, no atmosphere, nothing but infinite darkness set with the myriads of these acute and brilliant points and specks of light. Presently, when I looked again, the little earth seemed no bigger than the sun, and it dwindled and turned as I looked until, in a second's space (as it seemed to me), it was halved; and so it went on swiftly dwindling. Far away in the opposite direction, a little pinkish pin's head of light, shining steadily, was the planet Mars. I swam motionless in vacancy, and, without a trace of terror or astonishment, watched the speck of cosmic dust we call the world fall away from me.

Presently it dawned upon me that my sense of duration had changed: that my mind was moving not faster but infinitely slowlier, that between each separate impression there was a period of many days. The moon spun once round the earth as I noted this; and I perceived clearly the motion of Mars in his orbit. Moreover, it appeared as if the time between thought and thought grew steadily greater, until at last a thousand years was but a moment in my perception.

At first the constellations had shone motionless against the black background of infinite space; but presently it seemed as though the group of stars about Hercules and the Scorpion was contracting, while Orion and Aldebaran and their neighbours were scattering apart. Flashing suddenly out of the darkness there came a flying multitude of particles of rock, glittering like dust-specks in a sunbeam, and encomposed in a faintly luminous haze. They swirled all about me, and vanished again in a twinkling far behind. And then I saw that a bright spot of light, that shone a little to one side of my path, was growing very rapidly larger, and perceived that it was the planet Saturn rushing towards me. Larger and larger it grew, swallowing up the heavens behind it, and hiding every moment a fresh multitude of stars. I perceived its flattened, whirling body, its disc-like belt, and seven of its little satellites. It grew and grew, till it towered enormous; and then I plunged amid a streaming multitude of clashing stones and glancing dust-particles and gas-eddies, and saw for a moment the mighty triple belt like three concentric arches of moonlight above me, its shadow black on the boiling tumult below. These things happened in one-tenth of the time it takes to tell of them. The planet went by like a flash of lightning; for a few seconds it blotted out the sun, and there and then became a mere black, dwindling, winged patch against the light. The earth, the mother mote of my being, I could no longer see.

So with a, stately swiftness, in the profoundest silence, the solar system fell from me, as it had been a garment, until the sun was a mere star amid the multitude of stars, with its eddy of planet-specks, lost in the confused glittering of the remoter light. I was no longer a denizen of the solar system: I had come to the Outer Universe, I seemed to grasp and comprehend the whole world of matter. Ever more swiftly the stars closed in about the spot where Antares and Vega had vanished in a luminous haze, until that part of the sky had the semblance of a whirling mass of nebulæ, and ever before me yawned vaster gaps of vacant blackness and the stars shone fewer and fewer. It seemed as if I moved towards a point between Orion's belt and sword; and the void about that region opened vaster and vaster every second, an incredible gulf of nothingness, into which I was falling. Faster and ever faster the universe rushed by, a hurry of whirling motes at last, speeding silently into the void. Stars glowing brighter and brighter, with their circling planets catching the light in a ghostly fashion as I neared them, shone out and vanished again into inexistence; faint comets, clusters of meteorites, winking specks of matter, eddying light-points, whizzed past, some perhaps a hundred millions of miles or so from me at most, few nearer, travelling with unimaginable rapidity, shooting constellations, momentary darts of fire, through that black; enormous night. More than anything else it was like a dusty draught, sunbeam-lit. Broader, and wider, and deeper grew the starless space, the vacant Beyond, into which I was being drawn. At last a quarter of the heavens was black and blank and the whole headlong rush of stellar universe closed in behind me like a veil of light that is gathered together. I drove away from me like a monstrous jack-o'-lantern driven by the wind. I had come out into the wilderness of space. Ever the vacant blackness grew broader, until the hosts of the stars seemed only like a swarm of fiery specks hurrying away from me, inconceivably remote, and the darkness, the nothingness and emptiness, was about me on every side. Soon the little universe of matter, the cage of points in which I had begun to be, was dwindling, now to a whirling disc of luminous glittering, and now to one minute disc of hazy light. In a little while it would shrink to a point, and at last would vanish altogether.

Suddenly feeling came back, to me—feeling in the shape of overwhelming terror: such a dread of those dark vastitudes as no words can describe, a passionate resurgence of sympathy and social desire. Were there other souls, invisible to me as I to them, about me in the blackness? or was I indeed, even as I felt, alone? Had I passed out of being into something that was neither being nor not-being? The covering of the body, the covering of matter, had been torn from me, and the hallucinations of companionship and security. Everything was black and silent. I had ceased to be. I was nothing. There was nothing, save only that infinitesimal dot of light that dwindled in the gulf. I strained myself to hear and see, and for a while there was naught but infinite silence, intolerable darkness, horror, and despair.

Then I saw that about the spot of light into which the whole world of matter had shrunk there was a faint glow. And in a band on either side of that the darkness was not absolute. I watched it for ages, as it seemed to me, and through the long waiting the haze grew imperceptibly more distinct. And then about the band appeared an irregular cloud of the faintest, palest brown. I felt a passionate impatience; but the things grew brighter so slowly that they scarcely seemed to change.

What was unfolding itself? What was this strange reddish dawn in the interminable night of space?

The cloud's shape was grotesque. It seemed to be looped along its lower side into four projecting masses, and, above, it ended in a straight line. What phantom was it? I felt assured I had seen that figure before; but I could not think what, nor where, nor when it was. Then the realisation rushed upon me. *It was a clenched Hand.* I was alone in space, alone with this huge, shadowy Hand, upon which the whole Universe of Matter lay like an unconsidered speck of dust. It seemed as though I watched it through vast periods of time. On the forefinger glittered a ring; and the universe from which I had come was but a spot of light upon the ring's curvature. And the thing that the hand gripped had the likeness of a black rod. Through a long eternity I watched this Hand, with the ring and the rod, marvelling and fearing and waiting helplessly on what might follow. It seemed as though nothing could follow: that I should watch for ever, seeing only the Hand and the thing it held, and understanding nothing of its import. Was the whole universe but a refracting speck upon some greater Being? Were our worlds but the atoms of another universe, and those again of another, and so on through an endless progression? And what was I? Was I indeed immaterial? A vague persuasion of a body gathering about me came into my suspense. The abysmal darkness about the Hand filled with impalpable suggestions, with uncertain, fluctuating shapes.

Came a sound, like the sound of a tolling bell; faint, as if infinitely far, muffled as though heard through thick swathings of darkness: a deep, vibrating resonance, with vast gulfs of silence between each stroke. And the Hand appeared to tighten on the rod. And I saw far above the Hand, towards the apex of the darkness, a circle of dim phosphorescence, a ghostly sphere whence these sounds came throbbing; and at the last stroke the Hand vanished, for the hour had come, and I heard a noise of many waters. But the black rod remained as a great band across the sky. And then a voice, which seemed to run to the uttermost parts of space, spoke, saying, 'There will be no more pain.'

At that an almost intolerable gladness and radiance rushed upon me, and I saw the circle shining white and bright, and the rod black and shining, and many things else distinct and clear. And the circle was the face of the clock, and the rod the rail of my bed. Haddon was standing at the foot, against the rail, with a small pair of scissors on his fingers; and the hands of my clock on the mantel over his shoulder were clasped together over the hour of twelve. Mowbray was washing something in a basin at the octagonal table, and at my side I felt a subdued feeling that could scarce be spoken of as pain.

The operation had not killed me. And I perceived, suddenly that the dull melancholy of half a year was lifted from my mind.

THE PLATTNER STORY

WHETHER the story of Gottfried Plattner is to be credited or not, is a pretty question in the value of evidence. On the one hand, we have seven witnesses—to be perfectly exact, we have six and a half pairs of eyes, and one undeniable fact; and on the other we have—what is it?— prejudice, common sense, the inertia of opinion. Never were there seven more honest-seeming witnesses; never was there a more undeniable fact than the inversion of Gottfried Plattner's anatomical structure, and—never was there a more preposterous story than the one they have to tell! The most preposterous part of the story is the worthy Gottfried's contribution (for I count him as one of the seven). Heaven forbid that I should be led into giving countenance to superstition by a passion for impartiality, and so come to share the fate of Eusapia's patrons! Frankly, I believe there is something crooked about this business of Gottfried Plattner; but what that crooked factor is, I will admit as frankly, I do not know. I have been surprised at the credit accorded to the story in the most unexpected and authoritative quarters. The fairest way to the reader, however, will be for me to tell it without further comment.

Gottfried Plattner is, in spite of his name, a freeborn Englishman. His father was an Alsatian who came to England in the Sixties, married a respectable English girl of unexceptionable antecedents, and died, after a wholesome and uneventful life (devoted, I understand, chiefly to the laying of parquet flooring), in 1887. Gottfried's age is seven-and-twenty. He is, by virtue of his heritage of three languages, Modern Languages Master in a small private school in the South of England. To the casual observer he is singularly like any other Modern Languages Master in any other small private school. His costume is neither very costly nor very fashionable, but, on the other hand, it is not markedly cheap or shabby; his complexion, like his height and his bearing, is inconspicuous. You would notice perhaps that, like the majority of people, his face was not absolutely symmetrical, his right eye a little larger than the left, and his jaw a trifle heavier on the right side. If you, as an ordinary careless person, were to bare his chest and feel his heart beating, you would probably find it quite like the heart of anyone else. But here you and the trained observer would part company. If you found his heart quite ordinary, the trained observer would find it quite otherwise. And once the thing was pointed out to you, you too would perceive the peculiarity easily enough. It is that Gottfried's heart beats on the right side of his body.

Now that is not the only singularity of Gottfried's structure, although it is the only one that would appeal to the untrained mind. Careful sounding of Gottfried's internal arrangements, by a well-known surgeon, seems to point to the fact that all the other unsymmetrical parts of his body are similarly misplaced. The right lobe of his liver is on the left side, the left on his right; while his lungs, too, are similarly contraposed. What is still more singular, unless Gottfried is a consummate actor we must believe that his right hand has recently become his left. Since the occurrences we are about to consider (as impartially as possible), he has found the utmost difficulty in writing except from right to left across the paper with his left hand. He cannot throw with his right hand, he is perplexed at meal times between knife and fork, and his ideas of the rule of the road—he is a cyclist—are still a dangerous confusion. And there is not a scrap of evidence to show that before these occurrences Gottfried was at all left-handed.

There is yet another wonderful fact in this preposterous business. Gottfried produces three photographs of himself. You have him at the age of five or six, thrusting fat legs at you from under a plaid frock, and scowling. In that photograph his left eye is a little larger than his right, and his jaw is a trifle heavier on the left side. This is the reverse of his present living conditions. The photograph of Gottfried at fourteen seems to contradict these facts, but that is because it is one of those cheap 'Gem' photographs that were then in vogue, taken direct upon metal, and therefore reversing things just as a looking-glass would. The third photograph represents him at one-and-twenty, and confirms the record of the others. There seems here evidence of the strongest confirmatory character that Gottfried has exchanged his left side for his right. Yet how a human being can he so changed, short of a fantastic and pointless miracle, it is exceedingly hard to suggest.

In one way, of course, these facts might be explicable on the supposition that Plattner has undertaken an elaborate mystification on the strength of his heart's displacement. Photographs may be fudged, and left-handedness imitated. But the character of the man does not lend itself to any such theory. He is quiet, practical, unobtrusive, and thoroughly sane from the Nordau standpoint. He likes beer and smokes moderately, takes walking exercise daily, and has a healthily high estimate of the value of his teaching. He has a good but untrained tenor voice, and takes a pleasure in singing airs of a popular and cheerful character. He is fond, but not morbidly fond, of reading—chiefly fiction pervaded with a vaguely pious optimism,—sleeps well, and rarely dreams. He is, in fact, the very last person to evolve a fantastic fable. Indeed, so far from forcing this story upon the world, he has been singularly reticent on the matter. He meets inquirers with a certain engaging—bashfulness is almost the word, that disarms the most suspicious. He seems genuinely ashamed that anything so unusual has occurred to him.

It is to be regretted that Plattner's aversion to the idea of post-mortem dissection may postpone, perhaps for ever, the positive proof that his entire body has had its left and right sides transposed. Upon that fact mainly the credibility of his story hangs. There is no way of taking a man and moving him about *in space*, as ordinary people understand space, that will result in our changing his sides. Whatever you do, his right is still his right, his left his left. You can do that with a perfectly thin and flat thing, of course. If you were to cut a figure out of paper, any figure with a right and left side, you could change its sides simply by lifting it up and turning it over. But with a solid it is different. Mathematical theorists tell us that the only way in which the right and left sides of a solid body can be changed is by taking that body clean out of space as we know it,—taking it out of ordinary existence, that is, and turning it somewhere outside space. This is a little abstruse, no doubt, but anyone with a slight knowledge of mathematical theory will assure the reader of its truth. To put the thing in technical language, the curious inversion of Plattner's right and left sides is proof that he has moved out of our space into what is called the Fourth Dimension, and that he has returned again to our world. Unless we choose to consider ourselves the victims of an elaborate and motiveless fabrication, we are almost bound to believe that this has occurred.

So much for the tangible facts. We come now to the account of the phenomena that attended his temporary disappearance from the world. It appears that in the Sussexville Proprietary School, Plattner not only discharged the duties of Modern Languages Master, but also taught chemistry, commercial geography, book-keeping, shorthand, drawing, and any other additional subject to which the changing fancies of the boy's parents might direct attention. He knew little or nothing of these various subjects, but in secondary as distinguished from Board or elementary schools, knowledge in the teacher is, very properly, by no means so necessary as high moral character and gentlemanly tone. In chemistry he was particularly deficient, knowing, he says, nothing beyond the Three Gases (whatever the three gases may be). As, however, his pupils began by knowing nothing, and derived all their information from him, this caused him (or anyone) but little inconvenience for several terms. Then a little boy named Whibble joined the school, who had been educated, it seems, by some mischievous relative into an inquiring habit of mind. This little boy followed Plattner's lessons with marked and sustained interest, and in order to exhibit his zeal on the subject, brought at various times sub-stances for Plattner to analyse. Plattner, flattered by this evidence of his power to awaken interest and trusting to the boy's ignorance, analysed these and even made general statements as to their composition. Indeed he was so far stimulated by his pupil as to obtain a work upon analytical chemistry, and study it during his supervision of the evening's preparation. He was surprised to find chemistry quite an interesting subject.

So far the story is absolutely commonplace. But now the greenish powder comes upon the scene. The source of that greenish powder seems, unfortunately, lost. Master Whibble tells a tortuous story of finding it done up in a packet in a disused limekiln near the Downs. It would have been an excellent thing for Plattner, and possibly for Master Whibble's family, if a match could have been applied to that powder there and then. The young gentleman certainly did not bring it to school in a packet, but in a common eight-ounce graduated medi-cine bottle, plugged with masticated newspaper. He gave it to Plattner at the end of the afternoon school. Four boys had been detained after school prayers in order to complete some neglected tasks, and Plattner was supervising these in the small classroom in which the chemical teaching was conducted. The appliances for the practical teaching of chemistry in the Sussexville Proprietary School, as in most private schools in this country, are characterised by a severe simplicity. They are kept in a cupboard standing in a recess and having about the same capacity as a common travelling trunk. Plattner, being bored with his passive superintendence, seems to have welcomed the intervention of Whibble with his green powder as an agreeable diversion, and, unlocking this cupboard, proceeded at once with his analytical experiments. Whibble sat, luckily for himself, at a safe distance, regarding him. The four malefactors, feigning a profound absorption in their work, watched him furtively with the keenest interest. For even within the limits of the Three Gases, Plattner's practical chemistry was, I understand, temerarious.

They are practically unanimous in their account of Plattner's proceedings. He poured a little of the green powder into a test-tube, and tried the substance with water, hydrochloric acid, nitric acid, and sulphuric acid in succession. Getting no result, he emptied out a little heap—nearly half the bottleful, in fact—upon a slate and tried a match. He held the medicine bottle in his left hand. The stuff began to smoke and melt, and then—exploded with deafening violence and a blinding flash.

The five boys, seeing the flash and being prepared for catastrophes, ducked below their desks, and were none of them seriously hurt. The window was blown out into the playground, and the blackboard on its easel was upset. The slate was smashed to atoms. Some plaster fell from the ceiling. No other damage was done to the school edifice or appliances, and the boys at first, seeing nothing of Plattner, fancied he was knocked down and lying out of their sight below the desks. They jumped out of their places to go to his assistance, and were amazed to find the space empty. Being still confused by the sudden violence of the report, they hurried to the open door, under the impression that he must have been hurt, and have rushed out of the room. But Carson, the foremost, nearly collided in the doorway with the principal, Mr Lidgett.

Mr Lidgett is a corpulent, excitable man with one eye. The boys describe him as stumbling into the room mouthing some of those tempered expletives irritable schoolmasters accustom themselves to use—lest worse befall. 'Wretched mumchancer!' he said. 'Where's Mr Plattner?' The boys are agreed on the very words. ('Wobbler', 'snivelling puppy', and 'mumchancer' are, it seems, among the ordinary small change of Mr Lidgett's scholastic commerce.)

Where's Mr Plattner? That was a question that was to be repeated many times in the next few days. It really seemed as though that frantic hyperbole, 'blown to atoms,' had for once realised itself. There was not a visible particle of Plattner to be seen; not a drop of blood nor a stitch of clothing to be found. Apparently he had been blown clean out of existence and left not a wrack behind. Not so much as would cover a sixpenny piece, to quote a proverbial expression! The evidence of his absolute disappearance, as a consequence of that explosion, is indubitable.

It is not necessary to enlarge here upon the commotion excited in the Sussexville Proprietary School, and in Sussexville and elsewhere, by this event. It is quite possible, indeed, that some of the readers of these pages may recall the hearing of some remote and dying version of that excitement during the last summer holidays. Lidgett, it would seem, did everything in his power to suppress and minimise the story. He instituted a penalty of twenty-five lines for any mention of Plattner's name among the boys, and stated in the schoolroom that he was clearly aware of his assistant's whereabouts. He was afraid, he explains, that the possibility of an explosion happening, in spite of the elaborate precautions taken to minimise the practical teaching of chemistry, might injure the reputation of the school; and so might any mysterious quality in Plattner's departure. Indeed, he did everything in his power to make the occurrence seem as ordinary as possible. In particular, he cross-examined the five eyewitnesses of the occurrence so searchingly that they began to doubt the plain evidence of their senses. But, in spite of these efforts, the tale, in a magnified and distorted state, made a nine days' wonder in the district, and several parents withdrew their sons on colourable pretexts. Not the least remarkable point in the matter is the fact that a large number of people in the neighbourhood dreamed singularly vivid dreams of Plattner during the period of excitement before his return, and that these dreams had a curious uniformity. In almost all of them Plattner was seen, sometimes singly, sometimes in company, wandering about through a coruscating iridescence. In all cases his face was pale and distressed, and in some he gesticulated towards the dreamer. One or two of the boys, evidently under the influence of nightmare, fancied that Plattner approached them with remarkable swiftness, and seemed to look closely into their very eyes. Others fled with Plattner from the pursuit of vague and extraordinary creatures of a globular shape. But all these fancies were forgotten in inquiries and speculations when, on the Wednesday next but one after the Monday of the explosion, Plattner returned.

The circumstances of his return were as singular as those of his departure. So far as Mr Lidgett's somewhat choleric outline can be filled in from Plattner's hesitating statements, it would appear that on Wednesday evening, towards the hour of sunset, the former gentleman, having dismissed evening preparation, was engaged in his garden, picking and eating strawberries, a fruit of which he is inordinately fond. It is a large old-fashioned garden, secured from observation, fortunately, by a high and ivy-covered red-brick wall. Just as he was stooping over a particularly prolific plant, there was a flash in the air and a heavy thud, and before he could look round, some heavy body struck him violently from behind. He was pitched forward, crushing the strawberries he held in his hand, and with such force that his silk hat—Mr Lidgett adheres to the older ideas of scholastic costume—was driven violently down upon his forehead, and almost over one eye. This heavy missile, which slid over him sideways and collapsed into a sitting posture among the strawberry plants, proved to be our long-lost Mr Gottfried Plattner, in an extremely dishevelled condition. He was collarless and hatless, his linen was dirty, and there was blood upon his hands. Mr Lidgett was so indignant and surprised that he remained on all-fours, and with his hat jammed down on his eye, while he expostulated vehemently with Plattner for his disrespectful and unaccountable conduct.

This scarcely idyllic scene completes what I may call the exterior version of the Plattner story—its exoteric aspect. It is quite unnecessary to enter here into all the details of his dismissal by Mr Lidgett. Such details, with the full names and dates and references, will be found in the larger report of these occurrences that was laid before the Society for the Investigation of Abnormal Phenomena. The singular transposition of Plattner's right and left sides was scarcely observed for the first day or so, and then first in connection with his disposition to write from right to left across the blackboard. He concealed rather than ostended this curious confirmatory circumstance, as he considered it would unfavourably affect his prospects in a new situation. The displacement of his heart was discovered some months after, when he was having a tooth extracted under anaesthetics. He then, very unwillingly, allowed a cursory surgical examination to be made of himself, with a view to a brief account in the *Journal of Anatomy*. That exhausts the statement of the material facts; and we may now go on to consider Plattner's account of the matter.

But first let us clearly differentiate between the preceding portion of this story and what is to follow. All I have told thus far is established by such evidence as even a criminal lawyer would approve. Every one of the witnesses is still alive; the reader, if he have the leisure, may hunt the lads out tomorrow, or even brave the terrors of the redoubtable Lidgett, and cross-examine and trap and test to his heart's content; Gottfried Plattner, himself, and his twisted heart and his three photographs are producible. It may be taken as proved that he did disappear for nine days as the consequence of an explosion; that he returned almost as violently, under circumstances in their nature annoying to Mr Lidgett, whatever the details of those circumstances may be; and that he returned inverted, just as a reflection returns from a mirror. From the last fact, as I have already stated, it follows almost inevitably that Plattner, during those nine days, must have been in some state of existence altogether out of space. The evidence to these statements is, indeed, far stronger than that upon which most murderers are hanged. But for his own particular account of where he had been, with its confused explanations and well-nigh self-contradictory details, we have only Mr Gottfried Plattner's word. I do not wish to discredit that, but I must point out—what so many writers upon obscure psychic phenomena fail to do—that we are passing here from the practically undeniable to that kind of matter which any reasonable man is entitled to believe or reject as he thinks proper. The previous statements render it plausible; its discordance with common experience tilts it towards the incredible. I would prefer not to sway the beam of the reader's judgment either way, but simply to tell the story as Plattner told it me.

He gave me his narrative, I may state, at my house at Chislehurst; and so soon as he had left me that evening, I went into my study and wrote down everything as I remembered it. Subsequently he was good enough to read over a type-written copy, so that its substantial correctness is undeniable.

He states that at the moment of the explosion he distinctly thought he was killed. He felt lifted off his feet and driven forcibly backward. It is a curious fact for psychologists that he thought clearly during his backward flight, and wondered whether he should hit the chemistry cupboard or the blackboard easel. His heels struck ground, and he staggered and fell heavily into a sitting position on something soft and firm. For a moment the concussion stunned him. He became aware at once of a vivid scent of singed hair, and he seemed to hear the voice of Lidgett asking for him. You will understand that for a time his mind was greatly confused.

At first he was distinctly under the impression that he was still in the classroom. He perceived quite distinctly the surprise of the boys and the entry of Mr Lidgett. He is quite positive upon that score. He did not hear their remarks, but that he ascribed to the deafening effect of the experiment. Things about him seemed curiously dark and faint, but his mind explained that on the obvious but mistaken idea that the explosion had engendered a huge volume of dark smoke. Through the dimness the figures of Lidgett and the boys moved, as faint and silent as ghosts. Plattner's face still tingled with the stinging heat of the flash. He was, he says, 'all muddled'. His first definite thoughts seem to have been of his personal safety. He thought he was perhaps blinded and deafened. He felt his limbs and face in a gingerly manner. Then his perceptions grew clearer, and he was astonished to miss the old familiar desks and other schoolroom furniture about him. Only dim, uncertain, grey shapes stood in the place of these. Then came a thing that made him shout aloud, and awoke his stunned faculties to instant activity. *Two of the boys, gesticulating, walked one after the other clean through him!* Neither manifested the slightest consciousness of his presence. It is difficult to imagine the sensation he felt. They came against him, he says, with no more force than a wisp of mist.

Plattner's first thought after that was that he was dead. Having been brought up with thoroughly sound views in these matters, however, he was a little surprised to find his body still about him. His second conclusion was that he was not dead, but that the others were: that the explosion had destroyed the Sussexville Proprietary School and every soul in it except himself. But that, too, was scarcely satisfactory. He was thrown back upon astonished observation.

Everything about him was extraordinarily dark: at first it seemed to have an altogether ebony blackness. Overhead was a black firmament. The only touch of light in the scene was a faint greenish glow at the edge of the sky in one direction, which threw into prominence a horizon of undulating black hills. This, I say, was his impression at first. As his eye grew accustomed to the darkness, he began to distinguish a faint quality of differentiating greenish colour in the circumambient night. Against this background the furniture and occupants of the classroom, it seems, stood out like phosphorescent spectres, faint and impalpable. He extended his hand, and thrust it without an effort through the wall of the room by the fireplace.

He describes himself as making a strenuous effort to attract attention. He shouted to Lidgett, and tried to seize the boys as they went to and fro. He only desisted from these attempts when Mrs Lidgett, whom he as an Assistant Master naturally disliked, entered the room. He says the sensation of being in the world, and yet not a part of it, was an extraordinarily disagreeable one. He compared his feelings not inaptly to those of a cat watching a mouse through a window. Whenever he made a motion to communicate with the dim, familiar world about him, he found an invisible, incomprehensible barrier preventing intercourse.

He then turned his attention to his solid environment. He found the medicine bottle still unbroken in his hand, with the remainder of the green powder therein. He put this in his pocket, and began to feel about him. Apparently, he was sitting on a boulder of rock covered with a velvety moss. The dark country about him he was unable to see, the faint, misty picture of the schoolroom blotting it out, but he had a feeling (due perhaps to a cold wind) that he was near the crest of a hill, and that a steep valley fell away beneath his feet. The green glow along the edge of the sky seemed to be growing in extent and intensity. He stood up, rubbing his eyes.

It would seem that he made a few steps, going steeply downhill, and then stumbled, nearly fell, and sat down again upon a jagged mass of rock to watch the dawn. He became aware that the world about him was absolutely silent. It was as still as it was dark, and though there was a cold wind blowing up the hill-face, the rustle of grass, the soughing of the boughs that should have accompanied it, were absent. He could hear, therefore, if he could not see, that the hillside upon which he stood was rocky and desolate. The green grew brighter every moment, and as it did so a faint, transparent blood-red mingled with, but did not mitigate, the blackness of the sky overhead and the rocky desolations about him. Having regard to what follows, I am inclined to think that that redness may have been an optical effect due to contrast. Something black fluttered momentarily against the livid yellow-green of the lower sky, and then the thin and penetrating voice of a bell rose out of the black gulf below him. An oppressive expectation grew with the growing light.

It is probable that an hour or more elapsed while he sat there, the strange green light growing brighter every moment, and spreading slowly, in flamboyant fingers, upward towards the zenith. As it grew, the spectral vision of our world became relatively or absolutely fainter. Probably both, for the time must have been about that of our earthly sunset. So far as his vision of our world went, Plattner by his few steps downhill, had passed through the floor of the classroom, and was now, it seemed, sitting in mid-air in the larger schoolroom downstairs. He saw the boarders distinctly, but much more faintly than he had seen Lidgett. They were preparing their evening tasks, and he noticed with interest that several were cheating with their Euclid riders by means of a crib, a compilation whose existence he had hitherto never suspected. As the time passed they faded steadily, as steadily as the light of the green dawn increased.

Looking down into the valley, he saw that the light had crept far down its rocky sides, and that the profound blackness of the abyss was now broken by a minute green glow, like the light of a glow-worm. And almost immediately the limb of a huge heavenly body of blazing green rose over the basaltic undulations of the distant hills, and the monstrous hill-masses about him came out gaunt and desolate, in green light and deep, ruddy black shadows. He became aware of a vast number of ball-shaped objects drifting as thistledown drifts over the high ground. There were none of these nearer to him than the opposite side of the gorge. The bell below twanged quicker and quicker, with something like impatient insistence, and several lights moved hither and thither. The boys at work at their desks were now almost imperceptibly faint.

This extinction of our world, when the green sun of this other universe rose, is a curious point upon which Plattner insists. During the Other-World night it is difficult to move about, on account of the vividness with which the things of this world are visible. It becomes a riddle to explain why, if this is the case, we in this world catch no glimpse of the Other-World. It is due, perhaps, to the comparatively vivid illumination of this world of ours. Plattner describes the midday of the Other-World, at its brightest, as not being nearly so bright as this world at full moon, while its night is profoundly black. Consequently, the amount of light, even in an ordinary dark room, is sufficient to render the things of the Other-World invisible, on the same principle that faint phosphorescence is only visible in the profoundest darkness. I have tried, since he told me his story, to see something of the Other-World by sitting for a long space in a photographer's dark room at night. I have certainly seen indistinctly the form of greenish slopes and rocks, but only, I must admit, very indistinctly indeed. The reader may possibly be more successful. Plattner tells me that since his return he has seen and recognised places in the Other-World in his dreams, but this is probably due to his memory of these scenes. It seems quite possible that people with unusually keen eyesight may occasionally catch a glimpse of this strange Other-World about us.

However, this is a digression. As the green sun rose, a long street of black buildings became perceptible, though only darkly and indistinctly, in the gorge, and, after some hesitation, Plattner began to clamber down the precipitous descent towards them. The descent was long and exceedingly tedious, being so not only by the extraordinary steepness, but also by reason of the looseness of the boulders with which the whole face of the hill was strewn. The noise of his descent—now and then his heels struck fire from the rocks—seemed now the only sound in the universe, for the beating of the bell had ceased. As he drew nearer he perceived that the various edifices had a singular resemblance to tombs and mausoleums and monuments, saving only that they were all uniformly black instead of being white as most sepulchres are. And then he saw, crowding out of the largest building very much as people disperse from church, a number of pallid, rounded, pale-green figures. These scattered in several directions about the broad street of the place, some going through side alleys and reappearing upon the steepness of the hill, others entering some of the small black buildings which lined the way.

At the sight of these things drifting up towards him, Plattner stopped, staring. They were not walking, they were indeed limbless; and they had the appearance of human heads beneath which a tadpole-like body swung. He was too astonished at their strangeness, too full indeed of strangeness, to be seriously alarmed by them. They drove towards him, in front of the chill wind that was blowing uphill, much as soap-bubbles drive before a draught. And as he looked at the nearest of those approaching, he saw it was indeed a human head, albeit with singularly large eyes, and wearing such an expression of distress and anguish as he had never seen before upon mortal countenance. He was surprised to find that it did not turn to regard him, but seemed to be watching and following some unseen moving thing. For a moment he was puzzled, and then it occurred to him that this creature was watching with its enormous eyes something that was happening in the world he had just left. Nearer it came, and nearer, and he was too astonished to cry out. It made a very faint fretting sound as it came close to him. Then it struck his face with a gentle pat—its touch was very cold—and drove past him, and upward towards the crest of the hill.

An extraordinary conviction flashed across Plattner's mind that this head had a strong likeness to Lidgett. Then he turned his attention to the other heads that were now swarming thickly up the hillside. None made the slightest sign of recognition. One or two, indeed, came close to his head and almost followed the example of the first, but he dodged convulsively out of the way. Upon most of them he saw the same expression of unavailing regret he had seen upon the first, and heard the same faint sounds of wretchedness from them. One or two wept, and one rolling swiftly uphill wore an expression of diabolical rage. But others were cold, and several had a look of gratified interest in their eyes. One, at least, was almost in an ecstasy of happiness. Plattner does not remember that he recognised any more likenesses in those he saw at this time.

For several hours, perhaps, Plattner watched these strange things dispersing themselves over the hills, and not till long after they had ceased to issue from the clustering black buildings in the gorge did he resume his downward climb. The darkness about him increased so much that he had a difficulty in stepping true. Overhead the sky was now a bright pale green. He felt neither hunger nor thirst. Later, when he did, he found a chilly stream running down the centre of the gorge, and the rare moss upon the boulders, when he tried it at last in desperation, was good to eat.

He groped about among the tombs that ran down the gorge, seeking vaguely for some clue to these inexplicable things. After a long time, he came to the entrance of the big mausoleum-like building from which the heads had issued. In this he found a group of green lights burning upon a kind of basaltic altar, and a bell-rope from a belfry overhead hanging down into the centre of the place. Round the wall ran a lettering of fire in a character unknown to him. While he was still wondering at the purport of these things, he heard the receding tramp of heavy feet echoing far down the street. He ran out into the darkness again, but he could see nothing. He had a mind to pull the bell-rope, and finally decided to follow the footsteps. But although he ran far, he never overtook them; and his shouting was of no avail. The gorge seemed to extend an interminable distance. It was as dark as earthly starlight throughout its length, while the ghastly green day lay along the upper edge of its precipices. There were none of the heads, now, below. They were all, it seemed, busily occupied along the upper slopes. Looking up, he saw them drifting hither and thither, some hovering stationary, some flying swiftly through the air. It reminded him, he said, of 'big snowflakes'; only these were black and pale green.

In pursuing the firm, undeviating footsteps that he never overtook, in groping into new regions of this endless devil's dyke, in clambering up and down the pitiless heights, in wandering about the summits, and in watching the drifting faces, Plattner states that he spent the better part of seven or eight days. He did not keep count, he says. Though once or twice he found eyes watching him, he had word with no living soul. He slept among the rocks on the hillside. In the gorge things earthly were invisible, because, from the earthly standpoint, it was far underground. On the altitudes, so soon as the earthly day began, the world became visible to him. He found himself sometimes stumbling over the dark green rocks, or arresting himself on a precipitous brink, while all about him the green branches of the Sussexville lanes were swaying; or, again, he seemed to be walking through the Sussexville streets, or watching unseen the private business of some household. And then it was he discovered, that to almost every human being in our world there pertained some of these drifting heads; that everyone in the world is watched intermittently by these helpless disembodiments.

What are they—these Watchers of the Living? Plattner never learned. But two that presently found and followed him, were like his childhood's memory of his father and mother. Now and then other faces turned their eyes upon him: eyes like those of dead people who had swayed him, or injured him, or helped him in his youth and manhood. Whenever they looked at him, Plattner was overcome with a strange sense of responsibility. To his mother he ventured to speak; but she made no answer. She looked sadly, steadfastly, And tenderly— a little reproachfully, too, it seemed—into his eyes.

He simply tells this story: he does not endeavour to explain. We are left to surmise who these Watchers of the Living may be, or if they are indeed the Dead, why they should so closely and passionately watch a world they have left for ever. It may be—indeed to my mind it seems just—that, when our life has closed, when evil or good is no longer a choice for us, we may still have to witness the working out of the train of consequences we have laid. If human souls continue after death, then surely human interests continue after death. But that is merely my own guess at the meaning of the things seen. Plattner offers no interpretation, for none was given him. It is well the reader should understand this clearly. Day after day, with his head reeling, he wandered about this green-lit world outside the world, weary and, towards the end, weak and hungry. By day—by our earthly day, that is—the ghostly vision of the old familiar scenery of Sussexville, all about him, irked and worried him. He could not see where to put his feet, and ever and again with a chilly touch one of these Watching Souls would come against his face. And after dark the multitude of these Watchers about him, and their intent distress, confused his mind beyond describing. A great longing to return to the earthly life that was so near and yet so remote consumed him. The unearthliness of things about him produced a positively painful mental distress. He was worried beyond describing by his own particular followers. He would shout at them to desist from staring at him, scold at them, hurry away from them. They were always mute and intent. Run as he might over the uneven ground, they followed his destinies.

On the ninth day, towards evening, Plattner heard the invisible footsteps approaching, far away down the gorge. He was then wandering over the broad crest of the same hill upon which he had fallen in his entry into this strange Other-World of his. He turned to hurry down into the gorge, feeling his way hastily, and was arrested by the sight of the thing that was happening in a room in a back street near the school. Both of the people in the room he knew by sight. The windows were open, the blinds up, and the setting sun shone clearly into it, so that it came out quite brightly at first, a vivid oblong of room, lying like a magic-lantern picture upon the black landscape and the livid green dawn. In addition to the sunlight, a candle had just been lit in the room.

On the bed lay a lank man, his ghastly white face terrible upon the tumbled pillow. His clenched hands were raised above his head. A little table beside the bed carried a few medicine bottles, some toast and water, and an empty glass. Every now and then the lank man's lips fell apart, to indicate a word he could not articulate. But the woman did not notice that he wanted anything, because she was busy turning out papers from an old-fashioned bureau in the opposite corner of the room: At first the picture was very vivid indeed, but as the green dawn behind it grew brighter and brighter, so it became fainter and more and more transparent.

As the echoing footsteps paced nearer and nearer, those footsteps that sound so loud in that Other-World and come so silently in this, Plattner perceived about him a great multitude of dim faces gathering together out of the darkness and watching the two people in the room. Never before had he seen so many of the Watchers of the Living. A multitude had eyes only for the sufferer in the room, another multitude, in infinite anguish, watched the woman as she hunted with greedy eyes for something she could not find. They crowded about Plattner, they came across his sight and buffeted his face, the noise of their unavailing regrets was all about him. He saw clearly only now and then. At other times the pictures quivered dimly, through the veil of green reflections upon their movements. In the room it must have been very still, and Plattner says the candle flame streamed up into a perfectly vertical line of smoke, but in his ears each footfall and its echoes beat like a clap of thunder. And the faces! Two more particularly, near the woman's: one a woman's also, white and clear-featured, a face which might have once been cold and hard but which was now softened by the touch of a wisdom strange to earth. The other might have been the woman's father. Both were evidently absorbed in the contemplation of some act of hateful meanness, so it seemed, which they could no longer guard against and prevent. Behind were others, teachers it may be who had taught ill, friends whose influence had failed. And over the man, too—a multitude, but none that seemed to be parents or teachers! Faces that might once have been coarse, now purged to strength by sorrow! And in the forefront one face, a girlish one, neither angry nor remorseful but merely patient and weary, and, as it seemed to Plattner, waiting for relief. His powers of description fail him at the memory of this multitude of ghastly countenances. They gathered on the stroke of the bell. He saw them all in the space of a second. It would seem that he was so worked upon by his excitement that quite involuntarily his restless fingers took the bottle of green powder out of his pocket and held it before him. But he does not remember that.

Abruptly the footsteps ceased. He waited for the next and there was silence, and then suddenly, cutting through the unexpected stillness like a keen, thin blade, came the first stroke of the bell. At that the multitudinous faces swayed to and fro, and a louder crying began all about him. The woman did not hear; she was burning something now in the candle flame. At the second stroke everything grew dim, and a breath of wind, icy cold, blew through the host of watchers. They swirled about him like an eddy of dead leaves in the spring, and at the third stroke something was extended through them to the bed. You have heard of a beam of light. This was like a beam of darkness, and looking again at it, Plattner saw that it was a shadowy arm and hand.

The green sun was now topping the black desolations of the horizon, and the vision of the room was very faint. Plattner could see that the white of the bed struggled, and was convulsed; and that the woman looked round over her shoulder at it, startled.

The cloud of watchers lifted high like a puff of green dust before the wind, and swept swiftly downward towards the temple in the gorge. Then suddenly Plattner understood the meaning of the shadowy black arm that stretched across his shoulder and clutched its prey. He did not dare turn his head to see the Shadow behind the arm. With a violent effort, and covering his eyes, he set himself to run, made perhaps twenty strides, then slipped on a boulder and fell, He fell forward on his hands; and the bottle smashed and exploded as he touched the ground.

In another moment he found himself, stunned and bleeding, sitting face to face with Lidgett in the old walled garden behind the school.

There the story of Plattner's experiences ends. I have resisted, I believe successfully, the natural disposition of a writer of fiction to dress up incidents of this sort. I have told the thing as far as possible in the order in which Plattner told it to me. I have carefully avoided any attempt at style, effect, or construction. It would have been easy, for instance, to have worked the scene of the death-bed into a kind of plot in which Plattner might have been involved. But quite apart from the objectionableness of falsifying a most extraordinary true story, any such trite devices would spoil, to my mind, the peculiar effect of this dark world, with its livid green illumination and its drifting Watchers of the Living, which, unseen and unapproachable to us, is yet lying all about us.

It remains to add, that a death did actually occur in Vincent Terrace, just beyond the school garden, and, so far as can be proved, at the moment of Plattner's return. Deceased was a rate-collector and insurance agent. His widow, who was much younger than himself, married last month a Mr Whymper, a veterinary surgeon of Allbeeding. As the portion of this story given here has in various forms circulated orally in Sussexville, she has consented to my use of her name, on condition that I make it distinctly known that she emphatically contradicts every detail of Plattner's account of her husband's last moments. She burnt no will, she says, although Plattner never accused her of doing so: her husband made but one will, and that just after their marriage. Certainly, from a man who had never seen it, Plattner's account of the furniture of the room was curiously accurate.

One other thing, even at the risk of an irksome repetition, I must insist upon lest I seem to favour the credulous superstitious view. Plattner's absence from the world for nine days is, I think, proved. But that does not prove his story. It is quite conceivable that even outside space hallucinations may be possible. That, at least, the reader must bear distinctly in mind.

THE RED ROOM

'I CAN assure you,' said I, 'that it will take a very tangible ghost to frighten me.' And I stood up before the fire with my glass in my hand.

'It is your own choosing,' said the man with the withered arm, and glanced at me askance.

'Eight-and-twenty years,' said I, 'I have lived, and never a ghost have I seen as yet.'

The old woman sat staring hard into the fire, her pale eyes wide open. 'Ay,' she broke in; 'and eight-and-twenty years you have lived and never seen the likes of this house, I reckon. There's a many things to see, when one's still but eight-and-twenty.' She swayed her head slowly from side to side. 'A many things to see and sorrow for.'

I half suspected the old people were trying to enhance the spiritual terrors of their house by their droning insistence. I put down my empty glass on the table and looked about the room, and caught a glimpse of myself, abbreviated and broadened to an impossible sturdiness, in the queer old mirror at the end of the room. 'Well,' I said, 'if I see anything tonight, I shall be so much the wiser. For I come to the business with an open mind.'

'It's your own choosing,' said the man with the withered arm once more.

I heard the sound of a stick and a shambling step on the flags in the passage outside, and the door creaked on its hinges as a second old man entered, more bent, more wrinkled, more aged even than the first. He supported himself by a single crutch, his eyes were covered by a shade, and his lower lip, half averted, hung pale and pink from his decaying yellow teeth. He made straight for an arm-chair on the opposite side of the table, sat down clumsily, and began to cough. The man with the withered arm gave this new-comer a short glance of positive dislike; the old woman took no notice of his arrival, but remained with her eyes fixed steadily on the fire.

'I said—it's your own choosing,' said the man with the withered arm, when the coughing had ceased for a while.

'It's my own choosing,' I answered.

The man with the shade became aware of my presence for the first time, and threw his head back for a moment and sideways, to see me. I caught a momentary glimpse of his eyes, small and bright and inflamed. Then he began to cough and splutter again.

'Why don't you drink?' said the man with the withered arm, pushing the beer towards him. The man with the shade poured out a glassful with a shaky arm that splashed half as much again on the deal table. A monstrous shadow of him crouched upon the wall and mocked his action as he poured and drank. I must confess I had scarce expected these grotesque custodians. There is to my mind something inhuman in senility, something crouching and atavistic; the human qualities seem to drop from old people insensibly day by day. The three of them made me feel uncomfortable, with their gaunt silences, their bent carriage, their evident unfriendliness to me and to one another.

'If,' said I, 'you will show me to this haunted room of yours, I will make myself comfortable there,'

The old man with the cough jerked his head back so suddenly that it startled me, and shot another glance of his red eyes at me from under the shade; but no one answered me. I waited a minute, glancing from one to the other.

'If,' I said a little louder, 'if you will show me to this haunted room of yours, I will relieve you from the task of entertaining me.'

'There's a candle on the slab outside the door,' said the man with the withered arm, looking at my feet as he addressed me. 'But if you go to the red room tonight—'

('This night of all nights !' said the old woman.)

'You go alone.'

'Very well,' I answered. 'And which way do I go?'

'You go along the passage for a bit,' said he, 'until you come to a door, and through that is a spiral staircase, and halfway up that is a landing and another door covered with baize. Go through that and down the long corridor to the end, and the red room is on your left up the steps.'

'Have I got that right?' I said, and repeated his directions. He corrected me in one particular.

'And are you really going?' said the man with the shade, looking at me again for the third time, with that queer, unnatural tilting of the face.

('This night of all nights!' said the old woman.)

'It is what I came for,' I said, and moved towards the door. As I did so, the old man with the shade rose and staggered round the table, so as to be closer to the others and to the fire. At the door I turned and looked at them, and saw they were all close together, dark against the firelight, staring at me over their shoulders, with an intent expression on their ancient faces.

'Goodnight,' I said, setting the door open.

'It's your own choosing,' said the man with the withered arm.

I left the door wide open until the candle was well alight, and then I shut them in and walked down the chilly, echoing passage.

I must confess that the oddness of these three old pensioners in whose charge her ladyship had left the castle, and the deep toned, old-fashioned furniture of the housekeeper's room in which they foregathered, affected me in spite of my efforts to keep myself at a matter-of-fact phase. They seemed to belong to another age, an older age, an age when things spiritual were different from this of ours, less certain; an age when omens and witches were credible, and ghosts beyond denying. Their very existence was spectral; the cut of their clothing, fashions born in dead brains. The ornaments and conveniences of the room about them were ghostly—the thoughts of vanished men, which still haunted rather than participated in the world of today. But with an effort I sent such thoughts to the right-about. The long, draughty subterranean passage was chilly and dusty, and my candle flared and made the shadows cower and quiver. The echoes rang up and down the spiral staircase, and a shadow came sweeping up after me, and one fled before me into the darkness overhead. I came to the landing and stopped there for a moment, listening to a rustling that I fancied I heard; then, satisfied of the absolute silence, I pushed open the baize-covered door and stood in the corridor.

The effect was scarcely what I expected, for the moonlight, coming in by the great window on the grand staircase, picked out everything in vivid black shadow or silvery illumination. Everything was in its place: the house might have been deserted on the yesterday instead of eighteen months ago. There were candles in the sockets of the sconces, and whatever dust had gathered on the carpets or upon the polished flooring was distributed so evenly as to be invisible in the moonlight. I was about to advance, and stopped abruptly. A bronze group stood upon the landing, hidden from me by the corner of the wall, but its shadow fell with marvellous distinctness upon the white panelling, and gave me the impression of some one crouching to way-lay me. I stood rigid for half a minute perhaps. Then, with my hand in the pocket that held my revolver, I advanced, only to discover a Ganymede and Eagle glistening in the moonlight. That incident for a time restored my nerve, and a porcelain Chinaman on a buhl table, whose head rocked silently as I passed him, scarcely startled me.

The door to the red room and the steps up to it were in a shadowy corner. I moved my candle from side to side, in order to see clearly the nature of the recess in which I stood before opening the door. Here it was, thought I, that my predecessor was found, and the memory of that story gave me a sudden twinge of apprehension. I glanced over my shoulder at the Ganymede in the moonlight, and opened the door of the red room rather hastily, with my face half turned to the pallid silence of the landing.

I entered, closed the door behind me at once, turned the key I found in the lock within, and stood with the candle held aloft, survey-ing the scene of my vigil, the great red room of Lorraine Castle, in which the young duke had died. Or, rather, in which he had begun his dying, for he had opened the door and fallen headlong down the steps I had just ascended. That had been the end of his vigil, of his gallant attempt to conquer the ghostly tradition of the place; and never, I thought, had apoplexy better served the ends of superstition. And there were other and older stories that clung to the room, back to the half-credible beginning of it all, the tale of a timid wife and the tragic end that came to her husband's jest of frightening her. And looking around that large shadowy room, with its shadowy window bays, its recesses and alcoves, one could well understand the legends that had sprouted in its black corners, its germinating darkness. My candle was a little tongue of flame in its vastness, that failed to pierce the opposite end of the room, and left an ocean of mystery and suggestion beyond its island of light.

I resolved to make a systematic examination of the place at once, and dispel the fanciful suggestions of its obscurity before they obtained a hold upon me. After satisfying myself of the fastening of the door, I began to walk about the room, peering round each article of furniture, tucking up the valances of the bed, and opening its curtains wide. I pulled up the blinds and examined the fastenings of the several windows before closing the shutters, leant forward and looked up the blackness of the wide chimney, and tapped the dark oak panelling for any secret opening. There were two big mirrors in the room, each with a pair of sconces bearing candles, and on the mantel shelf, too, were more candles in china candlesticks. All these I lit one after the other. The fire was laid—an unexpected consideration from the old house-keeper—and I lit it, to keep down any disposition to shiver, and when it was burning well, I stood round with my back to it and regarded the room again. I had pulled up a chintz-covered arm-chair and a table, to form a kind of barricade before me, and on this lay my revolver ready to hand. My precise examination had done me good, but I still found the remoter darkness of the place, and its perfect stillness, too stimulating for the imagination. The echoing of the stir and crackling of the fire was no sort of comfort to me. The shadow in the alcove, at the end in particular, had that undefinable quality of a presence, that odd suggestion of a lurking living thing, that comes so easily in silence and solitude. At last, to reassure myself, I walked with a candle into it, and satisfied myself that there was nothing tangible there. I stood that candle upon the floor of the alcove, and left it in that position.

By this time I was in a state of considerable nervous tension, although to my reason there was no adequate cause for the condition. My mind, however, was perfectly clear. I postulated quite unreservedly that nothing supernatural could happen, and to pass the time I began to string some rhymes together, Ingoldsby fashion, of the original legend of the place. A few I spoke aloud, but the echoes were not pleasant. For the same reason I also abandoned, after a time, a conversation with myself upon the impossibility of ghosts and haunting. My mind reverted to the three old and distorted people downstairs, and I tried to keep it upon that topic. The sombre reds and blacks of the room troubled me; even with seven candles the place was merely dim. The one in the alcove flared in a draught, and the fire-flickering kept the shadows and penumbra perpetually shifting and stirring. Casting about for a remedy, I recalled the candles I had seen in the passage, and, with a slight effort, walked out into the moonlight, carrying a candle and leaving the door open, and presently returned with as many as ten. These I put in various knick-knacks of china with which the room was sparsely adorned, lit and placed where the shadows had lain

101

deepest, some on the floor, some in the window recesses, until at last my seventeen candles were so arranged that not an inch of the room but had the direct light of at least one of them. It occurred to me that when the ghost came, I could warn him not to trip over them, the room was now quite brightly illuminated. There was something very cheery and reassuring in these little streaming flames, and snuffing them gave me an occupation, and afforded a reassuring sense of the passage of time.

Even with that, however, the brooding expectation of the vigil weighed heavily upon me. It was after midnight that the candle in the alcove suddenly went out, and the black shadow sprang back to its place. I did not see the candle go out; I simply turned and saw that the darkness was there, as one might start and see the unexpected presence of a stranger. 'By Jove!' said I aloud; 'that draught's a strong one!' and, taking the matches from the table, I walked across the room in a leisurely manner to relight the corner again. My first match would not strike, and as I succeeded with the second, something seemed to blink on the wall before me. I turned my head involuntarily, and saw that the two candles on the little table by the fireplace were extinguished. I rose at once to my feet.

'Odd!' I said. 'Did I do that myself in a flash of absent-mindedness?'

I walked back, relit one, and as I did so, I saw the candle in the right sconce of one of the mirrors wink and go right out, and almost immediately its companion followed it. There was no mistake about it. The flame vanished, as if the wicks had been suddenly nipped between a finger and a thumb, leaving the wick neither glowing nor smoking, but black, While I stood gaping, the candle at the foot of the bed went out, and the shadows seemed to take another step towards me.

'This won't do!' said I, and first one and then another candle on the mantelshelf followed.

'What's up?' I cried, with a queer high note getting into my voice somehow. At that the candle on the wardrobe went out, and the one I had relit in the alcove followed.

'Steady on!' I said. 'These candles are wanted,' speaking with a half-hysterical facetiousness, and scratching away at a match the while for the mantel candlesticks. My hands trembled so much that twice I missed the rough paper of the matchbox. As the mantel emerged from darkness again, two candles in the remoter end of the window were eclipsed. But with the same match I also relit the larger mirror candles, and those on the floor near the doorway, so that for the moment I seemed to gain on the extinctions. But then in a volley there vanished four lights at once in different corners of the room, and I struck another match in quivering haste, and stood hesitating whither to take it.

As I stood undecided, an invisible hand seemed to sweep out the two candles on the table. With a cry of terror, I dashed at the alcove, then into the corner, and then into the window, relighting three, as two more vanished by the fireplace; then, perceiving a better way, I dropped the matches on the ironbound deed-box in the corner, and caught up the bedroom candlestick. With this I avoided the delay of striking matches; but for all that the steady process of extinction went on, and the shadows I feared and fought against returned, and crept in upon me, first a step gained on this side of me and then on that. It was like a ragged storm-cloud sweeping out the stars. Now and then one returned for a minute, and was lost again. I was now almost frantic with the horror of coming darkness, and my self-possession deserted me. I leaped panting and dishevelled from candle to candle, in a vain straggle against that remorseless advance.

I bruised myself on the thigh against the table, I sent a chair headlong, I stumbled and fell and whisked the cloth from the table in my fall. My candle rolled away from me, and I snatched another as I rose. Abruptly this was blown out, as I swung it off the table, by the wind of my sudden movement, and immediately the two remaining candles followed. But there was light still in the room, a red light that staved off the shadows from me. The fire! Of course, I could thrust my candle between the bars and relight it!

I turned to where the flames were dancing between the glowing coals, and splashing red reflections upon the furniture, made two steps towards the grate, and incontinently the flames dwindled and vanished, the glow vanished, the reflections rushed together and vanished, and as I thrust the candle between the bars, darkness closed upon me like the shutting of an eye, wrapped about me in a stifling embrace, sealed my vision, and crushed the last vestiges of reason from my brain. The candle fell from my hand. I flung out my arms in a vain effort to thrust that ponderous blackness away from me, and, lifting up my voice, screamed with all my might—once, twice, thrice. Then I think I must have staggered to my feet. I know I thought suddenly of the moonlit corridor, and, with my head bowed and my arms over my face, made a run for the door.

But I had forgotten the exact position of the door, and struck myself heavily against the corner of the bed. I staggered back, turned, and was either struck or struck myself against some other bulky furniture. I have a vague memory of battering myself thus, to and fro in the darkness, of a cramped struggle, and of my own wild crying as I darted to and fro, of a heavy blow at last upon my forehead, a horrible sensation of falling that lasted an age, of my last frantic effort to keep my footing, and then I remember no more.

I opened my eyes in daylight. My head was roughly bandaged, and the man with the withered arm was watching my face. I looked about me, trying to remember what had happened, and for a space I could not recollect. I turned to the corner, and saw the old woman, no longer abstracted, pouring out some drops of medicine from a little blue phial into a glass. 'Where am I? 'I asked. 'I seem to remember you, and yet I cannot remember who you are.'

They told me then, and I heard of the haunted Red Room as one who hears a tale. 'We found you at dawn,' said he, 'and there was blood on your forehead and lips.'

It was very slowly I recovered my memory of my experience. 'You believe now,' said the old man, 'that the room is haunted?' He spoke no longer as one who greets an intruder, but as one who grieves for a broken friend.

'Yes,' said I; 'the room is haunted.'

'And you have seen it. And we, who have lived here all our lives, have never set eyes upon it. Because we have never dared. . . . Tell us, is it truly the old earl who—'

'No,' said I; 'it is not.'

'I told you so,' said the old lady, with the glass in her hand. 'It is his poor young countess who was frightened—'

'It is not,' I said. 'There is neither ghost of earl nor ghost of countess in that room, there is no ghost there at all; but worse, far worse—'

'Well?' they said.

'The worst of all the things that haunt poor mortal man,' said I; 'and that is, in all its nakedness—*Fear*! Fear that will not have light nor sound, that will not bear with reason, that deafens and darkens and overwhelms. It followed me through the corridor, it fought against me in the room—'

I stopped abruptly. There was an interval of silence. My hand went up to my bandages.

Then the man with the shade sighed and spoke. 'That is it,' said he. 'I knew that was it. A Power of Darkness. To put such a curse upon a woman! It lurks there always. You can feel it even in the daytime, even of a bright summer's day, in the hangings, in the curtains, keeping behind you however you face about. In the dusk it creeps along the corridor and follows you, so that you dare not turn. There is Fear in that room of hers—black Fear, and there will be—so long as this house of sin endures.'

THE STORY OF THE LATE
MR ELVESHAM

I SET this story down, not expecting it will be believed, but, if possible, to prepare a way of escape for the next victim. He perhaps may profit by my misfortune. My own case, I know, is hopeless, and I am now in some measure prepared to meet my fate.

My name is Edward George Eden. I was born at Trentham, in Staffordshire, my father being employed in the gardens there. I lost my mother when I was three years old and my father when I was five, my uncle, George Eden, then adopting me as his own son. He was a single man, self-educated, and well-known in Birmingham as an enterprising journalist; he educated me generously, fired my ambition to succeed in the world, and at his death, which happened four years ago, left me his entire fortune, a matter of about five hundred pounds after all outgoing charges were paid. I was then eighteen. He advised me in his will to expend the money in completing my education. I had already chosen the profession of medicine, and through his posthumous generosity, and my good fortune in a scholarship competition, I became a medical student at University College, London. At the time of the beginning of my story I lodged at 11a University Street, in a little upper room, very shabbily furnished, and draughty, overlooking the back of Shoolbred's premises. I used this little room both to live in and sleep in, because I was anxious to eke out my means to the very last shillingsworth.

I was taking a pair of shoes to be mended at a shop in the Tottenham Court Road when I first encountered the little old man with the yellow face, with whom my life has now become so inextricably entangled. He was standing on the kerb, and staring at the number on the door in a doubtful way, as I opened it. His eyes—they were dull grey eyes, and reddish under the rims—fell to my face, and his countenance immediately assumed an expression of corrugated amiability.

'You come,' he said, 'apt to the moment. I had forgotten the number of your house. How do you do, Mr Eden?'

I was a little astonished at his familiar address, for I had never set eyes on the man before. I was annoyed, too, at his catching me with my boots under my arm. He noticed my lack of cordiality.

'Wonder who the deuce I am, eh? A friend, let me assure you. I have seen you before, though you haven't seen me. Is there anywhere where I can talk to you?'

I hesitated. The shabbiness of my room upstairs was not a matter for every stranger. 'Perhaps,' said I, 'we might walk down the street. I'm unfortunately prevented—' My gesture explained the sentence before I had spoken it.

'The very thing,' he said, and faced this way and then that. 'The street? Which way shall we go?' I slipped my boots down in the passage. 'Look here!' he said abruptly; 'this business of mine is a rigmarole. Come and lunch with me, Mr Eden. I'm an old man, a very old man, and not good at explanations, and what with my piping voice and the clatter of the traffic—'

He laid a persuasive skinny hand that trembled a little upon my arm.

I was not so old that an old man might not treat me to a lunch. Yet at the same time I was not altogether pleased by this abrupt invitation. 'I had rather—' I began. 'But *I* had rather,' he said, catching me up, 'and a certain civility is surely due to my grey hairs.' And so I consented, and went away with him.

He took me to Blavitski's; I had to walk slowly to accommodate myself to his paces; and over such a lunch as I had never tasted before, he fended off my leading questions, and I took a better note of his appearance. His clean-shaven face was lean and wrinkled, his shrivelled lips fell over a set of false teeth, and his white hair was thin and rather long; he seemed small to me—though, indeed, most people seemed small to me—and his shoulders were rounded and bent. And, watching him, I could not help but observe that he too was taking note of me, running his eyes, with a curious touch of greed in them, over me from my broad shoulders to my sun-tanned hands and up to my freckled face again. 'And now,' said he, as we lit our cigarettes, 'I must tell you of the business in hand.

'I must tell you, then, that I am an old man, a very old man.' He paused momentarily. 'And it happens that I have money that I must presently be leaving, and never a child have I to leave it to.' I thought of the confidence trick, and resolved I would be on the alert for the vestiges of my five hundred pounds. He proceeded to enlarge on his loneliness, and the trouble he had to find a proper disposition of his money. 'I have weighed this plan and that plan, charities, institutions, and scholarships, and libraries, and I have come to this conclusion at last'—he fixed his eyes on my face—'that I will find some young fellow, ambitious, pure-minded, and poor, healthy in body and healthy in mind, and, in short, make him my heir, give him all that I have.' He repeated, 'Give him all that I have. So that he will suddenly be lifted out of all the trouble and struggle in which his sympathies have been educated, to freedom and influence.'

I tried to seem disinterested. With a transparent hypocrisy, I said, 'And you want my help, my professional services maybe, to find that person.'

He smiled and looked at me over his cigarette, and I laughed at his quiet exposure of my modest pretence.

'What a career such a man might have!' he said. 'It fills me with envy to think how I have accumulated that another man may spend—

'But there are conditions, of course, burdens to be imposed. He must, for instance, take my name. You cannot expect everything without some return. And I must go into all the circumstances of his life before I can accept him. He must be sound. I must know his heredity, how his parents and grandparents died, have the strictest inquiries made into his private morals—'

This modified my secret congratulations a little. 'And do I understand,' said I, 'that I—?'

'Yes,' he said, almost fiercely. 'You. *You.*'

I answered never a word. My imagination was dancing wildly, my innate scepticism was useless to modify its transports. There was not a particle of gratitude in my mind—I did not know what to say nor how to say it. 'But why me in particular?' I said at last.

He had chanced to hear of me from Professor Haslar, he said, as a typically sound and sane young man, and he wished, as far as possible, to leave his money where health and integrity were assured.

That was my first meeting with the little old man. He was mysterious about himself; he would not give his name yet, he said, and after I had answered some questions of his, he left me at the Blavitski portal. I noticed that he drew a handful of gold coins from his pocket when it came to paying for the lunch. His insistence upon bodily health was curious. In accordance with an arrangement we had made I applied that day for a life policy in the Loyal Insurance Company for a large sum, and I was exhaustively overhauled by the medical advisers of that company in the subsequent week. Even that did not satisfy him, and he insisted I must be re-examined by the great Doctor Henderson. It was Friday in Whitsun week before he came to a decision. He called me down quite late in the evening—nearly nine it was—from cramming chemical equations for my Preliminary Scientific examination. He was standing in the passage under the feeble gas-lamp, and his face was a grotesque interplay of shadows. He seemed more bowed than when I had first seen him, and his cheeks had sunk in a little.

His voice shook with emotion. 'Everything is satisfactory, Mr Eden,' he said. 'Everything is quite, quite satisfactory. And this night of all nights, you must dine with me and celebrate your—accession.' He was interrupted by a cough. 'You won't have long to wait, either,' he said, wiping his handkerchief across his lips, and gripping my hand with his long bony claw that was disengaged. 'Certainly not very long to wait.'

We went into the street and called a cab. I remember every incident of that drive vividly, the swift easy motion, the contrast of gas and oil and electric light, the crowds of people in the streets, the place in Regent Street to which we went, and the sumptuous dinner we were served with there. I was disconcerted at first by the well-dressed waiter's glances at my rough clothes, bothered by the stones of the olives, but as the champagne warmed my blood, my confidence revived. At first the old man talked of himself. He had already told me his name in the cab; he was Egbert Elvesham, the great philosopher, whose name I had known since I was a lad at school. It seemed incredible to me that this man, whose intelligence had so early dominated mine, this great abstraction, should suddenly realise itself as this decrepit, familiar figure. I dare say every young fellow who has suddenly fallen among celebrities has felt something of my disappointment. He told me now of the future that the feeble streams of his life would presently leave dry for me, houses, copyrights, investments; I had never suspected that philosophers were so rich. He watched me drink and eat with a touch of envy. 'What a capacity for living you have!' he said; and then, with a sigh, a sigh of relief I could have thought it, 'It will not be long.'

'Ay,' said I, my head swimming now with champagne; 'I have a future perhaps—of a fairly agreeable sort, thanks to you. I shall now have the honour of your name. But you have a past. Such a past as is worth all my future.'

He shook his head and smiled, as I thought with half-sad appreciation of my flattering admiration. 'That future,' he said; 'would you in truth change it?' The waiter came with liqueurs. 'You will not perhaps mind taking my name, taking my position, but would you indeed—willingly—take my years?'

'With your achievements,' said I gallantly.

He smiled again. 'Kümmel—both,' he said to the waiter, and turned his attention to a little paper packet he had taken from his pocket. 'This hour,' said he, 'this after-dinner hour is the hour of small things. Here is a scrap of my unpublished wisdom.' He opened the packet with his shaking yellow fingers, and showed a little pinkish powder on the paper. This,' said he—' well, you must guess what it is. But Kümmel—put but a dash of this powder in it—is Himmel.' His large greyish eyes watched mine with an inscrutable expression.

It was a bit of a shock to me to find this great teacher gave his mind to the flavour of liqueurs. However, I feigned a great interest in his weakness, for I was drunk enough for such small sycophancy.

He parted the powder between the little glasses, and rising suddenly with a strange unexpected dignity, held out his hand towards me. I imitated his action, and the glasses rang. 'To a quick succession,' said he, and raised his glass towards his lips.

'Not that,' I said hastily. 'Not that.'

He paused, with the liqueur at the level of his chin, and his eyes blazing into mine.

'To a long life,' said I.

He hesitated. 'To a long life,' said he, with a sudden bark of laughter, and with eyes fixed on one another we tilted the little glasses. His eyes looked straight into mine, and as I drained the stuff off, I felt a curiously intense sensation. The first touch of it set my brain in a furious tumult; I seemed to feel an actual physical stirring in my skull, and a seething humming filled my ears. I did not notice the flavour in my mouth, the aroma that filled my throat; I saw only the grey intensity of his gaze that burnt into mine. The draught, the mental confusion, the noise and stirring in my head, seemed to last an interminable time. Curious vague impressions of half-forgotten things danced and vanished on the edge of my consciousness. At last he broke the spell. With a sudden explosive sigh he put down his glass.

'Well?' he said.

'It's glorious,' said I, though I had not tasted the stuff.

My head was spinning. I sat down. My brain was chaos. Then my perception grew clear and minute as though I saw things in a concave mirror. His manner seemed to have changed into something nervous and hasty. He pulled out his watch and grimaced at it. 'Eleven-seven! And tonight I must—Seven-twenty-five. Waterloo! I must go at once.' He called for the bill, and struggled with his coat. Officious waiters came to our assistance. In another moment I was wishing him goodbye over the apron of a cab, and still with an absurd feeling of minute distinctness, as though—how can I express it?—I not only saw but *felt* through an inverted opera-glass.

'That stuff,' he said. He put his hand to his forehead. 'I ought not to have given it to you. It will make your head split tomorrow. Wait a minute. Here.' He handed me out a little flat thing like a seidlitz-powder. 'Take that in water as you are going to bed. The other thing was a drug. Not till you're ready to go to bed, mind. It will clear your head. That's all. One more shake—Futurus!'

I gripped his shrivelled claw. 'Goodbye,' he said, and by the droop of his eyelids I judged he too was a little under the influence of that brain-twisting cordial.

He recollected something else with a start, felt in his breast-pocket, and produced another packet, this time a cylinder the size and shape of a shaving-stick. 'Here,' said he. 'I'd almost forgotten. Don't open this until I come tomorrow—but take it now.'

It was so heavy that I well-nigh dropped it. 'All ri'!' said I, and he grinned at me through the cab window as the cabman flicked his horse into wakefulness. It was a white packet he had given me, with red seals at either end and along its edge. 'If this isn't money,' said I, 'it's platinum or lead.'

I stuck it with elaborate care into my pocket, and with a whirling brain walked home through the Regent Street loiterers and the dark back streets beyond Portland Road. I remember the sensations of that walk very vividly, strange as they were. I was still so far myself that I could notice my strange mental state, and wonder whether this stuff I had had was opium—a drug beyond my experience. It is hard now to describe the peculiarity of my mental strangeness—mental doubling

111

vaguely expresses it. As I was walking up Regent Street I found in my mind a queer persuasion that it was Waterloo Station, and had an odd impulse to get into the Polytechnic as a man might get into a tram. I put a knuckle in my eye, and it was Regent Street. How can I express it? You see a skilful actor looking quietly at you, he pulls a grimace, and lo!—another person. Is it too extravagant if I tell you that it seemed to me as if Regent Street had, for the moment, done that? Then, being persuaded it was Regent Street again, I was oddly muddled about some fantastic reminiscences that cropped up. 'Thirty years ago,' thought I, 'it was here that I quarrelled with my brother.' Then I burst out laughing, to the astonishment and encouragement of a group of night prowlers. Thirty years ago I did not exist, and never in my life had I boasted a brother. The stuff was surely liquid folly, for the poignant regret for that lost brother still clung to me. Along Portland Road the madness took another turn. I began to recall vanished shops, and to compare the street with what it used to be. Confused, troubled thinking was comprehensible enough after the drink I had taken, but what puzzled me were these curiously vivid phantasmal memories that had crept into my mind; and not only the memories that had crept in, but also the memories that had slipped out. I stopped opposite Stevens', the natural history dealer's, and cudgelled my brains to think what he had to do with me. A bus went by, and sounded exactly like the rumbling of a train. I seemed to be dipped into some dark, remote pit for the recollection. 'Of course,' said I, at last, 'he has promised me three frogs tomorrow. Odd I should have forgotten.'

Do they still show children dissolving views? In those I remember one view would begin like a faint ghost, and grow and oust another. In just that way it seemed to me that a ghostly set of new sensations was struggling with those of my ordinary self.

I went on through Euston Road to Tottenham Court Road, puzzled, and a little frightened, and scarcely noticed the unusual way I was taking, for commonly I used to cut through the intervening network of back streets. I turned into University Street, to discover that I had forgotten my number. Only by a strong effort did I recall 11a, and even then it seemed to me that it was a thing some forgotten person had told me. I tried to steady my mind by recalling the incidents of the dinner, and for the life of me I could conjure up no picture of my host's face; I saw him only as a shadowy outline, as one might see oneself reflected in a window through which one was looking. In his place, however, I had a curious exterior vision of myself sitting at a table, flushed, bright-eyed, and talkative.

'I must take this other powder,' said I. 'This is getting impossible.'

I tried the wrong side of the hall for my candle and the matches, and had a doubt of which landing my room might be on. 'I'm drunk,' I said, 'that's certain,' and blundered needlessly on the staircase to sustain the proposition.

At the first glance my room seemed unfamiliar. 'What rot!' I said, and stared about me. I seemed to bring myself back by the effort and the odd phantasmal quality passed into the concrete familiar. There was the old looking-glass, with any notes on the albumens stuck in the corner of the frame, my old everyday suit of clothes pitched about the floor. And yet it was not so real after all. I felt an idiotic persuasion trying to creep into my mind, as it were, that I was in a railway carriage in a tram just stopping, that I was peering out of the window at some unknown station. I gripped the bed-rail firmly to reassure myself. 'It's clairvoyance, perhaps,' I said. 'I must write to the Psychical Research Society.'

I put the rouleau on my dressing-table, sat on my bed and began to take off my boots. It was as if the picture of my present sensations was painted over some other picture that was trying to show through. 'Curse it!' said I; 'my wits are going, or am I in two places at once?' Half undressed, I tossed the powder into a glass and drank it off. It effervesced, and became a fluorescent amber colour. Before I was in bed my mind was already tranquillised. I felt the pillow at my cheek, and thereupon I must have fallen asleep.

છ

I awoke abruptly out of a dream of strange beasts, and found myself lying on my back. Probably every one knows that dismal emotional dream from which one escapes, awake indeed but strangely cowed. There was a curious taste in my mouth, a tired feeling in my limbs, a sense of cutaneous discomfort. I lay with my head motionless on my pillow, expecting that my feeling of strangeness and terror would probably pass away, and that I should then doze off again to sleep. But instead of that, my uncanny sensations increased. At first I could perceive nothing wrong about me. There was a faint light in the room, so faint that it was the very next thing to darkness, and the furniture stood out in it as vague blots of absolute darkness. I stared with my eyes just over the bedclothes.

It came into my mind that some one had entered the room to rob me of my rouleau of money, but after lying for some moments, breathing regularly to simulate sleep, I realised this was mere fancy. Nevertheless, the uneasy assurance of something wrong kept fast hold of me. With an effort I raised my head from the pillow, and peered about me at the dark. What it was I could not conceive. I looked at the dim shapes around me, the greater and lesser darknesses that indicated curtains, table, fireplace, bookshelves, and so forth. Then I began to perceive something unfamiliar in the forms of the darkness. Had the bed turned round? Yonder should be the bookshelves, and something shrouded and pallid rose there, something that would not answer to the bookshelves, however I looked at it. It was far too big to be my shirt thrown on a chair.

Overcoming a childish terror I threw back the bedclothes and thrust my leg out of bed. Instead of coming out of my truckle-bed upon the floor, I found my foot scarcely reached the edge of the mattress. I made another step, as it were, and sat up on the edge of the bed. By the side of my bed should be the candle, and the matches upon the broken chair. I put out my hand and touched—nothing. I waved my hand in the darkness, and it came against some heavy hanging, soft and thick in texture, which gave a rustling noise at my touch. I grasped this and pulled it; it appeared to be a curtain suspended over the head of my bed.

I was now thoroughly awake, and beginning to realise that I was in a strange room. I was puzzled. I tried to recall the overnight circumstances, and I found them now, curiously enough, vivid in my memory: the supper, my reception of the little packages, my wonder whether I was intoxicated, my slow undressing, the coolness to my flushed face of my pillow. I felt a sudden distrust. Was that last night, or the night before? At any rate, this room was strange to me, and I could not imagine how I had got into it. The dim, pallid outline was growing paler, and I perceived it was a window, with the dark shape of an oval toilet-glass against the weak intimation of the dawn that filtered through the blind. I stood up, and was surprised by a curious feeling of weakness and unsteadiness. With trembling hands outstretched, I walked slowly towards the window, getting, nevertheless, a bruise on the knee from a chair by the way. I fumbled round the glass, which was large, with handsome brass sconces, to find the blind-cord. I could not find any. By chance I took hold of the tassel, and with the click of a spring the blind ran up.

I found myself looking out upon a scene that was altogether strange to me. The night was overcast, and through the flocculent grey of the heaped clouds there filtered a faint half-light of dawn. Just at the edge of the sky, the cloud-canopy had a blood-red rim. Below, everything was dark and indistinct, dim hills in the distance, a vague mass of buildings running up into pinnacles, trees like spilt ink, and below the window a tracery of black bushes and pale grey paths. It was so unfamiliar that for the moment I thought myself still dreaming. I felt the toilet-table; it appeared to be made of some polished wood, and was rather elaborately furnished—there were little cut-glass bottles and a brush upon it. There was also a queer little object, horse-shoe-shaped it felt, with smooth, hard projections, lying in a saucer. I could find no matches nor candlestick.

I turned my eyes to the room again. Now the blind was up, faint spectres of its furnishing came out of the darkness. There was a huge curtained bed, and the fireplace at its foot had a large white mantel with something of the shimmer of marble.

I leant against the toilet-table, shut my eyes and opened them again, and tried to think. The whole thing was far too real for dreaming. I was inclined to imagine there was still some hiatus in my memory as a consequence of my draught of that strange liqueur; that I had come into my inheritance perhaps, and suddenly lost my recollection of everything since my good fortune had been announced. Perhaps if I waited a little, things would be clearer to me again. Yet my dinner with old Elvesham was now singularly vivid and recent. The champagne, the observant waiters, the powder, and the liqueurs—I could have staked my soul it all happened a few hours ago.

And then occurred a thing so trivial and yet so terrible to me that I shiver now to think of that moment. I spoke aloud. I said, 'How the devil did I get here?' . . . *And the voice was not my own.*

It was not my own, it was thin, the articulation was slurred, the resonance of my facial bones was different. Then to reassure myself I ran one hand over the other, and felt loose folds of skin, the bony laxity of age. 'Surely,' I said in that horrible voice that had somehow established itself in my throat, 'surely this thing is a dream!' Almost as quickly as if I did it involuntarily, I thrust my fingers into my mouth.

My teeth had gone. My finger-tips ran on the flaccid surface of an even row of shrivelled gums. I was sick with dismay and disgust.

I felt then a passionate desire to see myself, to realise at once in its full horror the ghastly change that had come upon me. I tottered to the mantel, and felt along it for matches. As I did so, a barking cough sprang up in my throat, and I clutched the thick flannel nightdress I found about me. There were no matches there, and I suddenly realised that my extremities were cold. Sniffing and coughing, whimpering a little perhaps, I fumbled back to bed. 'It is surely a dream,' I whimpered to myself as I clambered back, 'surely a dream.' It was a senile repetition. I pulled the bedclothes over my shoulders, over my ears, I thrust my withered hand under the pillow, and determined to compose myself to sleep. Of course it was a dream. In the morning the dream would be over, and I should wake up strong and vigorous again to my youth and studies. I shut my eyes, breathed regularly, and, finding myself wakeful, began to count slowly through the powers of three.

But the thing I desired would not come. I could not get to sleep. And the persuasion of the inexorable reality of the change that had happened to me grew steadily. Presently I found myself with my eyes wide open, the powers of three forgotten, and my skinny fingers upon my shrivelled gums. I was indeed, suddenly and abruptly, an old man. I had in some unaccountable manner fallen through my life and come to old age, in some way I had been cheated of all the best of my life, of love, of struggle, of strength and hope. I grovelled into the pillow and tried to persuade myself that such hallucination was possible. Imperceptibly, steadily, the dawn grew clearer.

At last, despairing of further sleep, I sat up in bed and looked about me. A chill twilight rendered the whole chamber visible. It was spacious and well-furnished, better furnished than any room I had ever slept in before. A candle and matches became dimly visible upon a little pedestal in a recess. I threw back the bedclothes, and shivering with the rawness of the early morning, albeit it was summer-time, I got out and lit the candle. Then, trembling horribly so that the extinguisher rattled on its spike, I tottered to the glass and saw—*Elvesham's face*! It was none the less horrible because I had already dimly feared as much. He had already seemed physically weak and pitiful to me, but seen now, dressed only in a coarse flannel nightdress that fell apart and showed the stringy neck, seen now as my own body, I cannot describe its desolate decrepitude. The hollow cheeks, the straggling tail of dirty

grey hair, the rheumy bleared eyes, the quivering, shrivelled lips, the lower displaying a gleam of the pink interior lining, and those horrible dark gums showing. You who are mind and body together at your natural years, cannot imagine what this fiendish imprisonment meant to me. To be young and full of the desire and energy of youth, and to be caught, and presently to be crushed in this tottering ruin of a body.
. . .

But I wander from the course of my story. For some time I must have been stunned at this change that had come upon me. It was daylight when I did so far gather myself together as to think. In some inexplicable way I had been changed, though how, short of magic, the thing had been done, I could not say. And as I thought, the diabolical ingenuity of Elvesham came home to me. It seemed plain to me that as I found myself in his, so he must be in possession of my body, of my strength that is, and my future. But how to prove it? Then as I thought, the thing became so incredible even to me, that my mind reeled, and I had to pinch myself, to feel my toothless gums, to see myself in the glass, and touch the things about me before I could steady myself to face the facts again. Was all life hallucination? Was I indeed Elvesham, and he me? Had I been dreaming of Eden overnight? Was there any Eden? But if I was Elvesham, I should remember where I was on the previous morning, the name of the town in which I lived, what happened before the dream began. I struggled with my thoughts. I recalled the queer doubleness of my memories overnight. But now my mind was clear. Not the ghost of any memories but those proper to Eden could I raise.

'This way lies insanity!' I cried in my piping voice. I staggered to my feet, dragged my feeble, heavy limbs to the washhand-stand, and plunged my grey head into a basin of cold water. Then, towelling myself, I tried again. It was no good. I felt beyond all question that I was indeed Eden, not Elvesham. But Eden in Elvesham's body!

Had I been a man of any other age, I might have given myself up to my fate as one enchanted. But in these sceptical days miracles do not pass current. Here was some trick of psychology. What a drug and a steady stare could do, a drug and a steady stare, or some similar treatment, could surely undo. Men have lost their memories before. But to exchange memories as one does umbrellas! I laughed. Alas! not a healthy laugh, but a wheezing, senile titter. I could have fancied old Elvesham laughing at my plight, and a gust of petulant anger, unusual to me, swept across my feelings. I began dressing eagerly in the clothes I found lying about on the floor, and only realised when I was dressed that it was an evening suit I had assumed. I opened the wardrobe and found some ordinary clothes, a pair of plaid trousers, and an old-fashioned dressing-gown. I put a venerable smoking-cap on my venerable head, and, coughing a little from my exertions, tottered out upon the landing.

It was then perhaps a quarter to six, and the blinds were closely drawn and the house quite silent. The landing was a spacious one, a broad, richly-carpeted staircase went down into the darkness of the hall below, and before me a door ajar showed me a writing-desk, a revolving bookcase, the back of a study chair, and a fine array of bound books, shelf upon shelf.

'My study,' I mumbled, and walked across the landing. Then at the sound of my voice a thought struck me, and I went back to the bedroom and put in the set of false teeth. They slipped in with the ease of old habit. 'That's better,' said I, gnashing them, and so returned to the study.

The drawers of the writing-desk were locked. Its revolving top was also locked. I could see no indications of the keys, and there were none in the pockets of my trousers. I shuffled back at once to the bedroom, and went through the dress-suit, and afterwards the pockets of all the garments I could find. I was very eager; and one might have imagined that burglars had been at work, to see my room when I had done. Not only were there no keys to be found, but not a coin, nor a scrap of paper—save only the receipted bill of the overnight dinner.

A curious weariness asserted itself. I sat down and stared at the garments flung here and there, their pockets turned inside out. My first frenzy had already flickered out. Every moment I was beginning to realise the immense intelligence of the plans of my enemy, to see more and more clearly the hopelessness of my position. With an effort I rose and hurried into the study again. On the staircase was a housemaid pulling up the blinds. She stared, I think, at the expression of my face. I shut the door of the study behind me, and, seizing a poker, began an attack upon the desk. That is how they found me. The cover of the desk was split, the lock smashed, the letters torn out of the pigeon-holes and tossed about the room. In my senile rage I had flung about the pens and other such light stationery, and overturned the ink. Moreover, a large vase upon the mantel had got broken—I do not know how. I could find no cheque-book, no money, no indications of the slightest use for the recovery of my body. I was battering madly at the drawers, when the butler, backed by two women-servants, intruded upon me.

ଐ

That simply is the story of my change. No one will believe my frantic assertions. I am treated as one demented, and even at this moment I am under restraint. But I am sane, absolutely sane, and to prove it I have sat down to write this story minutely as the thing happened to me. I appeal to the reader, whether there is any trace of insanity in the style or method of the story he has been reading. I am a young man locked away in an old man's body. But the clear fact is incredible to every one. Naturally I appear demented to those who will not believe this, naturally I do not know the names of my secretaries, of the doctors who come to see me, of my servants and neighbours, of this town (wherever it is) where I find myself. Naturally I lose myself in my own house, and suffer inconveniences of every sort. Naturally I ask the oddest questions. Naturally I weep and cry out, and have paroxysms of despair. I have no money and no cheque-book. The bank will not recognise my signature, for I suppose that, allowing for the feeble muscles I now have, my handwriting is still Eden's. These people about me will not let me go to the bank personally. It seems, indeed, that there is no bank in this town, and that I have taken an account in some part of London. It seems that Elvesham kept the name of his solicitor secret from all his household—I can ascertain nothing. Elvesham was, of course, a profound student of mental science, and all my declarations of the facts of the case merely confirm the theory that my insanity is the outcome of overmuch brooding upon psychology. Dreams of the personal identity indeed! Two days ago I was a healthy youngster, with all life before me; now I am a furious old man, unkempt and desperate and miserable, prowling about a great luxurious strange house, watched, feared, and avoided as a lunatic by every one about me. And in London is Elvesham beginning life again in a vigorous body, and with all the accumulated knowledge and wisdom of threescore and ten. He has stolen my life.

What has happened I do not clearly know. In the study are volumes of manuscript notes referring chiefly to the psychology of memory, and parts of what may be either calculations or ciphers in symbols absolutely strange to me. In some passages there are indications that he was also occupied with the philosophy of mathematics. I take it he has transferred the whole of his memories, the accumulation that makes up his personality, from this old withered brain of his to mine, and, similarly, that he has transferred mine to his discarded tenement. Practically, that is, he has changed bodies. But how such a change may be possible is without the range of my philosophy. I have been a materialist for all my thinking life, but here, suddenly, is a clear case of man's detachability from matter.

One desperate experiment I am about to try. I sit writing here before putting the matter to issue. This morning, with the help of a table-knife that I had secreted at breakfast, I succeeded in breaking open a fairly obvious secret drawer in this wrecked writing-desk. I discovered nothing save a little green glass phial containing a white powder. Round the neck of the phial was a label, and thereon was written this one word, *'Release'*. This may be—is most probably, poison. I can understand Elvesham placing poison in my way, and I should be sure that it was his intention so to get rid of the only living witness against him, were it not for this careful concealment. The man has practically solved the problem of immortality. Save for the spite of chance, he will live in my body until it has aged, and then, again, throwing that aside, he will assume some other victim's youth and strength. When one remembers his heartlessness, it is terrible to think of the ever-growing experience, that . . . How long has he been leaping from body to body? . . . But I tire of writing. The powder appears to be soluble in water. The taste is not unpleasant.

∝

There the narrative found upon Mr Elvesham's desk ends. His dead body lay between the desk and the chair. The latter had been pushed back, probably by his last convulsions. The story was written in pencil, and in a crazy hand quite unlike his usual minute characters. There remain only two curious facts to record. Indisputably there was some connection between Eden and Elvesham, since the whole of Elvesham's property was bequeathed to the young man. But he never inherited. When Elvesham committed suicide, Eden was, strangely enough, already dead. Twenty-four hours before, he had been knocked down by a cab and killed instantly, at the crowded crossing at the inter-section of Gower Street and Euston Road. So that the only human being who could have thrown light upon this fantastic narrative is beyond the reach of questions.

THE APPLE

'I MUST get rid of it,' said the man in the corner of the carriage, abruptly breaking the silence.

Mr Hinchcliff looked up, hearing imperfectly. He had been lost in the rapt contemplation of the college cap tied by a string to his portmanteau handles—the outward and visible sign of his newly-gained pedagogic position—in the rapt appreciation of the college cap and the pleasant anticipations it excited. For Mr Hinchcliff had just matriculated at London University, and was going to be junior assistant at the Holmwood Grammar School—a very enviable position. He stared across the carriage at his fellow-traveller.

'Why not give it away?' said this person. 'Give it away! Why not?'

He was a tall, dark, sunburnt man with a pale face. His arms were folded tightly, and his feet were on the seat in front of him. He was pulling at a lank black moustache. He stared hard at his toes.

'Why not?' he said.

Mr Hinchcliff coughed.

The stranger lifted his eyes—they were curious, dark-grey eyes—and stared blankly at Mr Hinchcliff for the best part of a minute, perhaps. His expression grew to interest.

'Yes,' he said slowly. 'Why not? And end it.'

'I don't quite follow you, I'm afraid,' said Mr Hinchcliff, with another cough.

'You don't quite follow me?' said the stranger quite mechanically, his singular eyes wandering from Mr Hinchcliff to the bag with its ostentatiously displayed cap, and back to Mr Hinchcliff's downy face.

'You're so abrupt, you know,' apologised Mr Hinchcliff.

'Why shouldn't I?' said the stranger, following his thoughts. 'You are a student?' he said, addressing Mr Hinchcliff.

'I am—by Correspondence—of the London University,' said Mr Hinchcliff, with irrepressible pride, and feeling nervously at his tie.

'In pursuit of knowledge,' said the stranger, and suddenly took his feet off the seat, put his fist on his knees, and stared at Mr Hinchcliff as though he had never seen a student before. 'Yes,' he said, and flung out an index finger. Then he rose, took a bag from the hat-rack, and unlocked it. Quite silently he drew out something round and wrapped in a quantity of silver paper, and unfolded this carefully. He held it out towards Mr Hinchcliff—a small, very smooth, golden-yellow fruit.

Mr Hinchcliff's eyes and mouth were open. He did not offer to take this object—if he was intended to take it.

'That,' said this fantastic stranger, speaking very slowly, 'is the Apple of the Tree of Knowledge. Look at it—small, and bright, and wonderful—Knowledge—and I am going to give it to you.'

Mr Hinchcliff's mind worked painfully for a minute, and then the sufficient explanation, 'Mad!' flashed across his brain, and illuminated the whole situation. One humoured madmen. He put his head a little on one side.

'The Apple of the Tree of Knowledge, eh!' said Mr Hinchcliff, regarding it with a finely assumed air of interest, and then looking at the interlocutor. 'But don't you want to eat it yourself? And besides—how did you come by it?'

'It never fades. I have had it now three months. And it is ever bright and smooth and ripe and desirable, as you see it.' He laid his hand on his knee and regarded the fruit musingly. Then he began to wrap it again in the papers, as though he had abandoned his intention of giving it away.

'But how did you come by it?' said Mr Hinchcliff, who had his argumentative side. 'And how do you know that it is the Fruit of the Tree?'

'I bought this fruit,' said the stranger, 'three months ago—for a drink of water and a crust of bread. The man who gave it to me—because I kept the life in him—was an Armenian. Armenia! that wonderful country, the first of all countries, where the ark of the Flood remains to this day, buried in the glaciers of Mount Ararat. This man, I say, fleeing with others from the Kurds who had come upon them, went up into desolate places among the mountains-places beyond the common knowledge of men. And fleeing from imminent pursuit, they came to a slope high among the mountain-peaks, green with a grass like knife-blades, that cut and slashed most pitilessly at any one who went into it. The Kurds were close behind, and there was nothing for it but to plunge in, and the worst of it was that the paths they made through it at the price of their blood served for the Kurds to follow. Every one of the fugitives was killed save this Armenian and another. He heard the screams and cries of his friends, and the swish of the grass about those who were pursuing them—it was tall grass rising overhead. And then a shouting and answers, and when presently he paused, everything was still. He pushed out again, not understanding, cut and bleeding, until he came out on a steep slope of rocks below a precipice, and then he saw the grass was all on fire, and the smoke of it rose like a veil between him and his enemies.'

The stranger paused. 'Yes?' said Mr Hinchcliff. 'Yes?'

'There he was, all torn and bloody from the knife-blades of the grass, the rocks blazing under the afternoon sun—the sky molten brass—and the smoke of the fire driving towards him. He dared not stay there. Death he did not mind, but torture! Far away beyond the smoke he heard shouts and cries. Women screaming. So he went clambering up a gorge in the rocks—everywhere were bushes with dry branches that stuck like thorns among the leaves—until he clambered over the brow of a ridge that hid him. And then he met his companion, a shepherd, who had also escaped. And, counting cold and famine and thirst as nothing against the Kurds, they went on into the heights, and among the snow and ice. They wandered three whole days.

'The third day came the vision. I suppose hungry men often do see visions, but then there is this fruit.' He lifted the wrapped globe in his hand. 'And I have heard it, too, from other mountaineers who have known something of the legend. It was in the evening time, when the stars were increasing, that they came down a slope of polished rock into a huge dark valley all set about with strange, contorted trees, and in these trees hung little globes like glow-worm spheres, strange round yellow lights.

'Suddenly this valley was lit far away, many miles away, far down it, with a golden flame marching slowly athwart it, that made the stunted trees against it black as night, and turned the slopes all about them and their figures to the likeness of fiery gold. And at the vision they, knowing the legends of the mountains; instantly knew that it was Eden they saw, or the sentinel of Eden, and they fell upon their faces like men struck dead.

'When they dared to look again the valley was dark for a space, and then the light came again—returning, a burning amber.

'At that the shepherd sprang to his feet, and with a shout began to run down towards the light, but the other man was too fearful to follow him. He stood stunned, amazed, and terrified, watching his companion recede towards the marching glare. And hardly had the shepherd set out when there came a noise like thunder, the beating of invisible wings hurrying up the valley, and a great and terrible fear; and at that the man who gave me the fruit turned—if he might still escape. And hurrying headlong up the slope again, with that tumult sweeping after him, he stumbled against one of these stunted bushes, and a ripe fruit came off it into his hand. This fruit. Forthwith, the wings and the thunder rolled all about him. He fell and fainted, and when he came to his senses, he was back among the blackened ruins of his own village, and I and the others were attending to the wounded. A vision? But the golden fruit of the tree was still clutched in his hand. There were others there who knew the legend, knew what that strange fruit might be.' He paused. 'And this is it,' he said.

'It was a most extraordinary story to be told in a third-class carriage on a Sussex railway. It was as if the real was a mere veil to the fantastic, and here was the fantastic poking through. 'Is it?' was all Mr Hinchcliff could say.

'The legend,' said the stranger, 'tells that those thickets of dwarfed trees growing about the garden sprang from the apple that Adam carried in his hand when he and Eve were driven forth. He felt something in his hand, saw the half eaten apple, and flung it petulantly aside. And there they grow, in that desolate valley, girdled round with the everlasting snows, and there the fiery swords keep ward against the Judgment Day.'

'But I thought these things were'—Mr Hinchcliff paused—'fables —parables rather. Do you mean to tell me that there in Armenia—'

The stranger answered the unfinished question with the fruit in his open hand.

'But you don't know,' said Mr Hinchcliff, 'that that *is* the fruit of the Tree of Knowledge. The man may have had—a sort of mirage, say. Suppose—'

'Look at it,' said the stranger.

It was certainly a strange-looking globe, not really an apple, Mr Hinchcliff saw, and a curious glowing golden colour, almost as though light itself was wrought into its substance. As he looked at it, he began to see more vividly the desolate valley among the mountains, the

125

guarding swords of fire, the strange antiquities of the story he had just heard. He rubbed a knuckle into his eye. 'But—' said he.

'It has kept like that, smooth and full, three months. Longer than that it is now by some days. No drying, no withering, no decay.'

'And you yourself,' said Mr Hinchcliff, 'really believe that—'

'Is the Forbidden Fruit.'

There was no mistaking the earnestness of the man's manner and his perfect sanity. 'The Fruit of Knowledge,' he said.

'Suppose it was?' said Mr Hinchcliff, after a pause, still staring at it. 'But after all,' said Mr Hinchcliff, 'it's not my kind of knowledge—not the sort of knowledge. I mean, Adam and Eve have eaten it already.'

'We inherit their sins—not their knowledge,' said the stranger. 'That would make it all clear and bright again. We should see into everything, through everything, into the deepest meaning of everything—'

'Why don't you eat it, then?' said Mr Hinchcliff, with an inspiration.

'I took it intending to eat it,' said the stranger. 'Man has fallen. Merely to eat again could scarcely—

'Knowledge is power,' said Mr Hinchcliff.

'But is it happiness? I am older than you—more than twice as old. Time after time I have held this in my hand, and my heart has failed me at the thought of all that one might know, that terrible lucidity—Suppose suddenly all the world became pitilessly clear?'

'That, I think, would be a great advantage,' said Mr Hinchcliff, 'on the whole.'

'Suppose you saw into the hearts and minds of every one about you, into their most secret recesses—people you loved, whose love you valued?'

'You'd soon find out the humbugs,' said Mr Hinchcliff, greatly struck by the idea.

'And worse—to know yourself, bare of your most intimate illusions. To see yourself in your place. All that your lusts and weaknesses prevented your doing. No merciful perspective.'

'That might be an excellent thing too. "Know thyself," you know.'

'You are young,' said the stranger.

126

'If you don't care to eat it, and it bothers you, why don't you throw it away?'

'There again, perhaps, you will not understand me. To me, how could one throw away a thing like that, glowing, wonderful? Once one has it, one is bound. But, on the other hand, to *give* it away! To give it away to some one who thirsted after knowledge, who found no terror in the thought of that clear perception—'

'Of course,' said Mr Hinchcliff thoughtfully, 'it might be some sort of poisonous fruit.'

And then his eye caught something motionless, the end of a white board black-lettered outside the carriage window. '—MWOOD,' he saw. He started convulsively. 'Gracious!' said Mr Hinchcliff. 'Holm-wood!'—and the practical present blotted out the mystic realisations that had been stealing upon him.

In another moment he was opening the carriage-door, portmanteau in hand. The guard was already fluttering his green flag. Mr Hinchcliff jumped out. 'Here!' said a voice behind him, and he saw the dark eyes of the stranger shining and the golden fruit, bright and bare, held out of the open carriage-door. He took it instinctively, the train was already moving.

'*No!*' shouted the stranger, and made a snatch at it as if to take it back.

'Stand away,' cried a country porter, thrusting forward to close the door. The stranger shouted something Mr Hinchcliff did not catch, head and arm thrust excitedly out of the window, and then the shadow of the bridge fell on him, and in a trice he was hidden. Mr Hinchcliff stood astonished, staring at the end of the last waggon receding round the bend, and with the wonderful fruit in his hand. For the fraction of a minute his mind was confused, and then he became aware that two or three people on the platform were regarding him with interest. Was he not the new Grammar School master making his debut? It occurred to him that, so far as they could tell, the fruit might very well be the naive refreshment of an orange. He flushed at the thought, and thrust the fruit into his side pocket, where it bulged undesirably. But there was no help for it, so he went towards them, awkwardly concealing his sense of awkwardness, to ask the way to the Grammar School, and the means of getting his portmanteau and the two tin boxes which lay up the platform thither. Of all the odd and fantastic yarns to tell a fellow!

His luggage could be taken on a truck for sixpence, he found, and he could precede it on foot. He fancied an ironical note in the voices. He was painfully aware of his contour.

The curious earnestness of the man in the train, and the glamour of the story he told, had, for a time, diverted the current of Mr Hinch-cliff's thoughts. It drove like a mist before his immediate concerns. Fires that went to and fro! But the preoccupation of his new position, and the impression he was to produce upon Holmwood generally, and the school people in particular, returned upon him with reinvigorating power before he left the station and cleared his mental atmosphere. But it is extraordinary what an inconvenient thing the addition of a soft and rather brightly-golden fruit, not three inches in diameter, may prove to a sensitive youth on his best appearance. In the pocket of his black jacket it bulged dreadfully, spoilt the lines altogether. He passed a little old lady in black, and he felt her eye drop upon the excrescence at once. He was wearing one glove and carrying the other, together with his stick, so that to bear the fruit openly was impossible. In one place, where the road into the town seemed suitably secluded, he took his encumbrance out of his pocket and tried it in his hat. It was just too large, the hat wobbled ludicrously, and just as he was taking it out again, a butcher's boy came driving round the corner.

'Confound it!' said Mr Hinchcliff.

He would have eaten the thing, and attained omniscience there and then, but it would seem so silly to go into the town sucking a juicy fruit—and it certainly felt juicy. If one of the boys should come by, it might do him a serious injury with his discipline so to be seen. And the juice might make his face sticky and get upon his cuffs—or it might be an acid juice as potent as lemon, and take all the colour out of his clothes.

Then round a bend in the lane came two pleasant sunlit girlish figures. They were walking slowly towards the town and chattering—at any moment they might look round and see a hot-faced young man behind them carrying a kind of phosphorescent yellow tomato! They would be sure to laugh.

'Hang!' said Mr Hinchcliff, and with a swift jerk sent the encum-brance flying over the stone wall of an orchard that there abutted on the road. As it vanished, he felt a faint twinge of loss that lasted scarcely a moment. He adjusted the stick and glove in his hand, and walked on, erect and self-conscious, to pass the girls.

 C3

But in the darkness of the night Mr Hinchcliff had a dream, and saw the valley, and the flaming swords, and the contorted trees, and knew that it really was the Apple of the Tree of Knowledge that he had thrown regardlessly away. And he awoke very unhappy.

In the morning his regret had passed, but afterwards it returned and troubled him; never, however, when he was happy or busily occupied. At last, one moonlight night about eleven, when all Holmwood was quiet, his regrets returned with redoubled force, and therewith an impulse to adventure. He slipped out of the house and over the playground wall, went through the silent town to Station Lane, and climbed into the orchard where he had thrown the fruit. But nothing was to be found of it there among the dewy grass and the faint intangible globes of dandelion down.

THE CRYSTAL EGG

THERE was, until a year ago, a little and very grimy-looking shop near Seven Dials, over which, in weatherworn yellow lettering, the name of 'C. Cave, Naturalist and Dealer in Antiquities,' was inscribed. The contents of its window were curiously varied. They comprised some elephant tusks and an imperfect set of chessmen, beads and weapons, a box of eyes, two skulls of tigers and one human, several moth-eaten stuffed monkeys (one holding a lamp), an old-fashioned cabinet, a fly-blown ostrich egg or so, some fishing-tackle, and an extraordinarily dirty, empty glass fish-tank. There was also, at the moment the story begins, a mass of crystal, worked into the shape of an egg and brilliantly polished. And at that two people, who stood outside the window, were looking, one of them a tall, thin clergyman, the other a black-bearded young man of dusky complexion and unobtrusive costume. The dusky young man spoke with eager gesticulation, and seemed anxious for his companion to purchase the article.

While they were there Mr Cave came into his shop, his beard still wagging with the bread-and-butter of his tea. When he saw these men and the object of their regard, his countenance fell. He glanced guiltily over his shoulder, and softly shut the door. He was a little old man, with pale face and peculiar watery blue eyes; his hair was a dirty grey, and he wore a shabby blue frock-coat, an ancient silk hat, and carpet slippers very much down at heel. He remained watching the two men as they talked.

The clergyman went deep into his trouser pocket, examined a handful of money, and showed his teeth in an agreeable smile. Mr Cave seemed still more depressed when they came into the shop. The clergyman, without any ceremony, asked the price of the crystal egg. Mr Cave glanced nervously towards the door leading into the parlour, and said five pounds. The clergyman protested that the price was high, to his companion as well as to Mr Cave—it was, indeed, very much

130

more than Mr Cave had intended to ask, when he had stocked the article—and an attempt at bargaining ensued. Mr Cave stepped to the shop door, and held it open. 'Five pounds is my price,' he said, as though he wished to save himself the trouble of unprofitable discussion. As he did so, the upper portion of a woman's face appeared above the blind in the glass upper panel of the door leading into the parlour, and stared curiously at the two customers. 'Five pounds is my price,' said Mr Cave, with a quiver in his voice.

The swarthy young man had so far remained a spectator, watching Cave keenly. Now he spoke. 'Give him five pounds,' he said. The clergyman glanced at him to see if he were in earnest, and, when he looked at Mr Cave again, he saw that the latter's face was white. 'It's a lot of money,' said the clergyman, and, diving into his pocket, began counting his resources. He had little more than thirty shillings, and he appealed to his companion, with whom he seemed to be on terms of considerable intimacy. This gave Mr Cave an opportunity of collecting his thoughts, and he began to explain in an agitated manner that the crystal was not, as a matter of fact, entirely free for sale. His two customers were naturally surprised at this, and inquired why he had not thought of that before he began to bargain. Mr Cave became confused, but he stuck to his story, that the crystal was not in the market that afternoon, that a probable purchaser of it had already appeared. The two, treating this as an attempt to raise the price still further, made as if they would leave the shop. But at this point the parlour door opened, and the owner of the dark fringe and the little eyes appeared.

She was a coarse-featured, corpulent woman, younger and very much larger than Mr Cave; she walked heavily, and her face was flushed. 'That crystal *is* for sale,' she said. 'And five pounds is a good enough price for it. I can't think what you're about, Cave, not to take the gentleman's offer!'

Mr Cave, greatly perturbed by the irruption, looked angrily at her over the rims of his spectacles, and, without excessive assurance, asserted his right to manage his business in his own way. An altercation began. The two customers watched the scene with interest and some amusement, occasionally assisting Mrs Cave with suggestions. Mr Cave, hard driven, persisted in a confused and impossible story of an inquiry for the crystal that morning, and his agitation became painful. But he stuck to his point with extraordinary persistence. It was the young Oriental who ended this curious controversy. He proposed that they should call again in the course of two days—so as to give the alleged inquirer a fair chance. 'And then we must insist,' said the clergyman. 'Five pounds.' Mrs Cave took it on herself to apologise for her husband, explaining that he was sometimes 'a little odd,' and as the two customers left, the couple prepared for a free discussion of the incident in all its bearings.

Mrs Cave talked to her husband with singular directness. The poor little man, quivering with emotion, muddled himself between his stories, maintaining on the one hand that he had another customer in view, and on the other asserting that the crystal was honestly worth ten guineas. 'Why did you ask five pounds?' said his wife. 'Do let me manage my business my own way!' said Mr Cave.

Mr Cave had living with him a step-daughter and a step-son, and at supper that night the transaction was re-discussed. None of them had a high opinion of Mr Cave's business methods, and this action seemed a culminating folly.

'It's my opinion he's refused that crystal before,' said the step-son, a loose-limbed lout of eighteen.

'But *Five Pounds*!' said his step-daughter, an argumentative young woman of six-and-twenty.

Mr Cave's answers were wretched; he could only mumble weak assertions that he knew his own business best. They drove him from his half-eaten supper into the shop, to close it for the night, his ears aflame and tears of vexation behind his spectacles. 'Why had he left the crystal in the window so long? The folly of it!' That was the trouble closest in his mind. For a time he could see no way of evading sale.

After supper his step-daughter and step-son smartened themselves up and went out, and his wife retired upstairs to reflect upon the business aspects of the crystal, over a little sugar and lemon and so forth in hot water. Mr Cave went into the shop, and stayed there until late, ostensibly to make ornamental rockeries for gold-fish cases but really for a private purpose that will be better explained later. The next day Mrs Cave found that the crystal had been removed from the window, and was lying behind some second-hand books on angling. She replaced it in a conspicuous position. But she did not argue further about it, as a nervous headache disinclined her from debate. Mr Cave was always disinclined. The day passed disagreeably. Mr Cave was, if

132

anything, more absent-minded than usual, and uncommonly irritable withal. In the afternoon, when his wife was taking her customary sleep, he removed the crystal from the window again.

The next day Mr Cave had to deliver a consignment of dogfish at one of the hospital schools, where they were needed for dissection. In his absence Mrs Cave's mind reverted to the topic of the crystal, and the methods of expenditure suitable to a windfall of five pounds. She had already devised some very agreeable expedients, among others a dress of green silk for herself and a trip to Richmond, when a jangling of the front door bell summoned her into the shop. The customer was an examination coach who came to complain of the non-delivery of certain frogs asked for the previous day. Mrs Cave did not approve of this particular branch of Mr Cave's business, and the gentleman, who had called in a somewhat aggressive mood, retired after a brief exchange of words—entirely civil so far as he was concerned. Mrs Cave's eye then naturally turned to the window; for the sight of the crystal was an assurance of the five pounds and of her dreams. What was her surprise to find it gone!

She went to the place behind the locker on the counter, where she had discovered it the day before. It was not there; and she immediately began an eager search about the shop.

When Mr Cave returned from his business with the dog-fish, about a quarter to two in the afternoon, he found the shop in some confusion, and his wife, extremely exasperated and on her knees behind the counter, routing among his taxidermic material. Her face came up hot and angry over the counter, as the jangling bell announced his return, and she forthwith accused him of 'hiding it.'

'Hid *what*?' asked Mr Cave.

'The crystal!'

At that Mr Cave, apparently much surprised, rushed to the window. 'Isn't it here?' he said. 'Great Heavens! what has become of it?'

Just then, Mr Cave's step-son re-entered the shop from the inner room—he had come home a minute or so before Mr Cave—and he was blaspheming freely. He was apprenticed to a second-hand furniture dealer down the road, but he had his meals at home, and he was naturally annoyed to find no dinner ready.

But when he heard of the loss of the crystal, he forgot his meal, and his anger was diverted from his mother to his step-father. Their

133

first idea, of course, was that he had hidden it. But Mr Cave stoutly denied all knowledge of its fate—freely offering his bedabbled affidavit in the matter—and at last was worked up to the point of accusing, first, his wife and then his step-son of having taken it with a view to a private sale. So began an exceedingly acrimonious and emotional discussion, which ended for Mrs Cave in a peculiar nervous condition mid way between hysterics and amuck, and caused the step-son to be half an hour late at the furniture establishment in the afternoon. Mr Cave took refuge from his wife's emotions in the shop.

In the evening the matter was resumed, with less passion and in a judicial spirit, under the presidency of the step-daughter. The supper passed unhappily and culminated in a painful scene. Mr Cave gave way at last to extreme exasperation, and went out banging the front door violently. The rest of the family, having discussed him with the freedom his absence warranted, hunted the house from garret to cellar, hoping to light upon the crystal.

The next day the two customers called again. They were received by Mrs Cave almost in tears. It transpired that no one *could* imagine all that she had stood from Cave at various times in her married pilgrimage. . . . She also gave a garbled account of the disappearance. The clergyman and the Oriental laughed silently at one another, and said it was very extraordinary. As Mrs Cave seemed disposed to give them the complete history of her life, they made to leave the shop. Thereupon Mrs Cave, still clinging to hope, asked for the clergyman's address, so that, if she could get anything out of Cave, she might communicate it. The address was duly given, but apparently was afterwards mislaid. Mrs Cave can remember nothing about it.

In the evening of that day, the Caves seem to have exhausted their emotions, and Mr Cave, who had been out in the afternoon, supped in a gloomy isolation that contrasted pleasantly with the impassioned controversy of the previous days. For some time matters were very badly strained in the Cave household, but neither crystal nor customer reappeared.

Now, without mincing the matter, we must admit that Mr Cave was a liar. He knew perfectly well where the crystal was. It was in the rooms of Mr Jacoby Wace, Assistant Demonstrator at St Catherine's Hospital, Westbourne Street. It stood on the sideboard partially covered by a black velvet cloth, and beside a decanter of American whisky. It is from Mr Wace, indeed, that the particulars upon which this narrative is based were derived. Cave had taken off the thing to the hospital hidden in the dog-fish sack, and there had pressed the young investigator to keep it for him. Mr Wace was a little dubious at first. His relationship to Cave was peculiar. He had a taste for singular characters, and he had more than once invited the old man to smoke and drink in his rooms, and to unfold his rather amusing views of life in general and of his wife in particular. Mr Wace had encountered Mrs Cave, too, on occasions when Mr Cave was not at home to attend to him. He knew the constant interference to which Cave was subjected, and having weighed the story judicially, he decided to give the crystal a refuge. Mr Cave promised to explain the reasons for his remarkable affection for the crystal more fully on a later occasion, but he spoke distinctly of seeing visions therein. He called on Mr Wace the same evening.

He told a complicated story. The crystal he said had come into his possession with other oddments at the forced sale of another curiosity dealer's effects, and not knowing what its value might be, he had ticketed it at ten shillings. It had hung upon his hands at that price for same months, and he was thinking of 'reducing the figure,' when he made a singular discovery.

At that time his health was very bad—and it must be borne in mind that, throughout all this experience, his physical condition was one of ebb—and he was in considerable distress by reason of the negligence, the positive ill-treatment even, he received from his wife and step-children. His wife was vain, extravagant, unfeeling, and had a growing taste for private drinking; his step-daughter was mean and over-reaching; and his step-son had conceived a violent dislike for him, and lost no chance of showing it. The requirements of his business pressed heavily upon him, and Mr, Wace does not think that he was altogether free from occasional intemperance. He had begun life in a comfortable position, he was a man of fair education, and he suffered, for weeks at a stretch, from melancholia and insomnia. Afraid to disturb his family, he would slip quietly from his wife's side, when his thoughts became intolerable, and wander about the house. And about three o'clock one morning, late in August, chance directed him into the shop.

The dirty little place was impenetrably black except, in one spot, where he perceived an unusual glow of light. Approaching this, he discovered it to be the crystal egg, which was standing on the corner of the counter towards the window. A thin ray smote through a crack in the shutters, impinged upon the object, and seemed as it were to fill its entire interior.

It occurred to Mr Cave that this was not in accordance with the laws of optics as he had known them in his younger days. He could understand the rays being refracted by the crystal and coming to a focus in its interior, but this diffusion jarred with his physical conceptions. He approached the crystal nearly, peering into it and round it, with a transient revival of the scientific curiosity that in his youth had determined his choice of a calling. He was surprised to find the light not steady, but writhing within the substance of the egg, as though that object was a hollow sphere of some luminous vapour. In moving about to get different points of view, he suddenly found that he had come between it and the ray, and that the crystal none the less remained luminous. Greatly astonished, he lifted it out of the light ray and carried it to the darkest part of the shop. It remained bright for some four or five minutes, when it slowly faded and went out. He placed it in the thin streak of daylight, and its luminousness was almost immediately restored.

So far, at least, Mr Wace was able to verify the remarkable story of Mr Cave. He has himself repeatedly held this crystal in a ray of light (which had to be of a less diameter than one millimetre). And in a perfect darkness, such as could be produced by velvet wrapping, the crystal did undoubtedly appear very faintly phosphorescent. It would seem, however, that the luminousness was of some exceptional sort, and not equally visible to all eyes; for Mr Harbinger—whose name will be familiar to the scientific reader in connection with the Pasteur Institute—was quite unable to see any light whatever. And Mr Wace's own capacity for its appreciation was out of comparison inferior to that of Mr Cave's. Even with Mr Cave the power varied very considerably; his vision was most vivid during states of extreme weakness and fatigue.

Now from the outset this light in the crystal exercised an irresistible fascination upon Mr Cave. And it says more for his loneliness of soul than a volume of pathetic writing could do, that he told no human being of his curious observations. He seems to have been living in such an atmosphere of petty spite that to admit the existence of a pleasure would have been to risk the loss of it. He found that as the dawn advanced, and the amount of diffused light increased, the crystal became to all appearance non-luminous. And for some time he was unable to see anything in it, except at night-time, in dark corners of the shop.

But the use of an old velvet cloth, which he used as a background for a collection of minerals, occurred to him, and by doubling this, and putting it over his head and hands, he was able to get a sight of the luminous movement within the crystal even in the day-time. He was very cautious lest he should be thus discovered by his wife, and he practised this occupation only in the afternoons, while she was asleep upstairs, and then circumspectly in a hollow under the counter. And one day, turning the crystal about in his hands, he saw something. It came and went like a flash, but it gave him the impression that the object had for a moment opened to him the view of a wide and spacious and strange country; and, turning it about, he did, just as the light faded, see the same vision again.

Now, it would be tedious and unnecessary to state all the phases of Mr Cave's discovery from this point. Suffice that the effect was this: the crystal, being peered into at an angle of about 137 degrees from the direction of the illuminating ray, gave a clear and consistent picture of a wide and peculiar countryside. It was not dream-like at all; it produced a definite impression of reality, and the better the light the more real and solid it seemed. It was a moving picture: that is to say, certain objects moved in it, but slowly in an orderly manner like real things, and, according as the direction of the lighting and vision changed, the picture changed also. It must, indeed, have been like looking through an oval glass at a view, and turning the glass about to get at different aspects.

Mr Cave's statements, Mr Wace assures me, were extremely circumstantial, and entirely free from any of that emotional quality that taints hallucinatory impressions. But it must be remembered that all the efforts of Mr Wace to see any similar clarity in the faint opalescence of the crystal were wholly unsuccessful, try as he would. The difference in intensity of the impressions received by the two men was very great, and it is quite conceivable that what was a view to Mr Cave was a mere blurred nebulosity to Mr Wace.

The view, as Mr Cave described it, was invariably of an extensive plain, and he seemed always to be looking at it from a considerable height, as if from a tower or a mast. To the east and to the west the plain was bounded at a remote distance by vast reddish cliffs, which reminded him of those he had seen in some picture; but what the picture was Mr Wace was unable to ascertain. These cliffs passed north and south—he could tell the points of the compass by the stars that were visible of a night—receding in an almost illimitable perspective and fading into the mists of the distance before they met. He was nearer the eastern set of cliffs, on the occasion of his first vision the sun was rising over them, and black against the sunlight and pale against their shadow appeared a multitude of soaring forms that Mr Cave regarded as birds. A vast range of buildings spread below him; he seemed to be looking down upon them; and, as they approached the blurred and refracted edge of the picture, they became indistinct. There were also trees curious in shape, and in colouring a deep mossy green and an exquisite grey, beside a wide and shining canal. And something great and brilliantly coloured flew across the picture: But the first time Mr Cave saw these pictures he saw only in flashes, his hands shook, his head moved, the vision came and went, and grew foggy and indistinct. And at first he had the greatest difficulty in finding the picture again once the direction of it was lost.

His next clear vision, which came about a week after the first, the interval having yielded nothing but tantalising glimpses and some useful experience, showed him the view down the length of the valley. The view was different, but he had a curious persuasion, which his subsequent observations abundantly confirmed, that he was regarding this strange world from exactly the same spot, although he was looking in a different direction. The long façade of the great building whose roof he had looked down upon before, was now receding in perspective. He recognised the roof. In the front of the façade was a terrace of massive proportions and extraordinary length, and down the middle of the terrace, at certain intervals, stood huge but very graceful masts, bearing small shiny objects which reflected the setting sun. The import of these small objects did not occur to Mr Cave until some time after, as he was describing the scene to Mr Wace. The terrace overhung a thicket of the most luxuriant and graceful vegetation, and beyond this was a wide grassy lawn on which certain broad creatures, in form like beetles but enormously larger, reposed. Beyond this again was a richly decorated causeway of pinkish stone; and beyond that, and lined with dense *red* weeds, and passing up the valley exactly parallel with the distant cliffs, was a broad and mirror-like expanse of water. The air seemed full of squadrons of great birds, manoeuvring in stately curves;

and across the river was a multitude of splendid buildings, richly coloured and glittering with metallic tracery and facets, among a forest of moss-like and lichenous trees. And suddenly something flapped repeatedly across the vision, like the fluttering of a jewelled fan or the beating of a wing, and a face, or rather the upper part of a face with very large eyes, came as it were close to his own and as if on the other side of the crystal. Mr Cave was so startled and so impressed by the absolute reality of these eyes, that he drew his head back from the crystal to look behind it. He had become so absorbed in watching that he was quite surprised to find himself in the cool darkness of his little shop, with its familiar odour of methyl, mustiness, and decay. And, as he blinked about him, the glowing crystal faded, and went out.

Such were the first general impressions of Mr Cave. The story is curiously direct and circumstantial. From the outset, when the valley first flashed momentarily on his senses, his imagination was strangely affected, and, as he began to appreciate the details of the scene he saw, his wonder rose to the point of a passion. He went about his business listless and distraught, thinking only of the time when he should be able to return to his watching. And then a few weeks after his first sight of the valley came the two customers, the stress and excitement of their offer, and the narrow escape of the crystal from sale, as I have already told.

Now while the thing was Mr Cave's secret, it remained a mere wonder, a thing to creep to covertly and peep at, as a child might peep upon a forbidden garden. But Mr Wace has, for a young scientific investigator, a particularly lucid and consecutive habit of mind. Directly the crystal and its story came to him; and he had satisfied himself, by seeing the phosphorescence with his own eyes, that there really was a certain evidence for Mr Cave's statements, he proceeded to develop the matter systematically. Mr Cave was only too eager to come and feast his eyes on this wonderland he saw, and he came every night from half-past eight until half-past ten, and sometimes, in Mr Wace's absence, during the day. On Sunday afternoons, also, he came. From the outset Mr Wace made copious notes, and it was due to his scientific method that the relation between the direction from which the initiating ray entered the crystal and the orientation of the picture was proved. And, by covering the crystal in a box perforated only with a small aperture to admit the exciting ray, and by substituting black holland for his buff blinds, he greatly improved the conditions of the observations; so that in a little while they were able to survey the valley in any direction they desired.

So having cleared the way, we may give a brief account of this visionary world within the crystal. The things were in all cases seen by Mr Cave, and the method of working was invariably for him to watch the crystal and report what he saw, while Mr Wace (who as a science student had learnt the trick of writing in the dark) wrote a brief note of his report. When the crystal faded, it was put into its box in the proper position and the electric light turned on. Mr Wace asked questions, and suggested observations to clear up difficult points. Nothing, indeed, could have been less visionary and more matter-of-fact.

The attention of Mr Cave had been speedily directed to the bird-like creatures he had seen so abundantly present in each of his earlier visions. His first impression was soon corrected, and he considered for a time that they might represent a diurnal species of bat. Then he thought, grotesquely enough, that they might be cherubs. Their heads were round, and curiously human, and it was the eyes of one of them that had so startled him on his second observation. They had broad, silvery wings, not feathered, but glistening almost as brilliantly as new-killed fish and with the same subtle play of colour, and these wings were not built on the plan of bird-wing or bat, Mr Wace learned, but supported by curved ribs radiating from the body. (A sort of butterfly wing with curved ribs seems best to express their appearance.) The body was small, but fitted with two bunches of prehensile organs, like long tentacles, immediately under the mouth. Incredible as it appeared to Mr Wace, the persuasion at last became irresistible, that it was these creatures which owned the great quasi-human buildings and the magnificent garden that made the broad valley so splendid. And Mr Cave perceived that the buildings, with other peculiarities, had no doors, but that the great circular windows, which opened freely, gave the creatures egress and entrance. They would alight upon their tentacles, fold their wings to a smallness almost rod-like, and hop into the interior. But among them was a multitude of smaller-winged creatures, like great dragonflies and moths and flying beetles, and across the greensward brilliantly-coloured gigantic ground-beetles crawled lazily to and fro. Moreover, on the causeways and terraces, large-headed creatures similar to the greater winged flies, but wingless, were visible, hopping busily upon their hand-like tangle of tentacles.

Allusion has already been made to the glittering objects upon masts that stood upon the terrace of the nearer building. It dawned upon Mr Cave, after regarding one of these masts very fixedly on one particularly vivid day, that the glittering object there was a crystal exactly like that into which he peered. And a still more careful scrutiny convinced him that each one in a vista of nearly twenty carried a similar object.

Occasionally one of the large flying creatures would flutter up to one, and, folding its wings and coiling a number of its tentacles about the mast, would regard the crystal fixedly for a space—sometimes for as long as fifteen minutes. And a series of observations, made at the suggestion of Mr Wace, convinced both watchers that, so far as this visionary world was concerned, the crystal into which they peered actually stood at the summit of the end-most mast on the terrace, and that on one occasion at least one of these inhabitants of this other world had looked into Mr Cave's face while he was making these observations.

So much for the essential facts of this very singular story. Unless we dismiss it all as the ingenious fabrication of Mr Wace, we have to believe one of two things: either that Mr Cave's crystal was in two worlds at once, and that, while it was carried about in one, it remained stationary in the other, which seems altogether absurd; or else that it had some peculiar relation of sympathy with another and exactly similar crystal in this other world, so that what was seen in the interior of the one in this world was, under suitable conditions, visible to an observer in the corresponding crystal in the other world; and *vice versa*. At present, indeed, we do not know of any way in which two crystals could so come *en rapport*, but nowadays we know enough to understand that the thing is not altogether impossible. This view of the crystals as *en rapport* was the supposition that occurred to Mr Wace, and to me at least it seems extremely plausible. . . .

And where was this other world? On this, also, the alert intelligence of Mr Wace speedily threw light. After sunset, the sky darkened rapidly—there was a very brief twilight interval indeed—and the stars shone out. They were recognisably the same as those we see, arranged in the same constellations. Mr Cave recognised the Bear, the Pleiades, Aldebaran, and Sirius: so that the other world must be somewhere in the solar system, and, at the utmost, only a few hundreds of millions of miles from our own. Following up this clue, Mr Wace learned that the midnight sky was a darker blue even than our midwinter sky, and that the sun seemed a little smaller. *And there were two small moons!* 'like our moon but smaller, and quite differently masked' one of which moved so rapidly that its motion was clearly visible as one regarded it. These moons were never high in the sky, but vanished as they rose: that is, every time they revolved they were eclipsed because they were so near their primary planet. And all this answers quite completely, although Mr Cave did not know it, to what must be the condition of things on Mars.

Indeed, it seems an exceedingly plausible conclusion that peering into this crystal Mr Cave did actually see the planet Mars and its inhabitants. And, if that be the case, then the evening star that shone so brilliantly in the sky of that distant vision, was neither more nor less than our own familiar earth.

For a time the Martians—if they were Martians—do not seem to have known of Mr Cave's inspection. Once or twice one would come to peer, and go away very shortly to some other mast, as though the vision was unsatisfactory. During this time Mr Cave was able to watch the proceedings of these winged people without being disturbed by their attentions, and, although his report is necessarily vague and fragmentary, it is nevertheless very suggestive. Imagine the impression of humanity a Martian observer would get who, after a difficult process of preparation and with considerable fatigue to the eyes, was able to peer at London from the steeple of St Martin's Church for stretches, at longest, of four minutes at a time. Mr Cave was unable to ascertain if the winged Martians were the same as the Martians who hopped about the causeways and terraces, and if the latter could put on wings at will. He several times saw certain clumsy bipeds, dimly suggestive of apes, white and partially translucent, feeding among certain of the lichenous trees, and once some of these fled before one of the hopping, round-headed Martians. The latter caught one in its tentacles, and then the picture faded suddenly and left Mr Cave most tantalisingly in the dark. On another occasion a vast thing that Mr Cave thought at first was some gigantic insect, appeared advancing along the causeway beside the canal with extraordinary rapidity. As this drew nearer, Mr Cave perceived that it was a mechanism of shining metals and of extraordinary complexity. And then, when he looked again, it had passed out of sight.

After a time Mr Wace aspired to attract the attention of the Martians, and the next time that the strange eyes of one of them appeared close to the crystal Mr Cave cried out and sprang away, and they immediately turned on the light and began to gesticulate in a manner suggestive of signalling. But when at last Mr Cave examined the crystal again the Martian had departed.

Thus far these observations had progressed in early November, and then Mr Cave, feeling that the suspicions of his family about the crystal were allayed, began to take it to and fro with him in order that, as occasion arose in the daytime or night, he might comfort himself with what was fast becoming the most real thing in his existence.

In December Mr Wace's work in connection with a forthcoming examination became heavy, the sittings were reluctantly suspended for a week, and for ten or eleven days—he is not quite sure which—he saw nothing of Cave. He then grew anxious to resume these investigations, and, the stress of his seasonal labours being abated, he went down to Seven Dials. At the corner he noticed a shutter before a bird fancier's window, and then another at a cobbler's. Mr Cave's shop was closed.

He rapped and the door was opened by the step-son in black. He at once called Mrs Cave, who was, Mr Wace could not but observe, in cheap but ample widow's weeds of the most imposing pattern. Without any very great surprise Mr Wace learnt that Cave was dead, and already buried. She was in tears, and her voice was a little thick. She had just returned from Highgate. Her mind seemed occupied with her own prospects and the honourable details of the obsequies, but Mr Wace was at last able to learn the particulars of Cave's death. He had been found dead in his shop in the early morning, the day after his last visit to Mr Wace, and the crystal had been clasped in his stone-cold hands. His face was smiling, said Mrs Cave, and the velvet cloth from the minerals lay on the floor at his feet. He must have been dead five or six hours when he was found.

This came as a great shock to Wace, and he began to reproach himself bitterly for having neglected the plain symptoms of the old man's ill-health. But his chief thought was of the crystal. He approached that topic in a gingerly manner, because he knew Mrs Cave's peculiarities. He was dumbfounded to learn that it was sold.

Mrs Cave's first impulse, directly Cave's body had been taken upstairs, had been to write to the mad clergyman who had offered five pounds for the crystal, informing him of its recovery; but after a violent hunt in which her daughter joined her, they were convinced of the loss of his address. As they were without the means required to mourn and bury Cave in the elaborate style the dignity of an old Seven Dials inhabitant demands, they had appealed to a friendly fellow-tradesman in Great Portland Street. He had very kindly taken over a portion of the stock at a valuation. The valuation was his own and the crystal egg was included in one of the lots. Mr Wace, after a few suitable consolatory observations, a little off-handedly proffered perhaps, hurried at once to Great Portland Street. But there he learned that the crystal egg had already been sold to a tall, dark man in grey. And there the material facts in this curious, and to me at least very suggestive, story come abruptly to an end. The Great Portland Street dealer did not know who the tall dark man in grey was, nor had he observed him with sufficient attention to describe him minutely. He did not even know which way this person had gone after leaving the shop. For a time Mr Wace remained in the shop, trying the dealer's patience with hopeless questions, venting his own exasperation. And at last, realising abruptly that the whole thing had passed out of his hands, had vanished like a vision of the night, he returned to his own rooms, a little astonished to find the notes he had made still tangible and visible upon his untidy table.

His annoyance and disappointment were naturally very great. He made a second call (equally ineffectual) upon the Great Portland Street dealer, and he resorted to advertisements in such periodicals as were likely to come into the hands of a bric-a-brac collector. He also wrote letters to *The Daily Chronicle* and *Nature,* but both those periodicals, suspecting a hoax, asked him to reconsider his action before they printed, and he was advised that such a strange story, unfortunately so bare of supporting evidence, might imperil his reputation as an investigator. Moreover, the calls of his proper work were urgent. So that after a month or so, save for an occasional reminder to certain dealers, he had reluctantly to abandon the quest for the crystal egg, and from that day to this it remains undiscovered. Occasionally however, he tells me, and I can quite believe him, he has bursts of zeal in which he abandons his more urgent occupation and resumes the search.

Whether or not it will remain lost for ever, with the material and origin of it, are things equally speculative at the present time. If the present purchaser is a collector, one would have expected the inquiries of Mr Wace to have reached him through the dealers. He has been able to discover Mr Cave's clergyman and 'Oriental'—no other than the Rev. James Parker and the young Prince of Bosso-Kuni in Java. I am obliged to them for certain particulars. The object of the Prince was simply curiosity—and extravagance. He was so eager to buy, because Cave was so oddly reluctant to sell. It is just as possible that the buyer in the second instance was simply a casual purchaser and not a collector at all, and the crystal egg for all I know, may at the present moment be within a mile of me, decorating a drawing-room or serving as a paper-weight—its remarkable functions all unknown. Indeed, it is partly with the idea of such a possibility that I have thrown this narrative into a form that will give it a chance of being read by the ordinary consumer of fiction.

My own ideas in the matter are practically identical with those of Mr Wace. I believe the crystal on the mast in Mars and the crystal egg of Mr Cave's to be in some physical, but at present quite inexplicable, way *en rapport,* and we both believe further that the terrestrial crystal must have been—possibly at some remote date—sent hither from that planet, in order to give the Martians a near view of our affairs. Possibly the fellows to the crystals in the other masts are also on our globe. No theory of hallucination suffices for the facts.

THE PRESENCE BY THE FIRE

IT NEVER occurred to Reid that his wife lay dying until the very last day of her illness. He was a man of singularly healthy disposition, averse on principle to painful thoughts, and I doubt if in the whole of his married life his mind had dwelt for five minutes together on the possibility of his losing her.

They were both young, and intimate companions—such companions as many desire to be and few become. And perhaps it was her sense of the value of this rare companionship that made her, when first her health declined, run many an avoidable risk rather than leave him to go his way alone.

He was sorry that she was ill, sorry she should suffer, and he missed her, as she lay upstairs, in a thousand ways; but though the doctor was mindful to say all the 'preparatory' phrases of his profession, and though her sister spoke, as she conceived, quite plainly, it was as hard for him to understand that this was more than a temporary interruption of their life, as it would have been to believe that the sun would not rise again after tomorrow morning.

The day before she died he was restless, and after wandering about the house and taking a short walk, he occupied himself in planting out her evening primroses—a thing she had made a point of doing now for ten springs in succession. The garden she had always tended, he said, should not seem neglected when she came down again. He had rather his own work got in arrears than that this should happen.

The first realisation, when the doctor, finding all conventional euphemisms useless, told him the fact at last in stark, plain words, stunned him. Even then it is doubtful if he believed. He said not a word in answer, but the colour left his face, and the lines about his mouth hardened. And he walked softly and with white, expressionless features into her room.

146

He stood at the door-way, and looked for a minute at her thin little features, with the eyes closed and two little lines between the brows, then went and knelt by the bed and looked closely into her face. She did not move until he touched her hair and very softly whispered her name.

Then her eyes opened for a moment, and he saw that she knew him. Her lips moved, and it seemed that she whispered one of those foolish, tender little names that happy married folk delight in inventing for one another, and then she gathered her strength as if with an effort to speak distinctly. He bent mechanically and heard the last syllables of *au revoir*.

For a moment he did not clearly understand what the words were. That was all she said, and as for him, he answered not a word. He put his hand in hers, and she pressed it faintly and then more faintly. He kissed her forehead with dry lips, and the little lines of pain there faded slowly into peace.

For an hour they let him kneel, until the end had come; and all that time he never stirred. Then they had to tap his shoulder to rouse him from his rigour. He got up slowly, bent over her for a moment, looking down into her tranquil face, and then allowed them to lead him away.

That was how Reid parted from his wife, and for days after he behaved as a man who had been suddenly deprived of all initiative. He did no work; he went nowhere outside the house; he ate, drank and slept mechanically; and he did not even seem to suffer actively. For the most part, he sat stupidly at his desk or wandered about the big garden, looking with dull eyes at the little green buds that were now swiftly opening all about him. Not a soul ventured to speak to him of his loss, albeit those who did not know him might have judged his mood one of absolute apathy.

But nearly a week after the funeral the floodgates of his sorrow were opened. Quite suddenly the thing came upon him. Her sister heard him walk into the study and throw himself into a chair. Everything was still for a space, and then he sprang up again and she heard him wailing, 'Mary! Mary!' and then he ran, sobbing violently and stumbling, along the passage to his room. It was grotesquely like a little child that had suddenly been hurt.

He locked his door; and her sister, fearing what might happen, went along the passage. She thought of rapping at the door, but on second thoughts she refrained. After listening awhile she went away.

It was long after the first violence of his grief had passed that Reid first spoke of his feelings. He who had been a matter-of-fact materialist was converted, I found, to a belief in immortality by the pitiless logic of her uncompleted life. But I think it was an imperfect, a doubting, belief even at the best. And to strengthen it, perhaps, he began to show a growing interest in the inquiries of those who were sifting whatever evidence there may be of the return of those who are dead.

'For I want my wife now,' said he. 'I want her in this life. I want her about me—her comfort, her presence. What does it matter that I shall meet her again when I am changed, and she is changed? It was the dear trivialities, the little moments, the touch of her hand, the sound of her voice in the room with me, her distant singing in the garden, and her footfall on the stairs. If I could believe that,' he said, 'if I could believe—'

And in that spirit it was that he kept to the old home, and would scarcely bear that a thing within or without should be altered in any way. The white curtains that had been there the last autumn hung dirty in the windows, and the little desk that had been her own in the study stood there still, with the pen thrown down as he fancied she had left it.

'Here, if anywhere,' he said, 'she is at home. Here, if anywhere, her presence lives.'

Her sister left him when a housekeeper was obtained, and he went on living there alone, working little and communicating for the most part with these dead memories. After a time he loved nothing so much as to talk to her, and I think in those days that I was of service to him. He would take me about the house, pointing to this trivial thing and that; and telling me some little act of hers that he linked therewith. And he always spoke of her as one who still lived.

'She does' so and so, he would say; 'she likes' so and so. We would pace up and down the rich lawn of his house. 'My wife is particularly fond of those big white lilies,' he would say, 'and this year they are finer than ever.' So the summer passed and the autumn came.

And one day late in the evening he came to me, walking round the house and tapping at the French window of my study, and as he came in out of the night I noticed how deadly white and sunken his face was and how bright his eyes.

'I have seen her,' he said to me, in a low, clear voice. 'She has visited me. I knew she was watching me and near me. I have felt her presence for weeks and weeks. And now she has come.'

He was intensely excited, and it was some time before I could get any clear story from him.

He had been sitting by the fire in his study, musing, no doubt going over for the hundredth time, day by day and almost hour by hour as he was wont to do, one of the summer holidays they had spent together. He was staring, he said, into the glowing coals, and almost imperceptibly it was that there grew upon him the persuasion that he was not alone. The thought took shape slowly in his mind, but with a strange quality of absolute conviction, that she was sitting in the arm-chair in front of him, as she had done so often in the old days, and watching him a-dreaming. For a moment he did not dare to look up, lest he should find this a mere delusion.

Then slowly he raised his eyes. He was dimly aware of footsteps advancing along the passage as he did so. A wave of bitter disappointment swept over him as he saw the chair was empty, and this incontinently gave place to a tumult of surprise and joyful emotion. For he saw her—saw her distinctly. She was standing behind the chair, leaning over the back of it, and smiling the tender smile he knew so well. So in her life she had stood many a time and listened to him, smiling gently. The firelight played upon her face.

'I saw her as plainly as I see you,' he said. 'I saw the smile in her eyes, and my heart leapt out to her.'

For a moment he was motionless, entranced, and with an instantaneous appreciation of the transitoriness of this appearance. Then suddenly the door opened, the shadows in the room rushed headlong, and the housemaid came in with his lamp lit and without the shade—a dazzling glare of naked flame. The yellow light splashed over the room and brought out everything clear and vivid.

By mere reflex action he turned his head at the sound of the door-handle, and forthwith turned it back again. But the face he had longed for so patiently had vanished with the shadows before the light. Everything was abruptly plain and material. The girl replenished the fire, moved the arm-chair on one side, and took away the scuttle lining to refill it with coals. A curious bashfulness made Reid pretend to make

149

notes at his table until these offices were accomplished. Then he looked across the fireplace again, and the room was empty. The sense of her presence, too, had gone. He called upon her name again and again, rubbed his eyes, and tried to force her return by concentrating his mind upon her. But nothing availed. He could see her no more.

He allowed me to cross-examine him in the most detailed way upon this story. His manner was so sane, so convincing, and his honesty so indisputable, that I went to bed that night with my beliefs and disbeliefs greatly shaken. Hitherto I had doubted every ghost story I had heard; but here at last was one of a different quality. Indeed, I went to bed that night an unwilling convert to the belief in the phantasms of those who are dead and all that that belief implies.

My faith in Reid was confirmed by the fact that from late August, when this happened, until December he did not see the apparition again. Had it been an hallucination begotten of his own intense brooding it must inevitably have recurred. But it was presently to be proved beyond all question that the thing he saw was an exterior presence. Night after night he sat in his study, longing for the repetition of that strange experience; and at last, after many nights, he saw her for the second time.

It was earlier in the evening, but with the shorter winter days the room was already dark. Once more he looked into his study fire, and once more that fire glowed redly. Then there came the same sense of her presence, the same hesitation before he raised his eyes. But this time he looked over the chair at once and saw her without any flash of disappointment.

At the instant he felt not the faintest suspicion that his senses deceived him. For a moment he was dumb. He was seized with an intense longing to touch her hand. Then came into his head some half-forgotten story that one must speak first to a spirit. He leant forward.

'Mary!' he said very softly. But she neither moved nor spoke. And then suddenly it seemed that she grew less distinct.

'Mary!' he whispered, with a sudden pang of doubt. Her features grew unfamiliar.

Then suddenly he rose to his feet, and as he did so the making of the illusion was demonstrated. The high light on a vase that had been her cheek moved to the right; the shadow that had been her arm moved to the left.

Few people realise how little we actually see of what is before our eyes: a patch of light, a patch of shadow, and all the rest our memory and our imagination supply. A chance grouping of dim forms in the dusky firelit study had furnished all the suggestion his longing senses had required. His eyes and his heart and the humour of chance had cheated him.

He stood there staring. For a moment the disintegration of the figure filled him with a sense of grotesque horror and dismay. For a moment it seemed beyond the sanity of things. Then, as he realised the deception his senses had contrived, he sat down again, put his elbows on the table and buried his face in his hands.

About ten he came and told me. He told me in a clear hard voice, without a touch of emotion, recording a remarkable fact. 'As I told you the other thing, it is only right that I should tell you this,' he said.

Then he sat silently for a space. 'She will come no more,' he said at last. 'She will come no more.'

And suddenly he rose, and without a greeting, passed out into the night.

THE MAN WHO COULD WORK MIRACLES

A Pantoum in Prose

IT IS doubtful whether the gift was innate. For my own part, I think it
came to him suddenly. Indeed, until he was thirty he was a sceptic, and
did not believe in miraculous powers. And here, since it is the most
convenient place, I must mention that he was a little man, and had eyes
of a hot brown, very erect red hair, a moustache with ends that he
twisted up, and freckles. His name was George McWhirter Fotheringay—not the sort of name by any means to lead to any expectation of
miracles—and he was clerk at Gomshott's. He was greatly addicted to
assertive argument. It was while he was asserting the impossibility of
miracles that he had his first intimation of his extraordinary powers.
This particular argument was being held in the bar of the Long
Dragon, and Toddy Beamish was conducting the opposition by a
monotonous but effective 'So *you* say,' that drove Mr Fotheringay to
the very limit of his patience.

There were present, besides these two, a very dusty cyclist, landlord Cox, and Miss Maybridge, the perfectly respectable and rather
portly barmaid of the Dragon. Miss Maybridge was standing with her
back to Mr Fotheringay, washing glasses, the others were watching
him, more or less amused by the present ineffectiveness of the assertive
method. Goaded by the Torres Vedras tactics of Mr Beamish, Mr
Fotheringay determined to make an unusual rhetorical effort. 'Looky
here, Mr Beamish,' said Mr Fotheringay. 'Let us clearly understand
what a miracle is. It's something contrariwise to the course of Nature
done by power of Will, something what couldn't happen without being
specially willed.'

'So *you* say,' said Mr Beamish, repulsing him.

Mr Fotheringay appealed to the cyclist, who had hitherto been a
silent auditor, and received his assent—given with a hesitating cough

152

and a glance at Mr Beamish. The landlord would express no opinion, and Mr Fotheringay, returning to Mr Beamish, received the unexpected concession of a qualified assent to his definition of a miracle.

'For instance,' said Mr Fotheringay, greatly encouraged. 'Here would be a miracle. That lamp, in the natural course of nature, couldn't burn like that upsy-down, could it, Beamish?'

'*You* say it couldn't,' said Beamish.

'And you?' said Fotheringay. 'You don't mean to say—eh?'

'No,' said Beamish reluctantly. 'No, it couldn't.'

'Very well,' said Mr Fotheringay 'Then here comes some one, as it might be me, along here, and stands as it might be here, and says to that lamp, as I might do, collecting all my will—"Turn upsy-down without breaking, and go on burning steady," and—Hullo!'

It was enough to make any one say 'Hullo!' The impossible, the incredible, was visible to them all. The lamp hung inverted in the air, burning quietly with its flame pointing down. It was as solid, as indisputable as ever a lamp was, the prosaic common lamp of the Long Dragon bar.

Mr Fotheringay stood with an extended forefinger and the knitted brows of one anticipating a catastrophic smash. The cyclist, who was sitting next the lamp, ducked and jumped across the bar. Everybody jumped, more or less. Miss Maybridge turned and screamed. For nearly three seconds the lamp remained still. A faint cry of mental distress came from Mr Fotheringay. 'I can't keep it up,' he said, 'any longer.' He staggered back, and the inverted lamp suddenly flared, fell against the corner of the bar, bounced aside, smashed upon the floor, and went out.

It was lucky it had a metal receiver, or the whole place would have been in a blaze. Mr Cox was the first to speak, and his remark, shorn of needless excrescences, was to the effect that Fotheringay was a fool. Fotheringay was beyond disputing even so fundamental a proposition as that! He was astonished beyond measure at the thing that had occurred. The subsequent conversation threw absolutely no light on the matter so far as Fotheringay was concerned; the general opinion not only followed Mr Cox very closely but very vehemently. Every one accused Fotheringay of a silly trick, and presented him to himself as a foolish destroyer of comfort and security. His mind was in a tornado of perplexity, he was himself inclined to agree with them, and he made a remarkably ineffectual opposition to the proposal of his departure.

He went home flushed and heated, coat-collar crumpled, eyes smarting and ears red. He watched each of the ten street lamps nervously as he passed it. It was only when he found himself alone in his little bedroom in Church Row that he was able to grapple seriously with his memories of the occurrence, and ask, 'What on earth happened?'

He had removed his coat and boots, and was sitting on the bed with his hands in his pockets repeating the text of his defence for the seventeenth time, '*I* didn't want the confounded thing to upset,' when it occurred to him that at the precise moment he had said the commanding words he had inadvertently willed the thing he said, and that when he had seen the lamp in the air he had felt that it depended on him to maintain it there without being clear how this was to be done. He had not a particularly complex mind, or he might have stuck for a time at that 'inadvertently willed,' embracing, as it does, the abstrusest problems of voluntary action; but as it was, the idea came to him with a quite acceptable haziness. And from that, following, as I must admit, no clear logical path, he came to the test of experiment.

He pointed resolutely to his candle and collected his wind, though he felt he did a foolish thing. 'Be raised up,' he said. But in a second that feeling vanished. The candle was raised, hung in the air one giddy moment, and as Mr Fotheringay gasped, fell with a smash on his toilet-table, leaving him in darkness save for the expiring glow of its wick.

For a time Mr Fotheringay sat in the darkness, perfectly still. 'It did happen, after all,' he said. 'And 'ow I'm to explain it I *don't* know.' He sighed heavily, and began feeling in his pockets for a match. He could find none, and he rose and groped about the toilet-table. 'I wish I had a match,' he said. He resorted to his coat, and there were none there, and then it dawned upon him that miracles were possible even with matches. He extended a hand and scowled at it in the dark. 'Let there be a match in that hand,' he said. He felt some light object fall across his palm, and his fingers closed upon a match.

After several ineffectual attempts to light this, he discovered it was a safety-match. He threw it down, and then it occurred to him that he might have willed it lit. He did, and perceived it burning in the midst of his toilet-table mat. He caught it up hastily, and it went out. His perception of possibilities enlarged, and he felt for and replaced the candle in its candlestick. 'Here! *you* be lit,' said Mr Fotheringay, and forthwith the candle was flaring, and he saw a little black hole in the toilet-cover, with a wisp of smoke rising from it. For a time he stared from this to the little flame and back, and then looked up and met his own gaze in the looking-glass. By this help he communed with himself in silence for a time.

'How about miracles now?' said Mr Fotheringay at last, addressing his reflection.

The subsequent meditations of Mr Fotheringay were of a severe but confused description. So far as he could see, it was a case of pure willing with him. The nature of his first experiences disinclined him for any further experiments except of the most cautious type. But he lifted a sheet of paper, and turned a glass of water pink and then green, and he created a snail, which he miraculously annihilated, and got himself a miraculous new toothbrush. Somewhen in the small hours he had reached the fact that his will-power must be of a particularly rare and pungent quality, a fact of which he had certainly had inklings of before, but no certain assurance. The scare and perplexity of his first discovery was now qualified by pride in this evidence of singularity and by vague intimations of advantage. He became aware that the church clock was striking one, and as it did not occur to him that his daily duties at Gomshott's might be miraculously dispensed with, he resumed undressing, in order to get to bed without further delay. As he struggled to get his shirt over his head, he was struck with a brilliant idea. 'Let me be in bed,' he said, and found himself so. 'Undressed,' he stipulated; and, finding the sheets cold, added hastily, 'and in my nightshirt—no, in a nice soft woollen nightshirt. Ah!' he said with immense enjoyment. 'And now let me be comfortably asleep. . . .'

He awoke at his usual hour and was pensive all through breakfast-time, wondering whether his overnight experience might not be a particularly vivid dream. At length his mind turned again to cautious experiments. For instance, he had three eggs for breakfast; two his landlady had supplied, good, but shoppy, and one was a delicious fresh goose-egg, laid, cooked, and served by his extraordinary will. He hurried off to Gomshott's in a state of profound but carefully concealed excitement, and only remembered the shell of the third egg when his landlady spoke of it that night. All day he could do no work because of this astonishingly new self-knowledge, but this caused him

155

no inconvenience, because he made up for it miraculously in his last ten minutes.

As the day wore on his state of mind passed from wonder to elation, albeit the circumstances of his dismissal from the Long Dragon were still disagreeable to recall, and a garbled account of the matter that had reached his colleagues led to some badinage. It was evident he must be careful how he lifted frangible articles, but in other ways his gift promised more and more as he turned it over in his mind. He intended among other things to increase his personal property by unostentatious acts of creation. He called into existence a pair of very splendid diamond studs, and hastily annihilated them again as young Gomshott came across the counting-house to his desk. He was afraid young Gomshott might wonder how he had come by them. He saw quite clearly the gift required caution and watchfulness in its exercise, but so far as he could judge the difficulties attending its mastery would be no greater than those he had already faced in the study of cycling. It was that analogy, perhaps, quite as much as the feeling that he would be unwelcome in the Long Dragon, that drove him out after supper into the lane beyond the gas-works, to rehearse a few miracles in private.

There was possibly a certain want of originality in his attempts, for apart from his will-power Mr Fotheringay was not a very exceptional man. The miracle of Moses' rod came to his mind, but the night was dark and unfavourable to the proper control of large miraculous snakes. Then he recollected the story of 'Tannhäuser' that he had read on the back of the Philharmonic programme. That seemed to him singularly attractive and harmless. He stuck his walking-stick—a very nice Poona-Penang lawyer—into the turf that edged the footpath, and commanded the dry wood to blossom. The air was immediately full of the scent of roses, and by means of a match he saw for himself that this beautiful miracle was indeed accomplished. His satisfaction was ended by advancing footsteps. Afraid of a premature discovery of his powers, he addressed the blossoming stick hastily: 'Go back.' What he meant was 'Change back'; but of course he was confused. The stick receded at a considerable velocity, and incontinently came a cry of anger and a bad word from the approaching person. 'Who are you throwing brambles at, you fool?' cried a voice. 'That got me on the shin.'

'I'm sorry, old chap,' said Mr Fotheringay, and then realising the awkward nature of the explanation, caught nervously at his moustache. He saw Winch, one of the three Immering constables, advancing.

'What d'yer mean by it?' asked the constable. 'Hullo! It's you, is it? The gent that broke the lamp at the Long Dragon!'

'I don't mean anything by it,' said Mr Fotheringay. 'Nothing at all.'

'What d'yer do it for then?'

'Oh, bother!' said Mr Fotheringay.

'Bother indeed! D'yer know that stick hurt? What d'yer do it for, eh?'

For the moment Mr Fotheringay could not think what he had done it for. His silence seemed to irritate Mr Winch. 'You've been assaulting the police, young man, this time. 'That's what *you* done.'

'Look here, Mr Winch,' said Mr Fotheringay, annoyed and confused, 'I'm very sorry. The fact is—'

'Well?'

He could think of no way but the truth. 'I was working a miracle.' He tried to speak in an off-hand way, but try as he would he couldn't.

'Working a—! 'Ere, don't you talk rot. Working a miracle, indeed! Miracle! Well, that's downright funny! Why, you's the chap that don't believe in miracles. . . . Fact is, this is another of your silly conjuring tricks—that's what this is. Now, I tell you—'

But Mr Fotheringay never heard what Mr Winch was going to tell him. He realised he had given himself away, flung his valuable secret to all the winds of heaven. A violent gust of irritation swept him to action. He turned on the constable swiftly and fiercely. 'Here,' he said, 'I've had enough of this, I have! I'll show you a silly conjuring trick, I will! Go to Hades! Go now!'

He was alone!

Mr Fotheringay performed no more miracles that night, nor did he trouble to see what had become of his flowering stick. He returned to the town, scared and very quiet, and went to his bedroom. 'Lord!' he said, 'it's a powerful gift—an extremely powerful gift. I didn't hardly mean as much as that. Not really. . . . I wonder what Hades is like!'

He sat on the bed taking off his boots. Struck by a happy thought he transferred the constable to San Francisco, and without any more

157

interference with normal causation went soberly to bed. In the night he dreamt of the anger of Winch.

The next day Mr Fotheringay heard two interesting items of news. Someone had planted a most beautiful climbing rose against the elder Mr Gomshott's private house in the Lullaborough Road, and the river as far as Rawling's Mill was to be dragged for Constable Winch.

Mr Fotheringay was abstracted and thoughtful all that day, and performed no miracles except certain provisions for Winch, and the miracle of completing his day's work with punctual perfection in spite of all the bee-swarm of thoughts that hummed through his mind. And the extraordinary abstraction and meekness of his manner was remarked by several people, and made a matter for jesting. For the most part he was thinking of Winch.

On Sunday evening he went to chapel, and oddly enough, Mr Maydig, who took a certain interest in occult matters, preached about 'things that are not lawful.' Mr Fotheringay was not a regular chapel goer, but the system of assertive scepticism, to which I have already alluded, was now very much shaken. The tenor of the sermon threw an entirely new light on these novel gifts, and he suddenly decided to consult Mr Maydig immediately after the service. So soon as that was determined, he found himself wondering why he had not done so before.

Mr Maydig, a lean, excitable man with quite remarkably long wrists and neck, was gratified at a request for a private conversation from a young man whose carelessness in religious matters was a subject for general remark in the town. After a few necessary delays, he conducted him to the study of the Manse, which was contiguous to the chapel, seated him comfortably, and, standing in front of a cheerful fire—his legs threw a Rhodian arch of shadow on the opposite wall—requested Mr Fotheringay to state his business.

At first Mr Fotheringay was a little abashed, and found some difficulty in opening the matter. 'You will scarcely believe me, Mr Maydig, I am afraid' and so forth for some time. He tried a question at last, and asked Mr Maydig his opinion of miracles.

Mr Maydig was still saying 'Well' in an extremely judicial tone, when Mr Fotheringay interrupted again: 'You don't believe, I suppose, that some common sort of person—like myself, for instance—as it might be sitting here now, might have some sort of twist inside him that made him able to do things by his will.'

'It's possible,' said Mr Maydig. 'Something of the sort, perhaps, is possible.'

'If I might make free with something here, I think I might show you by a sort of experiment,' said Mr Fotheringay. 'Now, take that tobacco-jar on the table, for instance. What I want to know is whether what I am going to do with it is a miracle or not. Just half a minute, Mr Maydig, please.'

He knitted his brows, pointed to the tobacco-jar and said: 'Be a bowl of vi'lets.'

The tobacco-jar did as it was ordered.

Mr Maydig started violently at the change, and stood looking from the thaumaturgist to the bowl of flowers. He said nothing. Presently he ventured to lean over the table and smell the violets; they were fresh-picked and very fine ones. Then he stared at Mr Fotheringay again.

'How did you do that?' he asked.

Mr Fotheringay pulled his moustache. 'Just told it—and there you are. Is that a miracle, or is it black art, or what is it? And what do you think's the matter with me? That's what I want to ask.'

'It's a most extraordinary occurrence.'

'And this day last week I knew no more that I could do things like that than you did. It came quite sudden. It's something odd about my will, I suppose, and that's as far as I can see.'

'Is *that*—the only thing. Could you do other things besides that?'

'Lord, yes!' said Mr Fotheringay. 'Just anything.' He thought, and suddenly recalled a conjuring entertainment he had seen. 'Here!' He pointed. 'Change into a bowl of fish—no, not that—change into a glass bowl full of water with goldfish swimming in it. That's better! You see that, Mr Maydig?'

'It's astonishing. It's incredible. You are either a most extraordinary. . . . But no—'

'I could change it into anything,' said Mr Fotheringay. 'Just anything. Here! be a pigeon, will you?'

In another moment a blue pigeon was fluttering round the room and making Mr Maydig duck every time it came near him. 'Stop there, will you,' said Mr Fotheringay; and the pigeon hung motionless in the air. 'I could change it back to a bowl of flowers,' he said, and after replacing the pigeon on the table worked that miracle. 'I expect you will want your pipe in a bit,' he said, and restored the tobacco-jar.

159

Mr Maydig had followed all these later changes in a sort of ejaculatory silence. He stared at Mr Fotheringay and, in a very gingerly manner, picked up the tobacco-jar, examined it, replaced it on the table. '*Well!*' was the only expression of his feelings.

'Now, after that it's easier to explain what I came about,' said Mr Fotheringay; and proceeded to a lengthy and involved narrative of his strange experiences, beginning with the affair of the lamp in the Long Dragon and complicated by persistent allusions to Winch. As he went on, the transient pride Mr Maydig's consternation had caused passed away; he became the very ordinary Mr Fotheringay of everyday inter-course again. Mr Maydig listened intently, the tobacco-jar in his hand, and his bearing changed also with the course of the narrative. Presently, while Mr Fotheringay was dealing with the miracle of the third egg, the minister interrupted with a fluttering extended hand.

'It is possible,' he said. 'It is credible. It is amazing, of course, but it reconciles a number of difficulties. The power to work miracles is a gift—a peculiar quality like genius or second sight—hitherto it has come very rarely and to exceptional people. But in this case . . . I have always wondered at the miracles of Mahomet, and at Yogi's miracles, and the miracles of Madame Blavatsky. But, of course! Yes, it is simply a gift! It carries out so beautifully the arguments of that great thinker'—Mr Maydig's voice sank—'his Grace the Duke of Argyll. Here we plumb some profounder law—deeper than the ordinary laws of Nature. Yes—yes. Go on. Go on!'

Mr Fotheringay proceeded to tell of his misadventure with Winch, and Mr Maydig, no longer overawed or scared, began to jerk his limbs about and interject astonishment. 'It's this what troubled me most,' proceeded Mr Fotheringay; 'it's this I'm most mijitly in want of advice for; of course he's at San Francisco—wherever San Francisco may be—but of course it's awkward for both of us, as you'll see, Mr Maydig. I don't see how he can understand what has happened, and I dare say he's scared and exasperated something tremendous, and trying to get at me. I dare say he keeps on starting off to come here. I send him back, by a miracle, every few hours, when I think of it. And of course, that's a thing he won't be able to understand, and it's bound to annoy him; and, of course, if he takes a ticket every time it will cost him a lot of money. I done the best I could for him, but of course it's difficult for him to put himself in my place. I thought afterwards that his clothes might have got scorched, you know—if Hades is all it's supposed to be—before I shifted him. In that case I suppose they'd have locked him up in San Francisco. Of course I willed him a new suit of clothes on him directly I thought of it. But, you see, I'm already in a deuce of a tangle—'

Mr Maydig looked serious, 'I see you are in a tangle: Yes, it's a difficult position. How you are to end it. . . .' He became diffuse and inconclusive.

'However, we'll leave Winch for a little and discuss the larger question. I don't think this is a case of the black art or anything of the sort. I don't think there is any taint of criminality about it at all, Mr Fotheringay—none whatever, unless you are suppressing material facts. No, it's miracles—pure miracles—miracles, if I may say so, of the very highest class.'

He began to pace the hearthrug and gesticulate, while Mr Fotheringay sat with his arm on the table and his head on his arm, looking worried. 'I don't see how I'm to manage about Winch,' he said.

'A gift of working miracles—apparently a very powerful gift,' said Mr Maydig, 'will find a way about Winch—never fear. My dear Sir, you are a most important man—a man of the most astonishing possibilities. As evidence, for example! And in other ways, the things you may do . . .'

'Yes, *I've* thought of a thing or two,' said Mr Fotheringay. 'But— some of the things came a bit twisty. You saw that fish at first? Wrong sort of bowl and wrong sort of fish. And I thought I'd ask someone.'

'A proper course,' said Mr Maydig, 'a very proper course—altogether the proper course.' He stopped and looked at Mr Fotheringay. 'It's practically an unlimited gift. Let us test your powers, for instance. If they really *are* . . . If they really are all they seem to be.'

And so, incredible as it may seem, in the study of the little house behind the Congregational Chapel, on the evening of Sunday, November 10th 1896, Mr Fotheringay, egged on and inspired by Mr Maydig, began to work miracles. The reader's attention is specially and definitely called to the date. He will object, probably has already objected, that certain points in this story are improbable, that if any things of the sort already described had indeed occurred, they would have been in all the papers a year ago. The details immediately following he will find particularly hard to accept, because among other things they involve the conclusion that he or she, the reader in question, must have been killed in a violent and unprecedented manner more than a year ago. Now a miracle is nothing if not improbable, and as a matter of fact the reader *was* killed in a violent and unprecedented manner a year ago. In the subsequent course of this story that will become perfectly clear and credible, as every right-minded and reasonable reader will admit: But this is not the place for the end of the story, being but little beyond the hither side of the middle. And at first the miracles worked by Mr Fotheringay were timid little miracles—little things with the cups and parlour fitments, as feeble as the miracles of Theosophists, and, feeble as they were, they were received with awe by his collaborator. He would have preferred to settle the Winch business out of hand, but Mr Maydig would not let him. But after they had worked a dozen of these domestic trivialities, their sense of power grew, their imagination began to show signs of stimulation, and their ambition enlarged. Their first larger enterprise was due to hunger and the negligence of Mrs Minchin, Mr Maydig's housekeeper. The meal to which the minister conducted Mr Fotheringay was certainly ill-laid and uninviting as refreshment for two industrious miracle-workers; but they were seated, and Mr Maydig was descanting in sorrow rather than in anger upon his housekeeper's shortcomings, before it occurred to Mr Fotheringay that an opportunity lay before him. 'Don't you think, Mr Maydig,' he said, 'if it isn't a liberty, I—'

'My dear Mr Fotheringay! Of course! No—I didn't think.'

Mr Fotheringay waved his hand. 'What shall we have?' he said, in a large, inclusive spirit, and, at Mr Maydig's order, revised the supper very thoroughly. 'As for me,' he said, eyeing Mr Maydig's selection, 'I am always particularly fond of a tankard of stout and a nice Welsh rarebit, and I'll order that. I ain't much given to Burgundy,' and forthwith stout and Welsh rarebit promptly appeared at his command. They sat long at their supper, talking like equals, as Mr Fotheringay presently perceived with a glow of surprise and gratification, of all the miracles they would presently do. 'And, by the bye, Mr Maydig,' said Mr Fotheringay, 'I might perhaps be able to help you—in a domestic way.'

'Don't quite follow,' said Mr Maydig, pouring out a glass of miraculous old Burgundy.

Mr Fotheringay helped himself to a second Welsh rarebit out of vacancy, and took a mouthful. 'I was thinking,' he said, 'I might be able (*chum, chum*) to work (*chum, chum*) a miracle with Mrs Minchin (*chum, chum*)—make her a better woman.'

Mr Maydig put down the glass and looked doubtful. 'She's—She strongly objects to interference, you know, Mr Fotheringay. And—as a matter of fact—it's well past eleven and she's probably in bed and asleep. Do you think, on the whole—'

Mr Fotheringay considered these objections. 'I don't see that it shouldn't be done in her sleep.'

For a time Mr Maydig opposed the idea, and then he yielded. Mr Fotheringay issued his orders, and a little less at their ease, perhaps, the two gentlemen proceeded with their repast. Mr Maydig was enlarging on the changes he might expect in his housekeeper next day, with an optimism that seemed even to Mr Fotheringay's supper senses a little forced and hectic, when a series of confused noises from upstairs began. Their eyes exchanged interrogations, and Mr Maydig left the room hastily. Mr Fotheringay heard him calling up to his housekeeper and then his footsteps going softly up to her.

In a minute or so the minister returned, his step light, his face radiant. 'Wonderful!' he said, 'and touching! Most touching!'

He began pacing the hearthrug. 'A repentance—a most touching repentance—through the crack of the door. Poor woman! A most wonderful change! She had got up. She must have got up at once. She had got up out of her sleep to smash a private bottle of brandy in her box. And to confess it too! . . . But this gives us—it opens—a most amazing vista of possibilities. If we can work this miraculous change in *her* . . .'

'The thing's unlimited seemingly,' said Mr Fotheringay. 'And about Mr Winch—'

'Altogether unlimited.' And from the hearthrug Mr Maydig, waving the Winch difficulty aside, unfolded a series of wonderful proposals—proposals he invented as he went along.

Now what those proposals were does not concern the essentials of this story. Suffice it that they were designed in a spirit of infinite benevolence, the sort of benevolence that used to be called post-prandial. Suffice it, too, that the problem of Winch remained unsolved. Nor is it necessary to describe how far that series got to its fulfilment. There were astonishing changes. The small hours found Mr Maydig and Mr Fotheringay careering across the chilly market-square under the still moon, in a sort of ecstasy of thaumaturgy, Mr Maydig all flap and gesture, Mr Fotheringay short and bristling, and no longer abashed at his greatness. They had reformed every drunkard in the Parliamentary division, changed all the beer and alcohol to water (Mr

Maydig had overruled Mr Fotheringay on this point), they had, further, greatly improved the railway communication of the place,
drained Flinder's swamp, improved the soil of One Tree Hill, and
cured the Vicar's wart. And they were going to see what could be done
with the injured pier at South Bridge. 'The place' gasped Mr Maydig,
won't be the same place tomorrow. How surprised and thankful every
one will be!' And just at that moment the church clock struck three.

'I say,' said Mr Fotheringay, 'that's three o'clock! I must be getting back. I've got to be at business by eight. And besides, Mrs
Wimms—'

'We're only beginning,' said Mr Maydig, full of the sweetness of
unlimited power. 'We're only beginning. Think of all the good we're
doing. When people wake—'

'But—' said Mr Fotheringay.

Mr Maydig gripped his arm suddenly. His eyes were bright and
wild. 'My dear chap,' he said, 'there's no hurry. Look'—he pointed to
the moon at the zenith—'Joshua!'

'Joshua? 'said Mr Fotheringay.

'Joshua,' said Mr Maydig. 'Why not? Stop it.'

Mr Fotheringay looked at the moon.

'That's a bit tall,' he said after a pause.

'Why not?' said Mr Maydig. 'Of course it doesn't stop. You stop
the rotation of the earth, you know. Time stops. It isn't as if we were
doing harm.'

'H'm!' said Mr Fotheringay. 'Well.' He sighed. 'I'll try. Here—'

He buttoned up his jacket and addressed himself to the habitable
globe, with as good an assumption of confidence as lay in his power.
'Jest stop rotating, will you,' said Mr Fotheringay.

Incontinently he was flying head over heels through the air at the
rate of dozens of miles a minute. In spite of the innumerable circles he
was describing per second, he thought; for thought is wonderful—
sometimes as sluggish as flowing pitch, sometimes as instantaneous as
light. He thought in a second, and willed. 'Let me come down safe and
sound. Whatever else happens, let me down safe and sound.'

He willed it only just in time, for his clothes, heated by his rapid
flight through the air, were already beginning to singe. He came down
with a forcible, but by no means injurious bump in what appeared to
be a mound of fresh-turned earth. A large mass of metal and masonry,
extraordinarily like the clock-tower in the middle of the market-

square, hit the earth near him, ricochetted over him, and flew into stonework, bricks, and masonry, like a bursting bomb. A hurtling cow hit one of the large blocks and smashed like an egg. There was a crash that made all the most violent crashes of his past life seem like the sound of falling dust, and this was followed by a descending series of lesser crashes. A vast wind roared throughout earth and heaven, so that he could scarcely lift his head to look. For a while he was too breathless and astonished even to see where he was or what had happened. And his first movement was to feel his head and reassure himself that his streaming hair was still his own.

'Lord!' gasped Mr Fotheringay, scarce able to speak for the gale, 'I've had a squeak! What's gone wrong? Storms and thunder. And only a minute ago a fine night. It's Maydig set me on to this sort of thing. *What* a wind! If I go on fooling in this way I'm bound to have a thundering accident! . . .

'Where's Maydig?

'What a confounded mess everything's in!'

He looked about him so far as his flapping jacket would permit. The appearance of things was really extremely strange. 'The sky's all right anyhow,' said Mr Fotheringay. 'And that's about all that is all right. And even there it looks like a terrific gale coming up. But there's the moon overhead. Just as it was just now. Bright as midday. But as for the rest—Where's the village? 'Where's—where's anything? And what on earth set this wind a-blowing? *I* didn't order no wind.'

Mr Fotheringay struggled to get to his feet in vain, and after one failure, remained on all-fours, holding on. He surveyed the moonlit world to leeward, with the tails of his jacket streaming over his head. 'There's something seriously wrong,' said Mr Fotheringay. 'And what it is—goodness knows.'

Far and wide nothing was visible in the white glare through the haze of dust that drove before a screaming gale but tumbled masses of earth and heaps of inchoate ruins, no trees, no houses, no familiar shapes, only a wilderness of disorder vanishing at last into the darkness beneath the whirling columns and streamers, the lightnings and thunderings of a swiftly rising storm. Near him in the livid glare was something that might once have been an elm-tree, a smashed mass of splinters, shivered from boughs to base, and further a twisted mass of iron girders—only too evidently the viaduct—rose out of the piled confusion.

You see, when Mr Fotheringay had arrested the rotation of the solid globe, he had made no stipulation concerning the trifling movables upon its surface. And the earth spins so fast that the surface at its equator is travelling at rather more than a thousand miles an hour, and in these latitudes at more than half that pace. So that the village, and Mr Maydig, and Mr Fotheringay, and everybody and everything had been jerked violently forward at about nine miles per second—that is to say, much more violently than if they had been fired out of a cannon. And every human being, every living creature, every house, and every tree—all the world as we know it—had been so jerked and smashed and utterly destroyed. That was all.

These things Mr Fotheringay did not, of course, fully appreciate. But he perceived that his miracle had miscarried, and with that a great disgust of miracles came upon him. He was in darkness now, for the clouds had swept together and blotted out his momentary glimpse of the moon, and the air was full of fitful struggling tortured wraiths of hail. A great roaring of wind and waters filled earth and sky, and, peering under his hand through the dust and sleet to windward, he saw by the play of the lightnings a vast wall of water pouring towards him.

'Maydig!' screamed Mr Fotheringay's feeble voice amid the elemental uproar. 'Here!—Maydig!'

'Stop!' cried Mr Fotheringay to the advancing water. 'Oh, for goodness' sake, stop!'

'Just a moment,' said Mr Fotheringay to the lightnings and thunder. 'Stop jest a moment while I collect my thoughts. . . . And now what shall I do?' he said. What *shall* I do? Lord! I wish Maydig was about.'

'I know,' said Mr Fotheringay. 'And for goodness' sake let's have it right *this* time.'

He remained on all-fours, leaning against the wind, very intent to have everything right.

'Ah!' he said. 'Let nothing what I'm going to order happen until I say "Off!" . . . Lord! I wish I'd thought of that before!'

He lifted his little voice against the whirlwind, shouting louder and louder in the vain desire to hear himself speak. 'Now then!—here goes! Mind about that what I said just now. In the first place, when all I've got to say is done, let me lose my miraculous power, let my will become just like anybody else's will, and all these dangerous miracles be stopped. I don't like them. I'd rather I didn't work 'em. Ever so much. That's the first thing. And the second is—let me be back just before the miracles begin; let everything be just as it was before that blessed lamp turned up. It's a big job, but it's the last. Have you got it? No more miracles, everything as it was—me back in the Long Dragon just before I drank my half-pint. That's it! Yes.'

He dug his fingers into the mould, closed his eyes, and said 'Off!'

Everything became perfectly still. He perceived that he was standing erect.

'So *you* say,' said a voice.

He opened his eyes. He was in the bar of the Long Dragon, arguing about miracles with Toddy Beamish. He had a vague sense of some great thing forgotten that instantaneously passed. You see, except for the loss of his miraculous powers, everything was back as it had been; his mind and memory therefore were now just as they had been at the time when this story began. So that he knew absolutely nothing of all that is told here, knows nothing of all that is told here to this day. And among other things, of course, he still did not believe in miracles.

'I tell you that miracles, properly speaking, can't possibly happen,' he said, 'whatever you like to hold. And I'm prepared to prove it up to the hilt.'

'That's what you think,' said Toddy Beamish, and 'Prove it if you can.'

'Looky here, Mr Beamish,' said Mr Fotheringay. 'Let us clearly understand what a miracle is. It's something contrariwise to the course of Nature done by power of Will. . . .'

THE STOLEN BODY

MR BESSEL was the senior partner in the firm of Bessel, Hart, and Brown, of St Paul's Churchyard, and for many years he was well known among those interested in psychical research as a liberal-minded and conscientious investigator. He was an unmarried man, and instead of living in the suburbs, after the fashion of his class, he occupied rooms in the Albany, near Piccadilly. He was particularly interested in the questions of thought transference and of apparitions of the living, and in November, 1896, he commenced a series of experiments in conjunction with Mr Vincey, of Staple Inn, in order to test the alleged possibility of projecting an apparition of oneself by force of will through space.

Their experiments were conducted in the following manner: At a pre-arranged hour Mr Bessel shut himself in one of his rooms in the Albany and Mr Vincey in his sitting-room in Staple Inn, and each then fixed his mind as resolutely as possible on the other. Mr Bessel had acquired the art of self-hypnotism, and, so far as he could, he attempted first to hypnotise himself and then to project himself as a 'phantom of the living' across the intervening space of nearly two miles into Mr Vincey's apartment. On several evenings this was tried without any satisfactory result, but on the fifth or sixth occasion Mr Vincey did actually see or imagine he saw an apparition of Mr Bessel standing in his room. He states that the appearance, although brief, was very vivid and real. He noticed that Mr Bessel's face was white and his expression anxious, and, moreover, that his hair was disordered. For a moment Mr Vincey, in spite of his state of expectation, was too surprised to speak or move, and in that moment it seemed to him as though the figure glanced over its shoulder and incontinently vanished.

It had been arranged that an attempt should be made to photograph any phantasm seen, but Mr Vincey had not the instant presence of mind to snap the camera that lay ready on the table beside him, and when he did so he was too late. Greatly elated, however, even by this partial success, he made a note of the exact time, and at once took a cab to the Albany to inform Mr Bessel of this result.

He was surprised to find Mr Bessel's outer door standing open to the night, and the inner apartments lit and in an extraordinary disorder. An empty champagne magnum lay smashed upon the floor; its neck had been broken off against the inkpot on the bureau and lay beside it. An octagonal occasional table, which carried a bronze statuette and a number of choice books, had been rudely overturned, and down the primrose paper of the wall inky fingers had been drawn, as it seemed for the mere pleasure of defilement. One of the delicate chintz curtains had been violently torn from its rings and thrust upon the fire, so that the smell of its smouldering filled the room. Indeed the whole place was disarranged in the strangest fashion. For a few minutes Mr Vincey, who had entered sure of finding Mr Bessel in his easy chair awaiting him, could scarcely believe his eyes, and stood staring helplessly at these unanticipated things.

Then, full of a vague sense of calamity, he sought the porter at the entrance lodge. 'Where is Mr Bessel?' he asked. 'Do you know that all the furniture is broken in Mr Bessel's room?' The porter said nothing, but, obeying his gestures, came at once to Mr Bessel's apartment to see the state of affairs. 'This settles it,' he said, surveying the lunatic confusion. 'I didn't know of this. Mr Bessel's gone off. He's mad!'

He then proceeded to tell Mr Vincey that about half an hour previously, that is to say, at about the time of Mr Bessel's apparition in Mr Vincey's rooms, the missing gentleman had rushed out of the gates of the Albany into Vigo Street, hatless and with disordered hair, and had vanished into the direction of Bond Street. 'And as he went past me,' said the porter, 'he laughed—a sort of gasping laugh, with his mouth open and his eyes glaring—I tell you, sir, he fair scared me!—like this.'

According to his imitation it was anything but a pleasant laugh. 'He waved his hand, with all his fingers crooked and clawing—like that. And he said, in a sort of fierce whisper, "*Life*". Just that one word, "*Life*" '

'Dear me,' said Mr Vincey. 'Tut, tut,' and 'Dear me!' He could think of nothing else to say. He was naturally very much surprised. He turned from the room to the porter and from the porter to the room in the gravest perplexity. Beyond his suggestion that probably Mr Bessel would come back presently and explain what had happened, their conversation was unable to proceed. 'It might be a sudden tooth-ache,' said the porter, 'a very sudden and violent tooth-ache, jumping on him suddenly-like and driving him wild. I've broken things myself before now in such a case . . .' He thought. 'If it was, why should he say *"life"* to me as he went past?'

Mr Vincey did not know. Mr Bessel did not return, and at last Mr Vincey, having done some more helpless staring, and having addressed a note of brief inquiry and left it in a conspicuous position on the bureau, returned in a very perplexed frame of mind to his own premises in Staple Inn. This affair had given him a shock. He was at a loss to account for Mr Bessel's conduct on any sane hypothesis. He tried to read, but he could not do so; he went for a short walk, and was so preoccupied that he narrowly escaped a cab at the top of Chancery Lane; and at last—a full hour before his usual time—he went to bed. For a considerable time he could not sleep because of his memory of the silent confusion of Mr Bessel's apartment, and when at length he did attain an uneasy slumber it was at once disturbed by a very vivid and distressing dream of Mr Bessel.

He saw Mr Bessel gesticulating wildly, and with his face white and contorted. And, inexplicably mingled with his appearance, suggested perhaps by his gestures, was an intense fear, an urgency to act. He even believes that he heard the voice of his fellow experimenter calling distressfully to him, though at the time he considered this to be an illusion. The vivid impression remained though Mr Vincey awoke. For a space he lay awake and trembling in the darkness, possessed with that vague, unaccountable terror of unknown possibilities that comes out of dreams upon even the bravest men. But at last he roused himself, and turned over and went to sleep again, only for the dream to return with enhanced vividness.

He awoke with such a strong conviction that Mr Bessel was in overwhelming distress and need of help that sleep was no longer possible. He was persuaded that his friend had rushed out to some dire calamity. For a time he lay reasoning vainly against this belief, but at last he gave way to it. He arose, against all reason, lit his gas and dressed, and set out through the deserted streets—deserted, save for a noiseless policeman or so and the early news carts—towards Vigo Street to inquire if Mr Bessel had returned.

But he never got there. As he was going down Long Acre some unaccountable impulse turned him aside out of that street towards

Covent Garden, which was just waking to its nocturnal activities. He saw the market in front of him—a queer effect of glowing yellow lights and busy black figures. He became aware of a shouting, and perceived a figure turn the corner by the hotel and run swiftly towards him. He knew at once that it was Mr Bessel. But it was Mr Bessel transfigured. He was hatless and dishevelled, his collar was torn open, he grasped a bone-handled walking-cane near the ferrule end, and his mouth was pulled awry. And he ran, with agile strides, very rapidly. Their encounter was the affair of an instant. 'Bessel!' cried Vincey.

The running man gave no sign of recognition either of Mr Vincey or of his own name. Instead, he cut at his friend savagely with the stick, hitting him in the face within an inch of the eye. Mr Vincey, stunned and astonished, staggered back, lost his footing, and fell heavily on the pavement. It seemed to him that Mr Bessel leapt over him as he fell. When he looked again Mr Bessel had vanished, and a policeman and a number of garden porters and salesmen were rushing past towards Long Acre in hot pursuit.

With the assistance of several passers-by—for the whole street was speedily alive with running people—Mr Vincey struggled to his feet. He at once became the centre of a crowd greedy to see his injury. A multitude of voices competed to reassure him of his safety, and then to tell him of the behaviour of the madman, as they regarded Mr Bessel. He had suddenly appeared in the middle of the market screaming '*Life! Life!*' striking left and right with a bloodstained walking-stick, and dancing and shouting with laughter at each successful blow. A lad and two women had broken heads, and he had smashed a man's wrist; a little child had been knocked insensible, and for a time he had driven everyone before him, so furious and resolute had his behaviour been. Then he made a raid upon a coffee stall, hurled its paraffin flare through the window of the post office, and fled laughing, after stunning the foremost of the two policemen who had the pluck to charge him.

Mr Vincey's first impulse was naturally to join in the pursuit of his friend, in order if possible to save him from the violence of the indignant people. But his action was slow, the blow had half stunned him, and while this was still no more than a resolution came the news, shouted through the crowd, that Mr Bessel had eluded his pursuers. At first Mr Vincey could scarcely credit this, but the universality of the report, and presently the dignified return of two futile policemen, convinced him. After some aimless inquiries he returned towards Staple Inn, padding a handkerchief to a now very painful nose.

He was angry and astonished and perplexed. It appeared to him indisputable that Mr Bessel must have gone violently mad in the midst of his experiment in thought transference, but why that should make him appear with a sad white face in Mr Vincey's dreams seemed a problem beyond solution. He racked his brains in vain to explain this. It seemed to him at last that not simply Mr Bessel, but the order of things must be insane. But he could think of nothing to do. He shut himself carefully into his room, lit his fire—it was a gas fire with asbestos bricks—and, fearing fresh dreams if he went to bed, remained bathing his injured face, or holding up books in a vain attempt to read, until dawn. Throughout that vigil he had a curious persuasion that Mr Bessel was endeavouring to speak to him, but he would not let himself attend to any such belief.

About dawn, his physical fatigue asserted itself, and he went to bed and slept at last in spite of dreaming. He rose late; unrested and anxious and in considerable facial pain. The morning papers had no news of Mr Bessel's aberration—it had come too late for them. Mr Vincey's perplexities, to which the fever of his bruise added fresh irritation, became at last intolerable, and, after a fruitless visit to the Albany, he went down to St Paul's Churchyard to Mr Hart, Mr Bessel's partner, and so far as Mr Vincey knew, his nearest friend.

He was surprised to learn that Mr Hart, although he knew nothing of the outbreak, had also been disturbed by a vision, the very vision that Mr Vincey had seen—Mr Bessel, white and dishevelled, pleading earnestly by his gestures for help. That was his impression of the import of his signs. 'I was just going to look him up in the Albany when you arrived,' said Mr Hart. 'I was so sure of something being wrong with him.'

As the outcome of their consultation the two gentlemen decided to inquire at Scotland Yard for news of their missing friend. 'He is bound to be laid by the heels,' said Mr Hart. 'He can't go on at that pace for long.' But the police authorities had not laid Mr Bessel by the heels. They confirmed Mr Vincey's overnight experiences and added fresh circumstances, some of an even graver character than those he knew—a list of smashed glass along the upper half of Tottenham Court Road, an attack upon a policeman in Hampstead Road, and an atrocious assault upon a woman. All these outrages were committed between half-past twelve and a quarter to two in the morning, and between those hours—and, indeed, from the very moment of Mr Bessel's first rush from his rooms at half-past nine in the evening—they could trace the deepening violence of his fantastic career. For the last hour, at least from before one, that is, until a quarter to two, he had run amuck through London, eluding with amazing agility every effort to stop or capture him.

But after a quarter to two he had vanished. Up to that hour witnesses were multitudinous. Dozens of people had seen him, fled from him or pursued him, and then things suddenly came to an end. At a quarter to two he had been seen running down the Euston Road towards Baker Street, flourishing a can of burning colza oil and jerking splashes of flame therefrom at the windows of the houses he passed. But none of the policemen on Euston Road beyond the Waxwork Exhibition, nor any of those in the side streets down which he must have passed had he left the Euston Road, had seen anything of him. Abruptly he disappeared. Nothing of his subsequent doings came to light in spite of the keenest inquiry.

Here was a fresh astonishment for Mr Vincey. He had found considerable comfort in Mr Hart's conviction: 'He is bound to be laid by the heels before long,' and in that assurance he had been able to suspend his mental perplexities. But any fresh development seemed destined to add new impossibilities to a pile already heaped beyond the powers of his acceptance. He found himself doubting whether his memory might not have played him some grotesque trick, debating whether any of these things could possibly have happened; and in the afternoon he hunted up Mr Hart again to share the intolerable weight on his mind. He found Mr Hart engaged with a well-known private detective, but as that gentleman accomplished nothing in this case, we need not enlarge upon his proceedings.

All that day Mr Bessel's whereabouts eluded an unceasingly active inquiry, and all that night. And all that day there was a persuasion in the back of Mr Vincey's mind that Mr Bessel sought his attention, and all through the night Mr Bessel with a tear-stained face of anguish pursued him through his dreams. And whenever he saw Mr Bessel in his dreams he also saw a number of other faces, vague but malignant, that seemed to be pursuing Mr Bessel.

It was on the following day, Sunday, that Mr Vincey recalled certain remarkable stories of Mrs Bullock, the medium, who was then attracting attention for the first time in London. He determined to consult her. She was staying at the house of that well-known inquirer, Dr Wilson Paget, and Mr Vincey, although he had never met that gentleman before, repaired to him forthwith with the intention of invoking her help. But scarcely had he mentioned the name of Bessel when Doctor Paget interrupted him. 'Last night—just at the end,' he said, 'we had a communication.'

He left the room, and returned with a slate on which were certain words written in a handwriting, shaky indeed, but indisputably the handwriting of Mr Bessel !

'How did you get this?' said Mr Vincey. 'Do you mean?—'

'We got it last night,' said Doctor Paget. With numerous inter-ruptions from Mr Vincey, he proceeded to explain how the writing had been obtained. It appears that in her *séances*, Mrs Bullock passes into a condition of trance, her eyes rolling up in a strange way under her eyelids, and her body becoming rigid. She then begins to talk very rapidly, usually in voices other than her own. At the same time one or both of her hands may become active, and if slates and pencils are provided they will then write messages simultaneously with and quite independently of the flow of words from her mouth. By many she is considered an even mare remarkable medium than the celebrated Mrs Piper. It was one of these messages, the one written by her left hand, that Mr Vincey now had before him, It consisted of eight words writ-ten disconnectedly 'George Bessel . . . trial $excav^n$ . . . Baker Street . . . help . . . starvation.' Curiously enough, neither Doctor Paget nor the two other inquirers who were present had heard of the disappearance of Mr Bessel—the news of it appeared only in the evening papers of Saturday—and they had put the message aside with many others of a vague and enigmatical sort that Mrs Bullock has from time to time delivered.

When Doctor Paget heard Mr Vincey's story, he gave himself at once with great energy to the pursuit of this clue to the discovery of Mr Bessel. It would serve no useful purpose here to describe the inquiries of Mr Vincey and himself; suffice it that the clue was a genuine one, and that Mr Bessel was actually discovered by its aid.

He was found at the bottom of a detached shaft which had been sunk and abandoned at the commencement of the work for the new electric railway near Baker Street Station. His arm and leg and two ribs were broken. The shaft is protected by a hoarding nearly twenty feet high, and over this, incredible as it seems, Mr Bessel, a stout, middle-aged gentleman, must have scrambled in order to fall down the shaft. He was saturated in colza oil, and the smashed tin lay beside him, but luckily the flame had been extinguished by his fall. And his madness had passed from him altogether. But he was, of course, terribly enfeebled, and at the sight of his rescuers he gave way to hysterical weeping.

In view of the deplorable state of his flat, he was taken to the house of Dr Hatton in Upper Baker Street. Here he was subjected to a sedative treatment, and anything that might recall the violent crisis through which he had passed was carefully avoided. But on the second day he volunteered a statement.

Since that occasion Mr Bessel has several times repeated this statement—to myself among other people—varying the details as the narrator of real experiences always does, but never by any chance contradicting himself in any particular. And the statement he makes is in substance as follows.

In order to understand it clearly it is necessary to go back to his experiments with Mr Vincey before his remarkable attack. Mr Bessel's first attempts at self-projection, in his experiments with Mr Vincey, were, as the reader will remember, unsuccessful. But through all of them he was concentrating all his power and will upon getting out of the body—'willing it with all my might,' he says. At last, almost against expectation, came success. And Mr Bessel asserts that he, being alive, did actually, by an effort of will, leave his body and pass into some place or state outside this world.

The release was, he asserts, instantaneous. 'At one moment I was seated in my chair, with my eyes tightly shut, my hands gripping the arms of the chair, doing all I could to concentrate my mind on Vincey, and then I perceived myself outside my body—saw my body near me, but certainly not containing me, with the hands relaxing and the head drooping forward on the breast.'

Nothing shakes him in his assurance of that release. He describes in a quiet, matter-of-fact way the new sensation he experienced. He felt he had become impalpable—so much he had expected, but he had not expected to find himself enormously large. So, however, it would seem he became. 'I was a great cloud—if I may express it that way—anchored to my body. It appeared to me, at first, as if I had discovered a greater self of which the conscious being in my brain was only a little part. I saw the Albany and Piccadilly and Regent Street and all the rooms and places in the houses, very minute and very bright and distinct, spread out below me like a little city seen from a balloon. Every now and then vague shapes like drifting wreaths of smoke made the vision a little indistinct, but at first I paid little heed to them. The thing that astonished me most, and which astonishes me still, is that I saw quite distinctly the insides of the houses as well as the streets, saw little people dining and talking in the private houses, men and women dining, playing billiards, and drinking in restaurants and hotels, and several places of entertainment crammed with people. It was like watching the affairs of a glass hive.'

Such were Mr Bessel's exact words as I took them down when he told me the story. Quite forgetful of Mr Vincey, he remained for a space observing these things. Impelled by curiosity, he says, he stooped down, and with the shadowy arm he found himself possessed of attempted to touch a man walking along Vigo Street. But he could not do so, though his finger seemed to pass through the man. Something prevented his doing this, but what it was he finds it hard to describe. He compares the obstacle to a sheet of glass. 'I felt as a kitten may feel,' he said, 'when it goes for the first time to pat its reflection in a mirror.' Again and again, on the occasion when I heard him tell this story, Mr Bessel returned to that comparison of the sheet of glass. Yet it was not altogether a precise comparison, because, as the reader will speedily see, there were interruptions of this generally impermeable resistance, means of getting through the barrier to the material world again. But, naturally, there is a very great difficulty in expressing these unprecedented impressions in the language of everyday experience.

A thing that impressed him instantly, and which weighed upon him throughout all this experience, was the stillness of this place—he was in a world without sound.

At first Mr Bessel's mental state was an unemotional wonder. His thought chiefly concerned itself with where he might be. He was out of the body—out of his material body, at any rate—but that was not all. He believes, and I for one believe also, that he was somewhere out of space, as we understand it, altogether. By a strenuous effort of will he had passed out of his body into a world beyond this world, a world undreamt of, yet lying so close to it and so strangely situated with regard to it that all things on this earth are clearly visible both from without and from within in this other world about us. For a long time, as it seemed to him, this realisation occupied his mind to the exclusion

of all other matters, and then he recalled the engagement with Mr
Vincey, to which this astonishing experience was, after all, but a prel-
ude.

He turned his mind to locomotion in this new body in which he
found himself. For a time he was unable to shift himself from his
attachment to his earthly carcass. For a time this new strange cloud
body of his simply swayed, contracted, expanded, coiled, and writhed
with his efforts to free himself, and then quite suddenly the link that
bound him snapped. For a moment everything was hidden by what
appeared to be whirling spheres of dark vapour, and then through a
momentary gap he saw his drooping body collapse limply, saw his
lifeless head drop sideways, and found he was driving along like a huge
cloud in a strange place of shadowy clouds that had the luminous intri-
cacy of London spread like a model below.

But now he was aware that the fluctuating vapour about him was
something more than vapour, and the temerarious excitement of his
first essay was shot with fear. For he perceived, at first indistinctly, and
then suddenly very clearly, that he was surrounded by faces! that each
roll and coil of the seeming cloud-stuff was a face. And such faces!
Faces of thin shadow, faces of gaseous tenuity. Faces like those faces
that glare with intolerable strangeness upon the sleeper in the evil
hours of his dreams. Evil, greedy eyes that were full of a covetous curiosity, faces with knit brows and snarling, smiling lips; their vague
hands clutched at Mr Bessel as he passed, and the rest of their bodies
was but an elusive streak of trailing darkness. Never a word they said,
never a sound from the mouths that seemed to gibber. All about him
they pressed in that dreamy silence, passing freely through the dim
mistiness that was his body, gathering ever more numerously about
him. And the shadowy Mr Bessel, now suddenly fear-stricken, drove
through the silent, active multitude of eyes and clutching hands.

So inhuman were these faces, so malignant their staring eyes, and
shadowy, clawing gestures, that it did not occur to Mr Bessel to
attempt intercourse with these drifting creatures. Idiot phantoms, they
seemed, children of vain desire, beings unborn and forbidden the boon
of being, whose only expressions and gestures told of the envy and
craving for life that was their one link with existence.

It says much for his resolution that, amidst the swarming cloud of
these noiseless spirits of evil, he could still think of Mr Vincey. He
made a violent effort of will and found himself, he knew not how,

stooping towards Staple Inn, saw Vincey sitting attentive and alert in his arm-chair by the fire.

And clustering also about him, as they clustered ever about all that lives and breathes, was another multitude of these vain voiceless shadows, longing, desiring, seeking some loophole into life.

For a space Mr Bessel sought ineffectually to attract his friend's attention. He tried to get in front of his eyes, to move the objects in his room, to touch him. But Mr Vincey remained unaffected, ignorant of the being that was so close to his own. The strange something that Mr Bessel has compared to a sheet of glass separated them impermeably.

And at last Mr Bessel did a desperate thing. I have told how that in some strange way he could see not only the outside of a man as we see him, but within. He extended his shadowy hand and thrust his vague black fingers, as it seemed, through the heedless brain.

Then, suddenly, Mr Vincey started like a man who recalls his attention from wandering thoughts, and it seemed to Mr Bessel that a little dark-red body situated in the middle of Mr Vincey's brain swelled and glowed as he did so. Since that experience he has been shown anatomical figures of the brain, and he knows now that this is that useless structure, as doctors call it, the pineal eye. For, strange as it will seem to many, we have, deep in our brains—where it cannot possibly see any earthly light—an eye! At the time this, with the rest of the internal anatomy of the brain, was quite new to him. At the sight of its changed appearance, however, he thrust forth his finger, and, rather fearful still of the consequences, touched this little spot. And instantly Mr Vincey started, and Mr Bessel knew that he was seen.

And at that instant it came to Mr Bessel that evil had happened to his body, and behold! a great wind blew through all that world of shadows and tore him away. So strong was this persuasion that he thought no more of Mr Vincey, but turned about forthwith, and all the countless faces drove back with him like leaves before a gale. But he returned too late. In an instant he saw the body that he had left inert and collapsed—lying, indeed, like the body of a man just dead—had arisen, had arisen by virtue of some strength and will beyond his own. It stood with staring eyes, stretching its limbs in dubious fashion.

For a moment he watched it in wild dismay, and then he stooped towards it. But the pane of glass had closed against him again, and he was foiled. He beat himself passionately against this, and all about him the spirits of evil grinned and pointed and mocked. He gave way to furious anger. He compares himself to a bird that has fluttered heed-lessly into a room and is beating at the window-pane that holds it back from freedom.

And behold! the little body that had once been his was now dancing with delight. He saw it shouting, though he could not hear its shouts; he saw the violence of its movements grow. He watched it fling his cherished furniture about in the mad delight of existence, rend his books apart, smash bottles, drink heedlessly from the jagged fragments, leap and smite in a passionate acceptance of living. He watched these actions in paralysed astonishment. Then once more he hurled himself against the impassable barrier, and then, with all that crew of mocking ghosts about him, hurried back in dire confusion to Vincey to tell him of the outrage that had come upon him.

But the brain of Vincey was now closed against apparitions, and the disembodied Mr Bessel pursued him in vain as he hurried out into Holborn to call a cab. Foiled and terror-stricken, Mr Bessel swept back again, to find his desecrated body whooping in a glorious frenzy down the Burlington Arcade. . . .

And now the attentive reader begins to understand Mr Bessel's interpretation of the first part of this strange story. The being whose frantic rush through London had inflicted so much injury and disaster had indeed Mr Bessel's body, but it was not Mr Bessel. It was an evil spirit out of that strange world beyond existence, into which Mr Bessel had so rashly ventured. For twenty hours it held possession of him, and for all those twenty hours the dispossessed spirit-body of Mr Bessel was going to and fro in that unheard-of middle world of shad-ows seeking help in vain.

He spent many hours beating at the minds of Mr Vincey and of his friend Mr Hart. Each, as we know, he roused by his efforts. But the language that might convey his situation to these helpers across the gulf he did not know; his feeble fingers groped vainly and powerlessly in their brains. Once, indeed, as we have already told, he was able to turn Mr Vincey aside from his path so that he encountered the stolen body in its career, but he could not make him understand the thing that had happened: he was unable to draw any help from that encounter. . . .

All through those hours the persuasion was overwhelming in Mr Bessel's mind that presently his body would be killed by its furious tenant, and he would have to remain in this shadow-land for evermore.

So that those long hours were a growing agony of fear. And ever as he hurried to and fro in his ineffectual excitement innumerable spirits of that world about him mobbed him and confused his mind. And ever an envious applauding multitude poured after their successful fellow as he went upon his glorious career.

For that, it would seem, must be the life of these bodiless things of this world that is the shadow of our world. Ever they watch, coveting a way into a mortal body, in order that they may descend, as furies and frenzies, as violent lusts and mad, strange impulses, rejoicing in the body they have won. For Mr Bessel was not the only human soul in that place. Witness the fact that he met first one, and afterwards several shadows of men, men like himself, it seemed, who had lost their bodies even it may be as he had lost his, and wandered, despairingly, in that lost world that is neither life nor death. They could not speak because that world is silent, yet he knew them for men because of their dim human bodies, and because of the sadness of their faces.

But how they had come into that world he could not tell, nor where the bodies they had lost might be, whether they still raved about the earth, or whether they were closed for ever in death against return. That they were the spirits of the dead neither he nor I believe. But Doctor Wilson Paget thinks they are the rational souls of men who are lost in madness on the earth.

At last Mr Bessel chanced upon a place where a little crowd of such disembodied silent creatures was gathered, and thrusting through them he saw below a brightly-lit room, and four or five quiet gentlemen and a woman, a stoutish woman dressed in black bombazine and sitting awkwardly in a chair with her head thrown back. He knew her from her portraits to be Mrs Bullock, the medium. And he perceived that tracts and structures in her brain glowed and stirred as he had seen the pineal eye in the brain of Mr Vincey glow. The light was very fitful; sometimes it was a broad illumination, and sometimes merely a faint twilight spot, and it shifted slowly about her brain. She kept on talking and writing with one hand. And Mr Bessel saw that the crowding shadows of men about him, and a great multitude of the shadow spirits of that shadow land, were all striving and thrusting to touch the lighted regions of her brain. As one gained her brain or another was thrust away, her voice and the writing of her hand changed. So that what she said was disorderly and confused for the most part; now a fragment of one soul's message, and now a fragment of another's, and now she babbled the insane fancies of the spirits of vain desire. Then Mr Bessel understood that she spoke for the spirit that had touch of her, and he began to struggle very furiously towards her. But he was on the outside of the crowd and at that time he could not reach her, and at last, growing anxious, he went away to find what had happened meanwhile to his body.

For a long time he went to and fro seeking it in vain and fearing that it must have been killed, and then he found it at the bottom of the shaft in Baker Street, writhing furiously and cursing with pain. Its leg and arm and two ribs had been broken by its fall. Moreover, the evil spirit was angry because his time had been so short and because of the pain-making violent movements and casting his body about.

And at that Mr Bessel returned with redoubled earnestness to the room where the *séance* was going on, and so soon as he had thrust himself within sight of the place he saw one of the men who stood about the medium looking at his watch as if he meant that the *séance* should presently end. At that a great number of the shadows who had been striving turned away with gestures of despair. But the thought that the *séance* was almost over only made Mr Bessel the more earnest, and he struggled so stoutly with his will against the others that presently he gained the woman's brain. It chanced that just at that moment it glowed very brightly, and in that instant she wrote the message that Doctor Wilson Paget preserved. And then the other shadows and the cloud of evil spirits about him had thrust Mr Bessel away from her, and for all the rest of the *séance* he could regain her no more.

So he went back and watched through the long hours at the bottom of the shaft where the evil spirit lay in the stolen body it had maimed, writhing and cursing, and weeping and groaning, and learning the lesson of pain. And towards dawn the thing he had waited for happened, the brain glowed brightly and the evil spirit came out, and Mr Bessel entered the body he had feared he should never enter again. As he did so, the silence—the brooding silence—ended; he heard the tumult of traffic and the voices of people overhead, and that strange world that is the shadow of our world—the dark and silent shadows of ineffectual desire and the shadows of lost men—vanished clean away.

He lay there for the space of about three hours before he was found. And in spite of the pain and suffering of his wounds, and of the dim damp place in which he lay; in spite of the tears—wrung from him by his physical distress—his heart was full of gladness to know that he was nevertheless back once more in the kindly world of men.

A VISION OF JUDGMENT

1

BRU-A-A-A

I listened, not understanding.

Wa-ra-ra-ra.

'Good Lord!' said I, still only half awake. 'What an infernal shindy!'

Ra-ra-ra-ra-ra-ra-ra-ra-ra. Ta-ra-rra-ra.

'It's enough,' said I, 'to wake—' and stopped short. Where was I?

Ta-rra-rara—louder and louder.

'It's either some new invention—'

Toora-toora-toora! Deafening!

'No,' said I, speaking loud in order to hear myself. 'That's the Last Trump.'

Tooo-rraa!

2

The last note jerked me out of my grave like a hooked minnow.

I saw my monument (rather a mean little affair, and I wished I knew who'd done it), and the old elm tree and the sea view vanished like a puff of steam, and then all about me—a multitude no man could number, nations, tongues, kingdoms, peoples—children of all the ages, in an amphitheatral space as vast as the sky. And over against us, seated on a throne of dazzling white cloud, the Lord God and all the host of his angels. I recognised Azreal by his darkness and Michael by his sword, and the great angel who had blown the trumpet stood with the trumpet still half raised.

3

'Prompt,' said the little man beside me. 'Very prompt. Do you see the angel with the book?'

He was ducking and craning his head about to see over and under and between the souls that crowded round us. 'Everybody's here,' he said. 'Everybody. And now we shall know——

'There's Darwin,' he said, going off at a tangent. '*He'll* catch it! And there—you see?—that tall, important-looking man trying to catch the eye of the Lord God, that's the Duke. But there's a lot of people one doesn't know.

'Oh! there's Priggles, the publisher. I have always wondered about printers' overs. Priggles was a clever man. . . . But we shall know now—even about him.

'I shall hear all that. I shall get most of the fun before. . . . *My* letter's S.'

He drew the air in between his teeth.

'Historical characters, too. See? That's Henry the Eighth. There'll be a good bit of evidence. Oh, damn! He's Tudor.'

He lowered his voice. 'Notice this chap, just in front of us, all covered with hair. Paleolithic, you know. And there again—'

But I did not heed him, because I was looking at the Lord God.

4

'Is this *all*?' asked the Lord God.

The angel at the book—it was one of countless volumes, like the British Museum Reading-room Catalogue, glanced at us and seemed to count us in the instant.

'That's all,' he said, and added: 'It was, O God, a very little planet.'

The eyes of God surveyed us.

'Let us begin,' said the Lord God.

5

The angel opened the book and read a name. It was a name full of A's, and the echoes of it came back out of the uttermost parts of space. I did not catch it clearly, because the little man beside me said, in a sharp jerk, '*What's* that?' It sounded like 'Ahab' to me; but it could not have been the Ahab of Scripture.

Instantly a small black figure was lifted up to a puffy cloud at the very feet of God. It was a stiff little figure, dressed in rich outlandish robes and crowned, and it folded its arms and scowled.

'Well?' said God, looking down at him.

We were privileged to hear the reply, and indeed the acoustic properties of the place were marvellous.

'I plead guilty,' said the little figure.

'Tell them what you have done,' said the Lord God.

'I was a king,' said the little figure, 'a great king, and I was lustful and proud and cruel. I made wars, I devastated countries, I built palaces, and the mortar was the blood of men. Hear, O God, the witnesses against me, calling to you for vengeance. Hundreds and thousands of witnesses.' He waved his hands towards us. 'And worse! I took a prophet—one of your prophets—'

'One of my prophets,' said the Lord God.

'And because he would not bow to me, I tortured him for four days and nights, and in the end he died. I did more, O God, I blasphemed. I robbed you of your honours—'

'Robbed me of my honours,' said the Lord God.

'I caused myself to be worshipped in your stead. No evil was there but I practised it; no cruelty wherewith I did not stain my soul. And at last you smote me, O God!'

God raised his eyebrows slightly.

'And I was slain in battle. And so I stand before you, meet for your nethermost Hell! Out of your greatness daring no lies, daring no pleas, but telling the truth of my iniquities before all mankind.'

He ceased. His face I saw distinctly, and it seemed to me white and terrible and proud and strangely noble. I thought of Milton's Satan.

'Most of that is from the Obelisk,' said the Recording Angel, finger on page.

'It is,' said the Tyrannous Man, with a, faint touch of surprise.

Then suddenly God bent forward and took this man in his hand, and held him up on his palm as if to see him better. He was just a little dark stroke: in the middle of God's palm.

'*Did* he do all this?' said the Lord God.

The Recording Angel flattened his book with his hand.

'In a way,' said the Recording Angel, carelessly.

Now when I looked again at the little man his face had changed in a very curious manner. He was looking at the Recording Angel with a strange apprehension in his eyes, and one hand fluttered to his mouth. Just the movement of a muscle or so, and all that dignity of defiance was gone.

'Read,' said the Lord God.

And the angel read, explaining very carefully and fully all the wickedness of the Wicked Man. It was quite an intellectual treat.—A little 'daring' in places, I thought, but of course Heaven has its privileges. . . .

6

Everybody was laughing. Even the prophet of the Lord whom the Wicked Man had tortured had a smile on his face. The Wicked Man was really such a preposterous little fellow.

'And then,' read the Recording Angel, with a smile that set us all agog, 'one day, when he was a little irascible from over-eating, he—'

'Oh, not *that*,' cried the Wicked Man, 'nobody knew of *that*.

'It didn't happen,' screamed the Wicked Man. 'I was bad—I was really bad. Frequently bad, but there was nothing so silly—so absolutely silly—'

The angel went on reading.

'O God!' cried the Wicked Man. 'Don't let them know that! I'll repent! I'll apologise. . . .'

The Wicked Man on God's hand began to dance and weep. Suddenly shame overcame him. He made a wild rush to jump off the ball of God's little finger, but God stopped him by a dexterous turn of the wrist. Then he made a rush for the gap between hand and thumb, but the thumb closed. And all the while the angel went on reading—

reading. The Wicked Man rushed to and fro across God's palm, and then suddenly turned about and fled up the sleeve of God.

I expected God would turn him out, but the mercy of God is infinite.

The Recording Angel paused.

'Eh?' said the Recording Angel.

'Next,' said God, and before the Recording Angel could call upon the name a hairy creature in filthy rags stood upon God's palm.

7

'Has God got Hell up his sleeve then?' said the little man beside me.

'Is there a Hell?' I asked.

'If you notice,' he said—he peered between the feet of the great angels—'there's no particular indication of the Celestial City.'

' 'Ssh!' said a little woman near us, scowling. 'Hear this blessed Saint!'

8

'He was Lord of the Earth, but I was the prophet of the God of Heaven,' cried the Saint, 'and all the people marvelled at the sign. For I, O God, knew of the glories of thy Paradise. No pain, no hardship, gashing with knives, splinters thrust under my nails, strips of flesh flayed off, all for the glory and honour of God.'

God smiled.

'And at last I went, I in my rags and sores, smelling of my holy discomforts—'

Gabriel laughed abruptly.

'And lay outside his gates, as a sign, as a wonder—'

'As a perfect nuisance,' said the Recording Angel, and began to read, heedless of the fact that the Saint was still speaking of the gloriously unpleasant things he had done that Paradise might be his.

And behold, in that book the record of the Saint also was a revelation, a marvel.

It seemed not ten seconds before the Saint also was rushing to and fro over the great palm of God. Not ten seconds! And at last he also shrieked beneath that pitiless and cynical exposition, and fled also, even as the Wicked Man had fled, into the shadow of the sleeve. And it was permitted us to see into the shadow of the sleeve. And the two sat side by side, stark of all delusions, in the shadow of the robe of God's charity, like brothers.

And thither also I fled in my turn.

9

'And now,' said God, as he shook us out of his sleeve upon the planet he had given us to live upon, the planet that whirled about green Sirius for a sun, 'now that you understand me and each other a little better . . . try again.'

Then he and his great angels turned themselves about and suddenly had vanished.

The Throne had vanished.

All about me was a beautiful land, more beautiful than any I had ever seen before—waste, austere, and wonderful; and all about me were the enlightened souls of men in new clean bodies. . . .

A DREAM OF ARMAGEDDON

THE man with the white face entered the carriage at Rugby. He moved slowly in spite of the urgency of his porter, and even while he was still on the platform I noted how ill he seemed. He dropped into the corner over against me with a sigh, made an incomplete attempt to arrange his travelling shawl, and became motionless, with his eyes staring vacantly. Presently he was moved by a sense of my observation, looked up at me, and put out a spiritless hand for his newspaper. Then he glanced again in my direction.

I feigned to read. I feared I had unwittingly embarrassed him, and in a moment I was surprised to find him speaking.

'I beg your pardon?' said I.

'That book,' he repeated, pointing a lean finger, 'is about dreams.'

'Obviously,' I answered, for it was Fortnum-Roscoe's *Dream States,* and the title was on the cover.

He hung silent for a space as if he sought words. 'Yes,' he said at last, 'but they tell you nothing.'

I did not catch his meaning for a second.

'They don't know,' he added.

I looked a little more attentively at his face,

'There are dreams,' he said, 'and dreams.'

That sort of proposition I never dispute.

'I suppose—' he hesitated. 'Do you ever dream? I mean vividly.'

'I dream very little,' I answered. 'I doubt if I have three vivid dreams a year.'

'Ah!' he said, and seemed for a moment to collect his thoughts.

'Your dreams don't mix with your memories?' he asked abruptly. 'You don't find yourself in doubt; did this happen or did it not?'

'Hardly ever. Except just for a momentary hesitation now and then. I suppose few people do.'

'Does *he* say—' he indicated the book.

'Says it happens at times and gives the usual explanation about intensity of impression and the like to account for its not happening as a rule. I suppose you know something of these theories—'

'Very little—except that they are wrong.'

His emaciated hand played with the strap of the window for a time. I prepared to resume reading, and that seemed to precipitate his next remark. He leant forward almost as though he would touch me.

'Isn't there something called consecutive dreaming—that goes on night after night?'

'I believe there is. There are cases given in most books on mental trouble.'

'Mental trouble! Yes. I dare say there are. It's the right place for them. But what I mean—'He looked at his bony knuckles. 'Is that sort of thing always dreaming? Is it dreaming? Or is it something else? Mightn't it be something else?'

I should have snubbed his persistent conversation but for the drawn anxiety of his face. I remember now the look of his faded eyes and the lids red stained—perhaps you know that look.

'I'm not just arguing about a matter of opinion,' he said. 'The thing's killing me.'

'Dreams?'

'If you call them dreams. Night after night. Vivid!—so vivid . . . this—' (he indicated the landscape that went streaming by the window) 'seems unreal in comparison! I can scarcely remember who I am, what business I am on. . . .'

He paused. 'Even now—'

'The dream is always the same—do you mean?' I asked.

'It's over.'

'You mean?'

'I died.'

'Died?'

'Smashed and killed, and now, so much of me as that dream was, is dead. Dead for ever. I dreamt I was another man, you know, living in a different part of the world and in a different time. I dreamt that night after night. Night after night I woke into that other life. Fresh scenes and fresh happenings—until I came upon the last—'

'When you died?'

'When I died.'

'And since then—'

'No,' he said. 'Thank God! That was the end of the dream. . . .'

It was clear I was in for this dream. And after all, I had an hour before me, the light was fading fast, and Fortnum-Roscoe has a dreary way with him. 'Living in a different time,' I said: 'do you mean in some different age?'

'Yes.'

'Past?'

'No—to come—to come.'

'The year three thousand, for example?'

'I don't know what year it was. I did when I was asleep, when I was dreaming, that is, but not now—not now that I am awake. There's a lot of things I have forgotten since I woke out of these dreams, though I knew them at the time when I was—I suppose it was dreaming. They called the year differently from our way of calling the year. . . . What *did* they call it?' He put his hand to his forehead. 'No,' said he, 'I forget.'

He sat smiling weakly. For a moment I feared he did not mean to tell me his dream. As a rule I hate people who tell their dreams, but this struck me differently. I proffered assistance even. 'It began—' I suggested.

'It was vivid from the first. I seemed to wake up in it suddenly. And it's curious that in these dreams I am speaking of I never remembered this life I am living now. It seemed as if the dream life was enough while it lasted. Perhaps—But I will tell you how I find myself when I do my best to recall it all. I don't remember anything clearly until I found myself sitting in a sort of loggia looking out over the sea. I had been dozing, and suddenly I woke up—fresh and vivid—not a bit dreamlike—because the girl had stopped fanning me.'

'The girl?'

'Yes, the girl. You must not interrupt or you will put me out.'

He stopped abruptly. 'You won't think I'm mad?' he said.

'No,' I answered; 'you've been dreaming. Tell me your dream.'

'I woke up, I say, because the girl had stopped fanning me. I was not surprised to find myself there or anything of that sort, you understand. I did not feel I had fallen into it suddenly. I simply took it up at that point. Whatever memory I had of *this* life, this nineteenth-century life, faded as I woke, vanished like a dream. I knew all about myself, knew that my name was no longer Cooper but Hedon, and all about my position in the world. I've forgotten a lot since I woke—

191

there's a want of connection—but it was all quite clear and matter of fact then.'

He hesitated again, gripping the window strap, putting his face forward and looking up to me appealingly.

'This seems bosh to you?'

'No, no!' I cried. 'Go on. Tell me what this loggia was like.'

'It was not really a loggia—I don't know what to call it. It faced south. It was small. It was all in shadow except the semicircle above the balcony that showed the sky and sea and the corner where the girl stood. I was on a couch—it was a metal couch with light striped cushions—and the girl was leaning over the balcony with her back to me. The light of the sunrise fell on her ear and cheek. Her pretty white neck and the little curls that nestled there, and her white shoulder were in the sun, and all the grace of her body was in the cool blue shadow. She was dressed—how can I describe it? It was easy and flowing. And altogether there she stood, so that it came to me how beautiful and desirable she was, as though I had never seen her before And when at last I sighed and raised myself upon my arm she turned her face to me—'

He stopped.

'I have lived three-and-fifty years in this world. I have had mother, sisters, friends, wife and daughters—all their faces, the play of their faces, I know. But the face of this girl—it is much more real to me. I can bring it back into memory so that I see it again—I could draw it or paint it. And after all—'

He stopped—but I said nothing.

'The face of a dream—the face of a dream. She was beautiful. Not that beauty which is terrible, cold, and worshipful, like the beauty of a saint; nor that beauty that stirs fierce passions; but a sort of radiation, sweet lips that softened into smiles, and grave grey eyes. And she moved gracefully, she seemed to have part with all pleasant and gracious things—'

He stopped, and his face was downcast and hidden. Then he looked up at me and went on, making no further attempt to disguise his absolute belief in the reality of his story.

'You see, I had thrown up my plans and ambitions, thrown up all I had ever worked for or desired for her sake. I had been a master man away there in the north, with influence and property and a great reputation, but none of it had seemed worth having beside her. I had come to the place, this city of sunny pleasures, with her, and left all those things to wreck and ruin just to save a remnant at least of my life. While I had been in love with her before I knew that she had any care for me, before I had imagined that she would dare—that we should dare, all my life had seemed vain and hollow, dust and ashes. It *was* dust and ashes. Night after night and through the long days I had longed and desired—my soul had beaten against the thing forbidden!

'But it is impossible for one man to tell another just these things. It's emotion, it's a tint, a light that comes and goes. Only while it's there, everything changes, everything. The thing is I came away and left them in their Crisis to do what they could.'

'Left whom?' I asked, puzzled.

'The people up in the north there. You see—in this dream, anyhow—I had been a big man, the sort of man men come to trust in, to group themselves about. Millions of men who had never seen me were ready to do things and risk things because of their confidence in me. I had been playing that game for years, that big laborious game, that vague, monstrous political game amidst intrigues and betrayals, speech and agitation. It was a vast weltering world, and at last I had a sort of leadership against the Gang—you know it was called the Gang—a sort of compromise of scoundrelly projects and base ambitions and vast public emotional stupidities and catch-words—the Gang that kept the world noisy and blind year by year, and all the while that it was drifting, drifting towards infinite disaster. But I can't expect you to understand the shades and complications of the year—the year something or other ahead. I had it all down to the smallest details—in my dream. I suppose I had been dreaming of it before I awoke, and the fading outline of some queer new development I had imagined still hung about me as I rubbed my eyes. It was some grubby affair that made me thank God for the sunlight. I sat up on the couch and remained looking at the woman and rejoicing—rejoicing that I had came away out of all that tumult and folly and violence before it was too late. After all, I thought, this is life—love and beauty, desire and delight, are they not worth all those dismal struggles for vague, gigantic ends. And I blamed myself for having ever sought to be a leader when I might have given my days to love. But then, thought I, if I had not spent my early days sternly and austerely, I might have wasted myself upon vain and worthless women, and at the thought all my being went out in love and tenderness to my dear mistress, my dear lady, who had come at last and compelled me—compelled me by her invincible charm for me—to lay that life aside.

' "You are worth it," I said, speaking without intending her to hear; "you are worth it, my dearest one; worth pride and praise and all things. Love! to have *you* is worth them all together." And at the murmur of my voice she turned about.

' "Come and see," she cried—I can hear her now—"come and see the sunrise upon Monte Solaro."

'I remember how I sprang to my feet and joined her at the balcony. She put a white hand upon my shoulder and pointed towards great masses of limestone, flushing, as it were, into life. I looked. But first I noted the sunlight on her face caressing the lines of her cheeks and neck. How can I describe to you the scene we had before us? We were at Capri—'

'I have been there,' I said. 'I have clambered up Monte Solaro and drunk *vero Capri*—muddy stuff like cider—at the summit.'

'Ah!' said the man with the white face; 'then perhaps you can tell me—you will know if this was indeed Capri. For in this life I have never been there. Let me describe it. We were in a little room, one of a vast multitude of little rooms, very cool and sunny, hollowed out of the limestone of a sort of cape, very high above the sea. The whole island, you know, was one enormous hotel, complex beyond explaining, and on the other side there were miles of floating hotels, and huge floating stages to which the flying machines came. They called it a pleasure city. Of course, there was none of that in your time—rather, I should say, *is* none of that *now*. Of course. Now!—yes.

'Well, this room of ours was at the extremity of the cape, so that one could see east and west. Eastward was a great cliff—a thousand feet high perhaps—coldly grey except for one bright edge of gold, and beyond it the Isle of the Sirens, and a falling coast that faded and passed into the hot sunrise. And when one turned to the west, distinct and near was a little bay, a scimitar of beach still in shadow. And out of that shadow rose Solaro straight and tall, flushed and golden crested, like a beauty throned, and the white moon was floating behind her in the sky. And before us from east to west stretched the many-tinted sea all dotted with sailing boats.

'To the eastward, of course, these little boats were grey and very minute and clear, but to the westward they were little boats of gold—shining gold—almost like little flames. And just below us was a rock

194

with an arch worn through it. The blue sea-water broke to green and foam all round the rock, and a galley came gliding out of the arch.'

'I know that rock,' I said. 'I was nearly drowned there. It is called the Faraglioni.'

'*I Faraglioni*? Yes, *she* called it that,' answered the man with the white face. 'There was some story—but that—'

He put his hand to his forehead again. 'No,' he said, 'I forget that story.

'Well, that is the first thing I remember, the first dream I had, that shaded room and the beautiful air and sky and that dear lady of mine, with her shining arms and her graceful robe, and how we sat and talked in half whispers to one another. We talked in whispers not because there was anyone to hear, but because there was still such a freshness of mind between us that our thoughts were a little frightened, I think, to find themselves at last in words. And so they went softly.

'Presently we were hungry and we went from our apartment, going by a strange passage with a moving floor, until we came to the great breakfast room—there was a fountain and music. A pleasant and joyful place it was, with its sunlight and splashing, and the murmur of plucked strings. And we sat and ate and smiled at one another, and I would not heed a man who was watching me from a table near by.

'And afterwards we went on to the dancing-hall. But I cannot describe that hall. The place was enormous—larger than any building you have ever seen—and in one place there was the old gate of Capri, caught into the wall of a gallery high overhead. Light girders, stems and threads of gold, burst from the pillars like fountains, streamed like an Aurora across the roof and interlaced, like—like conjuring tricks. All about the great circle for the dancers there were beautiful figures, strange dragons, and intricate and wonderful grotesques bearing lights. The place was inundated with artificial light that shamed the newborn day. And as we went through the throng the people turned about and looked at us, for all through the world my name and face were known, and how I had suddenly thrown up pride and struggle to come to this place. And they looked also at the lady beside me, though half the story of how at last she had come to me was unknown or mistold. And few of the men who were there, I know, but judged me a happy man, in spite of all the shame and dishonour that had come upon my name.

'The air was full of music, full of harmonious scents, full of the rhythm of beautiful motions. Thousands of beautiful people swarmed about the hall, crowded the galleries, sat in a myriad recesses; they were dressed in splendid colours and crowned with flowers; thousands danced about the great circle beneath the white images of the ancient gods, and glorious processions of youths and maidens came and went. We two danced, not the dreary monotonies of your days—of this time, I mean—but dances that were beautiful, intoxicating. And even now I can see my lady dancing—dancing joyously. She danced, you know, with a serious face; she danced with a serious dignity, and yet she was smiling at me and caressing me—smiling and caressing with her eyes.

'The music was different,' he murmured. 'It went—I cannot describe it; but it was infinitely richer and more varied than any music that has ever come to me awake.

'And then—it was when we had done dancing—a man came to speak to me. He was a lean, resolute man, very soberly clad for that place, and already I had marked his face watching me in the breakfasting hall, and afterwards as we went along the passage I had avoided his eye. But now, as we sat in an alcove smiling at the pleasure of all the people who went to and fro across the shining floor, he came and touched me, and spoke to me so that I was forced to listen. And he asked that he might speak to me for a while apart.

' "No," I said. "I have no secrets from this lady. What do you want to tell me?"

'He said it was a trivial matter, or at least a dry matter, for a lady to hear.

' "Perhaps for me to hear," said I.

'He glanced at her, as though almost he would appeal to her. Then he asked me suddenly if I had heard of a great and avenging declaration that Evesham had made. Now, Evesham had always before been the man next to myself in the leadership of that great party in the north. He was a forcible, hard, and tactless man, and only I had been able to control and soften him. It was on his account even more than my own, I think, that the others had been so dismayed at my retreat. So this question about what he had done reawakened my old interest in the life I had put aside just for a moment.

' "I have taken no heed of any news for many days," I said. "What has Evesham been saying?"

'And with that the man began, nothing loth, and I must confess even I was struck by Evesham's reckless folly in the wild and threatening words he had used. And this messenger they had sent to me not only told me of Evesham's speech, but went on to ask counsel and to point out what need they had of me. While he talked, my lady sat a little forward and watched his face and mine.

'My old habits of scheming and organising reasserted themselves. I could even see myself suddenly returning to the north, and all the dramatic effect of it. All that this man said witnessed to the disorder of the party indeed, but not to its damage. I should go back stronger than I had come. And then I thought of my lady. You see—how can I tell you? There were certain peculiarities of our relationship—as things are I need not tell you about that—which would render her presence with me impossible. I should have had to leave her; indeed, I should have had to renounce her clearly and openly, if I was to do all that I could do in the north. And the man knew that, even as he talked to her and me, knew it as well as she did, that my steps to duty were—first, separation, then abandonment. At the touch of that thought my dream of a return was shattered. I turned on the man suddenly, as he was imagining his eloquence was gaining ground with me.

' "What have I to do with these things now?" I said. "I have done with them. Do you think I am coquetting with your people in coming here?"

' "No," he said; "but—"

' "Why cannot you leave me alone. I have done with these things. I have ceased to be anything but a private man."

' "Yes," he answered. "But have you thought?—this talk of war, these reckless challenges, these wild aggressions—"

'I stood up.

' "No," I cried. "I won't hear you. I took count of all those things, I weighed them—and I have come away.

'He seemed to consider the possibility of persistence. He looked from me to where the lady sat regarding us.

' "War," he, said, as if he were speaking to himself, and then turned slowly from me and walked away.

'I stood, caught in the whirl of thoughts his appeal had set going.

'I heard my lady's voice.

' "Dear," she said; "but if they have need of you—"

197

'She did not finish her sentence, she let it rest there. I turned to her sweet face, and the balance of my mood swayed and reeled.

' "They want me only to do the thing they dare not do themselves," I said. "If they distrust Evesham they must settle with him themselves."

'She looked at me doubtfully.

' "But war—" she said.

'I saw a doubt on her face that I had seen before, a doubt of herself and me, the first shadow of the discovery that, seen strongly and completely, must drive us apart for ever.

'Now I was an older mind than hers, and I could sway her to this belief or that.

' "My dear one," I said, "you must not trouble over these things. There will be no war. Certainly there will be no war. The age of wars is past. Trust me to know the justice of this case. They have no right upon me, dearest, and no one has a right upon me. I have been free to choose my life, and I have chosen this."

' "But *war*—," she said.

'I sat down beside her. I put an arm behind her and took her hand in mine. I set myself to drive that doubt away—I set myself to fill her mind with pleasant things again. I lied to her, and in lying to her I lied also to myself. And she was only too ready to believe me, only too ready to forget.

'Very soon the shadow had gone again, and we were hastening to our bathing-place in the Grotta del Bove Marino, where it was our custom to bathe every day. We swam and splashed one another, and in that buoyant water I seemed to become something lighter and stronger than a man. And at last we came out dripping and rejoicing and raced among the rocks. And then I put on a dry bathing-dress, and we sat to bask in the sun, and presently I nodded, resting my head against her knee, and she put her hand upon my hair and stroked it softly and I dozed. And behold! as it were with the snapping of the string of a violin, I was awakening, and I was in my own bed in Liverpool, in the life of today.

'Only for a time I could not believe that all these vivid moments had been no more than the substance of a dream.

'In truth, I could not believe it a dream for all the sobering reality of things about me. I bathed and dressed as it were by habit and as I shaved I argued why I of all men should leave the woman I loved to go back to fantastic politics in the hard and strenuous north. Even if Evesham did force the world back to war, what was that to me? I was a man with the heart of a man, and why should I feel the responsibility of a deity for the way the world might go?

'You know that is not quite the way I think about affairs, about my real affairs. I am a solicitor, you know, with a point of view.

'The vision was so real, you must understand, so utterly unlike a dream that I kept perpetually recalling trivial irrelevant details; even the ornament of a book-cover that lay on my wife's sewing-machine in the breakfast-room recalled with the utmost vividness the gilt line that ran about the seat in the alcove where I had talked with the messenger from my deserted party. Have you ever heard of a dream that had a quality like that?'

'Like—?'

'So that afterwards you remembered details you had forgotten.'

I thought. I had never noticed the point before, but he was right.

'Never,' I said. 'That is what you never seem to do with dreams.'

'No,' he answered. 'But that is just what I did. I am a solicitor, you must understand, in Liverpool, and I could not help wondering what the clients and business people I found myself talking to in my office would think if I told them suddenly I was in love with a girl who would be born a couple of hundred years or so hence, and worried about the politics of my great-great-great-grand-children. I was chiefly busy that day negotiating a ninety-nine-year building lease. It was a private builder in a hurry, and we wanted to tie him in every possible way. I had an interview with him, and he showed a certain want of temper that sent me to bed still irritated. That night I had no dream. Nor did I dream the next night, at least, to remember.

'Something of that intense reality of conviction vanished. I began to feel sure it was a dream. And then it came again.

'When the dream came again, nearly four days later, it was very different. I think it certain that four days had also elapsed in the dream. Many things had happened in the north, and the shadow of them was back again between us, and this time it was not so easily dispelled. I began I know with moody musings. Why, in spite of all, should I go back, go back for all the rest of my days to toil and stress, insults and perpetual dissatisfaction, simply to save hundreds of millions of common people, whom I did not love, whom too often I could do no other than despise, from the stress and anguish of war and infinite misrule? And after all I might fail. *They* all sought their own narrow ends, and why should not I—why should not I also live as a man? And out of such thoughts her voice summoned me, and I lifted my eyes.

'I found myself awake and walking. We had come out above the Pleasure City, we were near the summit of Monte Solaro and looking towards the bay. It was the late afternoon and very clear. Far away to the left Ischia hung in a golden haze between sea and sky, and Naples was coldly white against the hills, and before us was Vesuvius with a tall and slender streamer feathering at last towards the south, and the ruins of Torre Annunziata and Castellamare glittering and near.'

I interrupted suddenly: 'You have been to Capri, of course?'

'Only in this dream,' he said, 'only in this dream. All across the bay beyond Sorrento were the floating palaces of the Pleasure City moored and chained. And northward were the broad floating stages that received the aeroplanes. Aeroplanes fell out of the sky every afternoon, each bringing its thousands of pleasure-seekers from the uttermost parts of the earth to Capri and its delights. All these things, I say, stretched below.

'But we noticed them only incidentally because of an unusual sight that evening had to show. Five war aeroplanes that had long slumbered useless in the distant arsenals of the Rhinemouth were manoeuvring now in the eastward sky. Evesham had astonished the world by producing them and others, and sending them to circle here and there. It was the threat material in the great game of bluff he was playing, and it had taken even me by surprise. He was one of those incredibly stupid energetic people who seem sent by heaven to create disasters. His energy to the first glance seemed so wonderfully like capacity! But he had no imagination, no invention, only a stupid, vast, driving force of will, and a mad faith in his stupid idiot "luck" to pull him through. I remember how we stood out upon the headland watching the squadron circling far away, and how I weighed the full meaning of the sight, seeing clearly the way things must go. And then even it was not too late. I might have gone back, I think, and saved the world. The people of the north would follow me, I knew, granted only that in one thing I respected their moral standards. The east and south would trust me as they would trust no other northern man. And I knew I had only to put it to her and she would have let me go. . . . Not because she did not love me!

'Only I did not want to go; my will was all the other way about. I had so newly thrown off the incubus of responsibility: I was still so fresh a renegade from duty that the daylight clearness of what I *ought* to do had no power at all to touch my will. My will was to live, to gather pleasures and make my dear lady happy. But though this sense of vast neglected duties had no power to draw me, it could make me silent and preoccupied, it robbed the days I had spent of half their brightness and roused me into dark meditations in the silence of the night. And as I stood and watched Evesham's aeroplanes sweep to and fro—those birds of infinite ill omen—she stood beside me watching me, perceiving the trouble indeed, but not perceiving it clearly—her eyes questioning my face, her expression shaded with perplexity. Her face was grey because the sunset was fading out of the sky. It was no fault of hers that she held me. She had asked me to go from her, and again in the night time and with tears she had asked me to go.

'At last it was the sense of her that roused me from my mood. I turned upon her suddenly and challenged her to race down the mountain slopes. "No," she said, as if I jarred with her gravity; but I was resolved to end that gravity, and made her run—no one can be very grey and sad who is out of breath—and when she stumbled I ran with my hand beneath her arm. We ran down past a couple of men, who turned back staring in astonishment at my behaviour—they must have recognised my face. And halfway down the slope came a tumult in the air, clang-clank, clang-clank, and we stopped, and presently over the hill-crest those war things came flying one behind the other.'

The man seemed hesitating on the verge of a description.

'What were they like?' I asked.

'They had never fought,' he said. 'They were just like our iron-clads are nowadays; they had never fought. No one knew what they might do, with excited men inside them; few even cared to speculate. They were great driving things shaped like spear-heads with out a shaft, with a propeller in the place of the shaft.'

'Steel?'

'Not steel.'

'Aluminium?'

'No, no, nothing of that sort. An alloy that was very common—as common as brass, for example. It was called—let me see—' He squeezed his forehead with the fingers of one hand. 'I am forgetting everything,' he said.

'And they carried guns?'

'Little guns, firing high explosive shells. They fired the guns backwards, out of the base of the leaf, so to speak, and rammed with the beak. That was the theory, you know, but they had never been fought. No one could tell exactly what was going to happen. And meanwhile I suppose it was very fine to go whirling through the air like a flight of young swallows, swift and easy. I guess the captains tried not to think too clearly what the real thing would be like. And these flying war machines, you know, were only one sort of the endless war contrivances that had been invented and had fallen into abeyance during the long peace. There were all sorts of these things that people were routing out and furbishing up; infernal things, silly things; things that had never been tried; big engines, terrible explosives, great guns. You know the silly way of the ingenious sort of men who make these things; they turn 'em out as beavers build dams, and with no more sense of the rivers they're going to divert and the lands they're going to flood!

'As we went down the winding stepway to our hotel again, in the twilight, I foresaw it all: I saw how clearly and inevitably things were driving for war in Evesham's silly, violent hands, and I had some inkling of what war was bound to be under these new conditions. And even then, though I knew it was drawing near the limit of my opportunity, I could find no will to go back.'

He sighed.

'That was my last chance.

'We didn't go into the city until the sky was full of stars, so we walked out upon the high terrace, to and fro, and—she counselled me to go back.

' "My dearest," she said, and her sweet face looked up to me, "this is Death. This life you lead is Death. Go back to them, go back to your duty—"

'She began to weep, saying, between her sobs, and clinging to my arm as she said it, "Go back—Go back."

'Then suddenly she fell mute, and, glancing down at her face, I read in an instant the thing she had thought to do. It was one of those moments when one *sees*.

' "No!" I said.

' "No?" she asked, in surprise, and I think a little fearful at the answer to her thought.

' "Nothing," I said, "shall send me back. Nothing! I have chosen. Love, I have chosen, and the world must go. Whatever happens I will live this life—I will live for *you*! It—nothing shall turn me aside; nothing, my dear one. Even if you died—even if you died—"

' "Yes?" she murmured, softly.

' "Then—I also would die."

'And before she could speak again I began to talk, talking eloquently—as I *could* do in that life—talking to exalt love, to make the life we were living seem heroic and glorious; and the thing I was deserting something hard and enormously ignoble that it was a fine thing to set aside. I bent all my mind to throw that glamour upon it, seeking not only to convert her but myself to that. We talked, and she clung to me, torn too between all that she deemed noble and all that she knew was sweet. And at last I did make it heroic, made all the thickening disaster of the world only a sort of glorious setting to our unparalleled love, and we two poor foolish souls strutted there at last, clad in that splendid delusion, drunken rather with that glorious delusion, under the still stars.

'And so my moment passed.

'It was my last chance. Even as we went to and fro there, the leaders of the south and east were gathering their resolve, and the hot answer that shattered Evesham's bluffing for ever, took shape and waited. And all over Asia, and the ocean, and the South, the air and the wires were throbbing with their warnings to prepare—prepare.

'No one living, you know, knew what war was; no one could imagine, with all these new inventions, what horror war might bring. I believe most people still believed it would be a matter of bright uniforms and shouting charges and triumphs and flags and hands—in a time when half the world drew its food supply from regions ten thousand miles away—'

The man with the white face paused. I glanced at him, and his face was intent on the floor of the carriage. A little railway station, a string of loaded trucks, a signal-box, and the back of a cottage, shot by the carriage window, and a bridge passed with a clap of noise, echoing the tumult of the train.

'After that,' he said, 'I dreamt often. For three weeks of nights that dream was my life. And the worst of it was there were nights when I could not dream, when I lay tossing on a bed in this accursed life; and *there*—somewhere lost to me—things were happening—

momentous, terrible things. . . . I lived at nights—my days, my waking days, this life I am living now, became a faded, far-away dream, a drab setting, the cover of the book.'

He thought.

'I could tell you all, tell you every little thing in the dream, but as to what I did in the daytime—no. I could not tell—I do not remember. My memory—my memory has gone. The business of life slips from me—

He leant forward, and pressed his hands upon his eyes. For a long time he said nothing.

'And then?' said I.

'The war burst like a hurricane.'

He stared before him at unspeakable things.

'And then?' I urged again.

'One touch of unreality,' he said, in the low tone of a man who speaks to himself, 'and they would have been nightmares. But they were not nightmares—they were not nightmares. *No!*'

He was silent for so long that it dawned upon me that there was a danger of losing the rest of the story. But he went on talking again in the same tone of questioning self-communion.

'What was there to do but flight? I had not thought the war would touch Capri—I had seemed to see Capri as being out of it all, as the contrast to it all; but two nights after the whole place was shouting and bawling, every woman almost and every other man wore a badge—Evesham's badge—and there was no music but a jangling war-song over and over again, and everywhere men enlisting, and in the dancing halls they were drilling. The whole island was awhirl with rumours; it was said, again and again, that fighting had begun. I had not expected this. I had seen so little of the life of pleasure that I had failed to reckon with this violence of the amateurs. And as for me, I was out of it. I was like a man who might have prevented the firing of a magazine. The time had gone. I was no one; the vainest stripling with a badge counted for more than I. The crowd jostled us and bawled in our ears; that accursed song deafened us; a woman shrieked at my lady because no badge was on her, and we two went back to our own place again, ruffled and insulted—my lady white and silent, and I aquiver with rage. So furious was I, I could have quarrelled with her if I could have found one shade of accusation in her eyes.

'All my magnificence had gone from me. I walked up and down our rock cell, and outside was the darkling sea and a light to the southward that flared and passed and came again.

' "We must get out of this place," I said over and over. "I have made my choice, and I will have no hand in these troubles. I will have nothing of this war. We have taken our lives out of all these things. This is no refuge for us. Let us go."

'And the next day we were already in flight from the war that covered the world.

'And all the rest was Flight—all the rest was Flight.'

He mused darkly.

'How much was there of it?'

He made no answer.

'How many days?'

His face was white and drawn and his hands were clenched. He took no heed of my curiosity.

I tried to draw him back to his story with questions.

'Where did you go?' I said.

'When?'

'When you left Capri.'

'South-west,' he said, and glanced at me for a second. 'We went in a boat.'

'But I should have thought an aeroplane?'

'They had been seized.'

I questioned him no more. Presently I thought he was beginning again. He broke out in an argumentative monotone:

'But why should it be? If, indeed, this battle, this slaughter and stress *is* life, why have we this craving for pleasure and beauty? If there is no refuge, if there is no place of peace, and if all our dreams of quiet places are a folly and a snare, why have we such dreams? Surely it was no ignoble cravings, no base intentions, had brought us to this; it was Love had isolated us. Love had come to me with her eyes and robed in her beauty, more glorious than all else in life, in the very shape and colour of life, and summoned me away. I had silenced all the voices, I had answered all the questions—I had come to her. And suddenly there was nothing but War and Death!'

I had an inspiration. 'After all,' I said, 'it could have been only a dream.'

'A dream!' he cried, flaming upon me, 'a dream—when, even now—'

For the first time he became animated. A faint flush crept into his cheek. He raised his open hand and clenched it, and dropped it to his knee. He spoke, looking away from me, and for all the rest of the time he looked away. 'We are but phantoms,' he said, 'and the phantoms of phantoms, desires like cloud shadows and wills of straw that eddy in the wind; the days pass, use and wont carry us through as a train carries the shadow of its lights—so be it! But one thing is real and certain, one thing is no dreamstuff, but eternal and enduring. It is the centre of my life, and all other things about it are subordinate or altogether vain. I loved her, that woman of a dream. And she and I are dead together!

'A dream! How can it be a dream, when it has drenched a living life with unappeasable sorrow, when it makes all that I have lived for and cared for, worthless and unmeaning?

'Until that very moment when she was killed I believed we had still a chance of getting away,' he said. 'All through the night and morning that we sailed across the sea from Capri to Salerno, we talked of escape. We were full of hope, and it clung about us to the end, hope for the life together we should lead, out of it all, out of the battle and struggle, the wild and empty passions, the empty arbitrary "thou shalt" and "thou shalt not" of the world. We were uplifted, as though our quest was a holy thing, as though love for one another was a mission. . . .

'Even when from our boat we saw the fair face of that great rock Capri—already scarred and gashed by the gun emplacements and hiding-places that were to make it a fastness—we reckoned nothing of the imminent a slaughter, though the fury of preparation hung about in puffs and clouds of dust at a hundred points amidst the grey; but, indeed, I made a text of that and talked. There, you know, was the rock, still beautiful for all its scars, with its countless windows and arches and ways, tier upon tier, for a thousand feet, a vast carving of grey, broken by vine-clad terraces and lemon and orange groves and masses of agave and prickly pear, and puffs of almond blossom. And out under the archway that is built over the Marina Piccola other boats were coming; and as we came round the cape and within sight of the mainland, another string of boats came into view, driving before the wind towards the south-west. In a little while a multitude had come out, the remoter just specks of ultramarine in the shadow of the eastward cliff.

' "It is love and reason," I said, "fleeing from all this madness of war."

'And though we presently saw a squadron of aeroplanes flying across the southern sky we did not heed it. There it was—a line of dots in the sky—and then more, dotting the south-eastern horizon, and then still more, until all that quarter of the sky was stippled with blue specks. Now they were all thin little strokes of blue, and now one and now a multitude would heel and catch the sun and become short flashes of light. They came, rising and falling and growing larger like some huge flight of gulls or rooks or such-like birds, moving with a marvellous uniformity, and ever as they drew nearer they spread over a greater width of sky. The southward wing flung itself in an arrow-headed cloud athwart the sun. And then suddenly they swept round to the eastward and streamed eastward, growing smaller and smaller and clearer and clearer again until they vanished from the sky. And after that we noted to the northward and very high Evesham's fighting machines hanging high over Naples like an evening swarm of gnats.

'It seemed to have no more to do with us than a flight of birds.

'Even the mutter of guns far away in the south-east seemed to us to signify nothing. . . .

'Each day, each dream after that, we were still exalted, still seeking that refuge where we might live and love. Fatigue had come upon us, pain and many distresses. For though we were dusty and stained by our toilsome tramping, and half starved and with the horror of the dead men we had seen and the flight of the peasants—for very soon a gust of fighting swept up the peninsula—with these things haunting our minds it still resulted only in a deepening resolution to escape. Oh, but she was brave and patient! She who had never faced hardship and exposure had courage for herself—and me. We went to and fro seeking an outlet, over a country all commandeered and ransacked by the gathering hosts of war. Always we went on foot. At first there were other fugitives, but we did not mingle with them. Some escaped northward, some were caught in the torrent of peasantry that swept along the main roads, many gave themselves into the hands of the soldiery and were sent northward. Many of the men were impressed. But we kept away from these things; we had brought no money to bribe a passage north, and I feared for my lady at the hands of these conscript crowds. We had landed at Salerno, and we had been turned back from Cava, and we had tried to cross towards Taranto by a pass over Monte Alburno, but we had been driven back for want of food, and so we had come down among the marshes by Paestum, where those great temples stand alone. I had some vague idea that by Paestum it might be possible to find a boat or something, and take once more to sea. And there it was the battle overtook us

'A sort of soul-blindness had me. Plainly I could see that we were being hemmed in; that the great net of that giant Warfare had us in its toils. Many times we had seen the levies that had come down from the north going to and fro, and had come upon them in the distance amidst the mountains making ways for the ammunition and preparing the mounting of the guns. Once we fancied they had fired at us, taking us for spies—at any rate a shot had gone shuddering over us. Several times we had hidden in woods from hovering aeroplanes.

'But all these things do not matter now, these nights of flight and pain. . . . We were in an open place near those great temples at Paestum at last, on a blank stony place dotted with spiky bushes, empty and desolate and so flat that a grove of eucalyptus far away showed to the feet of its stems. Now I can see it! My lady was sitting down under a bush resting a little, for she was very weak and weary, and I was standing up watching to see if I could tell the distance of the firing that came and went. They were still, you know, fighting far from each other, with those terrible new weapons that had never before been used: guns that would carry beyond sight, and aeroplanes that would do—What *they* would do no man could foretell.

'I knew that we were between the two armies, and that they drew together. I knew we were in danger, and that we could not stop there and rest!

'Though all these things were in my mind, they were in the background. They seemed to be affairs beyond our concern. Chiefly, I was thinking of my lady. An aching distress filled me. For the first time she had owned herself beaten and had fallen a-weeping. Behind me I could hear her sobbing, but I would not turn round to her because I knew she had need of weeping, and had held herself so far and so long for me. It was well, I thought, that she would weep and rest and then we would toil on again, for I had no inkling of the thing that hung so near. Even now I can see her as she sat there, her lovely hair upon her shoulder, can mark again the deepening hollow of her cheek.

' "If we had parted," she said, "if I had let you go."

' "No," said I. "Even now, I do not repent. I will not repent; I made my choice, and I will hold on to the end."

'And then—

'Overhead in the sky flashed something and burst, and all about us I heard the bullets making a noise like a handful of peas suddenly thrown. They chipped the stones about us, and whirled fragments from the bricks and passed. . . .'

He put his hand to his mouth, and then moistened his lips.

'At the flash I had turned about. . .

'You know—she stood up—

'She stood up, you know, and moved a step towards me—

'As though she wanted to reach me—

'And she had been shot through the heart.'

He stopped and stared at me. I felt all that foolish incapacity an Englishman feels on such occasions. I met his eyes for a moment, and then stared out of the window. For a long space we kept silence. When at last I looked at him he was sitting back in his corner, his arms folded, and his teeth gnawing at his knuckles.

He bit his nail suddenly, and stared at it.

'I carried her,' he said, 'towards the temples, in my arms—as though it mattered. I don't know why. They seemed a sort of sanctuary, you know; they had lasted so long, I suppose.

'She must have died almost instantly. Only—I talked to her—all the way.'

Silence again.

'I have seen those temples,' I said abruptly, and indeed he had brought those still, sunlit arcades of worn sandstone very vividly before me.

'It was the brown one, the big brown one. I sat down on a fallen pillar and held her in my arms. . . . Silent after the first babble was over. And after a little while the lizards came out and ran about again, as though nothing unusual was going on, as though nothing had changed. . . . It was tremendously still there, the sun high and the shadows still; even the shadows of the weeds upon the entablature were still—in spite of the thudding and banging that went all about the sky.

'I seem to remember that the aeroplanes came up out of the south, and that the battle went away to the west. One aeroplane was struck, and overset and fell. I remember that—though it didn't interest me in the least. It didn't seem to signify. It was like a wounded gull, you know—flapping for a time in the water. I could see it down the aisle of the temple—a black thing in the bright blue water.

'Three or four times shells burst about the beach, and then that ceased. Each time that happened all the lizards scuttled in and hid for a space. That was all the mischief done, except that once a stray bullet gashed the stone hard by—made just a fresh bright surface.

'As the shadows grew longer, the stillness seemed greater.

'The curious thing,' he remarked, with the manner of a man who makes a trivial conversation, 'is that I didn't *think*—I didn't think at all. I sat with her in my arms amidst the stones—in a sort of lethargy—stagnant.

'And I don't remember waking up. I don't remember dressing that day. I know I found myself in my office, with my letters all slit open in front of me, and how I was struck by the absurdity of being there, seeing that in reality I was sitting, stunned, in that Paestum Temple with a dead woman in my arms. I read my letters like a machine. I have forgotten what they were about.'

He stopped, and there was a long silence.

Suddenly I perceived that we were running down the incline from Chalk Farm to Euston. I started at this passing of time. I turned on him with a brutal question, in the tone of 'Now or never.'

'And did you dream again?'

'Yes.'

He seemed to force himself to finish. His voice was very low.

'Once more, and as it were only for a few instants. I seemed to have suddenly awakened out of a great apathy, to have risen into a sitting position, and the body lay there on the stones beside me. A gaunt body. Not her, you know. So soon—it was not her. . . .

'I may have heard voices. I do not know. Only I knew clearly that men were coming into the solitude and that that was a last outrage.

'I stood up and walked through the temple, and then there came into sight—first one man with a yellow face, dressed in a uniform of dirty white, trimmed with blue, and then several, climbing to the crest of the old wall of the vanished city, and crouching there. They were little bright figures in the sunlight, and there they hung, weapon in hand, peering cautiously before them.

'And further away I saw others and then more at another point in the wall. It was a long lax line of men in open order.

'Presently the man I had first seen stood up and shouted a command, and his men came tumbling down the wall and into the high weeds towards the temple. He scrambled down with them and led them. He came facing towards me, and when he saw me he stopped.

'At first I had watched these men with a mere curiosity, but when I had seen they meant to come to the temple I was moved to forbid them. I shouted to the officer.

' "You must not come here," I cried, "*I* am here. I am here with my dead."

'He stared, and then shouted a question back to me in some unknown tongue.

'I repeated what I had said.

'He shouted again, and I folded my arms and stood still. Presently he spoke to his men and came forward. He carried a drawn sword.

'I signed to him to keep away, but he continued to advance. I told him again very patiently and clearly: "You must not come here. These are old temples and I am here with my dead.'

'Presently he was so close I could see his face clearly. It was a narrow face, with dull grey eyes, and a black moustache. He had a scar on his upper lip, and he was dirty and unshaven. He kept shouting un-intelligible things, questions, perhaps, at me.

'I know now that he was afraid of me, but at the time that did not occur to me. As I tried to explain to him, he interrupted me in imperious tones, bidding me, I suppose, stand aside.

'He made to go past me, and I caught hold of him.

'I saw his face change at my grip.

' "You fool," I cried. "Don't you know? She is dead!"

'He started back. He looked at me with cruel eyes. I saw a sort of exultant resolve leap into them—delight. Then, suddenly, with a scowl, he swept his sword back—*so*—and thrust.'

He stopped abruptly.

I became aware of a change in the rhythm of the train. The brakes lifted their voices and the carriage jarred and jerked. This present world insisted upon itself, became clamorous. I saw through the steamy window huge electric lights glaring down from tall masts upon a fog, saw rows of stationary empty carriages passing by; and then a signal-box, hoisting its constellation of green and red into the murky

London twilight, marched after them. I looked again at his drawn features.

'He ran me through the heart. It was with a sort of astonishment —no fear, no pain—but just amazement, that I felt it pierce me, felt the sword drive home into my body. It didn't hurt, you know. It didn't hurt at all.'

The yellow platform lights came into the field of view, passing first rapidly, then slowly, and at last stopping with a jerk. Dim shapes of men passed to and fro without.

'Euston!' cried a voice.

'Do you mean—'

'There was no pain, no sting or smart. Amazement and then darkness sweeping over everything. The hot, brutal face before me, the face of the man who had killed me, seemed to recede. It swept out of existence—'

'Euston!' clamoured the voices outside; 'Euston!'

The carriage door opened admitting a flood of sound, and a porter stood regarding us. The sounds of doors slamming, and the hoof-clatter of cab-horses, and behind these things the featureless remote roar of the London cobble-stones, came to my ears. A truckload of lighted lamps blazed along the platform.

'A darkness, a flood of darkness that opened and spread and blotted out all things.'

'Any luggage, sir?' said the porter.

'And that was the end?' I asked.

He seemed to hesitate. Then, almost inaudibly, he answered, '*No.*'

'You mean?'

'I couldn't get to her. She was there on the other side of the temple—And then—'

'Yes,' I insisted. 'Yes?'

'Nightmares,' he cried; 'nightmares indeed? My God! Great birds that fought and tore.'

THE NEW ACCELERATOR

CERTAINLY, if ever a man found a guinea when he was looking for a pin it is my good friend Professor Gibberne. I have heard before of investigators over-shooting the mark, but never quite to the extent that he has done. He has really, this time at any rate, without any touch of exaggeration in the phrase, found something to revolutionise human life. And that when he was simply seeking an all-round nervous stimulant to bring languid people up to the stresses of these pushful days. I have tasted the stuff now several times, and I cannot do better than describe the effect the thing had on me. That there are astonishing experiences in store for all in search of new sensations will become apparent enough.

Professor Gibberne, as many people know, is my neighbour in Folkestone. Unless my memory plays me a trick, his portrait at various ages has already appeared in *The Strand Magazine*—I think late in 1899; but I am unable to look it up because I have lent that volume to someone who has never sent it back. The reader may, perhaps recall the high forehead and the singularly long black eyebrows that give such a Mephistophelian touch to his face. He occupies one of those pleasant detached houses in the mixed style that make the western end of the Upper Sandgate Road so interesting. His is the one with the Flemish gables and the Moorish portico, and it is in the room with the mullioned bay window that he works when he is down here, and in which of an evening we have so often smoked and talked together. He is a mighty jester, but, besides, he likes to talk to me about his work; he is one of those men who find a help and stimulus in talking, and so I have been able to follow the conception of the New Accelerator right up from a very early stage. Of course, the greater portion of his experimental work is not done in Folkestone, but in Gower Street, in the fine new laboratory next to the hospital that he has been the first to use.

As everyone knows, or at least as all intelligent people know, the special department in which Gibberne has gained so great and deserved a reputation among physiologists is the action of drugs upon the nervous system. Upon soporifics, sedatives, and anaesthetics he is, I am told, unequalled. He is also a chemist of considerable eminence, and I suppose in the subtle and complex jungle of riddles that centres about the ganglion cell and the axis fibre there are little cleared places of his making, glades of illumination, that, until he sees fit to publish his results, are inaccessible to every other living man. And in the last few years he has been particularly assiduous upon this question of nervous stimulants, and already, before the discovery of the New Accelerator, very successful with them. Medical science has to thank him for at least three distinct and absolutely safe invigorators of unrivalled value to practising men. In cases of exhaustion the preparation known as Gibberne's B Syrup has, I suppose, saved more lives already than any lifeboat round the coast.

'But none of these things begin to satisfy me yet,' he told me nearly a year ago. 'Either they increase the central energy without affecting the nerves or they simply increase the available energy by lowering the nervous conductivity; and all of them are unequal and local in their operation. One wakes up the heart and viscera and leaves the brain stupefied, one gets at the brain champagne fashion and does nothing good for the solar plexus, and what I want—and what, if it's an earthly possibility, I mean to have—is a stimulant that stimulates all round, that wakes you up for a time from the crown of your head to the tip of your great toe, and makes you go two—or even three to everybody else's one. Eh? That's the thing I'm after.'

'It would tire a man,' I said.

'Not a doubt of it. And you'd eat double or treble—and all that. But just think what the thing would mean. Imagine yourself with a little phial like this—he held up a bottle of green glass and marked his points with it—'and in this precious phial is the power to think twice as fast, move twice as quickly, do twice an much work in a given time as you could otherwise do.'

'But is such a thing possible?'

'I believe so. If it isn't, I've wasted my time for a year. These various preparations of the hypophosphites, for example, seem to show that something of the sort. . . . Even if it was only one and a half times as fast it would do.'

214

'It *would* do,' I said.

'If you were a statesman in a corner, for example, time rushing up against you, something urgent to be done, eh?'

'He could dose his private secretary,' I said.

'And gain—double time. And think if you, for example, wanted to finish a book.'

'Usually,' I said, 'I wish I'd never begun 'em.'

'Or a doctor, driven to death, wants to sit down and think out a case. Or a barrister—or a man cramming for an examination.'

'Worth a guinea a drop,' said I, 'and more—to men like that.'

'And in a duel again,' said Gibberne, 'where it all depends on your quickness in pulling the trigger.'

'Or in fencing,' I echoed.

'You see,' said Gibberne, 'if I get it as an all-round thing it will really do you no harm at all—except perhaps to an infinitesimal degree it brings you nearer old age. You will just have lived twice to other people's once—'

'I suppose,' I meditated, 'in a duel—it would be fair?'

'That's a question for the seconds,' said Gibberne.

I harked back further. 'And you really think such a thing *is* possible?' I said.

'As possible,' said Gibberne, and glanced at something that went throbbing by the window, 'as a motorbus. As a matter of fact—'

He paused and smiled at me deeply, and tapped slowly on the edge of his desk with the green phial. 'I think I know the stuff. . . . Already I've got something coming.' The nervous smile upon his face betrayed the gravity of his revelation. He rarely talked of his actual experimental work unless things were very near the end. 'And it may be, it may be—I shouldn't be surprised—it may even do the thing at a greater rate than twice.'

'It will be rather a big thing,' I hazarded.

'It will be, I think, rather a big thing.'

But I don't think he quite knew what a big thing it was to be, for all that.

I remember we had several subsequent talks about the stuff. 'The New Accelerator' he called it, and his tone about it grew more confident on each occasion. Sometimes he talked nervously of unexpected physiological results its use might have, and then he would get a bit unhappy; at others he was frankly mercenary, and we debated long

215

and anxiously how the preparation might be turned to commercial account. 'It's a good thing,' said Gibberne, 'a tremendous thing. I know I'm giving the world something, and I think it only reasonable we should expect the world to pay. The dignity of science is all very well, but I think somehow I must have the monopoly of the stuff for, say, ten years. I don't see why *all* the fun in life should go to the dealers in ham.'

My own interest in the coming drug certainly did not wane in the time. I have always had a queer twist towards metaphysics in my mind. I have always been given to paradoxes about space and time, and it seemed to me that Gibberne was really preparing no less than the absolute acceleration of life. Suppose a man repeatedly dosed with such a preparation: he would live an active and record life indeed, but he would be an adult at eleven, middle-aged at twenty-five, and by thirty well on the road to senile decay. It seemed to me that so far Gibberne was only going to do for anyone who took his drug exactly what Nature has done for the Jews and Orientals, who are men in their, teens and aged by fifty, and quicker in thought and act than we are all the time. The marvel of drugs has always been great to my mind; you can madden a man, calm a man, make him incredibly strong and alert or a helpless log, quicken this passion and allay that, all by means of drugs, and here was a new miracle to be added to the strange armoury of phials the doctors use! But Gibberne was far too eager upon his technical points to enter very keenly into my aspect of the question.

It was the 7th or 8th of August when he told me the distillation that would decide his failure or success for a time was going forward as we talked, and was on the 10th that he told me the thing was done and the New Accelerator a tangible reality in the world. I met him as I was going up the Sandgate Hill towards Folkestone—I think I was going to get my hair cut and he came hurrying down to meet me—I suppose he was coming to my house to tell me at once of his success. I remember that his eyes were unusually bright and his face flushed, and I noted even then the swift alacrity of his step.

'It's done,' he cried, and gripped my hand, speaking very fast; 'it's more than done. Come up to my house and see.'

'Really?'

'Really!' he shouted: 'Incredibly! Come up and see.'

'And it does—twice?'

216

'It does more, much more. It scares me. Come up and see the stuff. Taste it! Try it! It's the most amazing stuff on earth. He gripped my arm and, walking at such a pace that he forced me into a trot, went shouting with me up the hill. A whole charabancful of people turned and stared at us in unison after the manner of people in charabancs. It was one of those hot, clear days that Folkestone sees so much of, every colour incredibly bright and every outline hard. There was a breeze, of course, but not so much breeze as sufficed under these conditions to keep me cool and dry. I panted for mercy.

'I'm not walking fast, am I?' cried Gibberne, and slackened his pace to a quick march.

'You've been taking some of this stuff,' I puffed.

'No,' he said. 'At the utmost a drop of water that stood in a beaker from which I had washed out the last traces of the stuff. I took some last night, you know. But that is ancient history, now.'

'And it goes twice?' I said, nearing his doorway in a grateful perspiration.

'It goes a thousand times, many thousand times!' cried Gibberne, with a dramatic gesture, flinging open his Early English carved oak gate.

'Phew!' said I, and followed him to the door.

'I don't know how many times it goes,' he said, with his latch-key in his hand.

'And you—'

'It throws all sorts of light on nervous physiology, it kicks the theory of vision into a perfectly new shape! . . . Heaven knows how many thousand times. We'll try all that after—The thing is to try the stuff now.'

'Try the stuff?' I said, as we went along the passage.

'Rather,' said Gibberne, turning on me in his study. 'There it is in that little green phial there! Unless you happen to be afraid?'

I am a careful man by nature, and only theoretically adventurous. I *was* afraid. But on the other hand there is pride.

'Well,' I haggled. 'You say you've tried it?'

'I've tried it,' he said, 'and I don't look hurt by it, do I? I don't even look livery and I *feel*—'

I sat down. 'Give me the potion,' I said. 'If the worst comes to the worst it will save having my hair cut, and that I think is one of the most hateful duties of a civilised man. How do you take the mixture?'

'With water,' said Gibberne, whacking down a carafe.

He stood up in front of his desk and regarded me in his easy chair; his manner was suddenly affected by a touch of the Harley Street specialist. 'It's rum stuff, you know,' he said.

I made a gesture with my hand.

'I must warn you in the first place as soon as you've got it down to shut your eyes, and open them very cautiously in a minute or so's time. One still sees. The sense of vision is a question of length of vibration, and not of multitude of impacts; but there's a kind of shock to the retina, a nasty giddy confusion just at the time if the eyes are open. Keep 'em shut.'

'Shut' I said. 'Good!'

And the next thing is, keep still. Don't begin to whack about. You may fetch something a nasty rap if you do. Remember you will be going several thousand times faster than you ever did before, heart, lungs, muscles, brain—everything—and you will hit hard without knowing it. You won't know it, you know. You'll feel just as you do now. Only everything in the world will seem to be going ever so many thousand times slower than it ever went before. That's what makes it so deuced queer.'

'Lor',' I said. 'And you mean—'

'You'll see,' said he, and took up a measure. He glanced at the material on his desk. 'Glasses,' he said, 'water. All here. Mustn't take too much for the first attempt.'

The little phial glucked out its precious contents. 'Don't forget what I told you,' he said, turning the contents of the measure into a glass in the manner of an Italian waiter measuring whisky. 'Sit with the eyes tightly shut and in absolute stillness for two minutes,' he said. 'Then you will hear me speak.'

He added an inch or so of water to the dose in each glass.

'By-the-bye,' he said, 'don't put your glass down. Keep it in your hand and rest your hand on your knee. Yes—so. And now—'

He raised his glass.

'The New Accelerator,' I said.

'The New Accelerator,' he answered, and we touched glasses and drank, and instantly I closed my eyes.

You know that blank non-existence into which one drops when one has taken 'gas'. For an indefinite interval it was like that. Then I heard Gibberne telling me to wake up, and I stirred and opened my eyes. There he stood as he had been standing, glass still in hand. It was empty, that was all the difference.

'Well?' said I.

'Nothing out of the way?'

'Nothing. A slight feeling of exhilaration, perhaps. Nothing more.'

'Sounds?'

'Things are still,' I said. 'By Jove! yes! They are still. Except the sort of faint pat, patter, like rain falling on different things. What is it?'

'Analysed sounds,' I think he said, but I am not sure. He glanced at the window. 'Have you ever seen a curtain before a window fixed in that way before?'

I followed his eyes, and there was the end of the curtain, frozen, as it were, corner high, in the act of flapping briskly in the breeze.

'No,' said I; 'that's odd.'

'And here,' he said, and opened the hand that held the glass. Naturally I winced, expecting the glass to smash. But so far from smashing it did not even seem to stir; it hung in mid-air—motionless. 'Roughly speaking,' said Gibberne, 'an object in these latitudes falls sixteen feet in the first second. This glass is falling sixteen feet in a second now. Only, you see, it hasn't been falling yet for the hundredth part of a second. That gives you some idea of the pace of my Accelerator.' And he waved his hand round and round, over and under the slowly sinking glass. Finally he took it by the bottom, pulled it down and placed it very carefully on the table. 'Eh?' he said to me, and laughed.

'That seems all right,' I said, and began very gingerly to raise myself from my chair. I felt perfectly well, very light and comfortable, and quite confident in my mind. I was going fast all over. My heart, for example, was beating a thousand times a second, but that caused me no discomfort at all. I looked out of the window. An immovable cyclist, head down and with a frozen puff of dust behind his driving-wheel, scorched to overtake a galloping charabanc that did not stir. I gaped in amazement at this incredible spectacle. 'Gibberne,' I cried, 'how long will this confounded stuff last?'

'Heaven knows!' he answered. 'Last time I took it I went to bed and slept it off. I tell you, I was frightened. It must have lasted some minutes, I think—it seemed like hours. But after a bit it slows down rather suddenly, I believe.'

I was proud to observe that I did not feel frightened—I suppose because there were two of us. 'Why shouldn't we go out?' I asked.

'Why not?'

'They'll see us.'

'Not they. Goodness, no! Why, we shall be going a thousand times faster than the quickest conjuring trick that was ever done. Come along! Which way shall we go? Window, or door?'

And out by the window we went.

Assuredly of all the strange experiences that I have ever had, or imagined, or read of other people having or imagining, that little raid I made with Gibberne on the Folkestone Leas, under the influence of the New Accelerator, was the strangest and maddest of all. We went out by his gate into the road, and there we made a minute examination of the statuesque passing traffic. The tops of the wheels and some of the legs of the horses of this charabanc, the end of the whip-lash and the lower jaw of the conductor—who was just beginning to yawn—were perceptibly in motion, but all the rest of the lumbering conveyance seemed still. And quite noiseless except for a faint rattling that came from one man's throat! And as parts of this frozen edifice there were a driver, you know, and a conductor, and eleven people! The effect as we walked about the thing began by being madly queer and ended by being—disagreeable. There they were, people like ourselves and yet not like ourselves, frozen in careless attitudes, caught in mid-gesture. A girl and a man smiled at one another, a leering smile that threatened to last for evermore; a woman in a floppy capelline rested her arm on the rail and stared at Gibberne's house with the unwinking stare of eternity; a man stroked his moustache like a figure of wax, and another stretched a tiresome stiff hand with extended fingers towards his loosened hat. We stared at them, we laughed at them, we made faces at them, and then a sort of disgust of them came upon us, and we turned away and walked round in front of the cyclist towards the Leas.

'Goodness!' cried Gibberne, suddenly; 'look there!'

He pointed, and there at the tip of his finger and sliding down the air with wings flapping slowly and at the speed of an exceptionally languid snail—was a bee.

And so we came out upon the Leas. There the thing seemed madder than ever. The band was playing in the upper stand, though all the sound it made for us was a low-pitched, wheezy rattle, a sort of prolonged last sigh that passed at times into a sound like the slow, muffled ticking of some monstrous clock. Frozen people stood erect; strange, silent, self-conscious-looking dummies hung unstably in mid-stride, promenading upon the grass. I passed close to a poodle dog suspended in the act of leaping, and watched the slow movement of his legs as he sank to earth. 'Lord, look *here*!' cried Gibberne, and we halted for a moment before a magnificent person in white faint-striped flannels, white shoes, and a Panama hat, who turned back to wink at two gaily dressed ladies he had passed. A wink, studied with such leisurely deliberation as we could afford, is an unattractive thing. It loses any duality of alert gaiety, and one remarks that the winking eye does not completely close, that under its drooping lid appears the lower edge of an eyeball and a line of white. 'Heaven give me memory,' said I, 'and I will never wink again.'

'Or smile,' said Gibberne, with his eye on the lady's answering teeth.

'It's infernally hot, somehow,' said I. 'Let's go slower.'

'Oh, come along!' said Gibberne

We picked our way among the bath-chairs in the path. Many of the people sitting in the chairs seemed almost natural in their passive poses, but the contorted scarlet of the bandsmen was not a restful thing to see. A purple-faced gentleman was frozen in the midst of a violent struggle to refold his newspaper against the wind; there were many evidences that all these people in their sluggish way were exposed to a considerable breeze, a breeze that had no existence so far as our sensations went. We came out and walked a little way from the crowd, and turned and regarded it. To see all that multitude changed to a picture, smitten rigid, as it were, into the semblance of realistic was, was impossibly wonderful. It was absurd, of course; but it filled me with an irrational, an exultant sense of superior advantage. Consider the wonder of it! All that I had said and thought and done since the stuff had begun to work in my veins had happened, so far as those people, so far as the world in general went, in the twinkling of an eye. 'The New Accelerator—' I began, but Gibberne interrupted me.

'There's that infernal old woman !' he said.

'What old woman?'

'Lives next door to me,' said Gibberne. 'Has a lapdog that yaps. Gods! The temptation is strong.'

There is something very boyish and impulsive about Gibberne at times. Before I could expostulate with him he had dashed forward, snatched the unfortunate animal out of visible existence, and was running violently with it towards the cliff of the Leas. It was most extraordinary. The little brute, you know, didn't bark or wriggle or make the slightest sign of vitality. It kept quite stiffly in an attitude of somnolent repose, and Gibberne held it by the neck. It was like running about with a dog of wood. 'Gibberne,' I cried, 'put it down!' Then I said something else. 'If you run like that, Gibberne,' I cried, 'you'll set your clothes on fire. Your linen trousers are going brown as it is!'

He clapped his hand on his thigh and stood hesitating on the verge. 'Gibberne,' I cried, coming up, 'put it down. This heat is too much! It's our running so! Two or three miles a second! Friction of the air!'

'What?' he said, glancing at the dog.

'Friction of the air,' I shouted. 'Friction of the air. Going too fast. Like meteorites and things. Too hot. And, Gibberne! Gibberne! I'm all over pricking and a sort of perspiration. You can see people stirring slightly. I believe the stuff's working off! Put that dog down.'

'Eh?' he said.

'It's working off,' I repeated. 'We're too hot and the stuff's working off! I'm wet through.'

He stared at me. Then at the band, the wheezy rattle of whose performance was certainly going faster. Then with a tremendous sweep of the arm he hurled the dog away from him and it went spinning upward, still inanimate and hung at last over the grouped parasols of a knot of shattering people. Gibberne was gripping my elbow. 'By Jove! he cried. 'I believe it is! A sort of hot pricking and—yes. That man's moving his pocket-handkerchief! Perceptibly. We must get out of this sharp.'

But we could not get out of it sharply enough. Luckily perhaps! For we might have run, and if we had run we should, I believe, have burst into flames. Almost certainly we should have burst into flames! You know we had neither of us thought of that. . . . But before we could even begin to run the action of the drug had ceased. It was the business of a minute fraction of a second. The effect of the New Accelerator passed like the drawing of a curtain, vanished in the movement of a hand. I heard Gibberne's voice in infinite alarm. 'Sit down,' he said, and flop, down upon the turf at the edge of the Leas I sat—scorching as I sat. There is a patch of burnt grass there still where I sat down. The whole stagnation seemed to wake up as I did so, the disarticulated vibration of the band rushed together into a blast of music, the promenaders put their feet down and walked their ways, the papers and flags began flapping, smiles passed into words, the winker finished his wink and went on his way complacently, and all the seated people moved and spoke.

The whole world had come alive again, was going as fast as we were, or rather we were going no faster than the rest of the world. It was like slowing down as one comes into a railway station. Everything seemed to spin round for a second or two, I had the most transient feeling of nausea, and that was all. And the little dog which had seemed to hang for a moment when the force of Gibberne's arm was expended fell with a swift acceleration clean through a lady's parasol!

That was the saving of us. Unless it was for one corpulent old gentleman in a bath-chair, who certainly did start at the sight of us and afterwards regarded us at intervals with a darkly suspicious eye, and finally, I believe, said something to his nurse about us, I doubt if a solitary person remarked our sudden appearance among them. Plop! We must have appeared abruptly. We ceased to smoulder almost at once, though the turf beneath me was uncomfortably hot. The attention of everyone—including even the Amusements' Association Band, which on this occasion, for the only time in its history, got out of tune—was arrested by the amazing fact, and the still more amazing yapping and uproar caused by the fact, that a respectable, over-fed lapdog sleeping quietly to the east of the bandstand should suddenly fall through the parasol of a lady on the west—in a slightly singed condition due to the extreme velocity of its movements through the air. In these absurd days, too, when we are all trying to be as psychic and silly and superstitions as possible! People got up and trod on other people, chairs were overturned, the Leas policeman ran. How the matter settled itself I do not know—we were much too anxious to disentangle ourselves from the affair and get out of range of the eye of the old gentleman in the bath-chair to make minute inquiries. As soon as we were sufficiently cool and sufficiently recovered from our giddiness and nausea and confusion of mind to do so we stood up and, skirting the crowd, directed our steps back along the road below the Metropole towards Gibberne's house. But amidst the din I heard very distinctly the gentleman who had been sitting beside the lady of the ruptured sunshade using quite unjustifiable threats and language to one of those chair-attendants who have 'Inspector' written on their caps. 'If you didn't throw the dog,' he said, 'who *did*?'

The sudden return of movement and familiar noises, and our natural anxiety about ourselves (our clothes were still dreadfully hot, and the fronts of the thighs of Gibberne's white trousers were scorched a drabbish brown), prevented the minute observations I should have liked to make on all these things. Indeed, I really made no observations of any scientific value on that return. The bee, of course, had gone. I looked for that cyclist, but he was already out of sight as we came into the Upper Sandgate Road or hidden from us by traffic; the charabanc, however, with its people now all alive and stirring, was clattering along at a spanking pace almost abreast of the nearer church.

We noted, however, that the window-sill on which we had stepped in getting out of the house was slightly singed, and that the impressions of our feet on the gravel of the path were unusually deep.

∾

So it was I had my first experience of the New Accelerator. Practically we had been running about and saying and doing all sorts of things in the space of a second or so of time. We had lived half an hour while the band had played, perhaps, two bars. But the effect it had upon us was that the whole world had stopped for our convenient inspection. Considering all things, and particularly, considering our rashness in venturing out of the house, the experience might certainly have been much more disagreeable than it was. It showed, no doubt, that Gibberne has still much to learn before his preparation is a manageable convenience, but its practicability it certainly demonstrated beyond all cavil.

Since that adventure he has been steadily bringing its use under control, and I have several times, and without the slightest bad result, taken measured doses under his direction; though I must confess I have not yet ventured abroad again while under its influence. I may mention, for example, that this story has been written at one sitting and without interruption, except for the nibbling of some chocolate, by its means. I began at 6.25, and my watch is now very nearly at the minute past the half-hour. The convenience of securing a long, uninterrupted spell of work in the midst of a day full of engagements cannot be exaggerated. Gibberne is now working at the quantitative handling of his preparation, with especial reference to its distinctive effects upon different types of constitution. He then hopes to find a Retarder with which to dilute its present rather excessive potency. The Retarder will, of course, have the reverse effect to the Accelerator; used alone it should enable the patient to spread a few seconds over many hours of ordinary time, and so to maintain an apathetic inaction, a glacier-like absence of alacrity, amidst the most animated or irritating surroundings. The two things together must necessarily work an entire revolution in civilised existence. It is the beginning of our escape from that Time Garment of which Carlyle speaks. While this Accelerator will enable us to concentrate ourselves with tremendous impact upon any moment or occasion that demands our utmost sense and vigour, the Retarder will enable us to pass in passive tranquillity through infinite hardship and tedium. Perhaps I am a little optimistic about the Retarder, which has indeed still to be discovered, but about the Accelerator there is no possible sort of doubt whatever. Its appearance upon the market in a convenient, controllable, and assimilable form is a matter of the next few months. It will be obtainable of all chemists and druggists, in small green bottles, at a high but, considering its extraordinary qualities, by no means excessive price. Gibberne's Nervous Accelerator it will be called, and he hopes to be able to supply it in three strengths: one in 200, one in 900, and one in 2000, distinguished by yellow, pink, and white labels respectively.

No doubt its use renders a great number of very extraordinary things possible; for, of course, the most remarkable and, possibly, even criminal proceedings may be effected with impunity by thus dodging, as it were, into the interstices of time. Like all potent preparations it will be liable to abuse. We have, however, discussed this aspect of the question very thoroughly, and we have decided that this is purely a matter of medical jurisprudence and altogether outside our province. We shall manufacture and sell the Accelerator, and, as for the consequences—we shall see.

THE INEXPERIENCED GHOST

THE scene amidst which Clayton told his last story comes back very vividly to my mind. There he sat, for the greater part of the time, in the corner of the authentic settle by the spacious open fire, and Sanderson sat beside him smoking the Broseley clay that bore his name. There was Evans, and that marvel among actors, Wish, who is also a modest man. We had all come down to the Mermaid Club that Saturday morning, except Clayton, who had slept there overnight— which indeed gave him the opening of his story. We had golfed until golfing was invisible; we had dined, and we were in that mood of tranquil kindliness when men will suffer a story. When Clayton began to tell one, we naturally supposed he was lying. It may be that indeed he was lying—of that the reader will speedily be able to judge as well as I. He began, it is true, with an air of matter-of-fact anecdote, but that we thought was only the incurable artifice of the man.

'I say!' he remarked, after a long consideration of the upward rain of sparks from the log that Sanderson had thumped, 'you know I was alone here last night?'

'Except for the domestics,' said Wish.

'Who sleep in the other wing,' said Clayton. 'Yes. Well—' He pulled at his cigar for some little time as though he still hesitated about his confidence. Then he said, quite quietly, 'I caught a ghost!'

'Caught a ghost, did you?' said Sanderson. 'Where is it?'

And Evans, who admires Clayton immensely and has been four weeks in America, shouted, '*Caught* a ghost, did you, Clayton? I'm glad of it! Tell us all about it right now.'

Clayton said he would in a minute, and asked him to shut the door.

He looked apologetically at me. 'There's no eavesdropping of course, but we don't want to upset our very excellent service with any rumours of ghosts in the place. There's too much shadow and oak panelling to trifle with that. And this, you know, wasn't a regular ghost. I don't think it will come again—ever.'

'You mean to say you didn't keep it?' said Sanderson.

'I hadn't the heart to,' said Clayton.

And Sanderson said he was surprised.

We laughed, and Clayton looked aggrieved. 'I know,' he said, with the flicker of a smile, 'but the fact is it really *was* a ghost, and I'm as sure of it as I am that I am talking to you now. I'm not joking. I mean what I say.'

Sanderson drew deeply at his pipe, with one reddish eye on Clayton, and then emitted a thin jet of smoke more eloquent than many words.

Clayton ignored the comment. 'It is the strangest thing that has ever happened in my life. You know I never believed in ghosts or anything of the sort, before, ever; and then, you know, I bag one in a corner; and the whole business is in my hands.'

He meditated still more profoundly and produced and began to pierce a second cigar with a curious little stabber he affected.

'You talked to it?' asked Wish.

'For the space, probably, of an hour.'

'Chatty?' I said, joining the party of the sceptics.

'The poor devil was in trouble,' said Clayton, bowed over his cigar-end and with the very faintest note of reproof.

'Sobbing?' someone asked.

Clayton heaved a realistic sigh at the memory, 'Good Lord!' he said; 'yes.' And then, 'Poor fellow! yes.'

'Where did you strike it?' asked Evans, in his best American accent.

'I never realised,' said Clayton, ignoring him, 'the poor sort of thing a ghost might be,' and he hung us up again for a time, while he sought for matches in his pocket and lit and warmed to his cigar.

'I took an advantage,' he reflected at last.

We were none of us in a hurry. 'A character,' he said, 'remains just the same character for all that it's been disembodied. That's a thing we too often forget. People with a certain strength or fixity of purpose may have ghosts of a certain strength and fixity of purpose—most haunting ghosts, you know, must be as one-idea'd as monomaniacs and as obstinate as mules to come back again and again. This poor creature wasn't.' He suddenly looked up rather queerly, and his eye went round the room. 'I say it,' he said, 'in all kindliness, but that is the plain truth of the case. Even at the first glance he struck me as weak.'

He punctuated with the help of his cigar.

'I came upon him, you know, in the long passage. His back was towards me and I saw him first. Right off I knew him for a ghost. He was transparent and whitish; clean through his chest I could see the glimmer of the little window at the end. And not only his physique but his attitude struck me as being weak. He looked, you know, as though he didn't know in the slightest whatever he meant to do. One hand was on the panelling and the other fluttered to his mouth. Like—*so!*'

'What sort of physique?' said Sanderson.

'Lean. You know that sort of young man's neck that has two great flutings down the back, here and here—so! And a little, meanish head with scrubby hair and rather bad ears. Shoulders bad, narrower than the hips; turndown collar, ready-made short jacket, trousers baggy and a little frayed at the heels. That's how he took me. I came very quietly up the staircase. I did not carry a light, you know—the candles are on the landing table and there is that lamp—and I was in my list slippers, and I saw him as I came up. I stopped dead at that—taking him in. I wasn't a bit afraid. I think that in most of these affairs one is never nearly so afraid or excited as one imagines one would be. I was surprised and interested. I thought, 'Good Lord! Here's a ghost at last! And I haven't believed for a moment in ghosts during the last five-and-twenty years.' '

'Um,' said Wish.

'I suppose I wasn't on the landing a moment before he found out I was there. He turned on me sharply, and I saw the face of an immature young man, a weak nose, a scrubby little moustache, a feeble chin. So for an instant we stood—he looking over his shoulder at me—and regarded one another. Then he seemed to remember his high calling. He turned round, drew himself up, projected his face, raised his arms, spread his hands in approved ghost fashion—came towards me. As he did so his little jaw dropped, and he emitted a faint, drawn-out "Boo." No, it wasn't—not a bit dreadful. I'd dined. I'd had a bottle of champagne, and being all alone, perhaps two or three—perhaps even four or five—whiskies, so I was as solid as rocks and no more frightened than if I'd been assailed by a frog. "Boo!" I said. "Nonsense. You don't belong to *this* place. What are you doing here?"

'I could see him wince. "Boo—oo," he said.

' "Boo—be hanged! Are you a member?" I said and just to show I didn't care a pin for him I stepped through a corner of him and made to light my candle. "Are you a member?" I repeated, looking at him sideways.

'He moved a little so as to stand clear of me, and his bearing became crestfallen. "No," he said, in answer to the persistent interrogation of my eye; "I'm not a member—I'm a ghost."

' "Well, that doesn't give you the run of the Mermaid Club. Is there anyone you want to see, or anything of that sort?' And doing it as steadily as possible for fear that he should mistake the carelessness of whisky for the distraction of fear, I got my candle alight. I turned on him, holding it. "What are you doing here?" I said.

'He had dropped his hands and stopped his booing, and there he stood, abashed and awkward, the ghost of a weak, silly, aimless young man. "I'm haunting," he said.

' "You haven't any business to," I said in a quiet voice.

' "I'm a ghost," he said, as if in defence.

' "That may be, but you haven't any business to haunt here. This is a respectable private club; people often stop here with nursemaids and children, and, going about in the careless way you do, some poor little mite could easily come upon you and be scared out of her wits. I suppose you didn't think of that?"

' "No, sir," he said, "I didn't."

' "You should have done. You haven't any claim on the place, have you? Weren't murdered here, or anything of that sort?"

' "None, sir; but I thought as it was old and oak-panelled—"

' "That's *no* excuse." I regarded him firmly. "Your corning here is a mistake," I said, in a tone of friendly superiority. I feigned to see if I had my matches. and then looked up at him frankly. "If I were you I wouldn't wait for cock-crow—I'd vanish right away."

He looked embarrassed. "The fact *is*, sir—"he began.

' "I'd vanish," I said, driving it home

' "The fact is, sir, that—somehow—I can't."

' "You *can't*?"

' "No, sir. There's something I've forgotten. I've been hanging about here since midnight last night, hiding in the cupboards of the empty bedrooms and things like that. I'm flurried. I've never come haunting before, and it seems to put me out."

' "Put you out?"

' "Yes, sir. I've tried to do it several times, and it doesn't come off. There's some little thing has slipped me, and I can't get back."

'That, you know, rather bowled me over. He looked at me in such an abject way that for the life of me I couldn't keep up quite the high hectoring vein I had adopted. "That's queer," I said, and as I spoke I fancied I heard someone moving about down below. "Come into my room and tell me more about it," I said. "I didn't, of course, understand this," and I tried to take him by the arm. But, of course, you might as well have tried to take hold of a puff of smoke! I had forgotten my number, I think; anyhow, I remember going into several bedrooms—it was lucky I was the only soul in that wing—until I saw my traps. "Here we are," I said, and sat down in the arm-chair; "sit down and tell me all about it. It seems to me you have got yourself into a jolly awkward position, old chap."

'Well, he said he wouldn't sit down; he'd prefer to flit up and down the room if it was all the same to me. And so he did, and in a little while we were deep in a long and serious talk. And presently, you know, something of those whiskies and sodas evaporated out of me, and I began to realise just a little what a thundering rum and weird business it was that I was in. There he was, semi-transparent—the proper conventional phantom, and noiseless except for his ghost of a voice—flitting to and fro in that nice, clean, chintz-hung old bedroom. You could see the gleam of the copper candlesticks through him, and the lights on the brass fender, and the corners of the framed engravings on the wall, and there he was telling me all about this wretched little life of his that had recently ended on earth. He hadn't a particularly honest face, you know, but being transparent, of course, he couldn't avoid telling the truth.'

'Eh?' said Wish, suddenly sitting up in his chair.

'What?' said Clayton.

'Being transparent—couldn't avoid telling the truth—I don't see it,' said Wish.

'*I* don't see it,' said Clayton, with inimitable assurance. 'But it *is* so, I can assure you nevertheless. I don't believe he got once a nail's breadth off the Bible truth. He told me how he had been killed—he went down into a London basement with a candle to look for a leakage of gas—and described himself as a senior English master in a London private school when that release occurred.'

'Poor wretch!' said I.

'That's what I thought, and the more he talked the more I thought it. There he was, purposeless in life and purposeless out of it. He talked of his father and mother and his schoolmaster, and all who had ever been anything to him in the world, meanly. He had been too sensitive, too nervous; none of them had ever valued him properly or understood him, he said. He had never had a real friend in the world, I think; he had never had a success. He had shirked games and failed examinations. "It's like that with some people," he said; "whenever I got into the examination-room or anywhere everything seemed to go." Engaged to be married of course—to another over-sensitive person, I suppose—when the indiscretion with the gas escape ended his affairs. "And where are you now?" I asked. "Not in—?"

'He wasn't clear on that point at all. The impression he gave me was of a sort of vague, intermediate state, a special reserve for souls too non-existent for anything so positive as either sin or virtue. I don't know. He was much too egotistical and unobservant to give me any clear idea of the kind of place, kind of country, there is on the Other Side of Things. Wherever he was, he seems to have fallen in with a set of kindred spirits: ghosts of weak Cockney young men, who were on a footing of Christian names, and among these there was certainly a lot of talk about "going haunting" and things like that. Yes—going haunting! They seemed to think "haunting" a tremendous adventure, and most of them funked it all the time. And so primed, you know, he had come.'

'But really!' said Wish to the fire.

'These are the impressions he gave me, anyhow,' said Clayton, modestly. 'I may, of course, have been in a rather uncritical state, but that was the sort of background he gave to himself. He kept flitting up and down, with his thin voice going—talking, talking about his wretched self, and never a word of clear, firm statement from first to last. He was thinner and sillier and more pointless than if he had been real and alive. Only then, you know, he would not have been in my bedroom here—if he *had* been alive. I should have kicked him out.'

'Of course,' said Evans, 'there *are* poor mortals like that.'

'And there's just as much chance of their having ghosts as the rest of us,' I admitted.

'What gave a sort of point to him, you know, was the fact that he did seem within limits to have found himself out. The mess he had made of haunting had depressed him terribly. He had been told it would be a "lark": he had come expecting it to be a "lark," and here it was, nothing but another failure added to his record! He proclaimed himself an utter out-and-out failure, He said, and I can quite believe it, that he had never tried to do anything all his life that he hadn't made a perfect mess of—and through all the wastes of eternity he never would. If he had had sympathy, perhaps—He paused at that, and stood regarding me. He remarked that, strange as it might seem to me, nobody, not anyone, ever, had given him the amount of sympathy I was doing now. I could see what he wanted straight away, and I determined to head him off at once. I may be a brute, you know, but being the Only Real Friend, the recipient of the confidences of one of these egotistical weaklings, ghost or body, is beyond my physical endurance. I got up briskly. "Don't you brood on these things too much," I said. "The thing you've got to do is to get out of this—get out of this sharp. You pull yourself together and *try*." "I can't," he said. "You try," I said, and try he did.'

'Try!' said Sanderson. '*How?*'

'Passes,' said Clayton.

'Passes?'

'Complicated series of gestures and passes with the hands. That's how he had come in and that's how he had to get out again. Lord! what a business I had!'

'But how could *any* series of passes—' I began.

'My dear man,' said Clayton, turning on me and putting a great emphasis on certain words, 'you want *everything* clear. I don't know *how*. All I know is that you *do*—that *he* did, anyhow, at least. After a fearful time, you know, he got his passes right and suddenly disappeared.'

'Did you,' said Sanderson slowly, 'observe the passes?'

'Yes,' said Clayton, and seemed to think. 'It was tremendously queer,' he said. 'There we were, I and this thin vague ghost, in that silent room, in this silent, empty inn, in this silent little Friday-night town. Not a sound except our voices and a faint panting he made when he swung. There was the bedroom candle, and one candle on the dressing-table alight, that was all—sometimes one or other would flare up into a tall, lean, astonished flame for a space. And queer things happened. "I can't," he said; "I shall never—!" And suddenly he sat down on a little chair at the foot of the bed and began to sob and sob. Lord! what a harrowing, whimpering thing he seemed!

' "You pull yourself together," I said, and tried to pat him on the back, and . . . my confounded hand went through him! By that time, you know, I wasn't nearly so—massive as I had been on the landing. I got the queerness of it full. I remember snatching back my hand out of him, as it were, with a little thrill, and walking over to the dressing-table. "You pull yourself together," I said to him, "and try." And in order to encourage and help him I began to try as well.'

'What!' said Sanderson, 'the passes?'

'Yes, the passes.'

'But—' I said, moved by an idea that eluded me for a space.

'This is interesting,' said Sanderson, with his finger in his pipe-bowl. 'You mean to say this ghost of yours gave way—'

'Did his level best to give away the whole confounded barrier? *Yes.*'

'He didn't,' said Wish; 'he couldn't. Or you'd have gone there too.'

'That's precisely it,' I said, finding my elusive idea put into words for me.

'That *is* precisely it,' said Clayton, with thoughtful eyes upon the fire.

For just a little while there was silence.

'And at last he did it?' said Sanderson.

'At last he did it. I had to keep him up to it hard, but he did it at last—rather suddenly. He despaired, we had a scene, and then he got up abruptly and asked me to go through the whole performance, slowly, so that he might see. "I believe," he said, "if I could *see* I should spot what was wrong at once." And he did. "*I* know," he said. "What do you know?" said I. "I know,' he repeated. Then he said, peevishly, "I *can't* do it, if you look at me—I really *can't;* it's been that, partly, all along. I'm such a nervous fellow that you put me out." Well, we had a bit of an argument. Naturally I wanted to see; but he was as obstinate as a mule, and suddenly I had come over as tired as a dog—he tired me out. "All right," I said, "I won't look at you," and turned towards the mirror, on the wardrobe, by the bed.

'He started off very fast. I tried to follow him by looking in the looking-glass, to see just what it was had hung. Round went his arms and his hands, so, and so, and so, and then with a rush came to the last gesture of all—you stand erect and open out your arms—and so, don't you know, he stood. And then he didn't! He didn't! He wasn't! I wheeled round from the looking-glass to him. There was nothing! I was alone, with the flaring candles and a staggering mind. What had happened? Had anything happened? Had I been dreaming? . . . And then, with an absurd note of finality about it, the clock upon the landing discovered the moment was ripe for striking *one*. So!—Ping! And I was as grave and sober as a judge, with all my champagne and whisky gone into the vast serene. Feeling queer, you know—confoundedly *queer*! Queer! Good Lord!'

He regarded his cigar-ash for a moment. 'That's all that happened,' he said.

'And then you went to bed?' asked Evans.

'What else was there to do?'

I looked Wish in the eye. We wanted to scoff, and there was something, something perhaps in Clayton's voice and manner, that hampered our desire.

'And about these passes?' said Sanderson

'I believe I could do them now.'

'Oh!' said Sanderson, and produced a pen-knife and set himself to grub the dottel out of the bowl of his clay.

'Why don't you do them now?' said Sanderson, shutting his penknife with a click.

'That's what I'm going to do,' said Clayton.

'They won't work,' said Evans.

'If they do—' I suggested.

'You know, I'd rather you didn't,' said Wish, stretching out his legs.

'Why?' asked Evans.

'I'd rather he didn't,' said Wish.

'But he hasn't got 'em right,' said Sanderson, plugging too much tobacco into his pipe.

'All the same, I'd rather he didn't,' said Wish.

We argued with Wish. He said that for Clayton to go through those gestures was like mocking a serious matter. 'But you don't believe—?' I said. Wish glanced at Clayton, who was staring into the fire, weighing something in his mind. 'I do—more than half, anyhow, I do,' said Wish.

'Clayton,' said I, 'you're too good a liar for us. Most of it was all right. But that disappearance . . . happened to be convincing. Tell us, it's a tale of cock and bull.'

He stood up without heeding me, took the middle of the hearth-rug, and faced me. For a moment he regarded his feet thoughtfully, and then for all the rest of the time his eyes were on the opposite wall, with an intent expression. He raised his two hands slowly to the level of his eyes and so began. . . .

Now, Sanderson is a Freemason, a member of the lodge of the Four Kings, which devotes itself so ably to the study and elucidation of all the mysteries of Masonry past and present, and among the students of this lodge Sanderson is by no means the least. He followed Clayton's motions with a singular interest in his reddish eye. 'That's not bad,' he said, when it was done. 'You really do, you know, put things together, Clayton, in a most amazing fashion. But there's one little detail out.'

'I know,' said Clayton. 'I believe I could tell you which.'

'Well?'

'This,' said Clayton, and did a queer little twist and writhing and thrust of the hands.

'Yes.'

'That, you know, was what *he* couldn't get right,' said Clayton. 'But how do *you*—?'

'Most of this business, and particularly how you invented it, I don't understand at all,' said Sanderson, 'but just that phase—I do.' He reflected. 'These happen to be a series of gestures—connected with a certain branch of esoteric Masonry—Probably you know. Or else—*How*?' He reflected still further. 'I do not see I can do any harm in telling you just the proper twist. After all, if you know, you know; if you don't, you don't.'

'I know nothing,' said Clayton, 'except what the poor devil let out last night.'

'Well, anyhow,' said Sanderson, and placed his churchwarden very carefully upon the shelf over the fireplace. Then very rapidly he gesticulated with his hands.

'So?' said Clayton, repeating.

'So,' said Sanderson, and took his pipe in hand again.

'Ah, *now*,' said Clayton, 'I can do the whole thing—right.'

He stood up before the waning fire and smiled at us all. But I think there was just a little hesitation in his smile. 'If I begin—' he said.

'I wouldn't begin,' said Wish.

'It's all right!' said Evans. 'Matter is indestructible. You don't think any jiggery-pokery of this sort is going to snatch Clayton into the world of shades. Not it! You may try, Clayton, so far as I'm concerned, until your arms drop off at the wrists.'

'I don't believe that,' said Wish, and stood up and put his arm on Clayton's shoulder. 'You've made me half believe in that story somehow, and I don't want to see the thing done.'

'Goodness!' said I, 'here's Wish frightened!'

'I am,' said Wish, with real or admirably feigned intensity. 'I believe that if he goes through these motions right he'll go.'

'He'll not do anything of the sort,' I cried. 'There's only one way out of this world for men, and Clayton is thirty years from that. Besides . . . And such a ghost! Do you think—?'

Wish interrupted me by moving. He walked out from among our chairs and stopped beside the table and stood there. 'Clayton,' he said, 'you're a fool.'

Clayton, with a humorous light in his eyes, smiled back at him. 'Wish,' he said, 'is right and all you others are wrong. I shall go. I shall get to the end of these passes, and as the last swish whistles through the air, Presto!—this hearthrug will be vacant, the room will be blank amazement, and a respectably dressed gentleman of fifteen stone will plump into the world of shades. I'm certain. So will you be. I decline to argue further. Let the thing be tried.'

'*No*,' said Wish, and made a step and ceased, and Clayton raised his hands once more to repeat the spirit's passing.

By that time, you know, we were all in a state of tension—largely because of the behaviour of Wish. We sat all of us with our eyes on Clayton—I, at least, with a sort of tight, stiff feeling about me as though from the back of my skull to the middle of my thighs my body had been changed to steel. And there, with a gravity that was imperturbably serene, Clayton bowed and swayed and waved his hands and arms before us. As he drew towards the end one piled up, one tingled in one's teeth. The last gesture, I have said, was to swing the arms out wide open, with the face held up. And when at last he swung out to this closing gesture I ceased even to breathe. It was ridiculous, of course, but you know that ghost-story feeling. It was after dinner, in a queer, old shadowy house. Would he, after all—?

There he stood for one stupendous moment, with his arms open and his upturned face, assured and bright, in the glare of the hanging lamp. We hung through that moment as if it were an age, and then came from all of us something that was half a sigh of infinite relief and half a reassuring '*No!*' For visibly—he wasn't going. It was all nonsense. He had told an idle story, and carried it almost to conviction, that was all! . . . And then in that moment the face of Clayton changed.

It changed. It changed as a lit house changes when its lights are suddenly extinguished. His eyes were suddenly eyes that were fixed, his smile was frozen on his lips, and he stood there still. He stood there, very gently swaying.

That moment, too, was an age. And then, you know, chairs were scraping, things were falling, and we were all moving. His knees seemed to give, and he fell forward, and Evans rose and caught him in his arms. . . .

It stunned us all. For a minute I suppose no one said a coherent thing. We believed it, yet could not believe. . . . I came out of a muddled stupefaction to find myself kneeling beside him, and his vest and shirt were torn open, and Sanderson's hand lay on his heart. . . .

Well—the simple fact before us could very well wait our convenience; there was no hurry for us to comprehend. It lay there for an hour; it lies athwart my memory, black and amazing still, to this day. Clayton had, indeed, passed into the world that lies so near to and so far from our own, and he had gone thither by the only road that mortal man may take. But whether he did indeed pass there by that poor ghost's incantation, or whether he was stricken suddenly by apoplexy in the midst of an idle tale—as the coroner's jury would have us believe—is no matter for my judging; it is just one of those inexplicable riddles that must remain unsolved until the final solution of all things shall come. All I certainly know is that, in the very moment, in the very instant, of concluding those passes, he changed, and staggered, and fell down before us—dead!

MR SKELMERSDALE
IN FAIRYLAND

'THERE'S a man in that shop,' said the Doctor, 'who has been in Fairyland.'

'Nonsense!' I said, and stared back at the shop. It was the usual village shop, post-office, telegraph wire on its brow, zinc pans and brushes outside, boots, shirtings, and potted meats in the window. 'Tell me about it,' I said, after a pause.

'*I* don't know,' said the Doctor. 'He's an ordinary sort of lout—Skelmersdale is his name. But everybody about here believes it like Bible truth.'

I reverted presently to the topic.

'I know nothing about it,' said the Doctor, 'and I don't *want* to know. I attended him for a broken finger—Married and Single cricket match—and that's when I struck the nonsense. That's all. But it shows you the sort of stuff I have to deal with, anyhow, eh? Nice to get modern sanitary ideas into a people like this!'

'Very,' I said in a mildly sympathetic tone, and he went on to tell me about that business of the Bonham drain. Things of that kind, I observe, are apt to weigh on the minds of Medical Officers of Health. I was as sympathetic as I knew how, and when he called the Bonham people 'asses,' I said they were 'thundering asses,' but even that did not allay him.

Afterwards, later in the summer, an urgent desire to seclude myself, while finishing my chapter on Spiritual Pathology—it was really, I believe, stiffer to write than it is to read—took me to Bignor. I lodged at a farmhouse, and presently found myself outside that little general shop again, in search of tobacco. 'Skelmersdale,' said I to myself at the sight of it, and went in.

I was served by a short, but shapely, young man, with a fair downy complexion, good small teeth, blue eyes, and a languid manner.

I scrutinised him curiously. Except for a touch of melancholy in his expression, he was nothing out of the common. He was in the shirt-sleeves and tucked-up apron of his trade, and a pencil was thrust behind his inoffensive ear. Athwart his black waistcoat was a gold chain, from which dangled a bent guinea.

'Nothing more today, sir?' he inquired. He leant forward over my bill as he spoke.

'Are you Mr Skelmersdale?' said I.

'I am, sir,' he said, without looking up.

'Is it true that you have been in Fairyland?'

He looked up at me for a moment with wrinkled brows, with an aggrieved, exasperated face. 'O SHUT it!' he said, and, after a moment of hostility, eye to eye, he went on adding up my bill. 'Four, six and a half,' he said, after a pause. 'Thank you, sir.'

So, unpropitiously, my acquaintance with Mr Skelmersdale began.

Well, I got from that to confidence—through a series of toilsome efforts. I picked him up again in the Village Room, where of a night I went to play billiards after my supper, and mitigate the extreme seclusion from my kind that was so helpful to work during the day. I contrived to play with him and afterwards to talk with him. I found the one subject to avoid was Fairyland. On everything else he was open and amiable in a commonplace sort of way, but on that he had been worried—it was a manifest taboo. Only once in the room did I hear the slightest allusion to his experience in his presence, and that was by a cross-grained farm hand who was losing to him. Skelmersdale had run a break into double figures, which, by the Bignor standards, was uncommonly good play. 'Steady on!' said his adversary. 'None of your fairy flukes!'

Skelmersdale stared at him for a moment, cue in hand, then flung it down and walked out of the room.

'Why can't you leave 'im alone?' said a respectable elder who had been enjoying the game, and in the general murmur of disapproval, the grin of satisfied wit faded from the ploughboy's face.

I scented my opportunity. 'What's this joke?' said I, 'about Fairyland?'

' 'Taint no joke about Fairyland, not to young Skelmersdale,' said the respectable elder, drinking.

A little man with rosy cheeks was more communicative. 'They *do* say, sir,' he said, 'that they took him into Aldington Knoll an' kep' him there a matter of three weeks.'

And with that the gathering was well under way. Once one sheep had started, others were ready enough to follow, and in a little time I had at least the exterior aspect of the Skelmersdale affair. Formerly, before he came to Bignor, he had been in that very similar little shop at Aldington Corner, and there whatever it was did happen had taken place. The story was clear that he had stayed out late one night on the Knoll and vanished for three weeks from the sight of men, and had returned with 'his cuffs as clean as when he started,' and his pockets full of dust and ashes. He returned in a state of moody wretchedness that only slowly passed away, and for many days he would give no account of where it was he had been. The girl he was engaged to at Clapton Hill tried to get it out of him, and threw him over partly because he refused, and partly because, as she said, he fairly gave her the ' 'ump'. And then when, some time after, he let out to some one carelessly that he had been in Fairyland and wanted to go back, and when the thing spread and the simple badinage of the countryside came into play, he threw up his situation abruptly, and came to Bignor to get out of the fuss. But as to what had happened in Fairyland none of these people knew. There the gathering in the Village Room went to pieces like a pack at fault. One said this, and another said that.

Their air in dealing with this marvel was ostensibly critical and sceptical, but I could see a considerable amount of belief showing through their guarded qualifications. I took a line of intelligent interest, tinged with a reasonable doubt of the whole story.

'If Fairyland's inside Aldington Knoll,' I said, 'why don't you dig it out?'

'That's what I says,' said the young ploughboy.

'There's a-many have tried to dig on Aldington Knoll,' said the respectable elder, solemnly, 'one time and another. But there's none as goes about today to tell what they got by digging.'

The unanimity of vague belief that surrounded me was rather impressive; I felt there must surely be *something* at the root of so much conviction, and the already pretty keen curiosity I felt about the real facts of the case was distinctly whetted. If these real facts were to be got from any one, they were to be got from Skelmersdale himself; and I set myself, therefore, still more assiduously to efface the first bad impression I had made and win his confidence to the pitch of voluntary speech. In that endeavour I had a social advantage. Being a person of affability and no apparent employment, and wearing tweeds and knickerbockers, I was naturally classed as an artist in Bignor, and in the remarkable code of social precedence prevalent in Bignor an artist ranks considerably higher than a grocer's assistant. Skelmersdale, like too many of his class, is something of a snob; he had told me to 'SHUT it' only under sudden, excessive provocation, and with, I am certain, a subsequent repentance; he was, I knew, quite glad to be seen walking about the village with me. In due course he accepted the proposal of a pipe and whisky in my rooms readily enough, and there, scenting by some happy instinct that there was trouble of the heart in this, and knowing that confidences beget confidences, I plied him with much of interest and suggestion from my real and fictitious past. And it was after the third whisky of the third visit of that sort, if I remember rightly, *apropos* of some artless expansion of a little affair that had touched and left me in my teens, that he did at last, of his own free will and motion, break the ice. 'It was like that with me,' he said, 'over there at Aldington. It's just that that's so rum. First I didn't care a bit and it was all her, and afterwards, when it was too late, it was, in a manner of speaking, all me.'

I forebore to jump upon this allusion, and so he presently threw out another, and in a little while he was making it as plain as daylight that the one thing he wanted to talk about now was this Fairyland adventure he had sat tight upon for so long. You see, I'd done the trick with him, and from being just another half-incredulous, would-be facetious stranger, I had, by all my wealth of shameless self-exposure, become the possible confidant. He had been bitten by the desire to show that he, too, had lived and felt many things, and the fever was upon him.

He was certainly confoundedly allusive at first, and my eagerness to clear him up with a few precise questions was only equalled and controlled by my anxiety not to get to this sort of thing too soon. But in another meeting or so the basis of confidence was complete; and from first to last I think I got most of the items and aspects—indeed, I got quite a number of times over almost everything that Mr Skelmersdale, with his very limited powers of narration, will ever be able to tell. And so I come to the story of his adventure, and I piece it all together again. Whether it really happened, whether he imagined it or dreamt it, or fell upon it in some strange hallucinatory trance, I do not profess to say. But that he invented it I will not for one moment entertain. The man simply and honestly believes the thing happened as he says it happened; he is transparently incapable of any lie so elaborate and sustained, and in the belief of the simple, yet often keenly penetrating, rustic minds about him I find a very strong confirmation of his sincerity. He believes—and nobody can produce any positive fact to falsify his belief. As for me, with this much of endorsement, I transmit his story—I am a little old now to justify or explain.

He says he went to sleep on Aldington Knoll about ten o'clock one night—it was quite possibly Midsummer Night, though he has never thought of the date, and he cannot be sure within a week or so—and it was a fine night and windless, with a rising moon. I have been at the pains to visit this Knoll thrice since his story grew up under my persuasions, and once I went there in the twilight summer moonrise on what was, perhaps, a similar night to that of his adventure. Jupiter was great and splendid above the moon, and in the north and north-west the sky was green and vividly bright over the sunken sun. The Knoll stands out bare and bleak under the sky, but surrounded at a little distance by dark thickets, and as I went up towards it there was a mighty starting and scampering of ghostly or quite invisible rabbits. Just over the crown of the Knoll, but nowhere else, was a multitudinous thin trumpeting of midges. The Knoll is, I believe, an artificial mound, the tumulus of some great prehistoric chieftain, and surely no man ever chose a more spacious prospect for a sepulchre. Eastward one sees along the hills to Hythe, and thence across the Channel to where, thirty miles and more, perhaps, away, the great white lights by Gris Nez and Boulogne wink and pass and shine. Westward lies the whole tumbled valley of the Weald, visible as far as Hindhead and Leith Hill, and the valley of the Stour opens the Downs in the north to interminable hills beyond Wye. All Romney Marsh lies southward at one's feet, Dymchurch and Romney and Lydd, Hastings and its hill are in the middle distance, and the hills multiply vaguely far beyond where Eastbourne rolls up to Beachy Head.

And out upon all this it was that Skelmersdale wandered, being troubled in his earlier love affair, and as he says, 'not caring *where* he went.' And there he sat down to think it over, and so, sulking and grieving, was overtaken by sleep. And so he fell into the fairies' power.

The quarrel that had upset him was some trivial matter enough between himself and the girl at Clapton hill to whom he was engaged. She was a farmer's daughter, said Skelmersdale, and 'very respectable,' and no doubt an excellent match for him; but both girl and lover were very young and with just that mutual jealousy, that intolerantly keen edge of criticism, that irrational hunger for a beautiful perfection, that life and wisdom do presently and most mercifully dull. What the precise matter of quarrel was I have no idea. She may have said she liked men in gaiters when he hadn't any gaiters on, or he may have said he liked her better in a different sort of hat, but however it began, it got by a series of clumsy stages to bitterness and tears. She no doubt got tearful and smeary, and he grew dusty and drooping, and she parted with invidious comparisons, grave doubts whether she ever had *really* cared for him, and a clear certainty she would never care again. And with this sort of thing upon his mind he came out upon Aldington Knoll grieving, and presently, after a long interval, perhaps, quite inexplicably fell asleep.

He woke to find himself on a softer turf than ever he had slept on before, and under the shade of very dark trees that completely hid the sky. Always, indeed, in Fairyland the sky is hidden, it seems. Except for one night when the fairies were dancing, Mr Skelmersdale, during all his time with them, never saw a star. And of that night I am in doubt whether he was in Fairyland proper or out where the rings and rushes are, in those low meadows near the railway line at Smeeth.

But it was light under these trees for all that, and on the leaves and amidst the turf shone a multitude of glow-worms, very bright and fine. Mr Skelmersdale's first impression was that he was *small,* and the next that quite a number of people still smaller were standing all about him. For some reason, he says, he was neither surprised nor frightened, but sat up quite deliberately and rubbed the sleep out of his eyes. And there all about him stood the smiling elves who had caught him sleeping under their privileges and had brought him into Fairyland.

What these elves were like I have failed to gather, so vague and imperfect is his vocabulary, and so unobservant of all minor detail does he seem to have been. They were clothed in something very light and beautiful, that was neither wool, nor silk, nor leaves, nor the petals of flowers. They stood all about him as he sat and waked, and down the glade towards him, down a glow-worm avenue and fronted by a star, came at once that Fairy Lady who is the chief personage of his memory and tale. Of her I gathered more. She was clothed in filmy green, and about her little waist was a broad silver girdle. Her hair waved back from her forehead on either side; there were curls not too wayward and yet astray, and on her brow was a little tiara, set with a single star. Her sleeves were some sort of open sleeves that gave little glimpses of her arms; her throat, I think, was a little displayed, because he speaks of the beauty of her neck and chin. There was a necklace of coral about her white throat, and in her breast a coral-coloured flower. She had the soft lines of a little child in her chin and cheeks and throat. And her eyes, I gather, were of a kindled brown, very soft and straight and sweet under her level brows. You see by these particulars how greatly this lady must have loomed in Mr Skelmersdale's picture. Certain things he tried to express and could not express; 'the way she moved,' he said several times; and I fancy a sort of demure joyousness radiated from this Lady.

And it was in the company of this delightful person, as the guest and chosen companion of this delightful person, that Mr Skelmersdale set out to be taken into the intimacies of Fairyland. She welcomed him gladly and a little warmly. I suspect a pressure of his hand in both of hers and a lit face to his. After all, ten years ago young Skelmersdale may have been a very comely youth. And once she took his arm, and once, I think, she led him by the hand adown the glade that the glow-worms lit.

Just how things chanced and happened there is no telling from Mr Skelmersdale's disarticulated skeleton of description. He gives little unsatisfactory glimpses of strange corners and doings, of places where there were many fairies together, of 'toadstool things that shone pink,' of fairy food, of which he could only say 'you should have tasted it!' and of fairy music, 'like a little musical box,' that came out of nodding flowers. There was a great open place where fairies rode and raced on 'things,' but what Mr Skelmersdale meant by 'these here things they rode,' there is no telling. Larvae, perhaps, or crickets, or the little beetles that elude us so abundantly. There was a place where water splashed and gigantic king-cups grew, and there in the hotter times the fairies bathed together. There were games being played and dancing and much elvish love-making, too, I think, among the moss branch thickets. There can be no doubt that the Fairy Lady made love to Mr Skelmersdale, and no doubt either that this young man set himself to resist her. A time came, indeed, when she sat on a bank beside him, in a quiet secluded place 'all smelling of vi'lets,' and talked to him of love.

'When her voice went low and she whispered,' said Mr Skelmersdale, 'and laid 'er 'and on my 'and, you know, and came close with a soft, warm friendly way she 'ad, it was as much as I could do to keep my 'ead.'

It seems he kept his head to a certain limited unfortunate extent. He saw ' 'ow the wind was blowing,' he says, and so, sitting there in a place all smelling of violets, with the touch of this lovely Fairy Lady about him, Mr Skelmersdale broke it to her gently—that he was engaged!

She had told him she loved him dearly, that he was a sweet human lad for her, and whatever he would ask of her he should have— even his heart's desire.

And Mr Skelmersdale, who, I fancy, tried hard to avoid looking at her little lips as they just dropped apart and came together, led up to the more intimate question by saying he would like enough capital to start a little shop. He'd just like to feel, he said, he had money enough to do that. I imagine a little surprise in those brown eyes he talked about, but she seemed sympathetic for all that, and she asked him many questions about the little shop, 'laughing like' all the time. So he got to the complete statement of his affianced position, and told her all about Millie.

'All?' said I.

'Everything,' said Mr Skelmersdale, 'just who she was, and where she lived, and everything about her. I sort of felt I 'ad to all the time, I did.'

' "Whatever you want you shall have," said the Fairy Lady. "That's as good as done. You shall feel you have the money just as you wish. And now, you know—*you must kiss me*." '

And Mr Skelmersdale pretended not to hear the latter part of her remark, and said she was very kind. That he really didn't deserve she should be so kind. And The Fairy Lady suddenly came quite close to him and whispered 'Kiss me!'

'And,' said Mr Skelmersdale, 'like a fool, I did.'

There are kisses and kisses, I am told, and this must have been quite the other sort from Millie's resonant signals of regard. There was something magic in that kiss; assuredly it marked a turning point. At any rate, this is one of the passages that he thought sufficiently important to describe most at length. I have tried to get it right, I have tried to disentangle it from the hints and gestures through which it came to me, but I have no doubt that it was all different from my telling and far finer and sweeter, in the soft filtered light and the subtly stirring silences of the fairy glades. The Fairy Lady asked him more about Millie, and was she very lovely, and so on—a great many times. As to Millie's loveliness, I conceive him answering that she was 'all right.' And then, or on some such occasion, the Fairy Lady told him she had fallen in love with him as he slept in the moonlight, and so he had been brought into Fairyland, and she had thought, not knowing of Millie, that perhaps he might chance to love her. 'But now you know you can't,' she said, 'so you must stop with me just a little while, and then you must go back to Millie.' She told him that, and you know Skelmersdale was already in love with her, but the pure inertia of his mind kept him in the way he was going. I imagine him sitting in a sort of stupefaction amidst all these glowing beautiful things, answering about his Millie and the little shop he projected and the need of a horse and cart. . . . And that absurd state of affairs must have gone on for days and days. I see this little lady, hovering about him and trying to amuse him, too dainty to understand his complexity and too tender to let him go. And he, you know, hypnotised as it were by his earthly position, went his way with her hither and thither, blind to everything in Fairy land but this wonderful intimacy that had come to him. It is hard, it is impossible, to give in print the effect of her radiant sweetness shining through the jungle of poor Skelmersdale's rough and broken sentences. To me, at least, she shone clear amidst the muddle of his story like a glow-worm in a tangle of weeds.

There must have been many days of things while all this was happening—and once, I say, they danced under the moonlight in the fairy rings that stud the meadows near Smeeth—but at last it all came to an end. She led him into a great cavernous place, lit by 'a red nightlight sort of thing,' where there were coffers piled on coffers, and cups and golden boxes, and a great heap of what certainly seemed to all Mr Skelmersdale's senses—coined gold. There were little gnomes amidst this wealth, who saluted her at her coming, and stood aside. And suddenly she turned on him there with brightly shining eyes.

'And now,' she said, 'you have been kind to stay with me so long, and it is time I let you go. You must go back to your Millie. You must go back to your Millie, and here—just as I promised you—they will give you gold.'

'She choked like,' said Mr Skelmersdale. 'At that, I had a sort of feeling—' (he touched his breastbone) 'as though I was fainting here. I felt pale, you know, and shivering, and even then—I 'adn't a thing to say.'

He paused. 'Yes,' I said.

The scene was beyond his describing. But I know that she kissed him goodbye.

'And you said nothing?'

'Nothing,' he said. 'I stood like a stuffed calf. She just looked back once, you know, and stood smiling like and crying—I could see the shine of her eyes—and then she was gone, and there was all these little fellows bustling about me, stuffing my 'ands and my pockets and the back of my collar and everywhere with gold.'

And then it was, when the Fairy Lady had vanished, that Mr Skelmersdale really understood and knew. He suddenly began plucking out the gold they were thrusting upon him, and shouting out at them to prevent their giving him more. ' "I don't *want* yer gold," I said. "I 'aven't done yet. I'm not going. I want to speak to that Fairy Lady again." I started off to go after her and they held me back. Yes, stuck their little 'ands against my middle and shoved me back. They kept giving me more and more gold until it was running all down my trouser legs and dropping out of my 'ands. "I don't *want* yer gold," I says to them, "I want just to speak to the Fairy Lady again." '

'And did you?'

'It came to a tussle.'

'Before you saw her?'

'I didn't see her. When I got out from them she wasn't anywhere to be seen.'

So he ran in search of her out of this red-lit cave, down a long grotto, seeking her, and thence he came out in a great and desolate place athwart which a swarm of will-o'-the-wisps were flying to and fro. And about him elves were dancing in derision, and the little gnomes came out of the cave after him, carrying gold in handfuls and casting it after him, shouting, 'Fairy love and fairy gold! Fairy love and fairy gold!'

And when he heard these words, came a great fear that it was all over, and he lifted up his voice and called to her by her name, and suddenly set himself to run down the slope from the mouth of the cavern, through a place of thorns and briers, calling after her very loudly and often. The elves danced about him unheeded, pinching him and pricking him, and the will-o'-the-wisps circled round him and dashed into his face, and the gnomes pursued him shouting and pelting him with fairy gold. As he ran with all this strange rout about him and distracting him, suddenly he was knee-deep in a swamp, and suddenly he was amidst thick twisted roots, and he caught his foot in one and stumbled and fell. . . .

He fell and he rolled over, and in that instant he found himself sprawling upon Aldington Knoll, all lonely under the stars.

He sat up sharply at once, he says, and found he was very stiff and cold, and his clothes were damp with dew. The first pallor of dawn and a chilly wind were coming up together. He could have believed the whole thing a strangely vivid dream until he thrust his hand into his side pocket and found it stuffed with ashes. Then he knew for certain it was fairy gold they had given him. He could feel all their pinches and pricks still, though there was never a bruise upon him. And in that manner, and so suddenly, Mr Skelmersdale came out of Fairyland back into this world of men. Even then he fancied the thing was but the matter of a night until he returned to the shop at Aldington Corner and discovered amidst their astonishment that he had been away three weeks.

'Lor! the trouble I 'ad!' said Mr Skelmersdale.

'How?'

'Explaining. I suppose you've never had anything like that to explain.'

'Never,' I said, and he expatiated for a time on the behaviour of this person and that. One name he avoided for a space.

'I expect she seemed changed?'

'Everyone was changed. Changed for good. Every one seemed big, you know, and coarse. And their voices seemed loud. Why, the sun, when it rose in the morning, fair hit me in the eye!'

'And Millie?' said I at last.

'I didn't seem to care a bit for seeing Millie,' he said.

'And Millie?'

'I didn't want to see Millie.'

'And when you did?'

'I came up against her Sunday, coming out of church. "Where you been?" she said, and I saw there was a row. *I* didn't care if there was. I seemed to forget about her even while she was there a-talking to me. She was just nothing. I couldn't make out whatever I 'ad seen in 'er ever, or what there could 'ave been. Sometimes when she wasn't about, I did get back a little, but never when she was there. Then it was always the other came up and blotted her out. . . . Any 'ow, it didn't break her heart.'

'Married?' I asked.

'Married 'er cousin,' said Mr Skelmersdale, and reflected on the pattern of the tablecloth for a space.

When he spoke again it was clear that his former sweetheart had clean vanished from his mind, and that the talk had brought back the Fairy Lady triumphant in his heart. He talked of her—soon he was letting out the oddest things, queer love secrets it would be treachery to repeat. I think, indeed, that was the queerest thing in the whole affair, to hear that neat little grocer man after his story was done, with a glass of whisky beside him and a cigar between his fingers, witnessing, with sorrow still, though now, indeed, with a time-blunted anguish, of the inappeasable hunger of the heart that presently came upon him. 'I couldn't eat,' he said, 'I couldn't sleep. I made mistakes in orders and got mixed with change. There she was day and night, drawing me and drawing me. Oh, I wanted her. Lord! how I wanted her! I was up there, most evenings I was up there on the Knoll, often even when it rained. I used to walk over the Knoll and round it and round it, calling for them to let me in. Shouting. Near blubbering I was at times. Daft I was and miserable. I kept on saying it was all a mistake. And every Sunday afternoon I went up there, wet and fine, though I knew as well as you do it wasn't no good by day. And I've tried to go to sleep there.'

He stopped sharply and decided to drink some whisky.

'I've tried to go to sleep there,' he said, and I could swear his lips trembled. 'I've tried to go to sleep there, often and often. And, you, know, I couldn't, sir—never. I've thought if I could go to sleep there, there might be something. . . . But I've sat up there and laid up there, and I couldn't—not for thinking and longing. It's the longing. . . . I've tried—'

He blew, drank up the rest of his whisky spasmodically, stood up suddenly and buttoned his jacket, staring closely and critically at the cheap oleographs beside the mantel meanwhile. The little black note-book in which he recorded the orders of his daily round projected stiffly from his breast pocket. When all the buttons were quite done, he patted his chest and turned on me suddenly. 'Well,' he said, 'I must be going.'

There was something in his eyes and manner that was too difficult for him to express in words. 'One gets talking,' he said at last at the door, and smiled wanly, and so vanished from my eyes. And that is the tale of Mr Skelmersdale in Fairyland just as he told it to me.

THE TRUTH ABOUT PYECRAFT

HE sits not a dozen yards away. If I glance over my shoulder I can see him. And if I catch his eye—and usually I catch his eye—it meets me with an expression—

It is mainly an imploring look—and yet with suspicion in it.

Confound his suspicion! If I wanted to tell on him I should have told long ago. I don't tell and I don't tell, and he ought to feel at his ease. As if anything so gross and fat as he could feel at ease! Who would believe me if I did tell?

Poor old Pyecraft! Great, uneasy jelly of substance! The fattest clubman in London.

He sits at one of the little club tables in the huge bay by the fire, stuffing. What is he stuffing? I glance judiciously and catch him biting at a round of hot buttered tea-cake, with his eyes on me. Confound him!—with his eyes on me!

That settles it, Pyecraft. Since you *will* be abject, since you *will* behave as though I was not a man of honour, here, right under your embedded eyes, I write the thing down—the plain truth about Pyecraft. The man I helped, the man I shielded, and who has requited me by making my club unendurable, absolutely unendurable, with his liquid appeal, with the perpetual 'don't tell' of his looks.

And, besides, why does he keep on eternally eating?

Well, here goes for the truth, the whole truth, and nothing but the truth!

Pyecraft—I made the acquaintance of Pyecraft in this very smoking-room. I was a young, nervous new member, and he saw it. I was sitting all alone, wishing I knew more of the members, and suddenly he came, a great rolling front of chins and abdomina, towards me, and grunted and sat down in a chair close by me and wheezed for a space, and scraped for a space with a match and lit a cigar, and then addressed me. I forget what he said—something about the matches not lighting properly, and afterwards as he talked he kept stopping the waiters one by one as they went by, and telling them about the matches in that thin, fluty voice he has. But, anyhow, it was in some such way we began our talking.

He talked about various things and came round to games. And thence to my figure and complexion. 'You ought to be a good cricketer,' he said. I suppose I am slender, slender to what some people would call lean, and I suppose I am rather dark, still—I am not ashamed of having a Hindu great-grandmother, but, for all that, I don't want casual strangers to see through me at a glance to *her*. So that I was set against Pyecraft from the beginning.

But he only talked about me in order to get to himself.

'I expect,' he said, 'you take no more exercise than I do, and probably you eat no less.' (Like all excessively obese people he fancied he ate nothing.) 'Yet'—and he smiled an oblique smile—'we differ.'

And then he began to talk about his fatness and his fatness; all he did for his fatness and all he was going to do for his fatness; what people had advised him to do for his fatness and what he had heard of people doing for fatness similar to his. '*A priori*,' he said, 'one would think a question of nutrition could be answered by dietary and a question of assimilation by drugs.' It was stifling. It was dumpling talk. It made me feel swelled to hear him.

One stands that sort of thing once in a way at a club, but a time came when I fancied I was standing too much. He took to me altogether too conspicuously. I could never go into the smoking-room but he would come wallowing towards me, and sometimes he came and gormandised round and about me while I had my lunch. He seemed at times almost to be clinging to me. He was a bore, but not so fearful a bore as to be limited to me; and from the first there was something in his manner—almost as though he knew, almost as though he penetrated to the fact that I *might*—that there was a remote, exceptional chance in me that no one else presented.

'I'd give anything to get it down,' he would say—'anything,' and peer at me over his vast cheeks and pant.

Poor old Pyecraft! He has just gonged, no doubt to order another buttered tea-cake!

He came to the actual thing one day. 'Our Pharmacopœia,' he said, 'our Western Pharmacopœia is anything but the last word of medical science. In the East, I've been told—'

He stopped and stared at me. It was like being at an aquarium.

I was quite suddenly angry with him. 'Look here,' I said, 'who told you about my great-grandmother's recipes?'

'Well,' he fenced.

'Every time we've met for a week,' I said—'and we've met pretty often—you've given me a broad hint or so about that little secret of mine.'

'Well,' he said, 'now the cat's out of the bag, I'll admit, yes, it is so. I had it—'

'From Pattison?'

'Indirectly,' he said, which I believe was lying, 'yes'

'Pattison,' I said, 'took that stuff at his own risk.'

He pursed his mouth and bowed.

'My great-grandmother's recipes,' I said, 'are queer things to handle. My father was near making me promise—'

'He didn't?'

'No. But he warned me. He himself used one—once.'

'Ah ! . . . But do you think—? Suppose—suppose there did happen to be one—'

'The things are curious documents,' I said. 'Even the smell of 'em. . . . No!'

But after going so far Pyecraft was resolved I should go farther. I was always a little afraid if I tried his patience too much he would fall on me suddenly and smother me. I own I was weak. But I was also annoyed with Pyecraft. I had got to that state of feeling for him that disposed me to say, 'Well, *take* the risk!' The little affair of Pattison to which I have alluded was a different matter altogether. What it was doesn't concern us now, but I knew, anyhow, that the particular recipe I used then was safe. The rest I didn't know so much about, and, on the whole, I was inclined to doubt their safety pretty completely.

Yet even if Pyecraft got poisoned—

I must confess the poisoning of Pyecraft struck me as an immense undertaking.

That evening I took that queer, odd-scented sandalwood box out of my safe and turned the rustling skins over. The gentleman who wrote the recipes for my great-grandmother evidently had a weakness for skins of a miscellaneous origin, and his handwriting was cramped to the last degree. Some of the things are quite unreadable to me—though my family, with its Indian Civil Service associations, has kept up a knowledge of Hindustani from generation to generation—and none are absolutely plain sailing. But I found the one that I knew was there soon enough, and sat on the floor by my safe for some time looking at it.

'Look here,' said I to Pyecraft next day, and snatched the slip away from his eager grasp.

'So far as I can make it out, this is a, recipe for Loss of Weight. ('Ah!' said Pyecraft.) I'm not absolutely sure, but I think it's that. And if you take my advice you'll leave it alone. Because, you know—I blacken my blood in your interest, Pyecraft—my ancestors on that side were, so far as I can gather, a jolly queer lot. See?'

'Let me try it,' said Pyecraft.

I leant back in my chair. My imagination made one mighty effort and fell flat within me. 'What in Heaven's name, Pyecraft,' I asked, 'do you think you'll look like when you get thin?'

He was impervious to reason. I made him promise never to say a word to me about his disgusting fatness again whatever happened—never, and then I handed him that little piece of skin.

'It's nasty stuff,' I said.

'No matter,' he said, and took it.

He goggled at it. 'But—but—' he said.

He had just discovered that it wasn't English.

'To the best of my ability,' I said, 'I will do you a translation.'

I did my best. After that we didn't speak for a fortnight. Whenever he approached me I frowned and motioned him away, and he respected our compact, but at the end of the fortnight he was as fat as ever. And then he got a word in.

'I must speak,' he said. 'It isn't fair. There's something wrong. It's done me no good. You're not doing your great-grandmother justice.'

'Where's the recipe?'

He produced it gingerly from his pocket-book.

I ran my eye over the items. 'Was the egg addled?' I asked.

'No. Ought it to have been?'

'That,' I said, 'goes without saying in all my poor dear, great-grandmother's recipes. When condition or quality is not specified you must get the worst. She was drastic or nothing. . . . And there's one or two possible alternatives to some of these other things. You got *fresh* rattlesnake venom?'

'I got a rattlesnake from Jamrach's. It cost—it cost—'

'That's your affair, anyhow. This last item—'

'I know a man who—'

'Yes. H'm. Well, I'll write the alternatives down. So far as I know the language, the spelling of this recipe is particularly atrocious. By the bye, dog here probably means pariah dog.'

For a month after that I saw Pyecraft constantly at the club and as fat and anxious as ever. He kept our treaty, but at times he broke the spirit of it by shaking his head despondently. Then one day in the cloakroom he said, 'Your great-grandmother—'

'Not a word against her,' I said; and he held his peace.

I could have fancied he had desisted, and I saw him one day talking to three new members about his fatness as though he was in search of ether recipes. And then, quite unexpectedly, his telegram came.

'Mr Formalyn!' bawled a page-boy under my nose, and I took the telegram and opened it at once.

'*For Heaven's sake come.—Pyecraft.*'

'H'm,' said I, and to tell the truth I was so pleased at the rehabilitation of my great-grandmother's reputation this evidently promised that I made a most excellent lunch.

I got Pyecraft's address from the hall porter. Pyecraft inhabited the upper half of a house in Bloomsbury, and I went there so soon as I had done my coffee and Trappistine. I did not wait to finish my cigar.

'Mr Pyecraft?' said I, at the front door.

They believed he was ill; he hadn't been out for two days.

'He expects me,' said I, and they sent me up.

I rang the bell at the lattice-door upon the landing.

'He shouldn't have tried it, anyhow,' I said to myself. 'A man who eats like a pig ought to look like a pig.'

An obviously worthy woman, with an anxious face and a carelessly placed cap, came and surveyed me through the lattice.

I gave my name and she opened his door for me in a dubious fashion.

'Well?' said I, as we stood together inside Pyecraft's piece of the landing.

' 'E said you was to come in if you came,' she said, and regarded me, making no motion to show me anywhere. And then, confidentially, ' 'E's locked in, sir.'

'Locked in?'

'Locked himself in yesterday morning and 'asn't let any one in since, sir. And ever and again *swearing*. Oh, my!'

I stared at the door she indicated by her glances. 'In there?' I said. 'Yes, sir.'

'What's up?'

She shook her head sadly. ' 'E keeps on calling for vittles sir. *'Eavy* vittles 'e wants. I get 'im what I can. Pork 'e's 'ad, sooit puddin', sossiges, noo bread. Everythink like that. Left outside, if you please, and me go away. 'E's eatin', sir, somethink *awful*.'

There came a piping bawl from inside the door; 'That Formalyn?'

'That you, Pyecraft?' I shouted, and went and banged the door.

'Tell her to go away.'

I did.

Then I could hear a curious pattering upon the door, almost like someone feeling for the handle in the dark, and Pyecraft's familiar grunts.

'It's all right,' I said, 'she's gone.'

But for a long time the door didn't open.

I heard the key turn. Then Pyecraft's voice said, 'Come in.'

I turned the handle and opened the door. Naturally I expected to see Pyecraft.

Well, you know, he wasn't there!

I never had such a shock in my life. There was his sitting-room in a state of untidy disorder, plates and dishes among the books and writing things, and several chairs overturned, but Pyecraft—

'It's all right, o' man; shut the door,' he said, and then I discovered him.

There he was right up close to the cornice in the corner by the door, as though someone had glued him to the ceiling. His face was anxious and angry. He panted and gesticulated. 'Shut the door,' he said. 'If that woman gets hold of it—'

I shut the door, and went and stood away from him and stared.

'If anything gives way and you tumble down,' I said, 'you'll break your neck, Pyecraft.'

'I wish I could,' he wheezed.

'A man of your age and weight getting up to kiddish gymnastics—'

'Don't,' he said, and looked agonised. 'Your damned great-grandmother—'

'Be careful,' I warned him.

'I'll tell you,' he said, and gesticulated.

'How the deuce,' said I, 'are you holding on up there?'

And then abruptly I realised that he was not holding on at all, that he was floating up there—just as a gas-filled bladder might have floated in the same position. He began a struggle to thrust himself away from the ceiling and to clamber down the wall to me. It's that prescription,' he panted, as he did so. 'Your great-gran—'

'*No!*' I cried.

He took hold of a framed engraving rather carelessly as he spoke and it gave way, and he flew back to the ceiling again, while the picture smashed on to the sofa. Bump he went against the ceiling, and I knew then why he was all over white on the more salient curves and angles of his person. He tried again more carefully, coming down by way of the mantel.

It was really a most extraordinary spectacle, that great, fat, apoplectic-looking man upside down and trying to get from the ceiling to the floor. 'That prescription,' he said. 'Too successful.'

'How?'

'Loss of weight—almost complete.'

And then, of course, I understood.

'By Jove, Pyecraft,' said I, 'what you wanted was a cure for fatness! But you always called it weight. You would call it weight.'

Somehow I was extremely delighted. I quite liked Pyecraft for the time. 'Let me help you!' I said, and took his hand and pulled him down. He kicked about, trying to get a foothold somewhere. It was very like holding a flag on a windy day.

'That table,' he said, pointing, 'is solid mahogany and very heavy. If you can put me under that—'

I did, and there he wallowed about like a captive balloon, while I stood on his hearthrug and talked to him.

I lit a cigar. 'Tell me,' I said, 'what happened?'

'I took it,' he said.

'How did it taste?'

'Oh, *beastly*!'

I should fancy they all did. Whether one regards the ingredients or the probable compound or the possible results, almost all my great-grandmother's remedies appear to me at least to be extraordinarily uninviting. For my own part—

'I took a little sip first.'

'Yes?'

'And as I felt lighter and better after an hour, I decided to take the draught.'

'My dear Pyecraft!'

'I held my nose,' he explained. 'And then I kept on getting lighter and lighter—and helpless, you know.'

He gave way suddenly to a burst of passion. 'What the goodness am I to *do*?' he said.

'There's one thing pretty evident,' I said, 'that you mustn't do. If you go out of doors you'll go up and up.' I waved an arm upward. 'They'd have to send Santos-Dumont after you to bring you down again.'

'I suppose it will wear off?'

I shook my head. 'I don't think you can count on that,' I said.

And then there was another burst of passion, and he kicked out at adjacent chairs and banged the floor. He behaved just as I should have expected a great, fat, self-indulgent man to behave under trying circumstances—that is to say, very badly. He spoke of me and of my great-grandmother with an utter want of discretion.

'I never asked you to take the stuff,' I said.

And generously disregarding the insults he was putting upon me, I sat down in his arm-chair and began to talk to him in a sober, friendly fashion.

I pointed out to him that this was a trouble he had brought upon himself, and that it had almost an air of poetical justice. He had eaten too much. This he disputed, and for a time we argued the point.

He became noisy and violent, so I desisted from this aspect of his lesson. 'And then,' said I, 'you committed the sin of euphuism. You called it, not Fat, which is just and inglorious, but Weight. You—'

He interrupted to say that he recognised all that. What was he to *do*?

I suggested he should adapt himself to his new conditions. So we came to the really sensible part of the business. I suggested that it would not be difficult for him to learn to walk about on the ceiling with his hands—

'I can't sleep,' he said.

But that was no great difficulty. It was quite possible, I pointed out, to make a shake-up under a wire mattress, fasten the under things on with tapes, and have a blanket, sheet, and coverlet to button at the side. He would have to confide in his housekeeper, I said; and after some squabbling he agreed to that. (Afterwards it was quite delightful to see the beautifully matter-of-fact way with which the good lady took all these amazing inversions.) He could have a library ladder in his room, and all his meals could be laid on the top of his bookcase. We also hit on an ingenious device by which he could get to the floor whenever he wanted, which was simply to put the *British Encyclopædia* (tenth edition) on the top of his open shelves. He just pulled out a couple of volumes and held on, and down he came. And we agreed there must be iron staples along the skirting, so that he could cling to those whenever he wanted to get about the room on the lower level.

As we got on with the thing I found myself almost keenly interested. It was I who called in the housekeeper and broke matters to her, and it was I chiefly who fixed up the inverted bed. In fact, I spent two whole days at his flat. I am a handy, interfering sort of man with a screwdriver, and I made all sorts of ingenious adaptations for him—ran a wire to bring his bells within reach, turned all his electric lights up instead of down, and so on. The whole affair was extremely curious and interesting to me, and it was delightful to think of Pyecraft like some great, fat blow-fly, crawling about on his ceiling and clambering round the lintel of his doors from one room to another, and never, never, never coming to the club any more. . . .

Then, you know, my fatal ingenuity got the better of me. I was sitting by his fire drinking his whisky, and he was up in his favourite corner by the cornice, tacking a Turkey carpet to the ceiling, when the idea struck me. 'By Jove, Pyecraft!' I said, 'all this is totally unnecessary.'

And before I could calculate the complete consequences of my notion I blurted it out. 'Lead underclothing,' said I, and the mischief was done.

Pyecraft received the thing almost in tears. 'To be right ways up again—' he said.

I gave him the whole secret before I saw where it would take me. 'Buy sheet lead,' I said, 'stamp it into discs. Sew 'em all over your underclothes until you have enough. Have lead-soled boots, carry a bag of solid lead, and the thing is done! Instead of being a prisoner here you may go abroad again, Pyecraft; you may travel—'

A still happier idea came to me. 'You need never fear a shipwreck. All you need do is just slip off some or all of your clothes, take the necessary amount of luggage in your hand, and float up in the air—'

In his emotion he dropped the tack-hammer within an ace of my head. 'By Jove!' he said, 'I shall be able to come back to the club again.'

The thing pulled me up short. 'By Jove!' I said, faintly. 'Yes. Of course—you will.'

He did. He does. There he sits behind me now, stuffing—as I live!—a third go of buttered tea-cake. And no one in the whole world knows—except his housekeeper and me—that he weighs practically nothing; that he is a mere boring mass of assimilatory matter, mere clouds in clothing, *niente, nefas,* the most inconsiderable of men. There he sits watching until I have done this writing. Then, if he can, he will waylay me. He will come billowing up to me. . . .

He will tell me over again all about it, how it feels, how it doesn't feel, how he sometimes hopes it is passing off a little. And always somewhere in that fat, abundant discourse he will say, 'The secret's keeping, eh? If any one know of it—I should be so ashamed. . . . Makes a fellow look such a fool, you know. Crawling about on a ceiling and all that. . . .

And now to elude Pyecraft, occupying, as he does, an admirable strategic position between me and the door.

THE MAGIC SHOP

I HAD seen the Magic Shop from afar several times; I had passed it once or twice, a shop window of alluring little objects, magic balls, magic hens, wonderful cones, ventriloquist dolls, the material of the basket trick, packs of cards that *looked* all right, and all that sort of thing, but never had I thought of going in until one day, almost without warning, Gip hauled me by my finger—right up to the window, and so conducted himself that there was nothing for it but to take him in. I had not thought the place was there, to tell the truth—a modest-sized frontage in Regent Street, between the picture shop and the place where the chicks run about just out of patent incubators—but there it was sure enough. I had fancied it was down nearer the Circus, or round the corner in Oxford Street, or even in Holborn; always over the way and a little inaccessible it had been, with something of the mirage in its position; but here it was now quite indisputably, and the fat end of Gip's pointing finger made a noise upon the glass.

'If I was rich,' said Gip, dabbing a finger at the Disappearing Egg, 'I'd buy myself that. And that' which was The Crying Baby, Very Human—'and that,' which was a mystery, and called, so a neat card asserted, 'Buy One and Astonish Your Friends.'

'Anything,' said Gip, 'will disappear under one of those cones. I have read about it in a book.

'And there, dadda, is the Vanishing Halfpenny—only they've put it this way up so's we can't see how it's done.'

Gip, dear boy, inherits his mother's breeding, and he did not propose to enter the shop or worry in any way; only, you know, quite unconsciously he lugged my finger doorward, and he made his interest clear.

'That,' he said, and pointed to the Magic Bottle.

'If you had that?' I said; at which promising inquiry he looked up with a sudden radiance.

'I could show it to Jessie,' he said, thoughtful as ever of others.

It's less than a hundred days to your birthday, Gibbles,' I said, and laid my hand on the door-handle.

Gip made no answer, but his grip tightened on my finger, and so we came into the shop.

It was no common shop this; it was a magic shop, and all the prancing precedence Gip would have taken in the matter of mere toys was wanting. He left the burthen of the conversation to me.

It was a little, narrow shop, not very well lit, and the doorbell pinged again with a plaintive note as we closed it behind us For a moment or so we were alone and could glance about us. There was a tiger in *papier-maché* on the glass case that covered the low counter—a grave, kind-eyed tiger that waggled his head in a methodical manner; there were several crystal spheres, a china hand holding magic cards, a stock of magic fish-bowls in various sizes, and an immodest magic hat that shamelessly displayed its springs. On the floor were magic mirrors: one to draw you out long and thin, one to swell your head and vanish your legs, and one to make you short and fat like a draught; and while we were laughing at these the shopman, as I suppose, came in.

At any rate, there he was behind the counter—a curious, sallow, dark man, with one ear larger than the other and a chin like the toe-cap of a boot.

'What can we have the pleasure?' he said, spreading his long, magic fingers on the glass case; and so with a start we were aware of him.

'I want,' I said, 'to buy my little boy a few simple tricks.'

'Legerdemain?' he asked. 'Mechanical? Domestic?'

'Anything amusing?' said I.

'Um!' said the shopman, and scratched his head for a moment as if thinking. Then, quite distinctly, he drew from his head a glass ball. 'Something in this way?' he said, and held it out.

The action was unexpected. I had seen the trick done at entertainments endless times before—it's part of the common stock of conjurers—but I had not expected it here. 'That's good,' I said, with a laugh.

'Isn't it?' said the shopman.

Gip stretched out his disengaged hand to take this object and found merely a blank palm.

'It's in your pocket,' said the shopman, and there it was!

'How much will that be?' I asked.

'We make no charge for glass balls,' said the shopman, politely. 'We get them'—he picked one out of his elbow as he spoke—'free.' He produced another from the back of his neck, and laid it beside its predecessor on the counter. Gip regarded his glass ball sagely, then directed a look of inquiry at the two on the counter, and finally brought his round-eyed scrutiny to the shopman, who smiled. You may have those too,' said the shopman, 'and if you *don't* mind, one from my mouth—*So!*'

Gip counselled me mutely for a moment, and then in a profound silence put away the four balls, resumed my reassuring finger, and nerved himself for the next event.

'We get all our smaller tricks in that way,' the shopman remarked.

I laughed in the manner of one who subscribes to a jest. 'Instead of going to the wholesale shop,' I said. 'Of course, it's cheaper.'

'In a way,' the shopman said. 'Though we pay in the end. But not so heavily—as people suppose. . . . Our larger tricks, and our daily provisions and all the other things we want, we get out of that hat. . . . And you know, sir, if you'll excuse my saying it, there *isn't* a wholesale shop, not for Genuine Magic goods, sir. I don't know if you noticed our inscription—the Genuine Magic Shop.' He drew a business-card from his cheek and handed it to me. 'Genuine,' he said, with his finger on the word, and added, 'There is absolutely no deception, sir.'

He seemed to be carrying out the joke pretty thoroughly, I thought.

He turned to Gip with a smile of remarkable affability. 'You, you know, are the Right Sort of Boy.'

I was surprised at his knowing that, because, in the interests of discipline, we keep it rather a secret even at home; but Gip received it in unflinching silence, keeping a steadfast eye on him.

It's only the Right Sort of Boy gets through that doorway.

And as if by way of illustration, there came a rattling at the door, and a squeaking little voice could be faintly heard. 'Nyar! I *warn'* a go in there, dadda, I WARN a go in there. Ny-a-a-ah!' and then the accents of a down-trodden parent, urging consolations and propitiations. 'It's locked, Edward,' he said.

'But it isn't,' said I.

'It is, sir,' said the shopman, 'always—for that sort of child,' and as he spoke we had a glimpse of the other youngster, a small, white face, pallid from sweet-eating and over-sapid food, and distorted by evil passions, a ruthless little egotist, pawing at the enchanted pane. 'It's no good, sir,' said the shopman, as I moved, with my natural helpfulness, doorward, and presently the spoilt child was carried off howling.

'How do you manage that?' I said, breathing more freely.

'Magic!' said the shopman, with a careless wave of the hand, and behold! sparks of coloured fire flew out of his fingers and vanished into the shadows of the shop.

'You were saying,' he said, addressing himself to Gip, 'before you came in, that you would like one of our 'Buy One and Astonish Your Friends' boxes?'

Gip, after a gallant effort, said 'Yes.'

'It's in your pocket.'

And leaning over the counter—he really had an extraordinarily long body—this amazing person produced the article in the customary conjurer's manner. 'Paper,' he said, and took a sheet out of the empty hat with the springs; 'string,' and behold his mouth was a string-box, from which he drew an unending thread, which when he had tied his parcel he bit off and, it seemed to me, swallowed the ball of string. And then he lit a candle at the nose of one of the ventriloquist's dummies, stuck one of his fingers (which had become sealing-wax red) into the flame, and so sealed the parcel. 'Then there was the Disappearing Egg,' he remarked, and produced one from within my coat-breast and packed it, and also The Crying Baby, Very Human. I handed each parcel to Gip as it was ready, and he clasped them to his chest.

He said very little, but his eyes were eloquent; the clutch of his arms was eloquent. He was the playground of unspeakable emotions. These, you know, were *real* Magics.

Then, with a start, I discovered something moving about in my hat—something soft and jumpy. I whipped it off, and a ruffled pigeon—no doubt a confederate—dropped out and ran on the counter, and went, I fancy, into a cardboard box behind the *papier-maché* tiger.

'Tut, tut!' said the shopman, dexterously relieving me of my head-dress; 'careless bird, and—as I live—nesting!'

He shook my hat, and shook out into his extended hand two or three eggs, a large marble, a watch, about half a dozen of the inevitable glass balls, and then crumpled, crinkled paper, more and more and more, talking all the time of the way in which people neglect to brush their hats *inside* as well as out, politely, of course, but with a certain personal application. All sorts of things accumulate, sir. . . . Not *you*, of course, in particular. . . . Nearly every customer. . . . Astonishing what they carry about with them. . . .' The crumpled paper rose and billowed on the counter more and more and more, until he was nearly hidden from us, until he was altogether hidden, and still his voice went on and on. 'We none of us know what the fair semblance of a human being may conceal, Sir. Are we all then no better than brushed exteriors, whited sepulchres—'

His voice stopped—exactly like when you hit a neighbour's gramophone with a well-aimed brick, the same instant silence, and the rustle of the paper stopped, and everything was still. . . .

'Have you done with my hat?' I said, after an interval.

There was no answer.

I stared at Gip, and Gip stared at me; and there were our distortions in the magic mirrors, looking very rum, and grave, and quiet. . . .

'I think we'll go now,' I said. 'Will you tell me how much all this comes to? . . .

'I say,' I said, on a rather louder note, 'I want the bill; and my hat, please,'

It might have been a sniff from behind the paper pile. . . .

'Let's look behind the counter, Gip,' I said. 'He's making fun of us.'

I led Gip round the head-wagging tiger, and what do you think there was behind the counter? No one at all? Only my hat on the floor, and a common conjurer's lop-eared white rabbit lost in meditation, and looking as stupid and crumpled as only a conjurer's rabbit can do. I resumed my hat, and the rabbit lolloped a lollop or so out of my way.

'Dadda!' said Gip, in a guilty whisper.

'What is it, Gip?' said I.

'I *do* like this shop, dadda.'

'So should I,' I said to myself, 'if the counter wouldn't suddenly extend itself to shut one of from the door.' But I didn't call Gip's attention to that. 'Pussy!' he said, with a hand out to the rabbit as it came lolloping past us; 'Pussy, do Gip a magic!' and his eyes followed it as it squeezed through a door I had certainly not remarked a moment before. Then this door opened wider, and the man with one ear larger than the other appeared again. He was smiling still, but his eye met mine with something between amusement and defiance. 'You'd like to see our show-room, sir,' he said, with an innocent suavity. Gip tugged my finger forward. I glanced at the counter and met the shopman's eye again. I was beginning to think the magic just a little too genuine. 'We haven't *very* much time,' I said. But somehow we were inside the showroom before I could finish that.

'All goods of the same quality,' said the shopman, rubbing his flexible hands together, 'and that is the Best. Nothing in the place that isn't genuine Magic, and warranted thoroughly rum. Excuse me, sir!'

I felt him pull at something that clung to my coat-sleeve, and then I saw he held a little, wriggling red demon by the tail—the little creature bit and fought and tried to get at his hand—and in a moment he tossed it carelessly behind a counter. No doubt the thing was only an image of twisted India-rubber, but for the moment—! And his gesture was exactly that of a man who handles some pretty biting bit of vermin. I glanced at Gip, but Gip was looking at a magic rocking-horse. I was glad he hadn't seen the thing. 'I say,' I said, in an undertone, and indicating Gip and the red demon with my eyes, 'you haven't many things like that about, have you?'

'None of ours! Probably brought it with you,' said the shopman—also in an undertone, and with a more dazzling smile than ever. 'Astonishing what people will carry about with them unawares!' And then to Gip, 'Do you see anything you fancy here?'

There were many things that Gip fancied there.

He turned to this astonishing tradesman with mingled confidence and respect. 'Is that a Magic Sword?' he said.

'A Magic Toy Sword. It neither bends, breaks, nor cuts the fingers. It renders the bearer invincible in battle against any one under eighteen. Half a crown to seven and sixpence, according to size. These panoplies on cards are for juvenile knights-errant and very useful—shield of safety, sandals of swiftness, helmet of invisibility.'

'Oh, dadda!' gasped Gip.

I tried to find out what they cost, but the shopman did not heed me. He had got Gip now; he had got him away from my finger; he had embarked upon the exposition of all his confounded stock, and nothing was going to stop him. Presently I saw with a qualm of distrust and something very like jealousy that Gip had hold of this person's finger as usually he has hold of mine. No doubt the fellow was interesting, I thought, and had an interestingly faked lot of stuff, really *good* faked stuff, still—

I wandered after them, saying very little, but keeping an eye on this prestidigital fellow. After all, Gip was enjoying it. And no doubt when the time came to go we should be able to go quite easily.

It was a long, rambling place, that show-room, a gallery broken up by stands and stalls and pillars, with archways leading off to other departments, in which the queerest-looking assistants loafed and stared at one, and with perplexing mirrors and curtains. So perplexing, indeed, were these that I was presently unable to make out the door by which we had come.

The shopman showed Gip magic trains that ran without steam or clockwork just as you set the signals, and then some very, very valuable boxes of soldiers that all came alive directly you took off the lid and said—I myself haven't a very quick ear and it was a tongue-twisting sound, but Gip—he has his mother's ear—got it in no time. 'Bravo!' said the shopman, putting the men back into the box unceremoniously and handing it to Gip. 'Now,' said the shopman, and in a moment Gip had made them all alive again.

'You'll take that box?' asked the shop man.

'We'll take that box,' said I, 'unless you charge its full value. In which case it would need a Trust Magnate—'

'Dear heart! *No!*' and the shopman swept the little men back again, shut the lid, waved the box in the air, and there it was, in brown paper, tied up and—*with Gip's full name and address on the Paper!*

The shopman laughed at my amazement.

'This is the genuine magic,' he said. 'The real thing.'

'It's almost too genuine for my taste,' I said again.

After that he fell to showing Gip tricks, odd tricks, and still odder the way they were done. He explained them, he turned them inside out, and there was the dear little chap nodding his busy bit of a head in the sagest manner.

I did not attend as well as I might. 'Hey, presto!' said the Magic Shopman, and then would come the clear, small 'Hey, presto!' of the boy. But I was distracted by other things. It was being borne in upon me just how tremendously rum this place was; it was, so to speak, inundated by a sense of rumness. There was something vaguely rum about the fixtures even, about the ceiling, about the floor, about the casually distributed chairs. I had a queer feeling that whenever I wasn't looking at them straight they went askew, and moved about, and played a noiseless puss-in-the-corner behind my back. And the cornice had a serpentine design with masks—masks altogether too expressive for proper plaster.

Then abruptly my attention was caught by one of the odd-looking assistants. He was some way off and evidently unaware of my presence—I saw a sort of three-quarter length of him over a pile of toys and through an arch—and, you know, he was leaning against a pillar in an idle sort of way doing the most horrid things with his features. The particular horrid thing he did was with his nose. He did it just as though he was idle and wanted to amuse himself. First of all it was a short, blobby nose, and then suddenly he shot it out like a telescope, and then out it flew and became thinner and thinner until it was like a long, red, flexible whip. Like a thing in a nightmare it was! He flourished it about and flung it forth as a fly-fisher flings his line.

My instant thought was that Gip mustn't see him. I turned about, and there was Gip quite preoccupied with the shopman, and thinking no evil. They were whispering together and looking at me. Gip was standing on a stool, and the shopman was holding a sort of big drum in his hand.

'Hide and seek, dadda!' cried Gip. 'You're He!'

And before I could do anything to prevent it, the shopman had clapped the big drum over him.

I saw what was up directly. 'Take that off,' I cried, 'this instant? You'll frighten the boy. Take it off!'

The shopman with the unequal ears did so without a word, and held the big cylinder towards me to show its emptiness. And the stool was vacant ! In that instant my boy had utterly disappeared! . . .

You know, perhaps, that sinister something that comes like a hand out of the unseen and grips your heart about. You know it takes your common self away and leaves you tense and deliberate, neither slow nor hasty, neither angry nor afraid. So it was with me.

I came up to this grinning shopman and kicked his stool aside.

'Stop this folly!' I said. 'Where is my boy?'

'You see,' he said, still displaying the drum's interior, 'there is no deception—'

I put out my hand to grip him, and he eluded me by a dexterous movement. I snatched again, and he turned from me and pushed open a door to escape. 'Stop!' I said, and he laughed, receding. I leapt after him—into utter darkness.

Thud!

'Lor' bless my 'eart! I didn't see you coming, sir!'

I was in Regent Street, and I had collided with a decent-looking working man; and a yard away, perhaps, and looking extremely perplexed with himself, was Gip. There was some sort of apology, and then Gip had turned and come to me with a bright little smile, as though for a moment he had missed me.

And he was carrying four parcels in his arm!

He secured immediate possession of my finger.

For the second I was rather at a loss. I stared round to see the door of the magic shop, and, behold, it was not there! There was no door, no shop, nothing, only the common pilaster between the shop where they sell pictures and the window with the chicks! . . .

I did the only thing possible in that mental tumult; I walked straight to the kerbstone and held up my umbrella for a cab.

' 'Ansoms,' said Gip, in a note of culminating exultation.

I helped him in, recalled my address with an effort, and got in also. Something unusual proclaimed itself in my tail-coat pocket, and I felt and discovered a glass ball. With a petulant expression I flung it into the street.

Gip said nothing.

For a space neither of us spoke.

'Dadda!' said Gip, at last, 'that *was* a proper shop!'

I came round with that to the problem of just how the whole thing had seemed to him. He looked completely undamaged—so far, good; he was neither scared nor unhinged, he was simply tremendously satisfied with the afternoon's entertainment, and there in his arms were the four parcels.

Confound it ! what could be in them?

'Um!' I said. 'Little boys can't go to shops like that every day.'

He received this with his usual stoicism, and for a moment I was sorry I was his father and not his mother, and so couldn't suddenly there, *coram publico*, in our hansom, kiss him. After all, I thought, the thing wasn't so very bad.

But it was only when we opened the parcels that I really began to be reassured. Three of them contained boxes of soldiers, quite ordinary lead soldiers, but of so good a quality as to make Gip altogether forget that originally these parcels had been Magic Tricks of the only genuine sort, and the fourth contained a kitten, a little living white kitten, in excellent health and appetite and temper.

I saw this unpacking with a sort of provisional relief. I hung about in the nursery for quite an unconscionable time. . . .

That happened six months ago. And now I am beginning to believe it is all right. The kitten had only the magic natural to all kittens, and the soldiers seem as steady a company as any colonel could desire. And Gip—?

The intelligent parent will understand that I have to go cautiously with Gip.

But I went so far as this one day. I said, 'How would you like your soldiers to come alive, Gip, and march about by themselves?'

'Mine do,' said Gip. 'I just have to say a word I know before I open the lid.'

'Then they march about alone?'

'Oh, *quite,* dadda. I shouldn't like them if they didn't do that.'

I displayed no unbecoming surprise, and since then I have taken occasion to drop in upon him once or twice, unannounced, when the soldiers were about, but so far I have never discovered them performing in anything like a magical manner. . . .

Its so difficult to tell.

There's also a question of finance. I have an incurable habit of paying bills. I have been up and down Regent Street several times, looking for that shop. I am inclined to think, indeed, that in that matter honour is satisfied, and that, since Gip's name and address are known to them, I may very well leave it to these people, whoever they may be, to send in their bill in their own time.

THE COUNTRY OF THE BLIND

THREE hundred miles and more from Chimborazo, one hundred from the snows of Cotopaxi, in the wildest wastes of Ecuador's Andes, there lies that mysterious mountain valley, cut off from the world of men, the Country of the Blind. Long years ago that valley lay so far open to the world that men might come at last through frightful gorges and over an icy pass into its equable meadows; and thither indeed men came, a family or so of Peruvian half-breeds fleeing from the lust and tyranny of an evil Spanish ruler. Then came the stupendous outbreak of Mindobamba, when it was night in Quito for seventeen days, and the water was boiling at Yaguachi and all the fish floating dying even as far as Guayaquil; everywhere along the Pacific slopes there were land-slips and swift thawings and sudden floods, and one whole side of the old Arauca crest slipped and came down in thunder, and cut off the Country of the Blind for ever from the exploring feet of men. But one of these early settlers had chanced to be on the hither side of the gorges when the world had so terribly shaken itself, and he perforce had to forget his wife and his child and all the friends and possessions he had left up there, and start life over again in the lower world. He started it again but ill, blindness overtook him, and he died of punish-ment in the mines; but the story he told begot a legend that lingers along the length of the Cordilleras of the Andes to this day.

He told of his reason for venturing back from that fastness, into which he had first been carried lashed to a llama, beside a vast bale of gear, when he was a child. The valley, he said, had in it all that the heart of man could desire—sweet water, pasture, an even climate, slopes of rich brown soil with tangles of a shrub that bore an excellent fruit, and on one side great hanging forests of pine that held the ava-lanches high. Far overhead, on three sides, vast cliffs of grey-green rock were capped by cliffs of ice; but the glacier stream came not to them but flowed away by the farther slopes, and only now and then huge masses fell on the valley side. In this valley it neither rained nor snowed, but the abundant springs gave a rich green pasture, that irrigation would spread over all the valley space. The settlers did well indeed there. Their beasts did well and multiplied, and but one thing marred their happiness. Yet it was enough to mar it greatly. A strange disease had come upon them, and had made all the children born to them there—and indeed, several older children also—blind. It was to seek some charm or antidote against this plague of blindness that he had with fatigue and danger and difficulty returned down the gorge. In those days, in such cases, men did not think of germs and infections, but of sins; and it seemed to him that the reason of this affliction must lie in the negligence of these priestless immigrants to set up a shrine so soon as they entered the valley. He wanted a shrine—a handsome, cheap, effectual shrine—to be erected in the valley; he wanted relics and such like potent things of faith, blessed objects and mysterious medals and prayers. In his wallet he had a bar of native silver for which he would not account; he insisted there was none in the valley with something of the insistence of an inexpert liar. They had all clubbed their money and ornaments together, having little need for such treasure up there, he said, to buy them holy help against their ill. I figure this dim-eyed young mountaineer, sunburnt, gaunt, and anxious, hat-brim clutched feverishly, a man all unused to the ways of the lower world, telling this story to some keen-eyed, attentive priest before the great convulsion; I can picture him presently seeking to return with pious and infallible remedies against that trouble, and the infinite dismay with which he must have faced the tumbled vastness where the gorge had once come out. But the rest of his story of mischances is lost to me, save that I know of his evil death after several years. Poor stray from that remoteness! The stream that had once made the gorge now bursts from the mouth of a rocky cave, and the legend his poor, ill-told story set going developed into the legend of a race of blind men somewhere 'over there' one may still hear today.

And amidst the little population of that now isolated and forgotten valley the disease ran its course. The old became groping and purblind, the young saw but dimly, and the children that were born to them saw never at all. But life was very easy in that snow-rimmed basin, lost to all the world, with neither thorns nor briars, with no evil insects nor any beasts save the gentle breed of llamas they had lugged and thrust and followed up the beds of the shrunken rivers in the gorges up which they had come. The seeing had become purblind so gradually that they scarcely noted their loss. They guided the sightless youngsters hither and thither until they knew the whole valley marvellously, and when at last sight died out among them the race lived on. They had even time to adapt themselves to the blind control of fire which they made carefully in stoves of stone. They were a simple strain of people at the first, unlettered, only slightly touched with the Spanish civilisation, but with something of a tradition of the arts of old Peru and of its lost philosophy. Generation followed generation. They forgot many things; they devised many things. Their tradition of the greater world they came from became mythical· in colour and uncertain. In all things save sight they were strong and able; and presently the chance of birth and heredity sent one who had an original mind and who could talk and persuade among them, and then afterwards another. These two passed, leaving their effects, and the little community grew in numbers and in understanding, and met and settled social and economic problems that arose. Generation followed generation. Generation followed generation. There came a time when a child was born who was fifteen generations from that ancestor who went out of the valley with a bar of silver to seek God's aid, and who never returned. Thereabouts it chanced that a man came into this community from the outer world. And this is the story of that man.

He was a mountaineer from the country near Quito, a man who had been down to the sea and had seen the world, a reader of books in an original way, an acute and enterprising man, and he was taken on by a party of Englishmen who had come out to Ecuador to climb mountains, to replace one of their three Swiss guides who had fallen ill. He climbed here and he climbed there, and then came the attempt on Parascotopetl, the Matterhorn of the Andes, in which he was lost to the outer world. The story of the accident has been written a dozen times. Pointer's narrative is the best. He tells how the party worked their difficult and almost vertical way up to the very foot of the last and greatest precipice, and how they built a night shelter amidst the snow upon a little shelf of rock, and, with a touch of real dramatic power, how presently they found Nunez had gone from them. They shouted and there was no reply; shouted and whistled, and for the rest of that night they slept no more.

As the morning broke they saw the traces of his fall. It was impossible he could have uttered a sound. He had slipped eastward towards the unknown side of the mountain; far below he had struck a steep slope of snow, and ploughed his way down it in the midst of a snow avalanche. His track went straight to the edge of a frightful precipice, and beyond that everything was hidden. Far, far below, and hazy with distance, they could see trees rising out of a narrow, shut-in valley—the lost Country of the Blind. But they did not know it was the lost Country of the Blind, nor distinguish it in any way from any other narrow streak of upland valley. Unnerved by this disaster, they abandoned their attempt in the afternoon, and Pointer was called away to the war before he could make another attack. To this day Parascotopetl lifts an unconquered crest, and Pointer's shelter crumbles unvisited amidst the snows.

And the man who fell survived.

At the end of the slope he fell a thousand feet, and came down in the midst of a cloud of snow upon a snow slope even steeper than the one above. Down this he was whirled, stunned and insensible, but without a bone broken in his body; and then at last came to gentler slopes, and at last rolled out and lay still, buried amidst a softening heap of the white masses that had accompanied and saved him. He came to himself with a dim fancy that he was ill in bed; then realised his position with a mountaineer's intelligence, and worked himself loose and, after a rest or so, out until he saw the stars. He rested flat upon his chest for a space, wondering where he was and what had happened to him. He explored his limbs, and discovered that several of his buttons were gone and his coat turned over his head. His knife had gone from his pocket and his hat was lost, though he had tied it under his chin. He recalled that he had been looking for loose stones to raise his piece of the shelter wall. His ice-axe had disappeared.

He decided he must have fallen, and looked up to see, exaggerated by the ghastly light of the rising moon, the tremendous flight he had taken. For a while he lay, gazing blankly at that vast pale cliff towering above, rising moment by moment out of a subsiding tide of darkness. Its phantasmal, mysterious beauty held him for a space, and then he was seized with a paroxysm of sobbing laughter. . . .

After a great interval of time he became aware that he was near the lower edge of the snow. Below, down what was now a moonlit and practicable slope, he saw the dark and broken appearance of rock-strewn turf. He struggled to his feet, aching in every joint and limb, got down painfully from the heaped loose snow about him, went downwards until he was on the turf, and there dropped rather than lay beside a boulder, drank deep from the flask in his inner pocket, and instantly fell asleep.

He was awakened by the singing of birds in the trees far below.

He sat up and perceived he was on a little alp at the foot of a vast precipice, that was grooved by the gully down which he and his snow had come. Over against him another wall of rock reared itself against the sky. The gorge between these precipices ran east and west and was full of the morning sunlight, which lit to the westward the mass of fallen mountain that closed the descending gorge. Below him it seemed there was a precipice equally steep, but behind the snow in the gully he found a sort of chimney-cleft dripping with snow-water down which a desperate man might venture. He found it easier than it seemed, and came at last to another desolate alp, and then after a rock climb of no particular difficulty to a steep slope of trees. He took his bearings and turned his face up the gorge, for he saw it opened out above upon green meadows, among which he now glimpsed quite distinctly a cluster of stone huts of unfamiliar fashion. At times his progress was like clambering along the face of a wall, and after a time the rising sun ceased to strike along the gorge, the voices of the singing birds died away, and the air grew cold and dark about him. But the distant valley with its houses was all the brighter for that. He came presently to talus, and among the rocks he noted—for he was an observant man—an unfamiliar fern that seemed to clutch out of the crevices with intense green hands. He picked a frond or so and gnawed its stalk and found it helpful.

About midday he came at last out of the throat of the gorge into the plain and the sunlight. He was stiff and weary; he sat down in the shadow of a rock, filled up his flask with water from a spring and drank it down, and remained for a time resting before he went on to the houses.

They were very strange to his eyes, and indeed the whole aspect of that valley became, as he regarded it, queerer and more unfamiliar. The greater part of its surface was lush green meadow, starred with many beautiful flowers, irrigated with extraordinary care, and bearing evidence of systematic cropping piece by piece. High up and ringing the valley about was a wall, and what appeared to be a circumferential water-channel, from which the little trickles of water that fed the meadow plants came, and on the higher slopes above this flocks of llamas cropped the scanty herbage. Sheds, apparently shelters or feeding-places for the llamas, stood against the boundary wall here and there. The irrigation streams ran together into a main channel down the centre of the valley, and this was enclosed on either side by a wall breast high. This gave a singularly urban quality to this secluded place, a quality that was greatly enhanced by the fact that a number of paths paved with black and white stones, and each with a curious little kerb at the side, ran hither and thither in an orderly manner. The houses of the central village were quite unlike the casual and higgledy-piggledy agglomeration of the mountain villages he knew; they stood in a continuous row on either side of a central street of astonishing cleanness; here and there their parti-coloured façade was pierced by a door, and not a solitary window broke their even frontage. They were parti-coloured with extraordinary irregularity; smeared with a sort of plaster that was sometimes grey, sometimes drab, sometimes slate-coloured or dark brown; and it was the sight of this wild plastering first brought the word 'blind' into the thoughts of the explorer. 'The good man who did that,' he thought, 'must have been as blind as a bat.'

He descended a steep place, and so came to the wall and channel that ran about the valley, near where the latter spouted out its surplus contents into the deeps of the gorge in a thin and wavering thread of cascade. He could now see a number of men and women resting on piled heaps of grass, as if taking a siesta, in the remoter part of the meadow, and nearer the village a number of recumbent children, and then nearer at hand three men carrying pails on yokes along a little path that ran from the encircling wall towards the houses. These latter were clad in garments of llama cloth and boots and belts of leather, and they wore caps of cloth with back and ear flaps. They followed one another in single file, walking slowly and yawning as they walked, like men who have been up all night. There was something so reassuringly prosperous and respectable in their bearing that after a moment's hesitation Nunez stood forward as conspicuously as possible upon his rock, and gave vent to a mighty shout that echoed round the valley.

The three men stopped, and moved their heads as though they were looking about them. They turned their faces this way and that, and Nunez gesticulated with freedom. But they did not appear to see him for all his gestures, and after a time, directing themselves towards the mountains far away to the right, they shouted as if in answer. Nunez bawled again, and then once more, and as he gestured ineffectually the word 'blind' came up to the top of his thoughts. 'The fools must be blind,' he said.

When at last, after much shouting and wrath, Nunez crossed the stream by a little bridge, came through a gate in the wall, and approached them, he was sure that they were blind. He was sure that this was the Country of the Blind, of which the legends told. Conviction had sprung upon him, and a sense of great and rather enviable adventure. The three stood side by side, not looking at him, but with their ears directed towards him, judging him by his unfamiliar steps. They stood close together like men a little afraid, and he could see their eyelids closed and sunken, as though the very balls beneath had shrunk away. There was an expression near awe on their faces.

'A man,' one said, in hardly recognisable Spanish—'a man it is—a man or a spirit—coming down from the rocks.'

But Nunez advanced with the confident steps of a youth who enters upon life. All the old stories of the lost valley and the Country of the Blind had come back to his mind, and through his thoughts ran this old proverb, as if it were a refrain—

'In the Country of the Blind the One-eyed Man is King.'

'In the Country of the Blind the One-eyed Man is King.'

And very civilly he gave them greeting. He talked to them and used his eyes.

'Where does he come from, brother Pedro?' asked one.

'Down out of the rocks.'

'Over the mountains I come,' said Nunez, 'out of the country beyond there—where men can see. From near Bogota, where there are a hundred thousand of people, and where the city passes out of sight.'

'Sight?' muttered Pedro. 'Sight?'

'He comes,' said the second blind man, 'out of the rocks.'

The cloth of their coats Nunez saw was curiously fashioned, each with a different sort of stitching.

They startled him by a simultaneous movement towards him, each with a hand outstretched. He stepped back from the advance of these spread fingers.

'Come hither,' said the third blind man, following his motion and clutching him neatly.

And they held Nunez and felt him over, saying no word further until they had done so.

'Carefully,' he cried, with a finger in his eye, and found they thought that organ, with its fluttering lids, a queer thing in him. They went over it again.

'A strange creature, Correa,' said the one called Pedro. 'Feel the coarseness of his hair. Like a llama's hair.'

'Rough he is as the rocks that begot him,' said Correa, investigating Nunez's unshaven chin with a soft and slightly moist hand. 'Perhaps he will grow finer.' Nunez struggled a little under their examination, but they gripped him firm.

'Carefully,' he said again.

'He speaks,' said the third man. 'Certainly he is a man.'

'Ugh!' said Pedro, at the roughness of his coat.

'And you have come into the world?' asked Pedro.

'*Out* of the world. Over mountains and glaciers; right over above there, half-way to the sun. Out of the great big world that goes down, twelve days' journey to the sea.'

They scarcely seemed to heed him. 'Our fathers have told us men may be made by the forces of Nature,' said Correa. 'It is the warmth of things and moisture, and rottenness—rottenness.'

'Let us lead him to the elders,' said Pedro.

'Shout first,' said Correa, 'lest the children be afraid. This is a marvellous occasion.'

So they shouted, and Pedro went first and took Nunez by the hand to lead him to the houses.

He drew his hand away. 'I can see,' he said.

'See?' said Correa.

'Yes, see,' said Nunez, turning towards him, and stumbled against Pedro's pail.

'His senses are still imperfect,' said the third blind man. 'He stumbles, and talks unmeaning words. Lead him by the hand.'

'As you will,' said Nunez, and was led along, laughing.

It seemed they knew nothing of sight.

Well, all in good time he would teach them.

He heard people shouting, and saw a number of figures gathering together in the middle roadway of the village.

He found it taxed his nerve and patience more than he had anticipated, that first encounter with the population of the Country of the Blind. The place seemed larger as he drew near to it, and the smeared plasterings queerer, and a crowd of children and men and women (the women and girls, he was pleased to note, had some of them quite sweet faces, for all that their eyes were shut and sunken) came about him, holding on to him, touching him with soft, sensitive hands, smelling at him and listening at every word he spoke. Some of the maidens and children, however, kept aloof as if afraid, and indeed his voice seemed coarse and rude beside their softer notes. They mobbed him. His three guides kept close to him with an effect of proprietorship, and said again and again, 'A wild man out of the rocks.'

'Bogota,' he said. 'Bogota. Over the mountain crests.'

'A wild man—using wild words,' said Pedro. 'Did you hear that—*Bogota*? His mind is hardly formed yet. He has only the beginnings of speech.'

A little boy nipped his hand. 'Bogota!' he said mockingly.

'Ay! A city to your village. I come from the great world—where men have eyes and see.'

'His name's Bogota,' they said.

'He stumbled,' said Correa, 'stumbled twice as we came hither.'

'Bring him to the elders.'

And they thrust him suddenly through a doorway into a room as black as pitch, save at the end there faintly glowed a fire. The crowd closed in behind him and shut out all but the faintest glimmer of day, and before he could arrest himself he had fallen headlong over the feet of a seated man. His arm out-flung, struck the face of someone else as he went down; he felt the soft impact of features and heard a cry of anger, and for a moment he struggled against a number of hands that clutched him. It was a one-sided fight. An inkling of the situation came to him, and he lay quiet.

'I fell down,' he said; 'I couldn't see in this pitchy darkness.'

There was a pause is if the unseen persons about him tried to understand his words. Then the voice of Correa said: 'He is but newly formed. He stumbles as he walks and mingles words that mean nothing with his speech.'

Others also said things about him that he heard or understood imperfectly.

'May I sit up?' he asked, in a pause. 'I will not struggle against you again.'

They consulted and let him rise.

The voice of an older man began to question him, and Nunez found himself trying to explain the great world out of which he had fallen, and the sky and mountains and sight and such-like marvels, to these elders who sat in darkness in the Country of the Blind. And they would believe and understand nothing whatever he told them, a thing quite outside his expectation. They would not even understand many of his words. For fourteen generations these people had been blind and cut off from all the seeing world; the names for all the things of sight had faded and changed; the story of the outer world was faded and changed to a child's story; and they had ceased to concern themselves with anything beyond the rocky slopes above their circling wall. Blind men of genius had arisen among them and questioned the shreds of belief and tradition they had brought with them from their seeing days, and had dismissed all these things as idle fancies, and replaced them with new and saner explanations. Much of their imagination had shrivelled with their eyes, and they had made for themselves new imaginations with their ever more sensitive ears and finger-tips. Slowly Nunez realised this; that his expectation of wonder and reverence at his origin and his gifts was not to be borne out; and after his poor attempt to explain sight to them had been set aside as the confused version of a new-made being describing the marvels of his incoherent sensations, he subsided, a little dashed, into listening to their instruction. And the eldest of the blind men explained to him life and philosophy and religion, how that the world (meaning their valley) had been first an empty hollow in the rocks, and then had come, first, inanimate things without the gift of touch, and llamas and a few creatures that had little sense, and then men, and at last angels, whom one could hear singing and making fluttering sounds, but whom no one could touch at all, which puzzled Nunez greatly until he thought of the birds.

He went on to tell Nunez how this time had been divided into the warm and the cold, which are the blind equivalents of day and night, and how it was good to sleep in the warm and work during the cold, so that now, but for his advent, the whole town of the blind would have been asleep. He said Nunez must have been specially created to learn and serve the wisdom they had acquired, and for all his mental incoherency and stumbling behaviour he must have courage, and do his best to learn, and at that all the people in the doorway murmured encouragingly. He said the night—for the blind call their day night—

was now far gone, and it behoved every one to go back to sleep. He asked Nunez if he knew how to sleep, and Nunez said he did, but that before sleep he wanted food.

They brought him food—llama's milk in a bowl, and rough salted bread—and led him into a lonely place to eat out of their hearing, and afterwards to slumber until the chill of the mountain evening aroused them to begin their day again. But Nunez slumbered not at all.

Instead, he sat up in the place where they had left him, resting his limbs and turning the unanticipated circumstances of his arrival over and over in his mind.

Every now and then he laughed, sometimes with amusement and sometimes with indignation.

'Unformed mind!' he said. 'Got no senses yet! They little know they've been insulting their heaven-sent king and master. I see I must bring them to reason. Let me think—let me think.'

He was still thinking when the sun set.

Nunez had an eye for all beautiful things, and it seemed to him that the glow upon the snowfields and glaciers that rose about the valley on every side was the most beautiful thing he had ever seen. His eyes went from that inaccessible glory to the village and irrigated fields, fast sinking into the twilight, and suddenly a wave of emotion took him, and he thanked God from the bottom of his heart that the power of sight had been given him.

He heard a voice calling to him from out of the village.

'Ya ho there, Bogota! Come hither!'

At that he stood up smiling. He would show these people once and for all what sight would do for a man. They would seek him, but not find him.

'You move not, Bogota,' said the voice.

He laughed noiselessly, and made two stealthy steps aside from the path.

'Trample not on the grass, Bogota; that is not allowed.'

Nunez had scarcely heard the sound he made himself. He stopped amazed.

The owner of the voice came running up the piebald path towards him.

He stepped back into the pathway. 'Here I am,' he said.

'Why did you not come when I called you?' said the blind man. 'Must you be led like a child? Cannot you hear the path as you walk?'

Nunez laughed. 'I can see it,' he said.

'There is no such word as *see*,' said the blind man, after a pause. 'Cease this folly, and follow the sound of my feet.'

Nunez followed, a little annoyed.

'My time will come,' he said.

'You'll learn,' the blind man answered. 'There is much to learn in the world.'

'Has no one told you, "In the Country of the Blind the One-eyed Man is King"?'

'What is blind?' asked the blind man carelessly over his shoulder.

Four days passed, and the fifth found the King of the Blind still incognito, as a clumsy and useless stranger among his subjects.

It was, he found, much more difficult to proclaim himself than he had supposed, and in the meantime, while he meditated his *coup d'état*, he did what he was told and learned the manners and customs of the Country of the Blind. He found working and going about at night a particularly irksome thing, and he decided that that should be the first thing he would change.

They led a simple laborious life, these people, with all the elements of virtue and happiness, as these things can be understood by men. They toiled, but not oppressively; they had food and clothing sufficient for their needs; they had days and seasons of rest; they made much of music and singing, and there was love among them, and little children.

It was marvellous with what confidence and precision they went about their ordered world. Everything, you see, had been made to fit their needs; each of the radiating paths of the valley area had a constant angle to the others, and was distinguished by a special notch upon its kerbing; all obstacles and irregularities of path or meadow had long since been cleared away; all their methods and procedure arose naturally from their special needs. Their senses had become marvellously acute; they could hear and judge the slightest gesture of a man a dozen paces away—could hear the very beating of his heart. Intonation had long replaced expression with them, and touches gesture, and their work with hoe and spade and fork was as free and confident as garden work can be. Their sense of smell was extraordinarily fine; they could distinguish individual differences as readily as a dog can, and they went about the tending of the llamas, who lived among the rocks above and came to the wall for food and shelter, with ease and confidence. It was only when at last Nunez sought to assert himself that he found how easy and confident their movements could be.

He rebelled only after he had tried persuasion.

He tried at first on several occasions to tell them of sight. 'Look you here, you people,' he said. 'There are things you do not understand in me.'

Once or twice one or two of them attended to him; they sat with faces downcast and ears turned intelligently towards him, and he did his best to tell them what it was to see. Among his hearers was a girl, with eyelids less red and sunken than the others, so that one could almost fancy she was hiding eyes, whom especially he hoped to persuade. He spoke of the beauties of sight, of watching the mountains, of the sky and the sunrise, and they heard him with amused incredulity that presently became condemnatory. They told him there were indeed no mountains at all, but that the end of the rocks where the llamas grazed was indeed the end of the world; thence sprang a cavernous roof of the universe, from which the dew and the avalanches fell; and when he maintained stoutly the world had neither end nor roof such as they supposed, they said his thoughts were wicked. So far as he could describe sky and clouds and stars to them it seemed to them a hideous void, a terrible blankness in the place of the smooth roof of things in which they believed—it was an article of faith with them that the cavern roof was exquisitely smooth to the touch. He saw that in some manner he shocked them, and gave up that aspect of the matter altogether, and tried to show them the practical value of sight. One morning he saw Pedro in the path called Seventeen and coming towards the central houses, but still too far off for hearing or scent, and he told them as much. 'In a little while,' he prophesied, 'Pedro will be here.' An old man remarked that Pedro had no business on path Seventeen, and then, as if in confirmation, that individual as he drew near turned and went transversely into path Ten, and so back with nimble paces towards the outer wall. They mocked Nunez when Pedro did not arrive, and afterwards, when he asked Pedro questions to clear his character, Pedro denied and outfaced him, and was afterwards hostile to him.

Then he induced them to let him go a long way up the sloping meadows towards the wall with one complacent individual, and to him he promised to describe all that happened among the houses. He noted certain goings and comings, but the things that really seemed to signify

to these people happened inside of or behind the windowless houses—
the only things they took note of to test him by—and of these, he
could see or tell nothing; and it was after the failure of this attempt,
and the ridicule they could not repress, that he resorted to force. He
thought of seizing a spade and suddenly smiting one or two of them to
earth, and so in fair combat showing the advantage of eyes. He went so
far with that resolution as to seize his spade, and then he discovered a
new thing about himself, and that was that it was impossible for him to
hit a blind man in cold blood.

He hesitated, and found them all aware that he snatched up the
spade. They stood alert, with their heads on one side, and bent ears
towards him for what he would do next.

'Put that spade down,' said one, and he felt a sort of helpless
horror. He came near obedience.

Then he thrust one backwards against a house wall, and fled past
him and out of the village.

He went athwart one of their meadows, leaving a track of tram-
pled grass behind his feet, and presently sat down by the side of one of
their ways. He felt something of the buoyancy that comes to all men in
the beginning of a fight, but more perplexity. He began to realise that
you cannot even fight happily with creatures who stand upon a different mental basis to yourself. Far away he saw a number of men carrying spades and sticks come out of the street of houses, and advance in a
spreading line along the several paths towards him. They advanced
slowly, speaking frequently to one another, and ever and again the
whole cordon would halt and sniff the air and listen.

The first time they did this Nunez laughed. But afterwards he did
not laugh.

One struck his trail in the meadow grass, and came stooping and
feeling his way along it.

For five minutes he watched the slow extension of the cordon,
and then his vague disposition to do something forthwith became
frantic. He stood up, went a pace or so towards the circumferential
wall, turned, and went back a little way. There they all stood in a crescent, still and listening.

He also stood still, gripping his spade very tightly in both hands.
Should he charge them?

The pulse in his ears ran into the rhythm of 'In the Country of the
Blind the One-eyed Man is King!'

Should he charge them?

He looked back at the high and unclimbable wall behind—unclimbable because of its smooth plastering, but withal pierced with many little doors, and at the approaching line of seekers. Behind these, others were now coming out of the street of houses.

Should he charge them?

'Bogota!' called one. 'Bogota! where are you?'

He gripped his spade still tighter, and advanced down the meadows toward the place of habitations, and directly he moved they converged upon him. 'I'll hit them if they touch me,' he swore; 'by Heaven, I will. I'll hit.' He called aloud, 'Look here, I'm going to do what I like in this valley. Do you hear? I'm going to do what I like and go where I like!'

They were moving in upon him quickly, groping, yet moving rapidly. It was like playing blind man's buff, with everyone blindfolded except one. 'Get hold of him' cried one. He found himself in the arc of a loose curve of pursuers. He felt suddenly he must be active and resolute.

'You don't understand,' he cried in a voice that was meant to be great and resolute, and which broke. 'You are blind, and I can see. Leave me alone!'

'Bogota! Put down that spade, and come off the grass!'

The last order, grotesque in its urban familiarity, produced a gust of anger.

'I'll hurt you,' he said, sobbing with emotion. 'By Heaven, I'll hurt you. Leave me alone!'

He began to run, not knowing clearly where to run. He ran from the nearest blind man, because it was a horror to hit him. He stopped, and then made a dash to escape from their closing ranks. He made for where a gap was wide, and the men on either side, with a quick perception of the approach of his pace rushed in on one another. He sprang forward, and then saw he must be caught, and *swish*! the spade had struck. He felt the soft thud of hand and arm, and the man was down with a yell of pain, and he was through.

Through! And then he was close to the street of houses again, and blind men, whirling spades and stakes, were running with a sort of reasoned swiftness hither and thither.

He heard steps behind him just in time, and found a tall man rushing forward and swiping at the sound of him. He lost his nerve, hurled his spade a yard wide at his antagonist, and whirled about and fled, fairly yelling as he dodged another.

He was panic-stricken. He ran furiously to and fro, dodging when there was no need to dodge, and in his anxiety to see on every side of him at once, stumbling. For a moment he was down and they heard his fall. Far away in the circumferential wall a little doorway looked like heaven, and he set off in a wild rush for it. He did not even look round at his pursuers until it was gained, and he had stumbled across the bridge, clambered a little way among the rocks, to the surprise and dismay of a young llama, who went leaping out of sight, and lay down sobbing for breath.

And so his *coup d'état* came to an end.

He stayed outside the wall of the valley of the Blind for two nights and days without food or shelter, and meditated upon the unexpected. During these meditations he repeated very frequently and always with a profounder note of derision the exploded proverb: 'In the Country of the Blind the One-Eyed Man is King.' He thought chiefly of ways of fighting and conquering these people, and it grew clear that for him no practicable way was possible. He had no weapons, and now it would be hard to get one.

The canker of civilisation had got to him even in Bogota, and he could not find it in himself to go down and assassinate a blind man. Of course, if he did that, he might then dictate terms on the threat of assassinating them all. But—sooner or later he must sleep! . . .

He tried also to find food among the pine trees, to be comfortable under pine boughs while the frost fell at night, and—with less confidence—to catch a llama by artifice in order to try to kill it—perhaps by hammering it with a stone—and so finally, perhaps, to eat some of it. But the llamas had a doubt of him and regarded him with distrustful brown eyes, and spat when he drew near. Fear came on him the second day and fits of shivering. Finally he crawled down to the wall of the Country of the Blind and tried to make terms. He crawled along by the stream, shouting, until two blind men came out to the gate and talked to him.

'I was mad,' he said. But I was only newly made.'

They said that was better.

He told them he was wiser now, and repented of all he had done.

Then he wept without intention, for he was very weak and ill now, and they took that as a favourable sign.

They asked him if he still thought he could '*see.*'

'No,' he said. 'That was folly. The word means nothing—less than nothing!'

They asked him what was overhead.

'About ten times ten the height of a man there is a roof above the world—of rock—and very, very smooth.' . . . He burst again into hysterical tears. 'Before you ask me any more, give me some food or I shall die.'

He expected dire punishments, but these blind people were capable of toleration. They regarded his rebellion as but one more proof of his general idiocy and inferiority; and after they had whipped him they appointed him to do the simplest and heaviest work they had for anyone to do, and he, seeing no other way of living, did submissively what he was told.

He was ill for some days, and they nursed him kindly. That refined his submission. But they insisted on his lying in the dark, and that was a great misery. And blind philosophers came and talked to him of the wicked levity of his mind, and reproved him so impressively for his doubts about the lid of rock that covered their cosmic casserole that he almost doubted whether indeed he was not the victim of hallucination in not seeing it overhead.

So Nunez became a citizen of the Country of the Blind, and these people ceased to be a generalised people and became individualities and familiar to him, while the world beyond the mountains became more and more remote and unreal. There was Yacob, his master, a kindly man when not annoyed; there was Pedro, Yacob's nephew; and there was Medina-saroté, who was the youngest daughter of Yacob. She was little esteemed in the world of the blind, because she had a clear-cut face, and lacked that satisfying, glossy smoothness that is the blind man's ideal of feminine beauty; but Nunez thought her beautiful at first, and presently the most beautiful thing in the whole creation. Her closed eyelids were not sunken and red after the common way of the valley, but lay as though they might open again at any moment; and she had long eyelashes, which were considered a grave disfigurement. And her voice was strong, and did not satisfy the acute hearing of the valley swains. So that she had no lover.

There came a time when Nunez thought that, could he win her, he would be resigned to live in the valley for all the rest of his days.

He watched her; he sought opportunities of doing her little services, and presently he found that she observed him. Once at a rest-day gathering they sat side by side in the dim starlight, and the music was sweet. His hand came upon hers and he dared to clasp it. Then very tenderly she returned his pressure. And one day, as they were at their meal in the darkness, he felt her hand very softly seeking him, and as it chanced the fire leaped then and he saw the tenderness of her face.

He sought to speak to her.

He went to her one day when she was sitting in the summer moonlight spinning. The light made her a thing of silver and mystery. He sat down at her feet and told her he loved her, and told her how beautiful she seemed to him. He had a lover's voice, he spoke with a tender reverence that came near to awe, and she had never before been touched by adoration. She made him no definite answer, but it was clear his words pleased her.

After that he talked to her whenever he could take an opportunity. The valley became the world for him, and the world beyond the mountains where men lived in sunlight seemed no more than a fairy tale he would some day pour into her ears. Very tentatively and timidly he spoke to her of sight.

Sight seemed to her the most poetical of fancies, and she listened to his description of the stars and the mountains and her own sweet white-lit beauty as though it was a guilty indulgence. She did not believe, she could only half understand, but she was mysteriously delighted, and it seemed to him that she completely understood.

His love lost its awe and took courage. Presently he was for demanding her of Yacob and the elders in marriage, but she became fearful and delayed. And it was one of her elder sisters who first told Yacob that Medina-saroté and Nunez were in love.

There was from the first very great opposition to the marriage of Nunez and Medina-saroté; not so much because they valued her as because they held him as a being apart, an idiot, incompetent thing below the permissible level of a man. Her sisters opposed it bitterly as bringing discredit on them all; and old Yacob, though he had formed a sort of liking for his clumsy, obedient serf, shook his head and said the thing could not be. The young men were all angry at the idea of corrupting the race, and one went so far as to revile and strike Nunez. He struck back. Then for the first time he found an advantage in seeing, even by twilight, and after that fight was over no one was disposed to raise a hand against him. But they still found his marriage impossible.

Old Yacob had a tenderness for his last little daughter, and was grieved to have her weep upon his shoulder.

'You see, my dear, he's an idiot. He has delusions; he can't do anything right.'

'I know,' wept Medina-saroté. 'But he's better than he was. He's getting better. And he's strong, dear father, and kind—stronger and kinder than any other man in the world. And he loves me—and, father, I love him.'

Old Yacob was greatly distressed to find her inconsolable, and, besides—what made it more distressing he liked Nunez for many things. So he went and sat in the windowless council-chamber with the other elders and watched the trend of the talk, and said, at the proper time, 'He's better than he was. Very likely, some day, we shall find him as sane as ourselves.'

Then afterwards one of the elders, who thought deeply, had an idea. He was the great doctor among these people, their medicine-man, and he had a very philosophical and inventive mind, and the idea of curing Nunez of his peculiarities appealed to him. One day when Yacob was present he returned to the topic of Nunez.

'I have examined Bogota,' he said, 'and the case is clearer to me. I think very probably he might be cured.'

'That is what I have always hoped,' said old Yacob.

'His brain is affected,' said the blind doctor.

The elders murmured assent.

'Now, *what* affects it?'

'Ah!' said old Yacob.

'*This*,' said the doctor, answering his own question. 'Those queer things that are called the eyes, and which exist to make an agreeable soft depression in the face, are diseased, in the case of Bogota, in such a way as to affect his brain. They are greatly distended, he has eyelashes, and his eyelids move, and consequently his brain is in a state of constant irritation and distraction.'

'Yes?' said old Yacob. 'Yes?'

'And I think I may say with reasonable certainty that, in order to cure him completely, all that we need do is a simple and easy surgical operation—namely, to remove these irritant bodies.'

'And then he will be sane?'

'Then he will be perfectly sane, and a quite admirable citizen.'

'Thank Heaven for science!' said old Yacob, and went forth at once to tell Nunez of his happy hopes.

But Nunez's manner of receiving the good news struck him as being cold and disappointing.

'One might think,' he said, 'from the tone you take, that you did not care for my daughter.'

It was Medina-saroté who persuaded Nunez to face the blind surgeons.

'*You* do not want me,' he said, 'to lose my gift of sight?'

She shook her head.

'My world is sight.'

Her head dropped lower.

'There are the beautiful things, the beautiful little things—the flowers, the lichens among the rocks, the lightness and softness on a piece of fur, the far sky with its drifting down of clouds, the sunsets and the stars. And there is you. For you alone it is good to have sight, to see your sweet, serene face, your kindly lips, your dear, beautiful hands folded together. . . . It is these eyes of mine you won, these eyes that hold me to you, that these idiots seek. Instead, I must touch you, hear you, and never see you again. I must come under that roof of rock and stone and darkness, that horrible roof under which your imagination stoops. . . . No; you would not have me do that?'

A disagreeable doubt had arisen in him. He stopped, and left the thing in question.

'I wish,' she said, 'sometime—' She paused.

'Yes?' said he, a little apprehensively.

'I wish sometimes—you would not talk like that.'

'Like what?'

'I know it's pretty—it's your imagination. I love it, but *now*—'

He felt cold. '*Now?*' he said faintly.

She sat quite still.

'You mean—you think—I should be better, better perhaps—'

He was realising things very swiftly. He felt anger, indeed, anger at the dull course of fate, but also sympathy for her lack of understanding—a sympathy near akin to pity.

'*Dear*,' he said, and he could see by her whiteness how intensely her spirit pressed against the things she could not say. He put his arms about her, he kissed her ear, and they sat for a time in silence.

'If I were to consent to this?' he said at last, in a voice that was very gentle.

She flung her arms about him, weeping wildly. 'Oh, if you would,' she sobbed, 'if only you would!'

For a week before the operation that was to raise him from his servitude and inferiority to the level of a blind citizen, Nunez knew nothing of sleep, and all through the warm sunlit hours, while the others slumbered happily, he sat brooding or wandered aimlessly, trying to bring his mind to bear on his dilemma. He had given his answer, he had given his consent, and still he was not sure. And at last work-time was over, the sun rose in splendour over the golden crests, and his last day of vision began for him. He had a few minutes with Medina-saroté before she went apart to sleep.

'Tomorrow,' he said, 'I shall see no more.'

'Dear heart!' she answered, and pressed his hands with all her strength.

'They will hurt you but little,' she said; 'and you are going through this pain—you are going through it, dear lover, for me. . . . Dear, if a woman's heart and life can do it, I will repay you. My dearest one, my dearest with the tender voice, I will repay.'

He was drenched in pity for himself and her.

He held her in his arms, and pressed his lips to hers, and looked on her sweet face for the last time. 'Goodbye!' he whispered at that dear sight, 'goodbye'

And then in silence he turned away from her.

She could hear his slow retreating footsteps, and something in the rhythm of them threw her into a passion of weeping.

He had fully meant to go to a lonely place where the meadows were beautiful with white narcissus, and there remain until the hour of his sacrifice should come, but as he went he lifted up his eyes and saw the morning, the morning like an angel in golden armour, marching down the steeps. . . .

It seemed to him that before this splendour he, and this blind world in the valley, and his love, and all, were no more than a pit of sin.

He did not turn aside as he had meant to do, but went on, and passed through the wall of the circumference and out upon the rocks, and his eyes were always upon the sunlit ice and snow.

He saw their infinite beauty, and his imagination soared over them to the things beyond he was now to resign for ever.

He thought of that great free world he was parted from, the world that was his own, and he had a vision of those further slopes, distance beyond distance, with Bogota, a place of multitudinous stirring beauty, a glory by day, a luminous mystery by night, a place of palaces and fountains and statues and white houses, lying beautifully in the middle distance. He thought how for a day or so one might come down through passes, drawing ever nearer and nearer to its busy streets and ways. He thought of the river journey, day by day, from great Bogota to the still vaster world beyond, through towns and villages, forest and desert places, the rushing river day by day, until its banks receded and the big steamers came splashing by, and one had reached the sea—the limitless sea, with its thousand islands, its thousands of islands, and its ships seen dimly far away in their incessant journeyings round and about that greater world. And there, unpent by mountains, one saw the sky—the sky, not such a disc as one saw it here, but an arch of immeasurable blue, a deep of deeps in which the circling stars were floating. . . .

His eyes scrutinised the great curtain of the mountains with a keener inquiry.

For example, if one went so, up that gully and to that chimney there, then one might come out high among those stunted pines that ran round in a sort of shelf and rose still higher and higher as it passed above the gorge. And then? That talus might be managed. Thence perhaps a climb might be found to take him up to the precipice that came below the snow; and if that chimney failed, then another farther to the east might serve his purpose better. And then? Then one would be out upon the amber-lit snow there, and half-way up to the crest of those beautiful desolations.

He glanced back at the village, then turned right round and regarded it steadfastly.

He thought of Medina-saroté, and she had become small and remote.

He turned again towards the mountain wall, down which the day had come to him.

Then very circumspectly he began to climb.

When sunset came he was no longer climbing, but he was far and high. He had been higher, but he was still very high. His clothes were torn, his limbs were blood-stained, he was bruised in many places, but he lay as if he were at his ease, and there was a smile on his face.

From where he rested the valley seemed as if it were in a pit nearly a mile below. Already it was dim with haze and shadow, though the mountain summits around him were things of light and fire. The mountain summits around him were things of light and fire, and the little details of the rocks near at hand were drenched with subtle beauty—a vein of green mineral piercing the grey, the flash of crystal faces here and there, a minute, minutely beautiful orange lichen close beside his face. There were deep mysterious shadows in the gorge, blue deepening into purple, and purple into a luminous darkness, and over-head was the illimitable vastness of the sky. But he heeded these things no longer, but lay quite inactive there, smiling as if he were satisfied merely to have escaped from the valley of the Blind in which he had thought to be King.

The glow of the sunset passed, and the night came, and still he lay peacefully contented under the cold stars.

THE DOOR IN THE WALL

1

ONE confidential evening, not three months ago, Lionel Wallace told me this story of the Door in the Wall. And at the time I thought that so far as he was concerned it was a true story.

He told it me with such a direct simplicity of conviction that I could not do otherwise than believe in him. But in the morning, in my own flat, I woke to a different atmosphere; and as I lay in bed and recalled the things he had told me, stripped of the glamour of his earnest slow voice, denuded of the focused, shaded table light, the shadowy atmosphere that wrapped about him and me, and the pleasant bright things, the dessert and glasses and napery of the dinner we had shared, making them for the time a bright little world quite cut off from every-day realities, I saw it all as frankly incredible. 'He was mystifying!' I said, and then: 'How well he did it! . . . It isn't quite the thing I should have expected him, of all people, to do well.'

Afterwards as I sat up in bed and sipped my morning tea, I found myself trying to account for the flavour of reality that perplexed me in his impossible reminiscences, by supposing they did in some way suggest, present, convey—I hardly know which word to use—experiences it was otherwise impossible to tell.

Well, I don't resort to that explanation now. I have got over my intervening doubts. I believe now, as I believed at the moment of telling, that Wallace did to the very best of his ability strip the truth of his secret for me. But whether he himself saw, or only thought he saw, whether he himself was the possessor of an inestimable privilege or the victim of a fantastic dream, I cannot pretend to guess. Even the facts of his death, which ended my doubts for ever, throw no light on that.

That much the reader must judge for himself.

I forget now what chance comment or criticism of mine, moved so reticent a man to confide in me. He was, I think, defending himself against an imputation of slackness and unreliability I had made in relation to a great public movement, in which he had disappointed me. But he plunged suddenly. 'I have,' he said, 'a preoccupation—'

'I know,' he went on, after a pause, 'I have been negligent. The fact is—it isn't a case of ghosts or apparitions—but—it's an odd thing to tell of, Redmond—I am haunted. I am haunted by something—that rather takes the light out of things, that fills me with longings.

He paused, checked by that English shyness that so often overcomes us when we would speak of moving or grave or beautiful things. 'You were at Saint Athelstan's all through,' he said, and for a moment that seemed to me quite irrelevant. 'Well'—and he paused. Then very haltingly at first, but afterwards more easily, he began to tell of the thing that was hidden in his life, the haunting memory of a beauty and a happiness that filled his heart with insatiable longings, that made all the interests and spectacle of worldly life seem dull and tedious and vain to him.

Now that I have the clue to it, the thing seems written visibly in his face. I have a photograph in which that look of detachment has been caught and intensified. It reminds me of what a woman once said of him—a woman who had loved him greatly. 'Suddenly,' she said, 'the interest goes out of him. He forgets you. He doesn't care a rap for you—under his very nose . . .'

Yet the interest was not always out of him, and when he was holding his attention to a thing Wallace could contrive to be an extremely successful man. His career, indeed, is set with successes. He left me behind him long ago; he soared up over my head, and cut a figure in the world that I couldn't cut anyhow. He was still a year short of forty, and they say now that he would have been in office and very probably in the new Cabinet if he had lived. At school he always beat me without effort—as it were by nature. We were at school together at Saint Athelstan's College in West Kensington for almost all our schooltime. He came into the school as my co-equal, but he left far above me, in a blaze of scholarships and brilliant performance. Yet I think I made a fair average running. And it was at school I heard first of the 'Door in the Wall'—that I was to hear of a second time only a month before his death.

To him at least the Door in the Wall was a real door, leading through a real wall to immortal realities. Of that I am now quite assured.

And it came into his life quite early, when he was a little fellow between five and six. I remember how, as he sat making his confession to me with a slow gravity, he reasoned and reckoned the date of it. 'There was,' he said, 'a crimson Virginia creeper in it—all one bright uniform crimson, in a clear amber sunshine against a white wall. That came into the impression somehow, though I don't clearly remember how, and there were horse-chestnut leaves upon the clean pavement outside the green door. They were blotched yellow and green, you know, not brown nor dirty, so that they must have been new fallen. I take it that means October. I look out for horse-chestnut leaves every year and I ought to know.

'If I'm right in that, I was about five years and four months old.'

He was, he said, rather a precocious little boy—he learned to talk at an abnormally early age, and he was so sane and 'old-fashioned,' as people say, that he was permitted an amount of initiative that most children scarcely attain by seven or eight. His mother died when he was two, and he was under the less vigilant and authoritative care of a nursery governess. His father was a stern, preoccupied lawyer, who gave him little attention and expected great things of him. For all his brightness he found life grey and dull, I think. And one day he wandered.

He could not recall the particular neglect that enabled him to get away, nor the course he took among the West Kensington roads. All that had faded among the incurable blurs of memory. But the white wall and the green door stood out quite distinctly.

As his memory of that childish experience ran, he did at the very first sight of that door experience a peculiar emotion, an attraction, a desire to get to the door and open it and walk in. And at the same time he had the clearest conviction that either it was unwise or it was wrong of him—he could not tell which—to yield to this attraction. He insisted upon it as a curious thing that he knew from the very beginning—unless memory has played him the queerest trick—that the door was unfastened, and that he could go in as he chose.

I seem to see the figure of that little boy, drawn and repelled. And it was very clear in his mind, too, though why it should be so was never explained, that his father would be very angry if he went in through that door.

Wallace described all these moments of hesitation to me with the utmost particularity. He went right past the door, and then, with his hands in his pockets and making an infantile attempt to whistle, strolled right along beyond the end of the wall. There he recalls a number of mean dirty shops, and particularly that of a plumber and decorator with a dusty disorder of earthenware pipes, sheet lead, ball taps, pattern books of wall paper, and tins of enamel. He stood pretending to examine these things, and *coveting,* passionately desiring, the green door.

Then, he said, he had a gust of emotion. He made a run for it, lest hesitation should grip him again; he went plump with outstretched hand through the green door and let it slam behind him. And so, in a trice, he came into the garden that has haunted all his life.

It was very difficult for Wallace to give me his full sense of that garden into which he came.

There was something in the very air of it that exhilarated, that gave one a sense of lightness and good happening and well-being; there was something in the sight of it that made all its colour clean and perfect and subtly luminous. In the instant of coming into it one was exquisitely glad—as only in rare moments, and when one is young and joyful one can be glad in this world. And everything was beautiful there. . . .

Wallace mused before he went on telling me. 'You see,' he said, with the doubtful inflection of a man who pauses at incredible things, 'there were two great panthers there. . . . Yes, spotted panthers. And I was not afraid. There was a long wide path with marble-edged flower-borders on either side, and these two huge velvety beasts were playing there with a ball. One looked up and came towards me, a little curious as it seemed. It came right up to me, rubbed its soft round ear very gently against the small hand I held out, and purred. It was, I tell you, an enchanted garden. I know. And the size? Oh! it stretched far and wide, this way and that. I believe there were hills far away. Heaven knows where West Kensington had suddenly got to. And somehow it was just like coming home.

You know, in the very moment the door swung to behind me, I forgot the road with its fallen chestnut leaves, its cabs and tradesmen's carts, I forgot the sort of gravitational pull back to the discipline and obedience of home, I forgot all hesitations and fear, forgot discretion, forgot all the intimate realities of this life. I became in a moment a very glad and wonder-happy little boy—in another world. It was a world with a different quality, a warmer, more penetrating and mellower light, with a faint clear gladness in its air, and wisps of sun-touched cloud in the blueness of its sky. And before me ran this long wide path, invitingly, with weedless beds on either side, rich with untended flowers, and these two great panthers. I put my little hands fearlessly on their soft fur, and caressed their round ears and the sensitive corners under their ears, and played with them, and it was as though they welcomed me home. There was a keen sense of home-coming in my mind, and when presently a tall, fair girl appeared in the pathway and came to meet me, smiling, and said, 'Well?' to me, and lifted me and kissed me, and put me down and led me by the hand, there was no amazement, but only an impression of delightful rightness, of being reminded of happy things that had in some strange way been overlooked. There were broad red steps, I remember, that came into view between spikes of delphinium, and up these we went to a great avenue between very old and shady dark trees. All down this avenue, you know, between the red chapped stems, were marble seats of honour and statuary, and very tame and friendly white doves.

'Along this cool avenue my girl-friend led me, looking down—I recall the pleasant lines, the finely-modelled chin of her sweet kind face—asking me questions in a soft, agreeable voice, and telling me things, pleasant things I know, though what they were I was never able to recall. . . . Presently a Capuchin monkey, very clean, with a fur of ruddy brown and kindly hazel eyes, came down a tree to us and ran beside me, looking up at me and grinning, and presently leaped to my shoulder. So we two went on our way in great happiness.'

He paused.

'Go on,' I said.

'I remember little things. We passed an old man musing among laurels, I remember, and a place gay with paroquets, and came through a broad shaded colonnade to a spacious cool palace, full of pleasant fountains, full of beautiful things, full of the quality and promise of heart's desire. And there were many things and many people, some that still seem to stand out clearly and some that are vaguer; but all these people were beautiful and kind. In some way—I don't know how—it was conveyed to me that they all were kind to me, glad to have me there, and filling me with gladness by their gestures, by the touch of their hands, by the welcome and love in their eyes. Yes—'

He mused for a while. 'Playmates I found there. That was very much to me, because I was a lonely little boy. They played delightful games in a grass-covered court where there was a sun-dial set about with flowers. And as one played one loved. . . .

'But—it's odd—there's a gap in my memory. I don't remember the games we played. I never remembered. Afterwards, as a child, I spent long hours trying, even with tears, to recall the form of that happiness. I wanted to play it all over again—in my nursery—by myself. No! All I remember is the happiness and two dear playfellows who were most with me. . . . Then presently came a sombre dark woman, with a grave, pale face and dreamy eyes, a sombre woman, wearing a soft long robe of pale purple, who carried a book, and beckoned and took me aside with her into a gallery above a hall—though my playmates were loth to have me go, and ceased their game and stood watching as I was carried away. "Come back to us!" they cried. "Come back to us soon!" I looked up at her face, but she heeded them not at all. Her face was very gentle and grave. She took me to a seat in the gallery, and I stood beside her, ready to look at her book as she opened it upon her knee. The pages fell open. She pointed, and I looked, marvelling, for in the living pages of that book I saw myself; it was a story about myself, and in it were all the things that had happened to me since ever I was born. . . .

'It was wonderful to me, because the pages of that book were not pictures, you understand, but realities.'

Wallace paused gravely—looked at me doubtfully.

'Go on,' I said. 'I understand.'

'They were realities—yes, they must have been; people moved and things came and went in them; my dear mother, whom I had near forgotten; then my father, stern and upright, the servants, the nursery, all the familiar things of home. Then the front door and the busy streets, with traffic to and fro. I looked and marvelled, and looked half doubtfully again into the woman's face and turned the pages over, skipping this and that, to see more of this book and more, and so at last I came to myself hovering and hesitating outside the green door in the long white wall, and felt again the conflict and the fear,

' "And next?" I cried, and would have turned on, but the cool hand of the grave woman delayed me.

' "Next?" I insisted, and struggled gently with her hand, pulling up her fingers with all my childish strength, and as she yielded and the page came over she bent down upon me like a shadow and kissed my brow.

'But the page did not show the enchanted garden, nor the panthers, nor the girl who had led me by the hand, nor the playfellows who had been so loth to let me go. It showed a long grey street in West Kensington, in that chill hour of afternoon before the lamps are lit; and I was there, a wretched little figure, weeping aloud, for all that I could do to restrain myself, and I was weeping because I could not return to my dear playfellows who had called after me, "Come back to us! Come back to us soon!" I was there. This was no page in a book, but harsh reality; that enchanted place and the restraining hand of the grave mother at whose knee I stood had gone—whither had they gone?'

He halted again, and remained for a time staring into the fire.

'Oh! the woefulness of that return!' he murmured.

'Well?' I said, after a minute or so.

'Poor little wretch I was!—brought back to this grey world again! As I realised the fullness of what had happened to me, I gave way to quite ungovernable grief. And the shame and humiliation of that public weeping and my disgraceful homecoming remain with me still. I see again the benevolent-looking old gentleman in gold spectacles who stopped and spoke to me—prodding me first with his umbrella. "Poor little chap," said he; "and are you lost then?"—and me a London boy of five and more! And he must needs bring in a kindly young police-man and make a crowd of me, and so march me home. Sobbing, conspicuous, and frightened, I came back from the enchanted garden to the steps of my father's house.

'That is as well as I can remember my vision of that garden—the garden that haunts me still. Of course, I can convey nothing of that indescribable quality of translucent unreality, that *difference* from the common things of experience that hung about it all; but that—that is what happened. If it was a dream, I am sure it was a day-time and alto-gether extraordinary dream. . . . H'm!—naturally there followed a terrible questioning, by my aunt, my father, the nurse, the governess—every one. . . .

'I tried to tell them, and my father gave me my first thrashing for telling lies. When afterwards I tried to tell my aunt, she punished me again for my wicked persistence. Then, as I said, every one was forbidden to listen to me, to hear a word about it. Even my fairy-tale books were taken away from me for a time—because I was too "imaginative." Eh? Yes, they did that! My father belonged to the old school. . . . And my story was driven back upon myself. I whispered it to my pillow— my pillow that was often damp and salt to my whispering lips with childish tears. And I added always to my official and less fervent prayers this one heartfelt request: "Please God I may dream of the garden. Oh! take me back to my garden! Take me back to my garden!" I dreamt often of the garden. I may have added to it, I may have changed it; I do not know. . . . All this, you understand, is an attempt to reconstruct from fragmentary memories a very early experience. Between that and the other consecutive memories of my boyhood there is a gulf. A time came when it seemed impossible I should ever speak of that wonder glimpse again.'

I asked him an obvious question.

'No,' he said. 'I don't remember that I ever attempted to find my way back to the garden in those early years. This seems odd to me now, but I think that very probably a closer watch was kept on my movements after this misadventure to prevent my going astray. No, it wasn't till you knew me that I tried for the garden again. And I believe there was a period—incredible as it seems now—when I forgot the garden altogether—when I was about eight or nine it may have been. Do you remember me as a kid at Saint Athelstan's?'

'Rather!'

'I didn't show any signs, did I, in those days of having a secret dream?'

2

He looked up with a sudden smile.

'Did you ever play North-West Passage with me? . . . No, of course you didn't come my way!'

'It was a sort of game,' he went on, 'that every imaginative child plays all day. The idea was the discovery of a North-West Passage to school. The way to school was plain enough; the game consisted in finding some way that wasn't plain, starting off ten minutes early in some almost hopeless direction, and working my way round through unaccustomed streets to my goal. And one day I got entangled among some rather low-class streets on the other side of Campden Hill, and I began to think that for once the game would be against me and that I should get to school late. I tried rather desperately a street that seemed a cul-de-sac, and found a passage at the end. I hurried through that with renewed hope. 'I shall do it yet,' I said, and passed a row of frowsy little shops that were inexplicably familiar to me, and behold! there was my long white wall and the green door that led to the enchanted garden!

'The thing whacked upon me suddenly. Then, after all, that garden, that wonderful garden, wasn't a dream!'

He paused.

'I suppose my second experience with the green door marks the world of difference there is between the busy life of a schoolboy and the infinite leisure of a child. Anyhow, this second time I didn't for a moment think of going in straight away. You see—For one thing, my mind was full of the idea of getting to school in time—set on not breaking my record for punctuality. I must surely have felt *some* little desire at least to try the door—yes. I must have felt that. . . . But I seem to remember the attraction of the door mainly as another obstacle to my overmastering determination to get to school. I was immensely interested by this discovery I had made, of course—I went on with my mind full of it—but I went on. It didn't check me. I ran past, tugging out my watch, found I had ten minutes still to spare, and then I was going downhill into familiar surroundings. I got to school, breathless, it is true, and wet with perspiration, but in time. I can remember hanging up my coat and hat. . . . Went right by it and left it behind me. Odd, eh?'

He looked at me thoughtfully. 'Of course I didn't know then that it wouldn't always be there. Schoolboys have limited imaginations. I suppose I thought it was an awfully jolly thing to have it there, to know my way back to it; but there was the school tugging at me. I expect I was a good deal distraught and inattentive that morning, recalling what I could of the beautiful strange people I should presently see again. Oddly enough I had no doubt in my mind that they would be glad to see me. . . . Yes, I must have thought of the garden that morning just as a jolly sort of place to which one might resort in the interludes of a strenuous scholastic career.

'I didn't go that day at all. The next day was a half holiday, and that may have weighed with me. Perhaps, too, my state of inattention brought down impositions upon me, and docked the margin of time necessary for the detour. I don't know. What I do know is that in the meantime the enchanted garden was so much upon my mind that I could not keep it to myself.

'I told—what was his name?—a ferrety-looking youngster we used to call Squiff.'

'Young Hopkins,' said I.

'Hopkins it was. I did not like telling him. I had a feeling that in some way it was against the rules to tell him, but I did. He was walking part of the way home with me; he was talkative, and if we had not talked about the enchanted garden we should have talked of something else, and it was intolerable to me to think about any other subject. So I blabbed.

'Well, he told my secret. The next day in the play interval I found myself surrounded by half a dozen bigger boys, half teasing, and wholly curious to hear more of the enchanted garden. There was that big Fawcett—you remember him?—and Carnaby and Morley Reynolds. You weren't there by any chance? No, I think I should have remembered if you were. . . .

'A boy is a creature of odd feelings. I was, I really believe, in spite of my secret self-disgust, a little flattered to have the attention of these big fellows. I remember particularly a moment of pleasure caused by the praise of Crawshaw—you remember Crawshaw major, the son of Crawshaw the composer?—who said it was the best lie he had ever heard. But at the same time there was a really painful undertow of shame at telling what I felt was indeed a sacred secret. That beast Fawcett made a joke about the girl in green—'

Wallace's voice sank with the keen memory of that shame. 'I pretended not to hear,' he said. 'Well, then Carnaby suddenly called me a young liar, and disputed with me when I said the thing was true. I said I knew where to find the green door, could lead them all there in ten minutes. Carnaby became outrageously virtuous, and said I'd have to—and bear out my words or suffer. Did you ever have Carnaby twist your arm? Then perhaps you'll understand how it went with me. I swore my story was true. There was nobody in the school then to save a chap from Carnaby, though Crawshaw put in a word or so. Carnaby had got his game. I grew excited and red-eared, and a little frightened.

I behaved altogether like a silly little chap, and the outcome of it all was that instead of starting alone for my enchanted garden, I led the way presently—cheeks flushed, ears hot, eyes smarting, and my soul one burning misery and shame—for a party of six mocking, curious, and threatening schoolfellows.

'We never found the white wall and the green door. . . .'

'You mean—?'

'I mean I couldn't find it. I would have found it if I could.

'And afterwards when I could go alone I couldn't find it. I never found it. I seem now to have been always looking for it through my schoolboy days, but I never came upon it—never.'

'Did the fellows—make it disagreeable?'

'Beastly. . . . Carnaby held a council over me for wanton lying. I remember how I sneaked home and upstairs to hide the marks of my blubbering. But when I cried myself to sleep at last it wasn't for Carnaby, but for the garden, for the beautiful afternoon I had hoped for, for the sweet friendly women and the waiting playfellows, and the game I had hoped to learn again, that beautiful forgotten game. . . .

'I believe firmly that if I had not told—. . . I had bad times after that—crying at night and wool-gathering by day. For two terms I slacked and had bad reports. Do you remember? Of course you would. It was *you*—your beating me in mathematics that brought me back to the grind again.'

3

For a time my friend stared silently into the red heart of the fire. Then he said: 'I never saw it again until I was seventeen.

'It leaped upon me for the third time—as I was driving to Paddington on my way to Oxford and a scholarship. I had just one momentary glimpse. I was leaning over the apron of my hansom smoking a cigarette, and no doubt thinking myself no end of a man of the world, and suddenly there was the door, the wall, the dear sense of unforgettable and still attainable things.

'We clattered by—I too taken by surprise to stop my cab until we were well past and round a corner. Then I had a queer moment, a double and divergent movement of my will: I tapped the little door in the roof of the cab, and brought my arm down to pull out my watch.

'Yes, sir!' said the cabman, smartly. 'Er—well—it's nothing,' I cried. '*My* mistake! We haven't much time! Go on!' And he went on. . . .

'I got my scholarship. And the night after I was told of that, I sat over my fire in my little upper room, my study, in my father's house, with his praise—his rare praise—and his sound counsels ringing in my ears, and I smoked my favourite pipe—the formidable bulldog of adolescence—and thought of that door in the long white wall. 'If I had stopped,' I thought, 'I should have missed my scholarship, I should have missed Oxford—muddled all the fine career before me! I begin to see things better! I fell musing deeply, but I did not doubt then this career of mine was a thing that merited sacrifice.

'Those dear friends and that clear atmosphere seemed very sweet to me, very fine but remote. My grip was fixing now upon the world. I saw another door opening—the door of my career.'

He stared again into the fire. Its red light picked out a stubborn strength in his face for just one flickering moment, and then it vanished again.

'Well,' he said and sighed, 'I have served that career. I have done—much work, much hard work. But I have dreamt of the enchanted garden a thousand dreams, and seen its door, or at least glimpsed its door, four times since then. Yes—four times. For a while this world was so bright and interesting, seemed so full of meaning and opportunity, that the half-effaced charm of the garden was by comparison gentle and remote. Who wants to pat panthers on the way to dinner with pretty women and distinguished men? I came down to London from Oxford, a man of bold promise that I have done something to redeem. Something—and yet there have been disappointments. . . .

'Twice I have been in love—I will not dwell on that—but once, as I went to some one who, I knew, doubted whether I dared to come, I took a short cut at a venture through an unfrequented road near Earl's Court, and so happened on a white wall and a familiar green door. 'Odd!' said I to myself, 'but I thought this place was on Campden Hill. It's the place I never could find somehow—like counting Stonehenge—the place of that queer day-dream of mine.' And I went by it intent upon my purpose. It had no appeal to me that afternoon.

'I had just a moment's impulse to try the door, three steps aside were needed at the most—though I was sure enough in my heart that it would open to me—and then I thought that doing so might delay me on the way to that appointment in which my honour was involved. Afterwards I was sorry for my punctuality—I might at least have peeped in and waved a hand to those panthers, but I knew enough by this time not to seek again belatedly that which is not found by seeking. Yes, that time made me very sorry. . . .

'Years of hard work after that, and never a sight of the door. It's only recently it has come back to me. With it has come a sense as though some thin tarnish had spread itself over my world. I began to think of it as a sorrowful and bitter thing that I should never see that door again. Perhaps I was suffering a little from overwork—perhaps it was what I've heard spoken of as the feeling of forty. I don't know. But certainly the keen brightness that makes effort easy has gone out of things recently, and that just at a time—with all these new political developments—when I ought to be working. Odd, isn't it? But I do begin to find life toilsome, its rewards, as I come near them, cheap. I began a little while ago to want the garden quite badly. Yes—and I've seen it three times.'

'The garden?'

'No—the door! And I haven't gone in!'

He leaned over the table to me, with an enormous sorrow in his voice as he spoke. 'Thrice I have had my chance—*thrice*! If ever that door offers itself to me again, I swore, I will go in, out of this dust and heat, out of this dry glitter of vanity, out of these toilsome futilities. I will go and never return. This time I will stay. . . . I swore it, and when the time came—I *didn't go*.

'Three times in one year have I passed that door and failed to enter. Three times in the last year.

'The first time was on the night of the snatch division on the Tenants' Redemption Bill, on which the Government was saved by a majority of three. You remember? No one on our side—perhaps very few on the opposite side—expected the end that night. Then the debate collapsed like eggshells. I and Hotchkiss were dining with his cousin at Brentford; we were both unpaired, and we were called up by telephone, and set off at once in his cousin's motor. We got in barely in time, and on the way we passed my wall and door—livid in the moonlight, blotched with hot yellow as the glare of our lamps lit it, but unmistakable. 'My God!' cried I. 'What?' said Hotchkiss. 'Nothing!' I answered, and the moment passed.

'I've made a great sacrifice,' I told the whip as I got in. 'They all have,' he said, and hurried by.

'I do not see how I could have done otherwise then. And the next occasion was as I rushed to my father's bedside to bid that stern old man farewell. Then, too, the claims of life were imperative. But the third time was different; it happened a week ago. It fills me with hot remorse to recall it. I was with Gurker and Ralphs—it's no secret now, you know, that I've had my talk with Gurker. We had been dining at Frobisher's, and the talk had become intimate between us. The question of my place in the reconstructed Ministry lay always just over the boundary of the discussion. Yes—yes. That's all settled. It needn't be talked about yet, but there's no reason to keep a secret from you. . . . Yes—thanks! thanks! But let me tell you my story.

'Then, on that night things were very much in the air. My position was a very delicate one. I was keenly anxious to get some definite word from Gurker, but was hampered by Ralphs' presence. I was using the best power of my brain to keep that light and careless talk not too obviously directed to the point that concerned me. I had to. Ralphs' behaviour since has more than justified my caution. . . . Ralphs, I knew, would leave us beyond the Kensington High Street, and then I could surprise Gurker by a sudden frankness. One has some times to resort to these little devices. . . . And then it was that in the margin of my field of vision I became aware once more of the white wall, the green door before us down the road.

'We passed it talking. I passed it. I can still see the shadow of Gurker's marked profile, his opera hat tilted forward over his prominent nose, the many folds of his neck wrap going before my shadow and Ralphs' as we sauntered past.

'I passed within twenty inches of the door. 'If I say goodnight to them, and go in,' I asked myself, 'what will happen?' And I was all a-tingle for that word with Gurker.

I could not answer that question in the tangle of my other problems. 'They will think me mad,' I thought. 'And suppose I vanish now!—Amazing disappearance of a prominent politician!' That weighed with me. A thousand inconceivably petty worldlinesses weighed with me in that crisis.'

Then he turned on me with a sorrowful smile, and, speaking slowly, 'Here I am!' he said.

'Here I am!' he repeated, 'and my chance has gone from me. Three times in one year the door has been offered me—the door that goes into peace, into delight, into a beauty beyond dreaming, a kindness no man on earth can know. And I have rejected it, Redmond, and it has gone—'

'How do you know?'

'I know. I know. I am left now to work it out, to stick to the tasks that held me so strongly when my moments came. You say I have success—this vulgar, tawdry, irksome, envied thing. I have it.' He had a walnut in his big hand. 'If that was my success,' he said, and crushed it, and held it out for me to see.

'Let me tell you something, Redmond. This loss is destroying me. For two months, for ten weeks nearly now, I have done no work at all, except the most necessary and urgent duties. My soul is full of inappeasable regrets. At nights—when it is less likely I shall be recognised—I go out. I wander. Yes. I wonder what people would think of that if they knew. A Cabinet Minister, the responsible head of that most vital of all departments, wandering alone—grieving—sometimes near audibly lamenting—for a door, for a garden!'

4

I can see now his rather pallid face, and the unfamiliar sombre fire that had come into his eyes. I see him very vividly tonight. I sit recalling his words, his tones, and last evening's *Westminster Gazette* still lies on my sofa, containing the notice of his death. At lunch today the club was busy with his death. We talked of nothing else.

They found his body very early yesterday morning in a deep excavation near East Kensington Station. It is one of two shafts that have been made in connection with an extension of the railway southward. It is protected from the intrusion of the public by a hoarding upon the high road, in which a small doorway has been cut for the convenience of some of the workmen who live in that direction. The doorway was left unfastened through a misunderstanding between two gangers, and through it he made his way.

My mind is darkened with questions and riddles.

It would seem he walked all the way from the House that night—he has frequently walked home during the past Session—and so it is I figure his dark form coming along the late and empty streets, wrapped up, intent. And then did the pale electric lights near the station cheat the rough planking into a semblance of white? Did that fatal unfastened door awaken some memory?

Was there, after all, ever any green door in the wall at all?

I do not know. I have told his story as he told it to me. There are times when I believe that Wallace was no more than the victim of the coincidence between a rare but not unprecedented type of hallucination and a careless trap, but that indeed is not my profoundest belief. You may think me superstitious, if you will, and foolish; but, indeed, I am more than half convinced that he had, in truth, an abnormal gift, and a sense, something—I know not what—that in the guise of wall and door offered him an outlet, a secret and peculiar passage of escape into another and altogether more beautiful world. At any rate, you will say, it betrayed him in the end. But did it betray him? There you touch the inmost mystery of these dreamers, these men of vision and the imagination. We see our world fair and common, the hoarding and the pit. By our daylight standard he walked out of security into darkness, danger, and death.

But did he see like that?

THE BEAUTIFUL SUIT

THERE was once a little man whose mother made him a beautiful suit of clothes. It was green and gold, and woven so that I cannot describe how delicate and fine it was, and there was a tie of orange fluffiness that tied up under his chin. And the buttons in their newness shone like stars. He was proud and pleased by his suit beyond measure, and stood before the long looking-glass when first he put it on, so astonished and delighted with it that he could hardly turn himself away.

He wanted to wear it everywhere, and show it to all sorts of people. He thought over all the places he had ever visited, and all the scenes he had ever heard described, and tried to imagine what the feel of it would be if he were to go now to those scenes and places wearing his shining suit, and he wanted to go out forthwith into the long grass and the hot sunshine of the meadow wearing it. Just to wear it! But his mother told him. 'No.' She told him he must take great care of his suit, for never would he have another nearly so fine; he must save it and save it, and only wear it on rare and great occasions. It was his wedding-suit, she said. And she took the buttons and twisted them up with tissue paper for fear their bright newness should be tarnished, and she tacked little guards over the cuffs and elbows, and wherever the suit was most likely to come to harm. He hated and resisted these things, but what could he do? And at last her warnings and persuasions had effect, and he consented to take off his beautiful suit and fold it into its proper creases, and put it away. It was almost as though he gave it up again. But he was always thinking of wearing it, and of the supreme occasions when someday it might be worn without the guards, without the tissue paper on the buttons, utterly and delightfully never caring, beautiful beyond measure.

One night, when he was dreaming of it after his habit, he dreamt he took the tissue paper from one of the buttons, and found its brightness a little faded, and that distressed him mightily in his dream. He polished the poor faded button and polished it, and, if anything, it grew duller. He woke up and lay awake, thinking of the brightness slightly dulled, and wondering how he would feel if perhaps when the great occasion (whatever it might be) should arrive, one button should chance to be ever so little short of its first glittering freshness, and for days and days that thought remained with him distressingly. And when next his mother let him wear his suit, he was tempted and nearly gave way to the temptation just to fumble off a bit of tissue paper and see if indeed the buttons were keeping as bright as ever.

He went trimly along on his way to church, full of this wild desire. For you must know his mother did, with repeated and careful warnings, let him wear his suit at times, on Sundays, for example, to and fro from church, when there was no threatening of rain, no dust blowing, nor anything to injure it, with its buttons covered and its protections tacked upon it, and a sunshade in his hand to shadow it if there seemed too strong a sunlight for its colours. And always, after such occasions, he brushed it over and folded it exquisitely as she had taught him, and put it away again.

Now all these restrictions his mother set to the wearing of his suit he obeyed, always he obeyed them, until one strange night he woke up and saw the moonlight shining outside his window. It seemed to him the moonlight was not common moonlight, nor the night a common night, and for awhile he lay quite drowsily, with this odd persuasion in his mind. Thought joined on to thought like things that whisper warmly in the shadows. Then he sat up in his little bed suddenly very alert, with his heart beating very fast, and a quiver in his body from top to toe. He had made up his mind. He knew that now he was going to wear his suit as it should be worn. He had no doubt in the matter. He was afraid, terribly afraid, but glad, glad.

He got out of his bed and stood for a moment by the window looking at the moonshine-flooded garden, and trembling at the thing he meant to do. The air was full of a minute clamour of crickets and murmurings, of the infinitesimal shoutings of little living things. He went very gently across the croaking boards, for fear that he might wake the sleeping house, to the big dark clothes-press wherein his beautiful suit lay folded, and he took it out garment by garment, and softly and very eagerly tore off its tissue-paper covering and its tacked protections until there it was, perfect and delightful as he had seen it when first his mother had given it to him—a long time it seemed ago.

Not a button had tarnished, not a thread had faded on this dear suit of his; he was glad enough for weeping as in a noiseless hurry he put it on. And then back he went, soft and quick, to the window that looked out upon the garden, and stood there for a minute, shining in the moonlight, with his buttons twinkling like stars, before he got out on the sill, and, making as little of a rustling as he could, clambered down to the garden path below. He stood before his mother's house, and it was white and nearly as plain as by day, with every window-blind but his own shut like an eye that sleeps. The trees cast still shadows like intricate black lace upon the wall.

The garden in the moonlight was very different from the garden by day; moonshine was tangled in the hedges and stretched in phantom cobwebs from spray to spray. Every flower was gleaming white or crimson black, and the air was a-quiver with the thridding of small crickets and nightingales singing unseen in the depths of the trees.

There was no darkness in the world, but only warm, mysterious shadows, and all the leaves and spikes were edged and lined with iridescent jewels of dew. The night was warmer than any night had ever been, the heavens by some miracle at once vaster and nearer, and, spite of the great ivory-tinted moon that ruled the world, the sky was full of stars.

The little man did not shout nor sing for all his infinite gladness. He stood for a time like one awe-stricken, and then, with a queer small cry and holding out his arms, he ran out as if he would embrace at once the whole round immensity of the world. He did not follow the neat set paths that cut the garden squarely, but thrust across the beds and through the wet, tall, scented herbs, through the night-stock and the nicotine and the clusters of phantom white mallow flowers and through the thickets of southernwood and lavender, and knee-deep across a wide space of mignonette. He came to the great hedge, and he thrust his way through it; and though the thorns of the brambles scored him deeply and tore threads from his wonderful suit, and though burrs and goose-grass and havers caught and clung to him, he did not care. He did not care, for he knew it was all part of the wearing for which he had longed. 'I am glad I put on my suit,' he said; 'I am glad I wore my suit.'

Beyond the hedge he came to the duck-pond, or at least to what was the duck-pond by day. But by night it was a great bowl of silver moonshine all noisy with singing frogs, of wonderful silver moonshine twisted and clotted with strange patternings, and the little man ran down into its waters between the thin black rushes, knee-deep and waist-deep and to his shoulders, smiting the water to black and shining wavelets with either hand, swaying and shivering wavelets, amidst which the stars were netted in the tangled reflections of the brooding trees upon the bank. He waded until he swam, and so he crossed the pond and came out upon the other side, trailing, as it seemed to him, not duckweed, but very silver in long, clinging, dripping masses. And up he went through the transfigured tangles of the willow-herb and the uncut seeding grasses of the farther bank. He came glad and breathless into the high road. 'I am glad,' he said, 'beyond measure, that I had the clothes that fitted this occasion.'

The high road ran straight as an arrow flies, straight into the deep-blue pit of sky beneath the moon, a white and shining road between the singing nightingales, and along it he went, running now and leaping, and now walking and rejoicing, in the clothes his mother had made for him with tireless, loving hands. The road was deep in dust, but that for him was only soft whiteness; and as he went a great dim moth came fluttering round his wet and shimmering and hastening figure. At first he did not heed the moth, and then he waved his hands at it, and made a sort of dance with it as it circled round his head. 'Soft moth!' he cried, 'dear moth! And wonderful night, wonderful night of the world! Do you think my clothes are beautiful, dear moth? As beautiful as your scales and all this silver vesture of the earth and sky?'

And the moth circled closer and closer until at last its velvet wings just brushed his lips. . . .

And next morning they found him dead, with his neck broken, in the bottom of the stone pit, with his beautiful clothes a little bloody, and foul and stained with the duckweed from the pond. But his face was a face of such happiness that, had you seen it, you would have understood indeed how that he had died happy, never knowing that cool and streaming silver for the duckweed in the pond.

THE WILD ASSES OF THE DEVIL

I

THERE was once an Author who pursued fame and prosperity in a pleasant villa on the south coast of England. He wrote stories of an acceptable nature and rejoiced in a growing public esteem, carefully offending no one and seeking only to please. He had married under circumstances of qualified and tolerable romance a lady who wrote occasional but otherwise regular verse, he was the father of a little daughter, whose reported sayings added much to his popularity, and some of the very best people in the land asked him to dinner. He was a deputy-lieutenant and a friend of the Prime Minister, a literary knighthood was no remote possibility for him, and even the Nobel Prize, given a sufficient longevity, was not altogether beyond his hopes. And this amount of prosperity had not betrayed him into any un-English pride. He remembered that manliness and simplicity which are expected from authors. He smoked pipes and not the excellent cigars he could have afforded. He kept his hair cut and never posed. He did not hold himself aloof from people of the inferior and less successful classes. He habitually travelled third class in order to study the characters he put into his delightful novels; he went for long walks and sat in inns, accosting people; he drew out his gardener. And though he worked steadily, he did not give up the care of his body, which threatened a certain plumpness and what is more to the point, a localised plumpness, not generally spread over the system but exaggerating the anterior equator. This expansion was his only care. He thought about fitness and played tennis, and every day, wet or fine, he went for at least an hour's walk. . . .

Yet this man, so representative of Edwardian literature—for it is in the reign of good King Edward the story begins—in spite of his enviable achievements and prospects, was doomed to the most exhausting and dubious adventures before his life came to its unhonoured end. . . .

Because I have not told you everything about him. Sometimes—in the morning sometimes—he would be irritable and have quarrels with his shaving things, and there were extraordinary moods when it would seem to him that living quite beautifully in a pleasant villa and being well-off and famous, and writing books that were always good-humoured and grammatical and a little distinguished in an inoffensive way, was about as boring and intolerable a life as any creature with a soul to be damned could possibly pursue. Which shows only that God in putting him together had not forgotten that viscus the liver which is usual on such occasions. . . .

The winter at the seaside is less agreeable and more bracing than the summer, and there were days when this Author had almost to force himself through the wholesome, necessary routines of his life, when the south-west wind savaged his villa and roared in the chimneys and slapped its windows with gustful of rain and promised to wet that Author thoroughly and exasperatingly down his neck and round his wrists and ankles directly he put his nose outside his door. And the grey waves he saw from his window came rolling inshore under the hurrying grey rain-bursts, line after line, to smash along the undercliff into vast, feathering fountains of foam and sud and send a salt-tasting spin-drift into his eyes. But manfully he would put on his puttees and his waterproof cape and his biggest brierwood pipe, and out he would go into the whurry-balloo of it all, knowing that so he would be all the brighter for his nice story-writing after tea.

On such a day he went out. He went out very resolutely along the seaside gardens of gravel and tamarisk and privet, resolved to oblige himself to go right past the harbour and up to the top of the east cliff before ever he turned his face back to the comforts of fire and wife and tea and buttered toast. . . .

And somewhere, perhaps half a mile away from home, he became aware of a queer character trying to keep abreast of him.

His impression was of a very miserable black man in the greasy, blue-black garments of a stoker, a lascar probably from a steamship in the harbour, and going with a sort of lame hobble.

As he passed this individual the Author had a transitory thought of how much Authors don't know in the world, how much, for instance, this shivering, cringing body might be hiding within itself, of inestimable value as 'local colour' if only one could get hold of it for 'putting into' one's large acceptable novels. Why doesn't one sometimes tap these sources? Kipling, for example, used to do so, with most successful results. . . . And then the Author became aware that this enigma was hurrying to overtake him. He slackened his pace. . . .

The creature wasn't asking for a light; it was begging for a box of matches. And what was odd, in quite good English.

The Author surveyed the beggar and slapped his pockets. Never had he seen so miserable a face. It was by no means a prepossessing face, with its aquiline nose, its sloping brows, its dark, deep, bloodshot eyes much too close together, its V-shaped, dishonest mouth and drenched chin-tuft. And yet it was attractively animal and pitiful. The idea flashed suddenly into the Author's head: 'Why not, instead of going on, thinking emptily, through this beastly weather—why not take this man back home now, to the warm, dry study, and give him a hot drink and something to smoke, and *draw him out?*'

Get something technical and first-hand that would rather score off Kipling.

'It's damnably cold!' he shouted, in a sort of hearty, forecastle voice.

'It's worse than that,' said the strange stoker.

'It's a hell of a day!' said the Author, more forcible than ever.

'Don't remind me of hell,' said the stoker, in a voice of inappeasable regret.

The Author slapped his pockets again. 'You've got an infernal cold. Look here, my man—confound it! would you like a hot grog? . . .'

2

The scene shifts to the Author's study—a blazing coal fire, the stoker sitting dripping and steaming before it, with his feet inside the fender, while the Author fusses about the room, directing the preparation of hot drinks. The Author is acutely aware not only of the stoker but of himself. The stoker has probably never been in the home of an Author before; he is probably awestricken at the array of books, at the comfort, convenience, and efficiency of the home, at the pleasant personality entertaining him. . . . Meanwhile the Author does not forget that the stoker is material, is 'copy,' is being watched, *observed*. So he poses and watches, until presently he forgets to pose in his astonishment at the thing he is observing. Because this stoker is rummier than a stoker ought to be—

He does not simply accept a hot drink; he informs his host just how hot the drink must be to satisfy him.

'Isn't there something you could put in it—something called red pepper? I've tasted that once or twice. It's good. If you could put in a bit of red pepper.'

'If you can stand that sort of thing?'

'And if there isn't much water, can't you set light to the stuff? Or let me drink it boiling, out of a pannikin or something? Pepper and all.'

Wonderful fellows, these stokers! The Author went to the bell and asked for red pepper.

And then as he came back to the fire he saw something that he instantly dismissed as an optical illusion, as a mirage effect of the clouds of steam his guest was disengaging. The stoker was sitting, all crouched up, as close over the fire as he could contrive; and he was holding his black hands, not to the fire but *in* the fire, holding them pressed flat against two red, glowing masses of coal. . . . He glanced over his shoulder at the Author with a guilty start, and then instantly the Author perceived that the hands were five or six inches away from the coal.

Then came smoking. The Author produced one of his big cigars— for although a conscientious pipe-smoker himself he gave people cigars; and then, again struck by something odd, he went off into a corner of the room where a little oval mirror gave him a means of watching the stoker undetected. And this is what he saw.

He saw the stoker, after a furtive glance at him, deliberately turn the cigar round, place the lighted end in his mouth, inhale strongly, and blow a torrent of sparks and smoke out of his nose. His firelit face as he did this expressed a diabolical relief. Then very hastily he reversed the cigar again, and turned round to look at the Author. The Author turned slowly towards him.

'You like that cigar?' he asked, after one of those mutual pauses that break down a pretence.

'It's admirable.'

'Why do you smoke it the other way round?'

The stoker perceived he was caught. 'It's a stokehole trick,' he said. 'Do you mind if I do it? I didn't think you saw.'

317

'Pray smoke just as you like,' said the Author, and advanced to watch the operation.

It was exactly like the fire-eater at the village fair. The man stuck the burning cigar into his mouth and blew sparks out of his nostrils. 'Ah!' he said, with a note of genuine satisfaction. And then, with the cigar still burning in the corner of his mouth, he turned to the fire and *began to rearrange the burning coals with his hands* so as to pile up a great glowing mass. He picked up flaming and white-hot lumps as one might pick up lumps of sugar. The Author watched him, dumb-founded.

'I say!' he cried. 'You stokers get a bit tough.'

The stoker dropped the glowing piece of coal in his hand. 'I forgot,' he said, and sat back a little.

'Isn't that a bit—*extra?*' asked the Author, regarding him. 'Isn't that some sort of trick?'

'We get so tough down there,' said the stoker, and paused discreetly as the servant came in with the red pepper.

'Now you can drink,' said the Author, and set himself to mix a drink of a pungency that he would have considered murderous ten minutes before. When he had done, the stoker reached over and added more red pepper.

'I don't quite see how it is your hand doesn't burn,' said the Author as the stoker drank. The stoker shook his head over the uptilted glass.

'Incombustible,' he said, putting it down. 'Could I have just a tiny drop more? Just brandy and pepper, if you *don't* mind. Set alight. I don't care for water except when it's superheated steam.'

And as the Author poured out another stiff glass of this incandescent brew, the stoker put up his hand and scratched the matted black hair over his temple. Then instantly he desisted and sat looking wickedly at the Author, while the Author stared at him aghast. For at the corner of his square, high, narrow forehead, revealed for an instant by the thrusting back of the hair, a curious stumpy excrescence had been visible; and the top of his ear—he had a pointed top to his ear!

'A-a-a-a-h!' said the Author, with dilated eyes.

'A-a-a-a-h!' said the stoker, in hopeless distress.

'But you aren't—!'

'I know—I know I'm not. I know. . . . I'm a devil. A poor, lost, homeless devil.'

And suddenly, with a gesture of indescribable despair, the apparent stoker buried his face in his hands and burst into tears.

'Only man who's ever been decently kind to me,' he sobbed. 'And now—you'll chuck me out again into the beastly wet and cold. . . . Beautiful fire. . . . Nice drink. . . . Almost home-like. . . . Just to torment me. . . . Boo-ooh!'

And let it be recorded to the credit of our little Author, that he did overcome his momentary horror, that he did go quickly round the table, and that he patted that dirty stoker's shoulder.

'There!' he said. 'There! Don't mind my rudeness. Have another nice drink. Have a hell of a drink. I won't turn you out if you're unhappy—on a day like this. Have just a mouthful of pepper, man, and pull yourself together.'

And suddenly the poor devil caught hold of his arm. 'Nobody good to me,' he sobbed. 'Nobody good to me.' And his tears ran down over the Author's plump little hand—scalding tears.

3

All really wonderful things happen rather suddenly and without any great emphasis upon their wonderfulness, and this was no exception to the general rule. This Author went on comforting his devil as though this was nothing more than a chance encounter with an unhappy child, and the devil let his grief and discomfort have vent in a manner that seemed at the time as natural as anything could be. He was clearly a devil of feeble character and uncertain purpose, much broken down by harshness and cruelty, and it throws a curious light upon the general state of misconception with regard to matters diabolical that it came as a quite pitiful discovery to our Author that a devil could be unhappy and heart-broken. For a long time his most earnest and persistent questioning could gather nothing except that his guest was an exile from a land of great warmth and considerable entertainment, and it was only after considerable further applications of brandy and pepper that the sobbing confidences of the poor creature grew into the form of a coherent and understandable narrative.

And then it became apparent that this person was one of the very lowest types of infernal denizen, and that his role in the dark realms of Dis had been that of watcher and minder of a herd of sinister beings hitherto unknown to our Author, the Devil's Wild Asses, which pastured in a stretch of meadows near the Styx. They were, he gathered, unruly, dangerous, and enterprising beasts, amenable only to a certain formula of expletives, which instantly reduced them to obedience. These expletives the stoker-devil would not repeat; to do so except when actually addressing one of the Wild Asses would, he explained, involve torments of the most terrible description. The bare thought of them gave him a shivering fit. But he gave the Author to understand that to crack these curses as one drove the Wild Asses to and from their grazing on the Elysian fields was a by no means disagreeable amusement. The ass-herds would try who could crack the loudest until the welkin rang.

And speaking of these things, the poor creature gave a picture of diabolical life that impressed the Author as by no means unpleasant for any one with a suitable constitution. It was like the Idylls of Theocritus done in fire; the devils drove their charges along burning lanes and sat gossiping in hedges of flames, rejoicing in the warm dry breezes (which it seems are rendered peculiarly bracing by the faint flavour of brimstone in the air), and watching the harpies and furies and witches circling in the perpetual afterglow of that inferior sky. And ever and again there would be holidays, and one would take one's lunch and wander over the sulphur craters picking flowers of sulphur or fishing for the souls of usurers and publishers and house-agents and land-agents in the lakes of boiling pitch. It was good sport, for the usurers and publishers and house-agents and land-agents were always eager to be caught; they crowded round the hooks and fought violently for the bait, and protested vehemently and entertainingly against the Rules and Regulations that compelled their instant return to the lake of fire.

And sometimes when he was on holiday this particular devil would go through the saltpetre dunes, where the witches' brooms grow and the blasted heath is in flower, to the landing-place of the ferry whence the Great Road runs through the shops and banks of the Via Dolorosa to the New Judgement Hall, and watch the crowds of damned arriving by the steam ferry-boats of the Consolidated Charon Company. This steamboat-gazing seems about as popular down there as it is at Folkestone. Almost every day notable people arrive, and, as the devils are very well informed about terrestrial affairs—for of course all the earthly newspapers go straight to hell—whatever else could one expect?—they get ovations of an almost undergraduate intensity. At times you can hear their cheering or booing, as the case may be, right away on the pastures where the Wild Asses feed. And that had been this particular devil's undoing.

He had always been interested in the career of the Rt. Hon. W.E. Gladstone. . . .

He was minding the Wild Asses. He knew the risks. He knew the penalties. But when he heard the vast uproar, when he heard the eager voices in the lane of fire saying, 'It's Gladstone at last!' when he saw how quietly and unsuspiciously the Wild Asses cropped their pasture, the temptation was too much. He slipped away. He saw the great Englishman landed after a slight struggle. He joined in the outcry of 'Speech! Speech!' He heard the first delicious promise of a Home Rule movement which should break the last feeble links of Celestial Control. . . .

And meanwhile the Wild Asses escaped—according to the rules and the prophecies. . . .

4

The little Author sat and listened to this tale of a wonder that never for a moment struck him as incredible. And outside his rain-lashed window the strung-out fishing smacks pitched and rolled on their way home to Folkestone harbour. . . .

The Wild Asses escaped.

They got away to the world. And his superior officers took the poor herdsman and tried him and bullied him and passed this judgement upon him: that he must go to the earth and find the Wild Asses, and say to them that certain string of oaths that otherwise must never be repeated, and so control them and bring them back to hell. That— or else one pinch of salt on their tails. It did not matter which. One by one he must bring them back, driving them by spell and curse to the cattle-boat of the ferry. And until he had caught and brought them all back he might never return again to the warmth and comfort of his accustomed life. That was his sentence and punishment. And they put him into a shrapnel shell and fired him out among the stars, and when he had a little recovered he pulled himself together and made his way to the world.

But he never found his Wild Asses and after a little time he gave up trying.

He gave up trying because the Wild Asses, once they had got out of control, developed the most amazing gifts. They could, for instance, disguise themselves with any sort of human shape, and the only way in which they differed then from a normal human being was—according to the printed paper of instructions that had been given to their custodian when he was fired out—that 'their general conduct remains that of a Wild Ass of the Devil.'

'And what interpretation can we put upon *that*?' he asked the listening Author.

And there was one night in the year—Walpurgis Night—when the Wild Asses became visibly great black wild asses and kicked up their hind legs and brayed. They had to. 'But then, of course,' said the devil, 'they would take care to shut themselves up somewhere when they felt that coming on.'

Like most weak characters, the stoker devil was intensely egotistical. He was anxious to dwell upon his own miseries and discomforts and difficulties and the general injustice of his treatment, and he was careless and casually indicative about the peculiarities of the Wild Asses, the matter which most excited and interested the Author. He bored on with his doleful story, and the Author had to interrupt with questions again and again in order to get any clear idea of the situation.

The devil's main excuse for his nervelessness was his profound ignorance of human nature. 'So far as I can see,' he said, 'they might all be Wild Asses. I tried it once—'

'Tried what?'

'The formula. You know.'

'Yes?'

'On a man named Sir Edward Carson.'

'Well?'

'Ugh!' said the devil.

'Punishment?'

'Don't speak of it. He was just a professional lawyer-politician who had lost his sense of values. . . . How was *I* to know? . . . But our people certainly know how to hurt. . . .'

After that it would seem this poor devil desisted absolutely from any attempt to recover his lost charges. He just tried to live for the moment and make his earthly existence as tolerable as possible. It was clear he hated the world. He found it cold, wet, draughty. . . . I can't understand why everybody insists upon living outside of it,' he said. 'If you went inside—'

He sought warmth and dryness. For a time he found a kind of contentment in charge of the upcast furnace of a mine, and then he was superseded by an electric-fan. While in this position he read a vivid account of the intense heat in the Red Sea, and he was struck by the idea that if he could get a job as stoker upon an Indian liner he might snatch some days of real happiness during that portion of the voyage. For some time his natural ineptitude prevented his realising this project, but at last, after some bitter experiences of homelessness during a London December, he had been able to ship on an Indiaward boat—only to get stranded in Folkestone in consequence of a propeller breakdown. And so here he was!

He paused.

'But about these Wild Asses?' said the Author.

The mournful, dark eyes looked at him hopelessly.

'Mightn't they do a lot of mischief?' asked the Author.

'They'll do no end of mischief,' said the despondent devil.

'Ultimately you'll catch it for that?'

'Ugh!' said the stoker, trying not to think of it.

5

Now the spirit of romantic adventure slumbers in the most unexpected places, and I have already told you of our plump Author's discontents. He had been like a smouldering bomb for some years. Now, he burst out. He suddenly became excited, energetic, stimulating, uplifting.

He stood over the drooping devil.

'But my dear chap!' he said. 'You must pull yourself together. You must do better than this. These confounded brutes may be doing all sorts of mischief. While you—shirk. . . .'

And so on. Real ginger.

'If I had some one to go with me. Some one who knew his way about.'

The Author took whisky in the excitement of the moment. He began to move very rapidly about his room and make short, sharp gestures. You know how this sort of emotion wells up at times. 'We must work from some central place,' said the Author. 'To begin with, London perhaps.'

It was not two hours later that they started, this Author and this devil he had taken to himself, upon a mission. They went out in overcoats and warm underclothing—the Author gave the devil a thorough outfit, a double lot of Jaeger's extra thick—and they were resolved to find the Wild Asses of the Devil and send them back to hell, or at least the Author was, in the shortest possible time. In the picture you will see him with a field-glass slung under his arm, the better to watch suspected cases; in his pocket, wrapped in oiled paper, is a lot of salt to use if by chance he finds a Wild Ass when the devil and his string of oaths is not at hand. So he started. And when he had caught and done for the Wild Asses, then the Author supposed that he would come back to his nice little villa and his nice little wife, and to his little daughter who said the amusing things, and to his popularity, his large gilt-edged popularity, and—except for an added prestige—be just exactly the man he had always been. Little knowing that whosoever takes unto himself a devil and goes out upon a quest, goes out upon a quest from which there is no returning

Nevermore.

THE STORY OF THE LAST TRUMP

I

THE story of the Last Trump begins in Heaven and it ends in all sorts of places round about the world. . . .

Heaven, you must know, is a kindly place, and the blessed ones do not go on for ever singing Alleluia, whatever you may have been told. For they too are finite creatures, and must be fed with their eternity in little bits, as one feeds a chick or a child. So that there are mornings and changes and freshness, there is time to condition their lives. And the children are still children, gravely eager about their playing and ready always for new things; just children they are, but blessed as you see them in the pictures beneath the careless feet of the Lord God. And one of these blessed children routing about in an attic—for Heaven is, of course, full of the most heavenly attics, seeing that it has children—came upon a number of instruments stored away, and laid its little chubby hands upon them. . . .

Now indeed I cannot tell what these instruments were, for to do so would be to invade mysteries. . . . But one I may tell of, and that was a great brazen trumpet which the Lord God had made when He made the world—for the Lord God finishes all His jobs—to blow when the time for our judgement came round. And He had made it and left it; there it was, and everything was settled exactly as the Doctrine of Predestination declares. And this blessed child conceived one of those unaccountable passions of childhood for its smoothness and brassiness, and he played with it and tried to blow it, and trailed it about with him out of the attic into the gay and golden streets, and, after many fitful wanderings to those celestial battlements of crystal of which you have doubtless read. And there the blessed child fell to counting the stars, and forgot all about the Trumpet beside him until a flourish of his elbow sent it over. . . .

325

Down fell the trump, spinning as it fell, and for a day or so, which seemed but moments in heaven, the blessed child watched its fall until it was a glittering little speck of brightness. . . .

When it looked a second, time the trump was gone. . . .

I do not know what happened to that child when at last it was time for Judgement Day and that shining trumpet was missed. I know that Judgement Day is long overpassed, because of the wickedness of the world; I think perhaps it was in A.D. 1000 when the expected Day should have dawned that never came, but no other heavenly particulars do I know at all, because now my scene changes to the narrow ways of this Earth. . . . And the Prologue in Heaven ends.

2

And now the scene is a dingy little shop in Caledonian Market, where things of an incredible worthlessness lie in wait for such as seek after an impossible cheapness. In the window, as though it had always been there and never anywhere else, lies a long, battered discoloured trumpet of brass that no prospective purchaser has ever been able to sound. In it mice shelter, and dust and fluff have gathered after the fashion of this world. The keeper of the shop is a very old man, and he bought the shop long ago, but already this trumpet was there; he has no idea whence it came, nor its country or origin, nor anything about it. But once in a moment of enterprise that led to nothing he decided to call it an Ancient Ceremonial Shawm, though he ought to have known that whatever a shawm may be the last thing it was likely to be is a trumpet, seeing that they are always mentioned together. And above it hung concertinas and melodeons and cornets and tin whistles and mouth-organs and all that rubbish of musical instruments which delight the hearts of the poor. Until one day two blackened young men from the big motor works in the Pansophist Road stood outside the window and argued.

They argued about these instruments in stock and how you made these instruments sound, because they were fond of argument, and one asserted and the other denied that he could make every instrument in the place sound a note. And the argument rose high, and led to a bet.

'Supposing, of course, that the instrument is in order,' said Hoskin, who was betting he could.

'That's understood,' said Briggs.

And then they called as witnesses certain other young and black and greasy men in the same employment, and after much argument and discussion that lasted through the afternoon, they went in to the little old dealer about teatime, just as he was putting a blear-eyed, stinking paraffin-lamp to throw an unfavourable light upon his always very unattractive window. And after great difficulty they arranged that for the sum of one shilling, paid in advance, Hoskin should have a try at every instrument in the shop that Briggs chose to indicate.

And the trial began.

The third instrument that was pitched upon by Briggs for the trial was the strange trumpet that lay at the bottom of the window, the trumpet that you, who have read the Introduction, know was the trumpet for the Last Trump. And Hoskin tried and tried again, and then, blowing desperately, hurt his ears. But he could get no sound from the trumpet. Then he examined the trumpet more carefully and discovered the mice and fluff and other things in it, and demanded that it should be cleaned; and the old dealer, nothing loth, knowing they were used to automobile-horns and such-like instruments, agreed to let them clean it on condition that they left it shiney. So the young men, after making a suitable deposit (which, as you shall hear, was presently confiscated), went off with the trumpet, proposing to clean it next day at the works and polish it with the peculiarly excellent brass polish employed upon the honk-honk horns of the firm. And this they did, and Hoskin tried again.

But he tried in vain. Whereupon there arose a great argument about the trumpet, whether it was in order or not, whether it was possible for any one to sound it. For if not, then clearly it was outside the condition of the bet.

Others among the young men tried it, including two who played wind instruments in a band and were musically knowing men. After their own failure they were strongly on the side of Hoskin and strongly against Briggs, and most of the other young men were of the same opinion.

'Not a bit of it,' said Briggs, who was a man of resource. '*I*'ll show you that it can be sounded.'

And taking the instrument in his hand, he went towards a peculiarly powerful foot blow-pipe that stood at the far end of the toolshed. 'Good old Briggs!' said one of the other young men, and opinion veered about.

Briggs removed the blow-pipe from its bellows and tube, and then adjusted the tube very carefully to the mouthpiece of the trumpet. Then with great deliberation he produced a piece of bees-waxed string from a number of other strange and filthy contents in his pocket and tied the tube to the mouthpiece. And then he began to work the treadle of the bellows.

'Good old Briggs!' said the one who had previously admired him.

And then something incomprehensible happened.

It was a flash. Whatever else it was, it was a flash. And a sound that seemed to coincide exactly with the flash.

Afterwards the young men agreed to it that the trumpet blew to bits. It blew to bits and vanished, and they were all flung upon their faces—not backward, be it noted, but on their faces—and Briggs was stunned and scared. The toolshed windows were broken and the various apparatus and cars around were much displaced, and no *traces of the trumpet were ever discovered*.

That last particular puzzled and perplexed poor Briggs very much. It puzzled and perplexed him the more because he had had an impression, so extraordinary, so incredible, that he was never able to describe it to any other living person. But his impression was this: that the flash that came with the sound came, not from the trumpet but to it, that it smote down to it and took it, and that its shape was in the exact likeness of a hand and arm of fire.

3

And that was not all, that was not the only strange thing about the disappearance of that battered trumpet. There was something else, even more difficult to describe, an effect as though for one instant something opened. . . .

The young men who worked with Hoskin and Briggs had that clearness of mind which comes of dealing with machinery, and they all felt this indescribable something else, as if for an instant the world wasn't the world, but something lit and wonderful, larger—

This is what one of them said of it.

'I felt,' he said, 'just for a minute—as though I was blown to Kingdom Come.'

'It is just how it took me,' said another. ' "Lord," I says, "here's Judgement Day!" and then there I was sprawling among the files. . . .'

But none of the others felt that they could say anything more definite than that.

4

Moreover, there was a storm. All over the world there was a storm that puzzled meteorology, a moment's gale that left the atmosphere in a state of wild swaygog, rains, tornadoes, depressions, irregularities for weeks. News came of it from all the quarters of the earth.

All over China, for example, that land of cherished graves, there was a duststorm, dust leaped into the air. A kind of earthquake shook Europe—an earthquake that seemed to have at heart the peculiar interests of Mr Algernon Ashton; everywhere it cracked mausoleums and shivered the pavements of cathedrals, swished the flower-beds of cemeteries, and tossed tombstones aside. A crematorium in Texas blew up. The sea was greatly agitated, and the beautiful harbour of Sydney, in Australia, was seen to be littered with sharks floating upside down in manifest distress. . . .

And all about the world a sound was heard like the sound of a trumpet instantly cut short.

5

But this much is only the superficial dressing of the story. The reality is something different. It is this: that in an instant, and for an instant, the dead lived, and all that are alive in the world did for a moment see the Lord God and all His powers, His hosts of angels, and all His array looking down upon them. They saw Him as one sees by a flash of lightning in the darkness, and then instantly the world was opaque again, limited, petty, habitual. That is the tremendous reality of this story. Such glimpses have happened in individual cases before. The Lives of the saints abound in them. Such a glimpse it was that came to Devindranath Tagore upon the burning ghat at Benares. But this was not an individual but a world experience; the flash came to every one. Not always was it quite the same, and thereby the doubter found his denials, when presently a sort of discussion broke out in the obscurer Press. For this one testified that it seemed that 'One stood very near to me,' and another saw 'all the hosts of heaven flame up towards the Throne.'

And there were others who had a vision of brooding watchers, and others who imagined great sentinels before a veiled figure, and some one who felt nothing more divine than a sensation of happiness and freedom such as one gets from a sudden burst of sunshine in the spring. . . . So that one is forced to believe that something more than wonderfully wonderful, something altogether strange, was seen, and that all these various things that people thought they saw were only interpretations drawn from their experiences and their imaginations. It was a light, it was beauty, it was high and solemn, it made this world seem a flimsy transparency.

Then it had vanished. . . .

And people were left with the question of what they had seen, and just how much it mattered.

6

A little old lady sat by the fire in a small sitting-room in West Kensington. Her cat was in her lap, her spectacles were on her nose; she was reading the morning's paper, and beside her, on a little occasional table, was her tea and a buttered muffin. She had finished the crimes and she was reading about the Royal Family. When she had read all there was to read about the Royal Family, she put down the paper, deposited the cat on the hearthrug, and turned to her tea. She had poured out her first cup and she had just taken up a quadrant of muffin when the trump and the flash came. Through its instant duration she remained motionless with the quadrant of muffin poised halfway to her mouth. Then very slowly she put the morsel down.

'Now what was that?' she said.

She surveyed the cat, but the cat was quite calm. Then she looked very, very hard at her lamp. It was a patent safety lamp, and had always behaved very well. Then she stared at the window, but the curtains were drawn and everything was in order.

'One might think I was going to be ill,' she said, and resumed her toast.

7

Not far away from this old lady, not more than three-quarters of a mile at most, sat Mr Parchester in his luxurious study, writing a perfectly beautiful, sustaining, sermon about the Need of Faith in God. He was a handsome, earnest, modern preacher, he was rector of one of our big West End churches, and he had amassed a large, fashionable congregation. Every Sunday, and at convenient intervals during the week, he fought against Modern Materialism, Scientific Education, Excessive Puritanism, Pragmatism, Doubt, Levity, Selfish Individualism, Further Relaxation of the Divorce Laws, all the Evils of our Time—and anything else that was unpopular. He believed quite simply, he said, in all the old, simple, kindly things. 'He had the face of a saint, but he had rendered this generally acceptable by growing side whiskers. And nothing could tame the beauty of his voice.

He was an enormous asset in the spiritual life of the metropolis— to give it no harsher name—and his fluent periods had restored faith and courage to many a poor soul hovering on the brink of the dark river of thought. . . .

And just as beautiful Christian maidens played a wonderful part in the last days of Pompeii, in winning proud Roman hearts to a hated and despised faith, so Mr Parchester's naturally graceful gestures, and his simple, melodious, trumpet voice won back scores of our half-pagan rich women to church attendance and the social work of which his church was the centre. . . .

And now by the light of an exquisitely shaded electric lamp he was writing this sermon of quiet, confident belief (with occasional hard smacks, perfect stingers in fact, at current unbelief and rival leaders of opinion) in the simple, divine faith of our fathers. . . .

When there came this truncated trump and this vision. . . .

8

Of all the innumerable multitudes who for the infinitesimal fraction of a second had this glimpse of the Divinity, none were so blankly and profoundly astonished as Mr Parchester. For—it may be because of his subtly spiritual nature—he *saw*, and seeing believed. He dropped his pen and let it roll across his manuscript, he sat stunned, every drop of blood fled from his face and his lips and his eyes dilated.

While he had just been writing and arguing about God, there *was* God!

The curtain had been snatched back for an instant; it had fallen again; but his mind had taken a photographic impression of everything that he had seen—the grave presences, the hierarchy, the effulgence, the vast concourse, the terrible, gentle eyes. He felt it, as though the vision still continued, behind the bookcases, behind the pictured wall and the curtained window: *even now there was judgement!*

For quite a long time he sat, incapable of more than apprehending this supreme realisation. His hands were held out limply upon the desk before him. And then very slowly his staring eyes came back to immediate things, and fell upon the scattered manuscript on which he had been engaged. He read an unfinished sentence and slowly recovered its intention. As he did so, a picture of his congregation came to him as he saw it from the pulpit during his evening sermon, as he had intended to see it on the Sunday evening that was at hand, with Lady Rupert in her sitting and Lady Blex in hers and Mrs Munbridge, the rich and in her Jewish way very attractive Mrs Munbridge, running them close in her adoration, and each with one or two friends they had brought to adore him, and behind them the Hexhams, and the Wassinghams and behind them others and others and others, ranks and ranks of people, and the galleries on either side packed with worshippers of a less dominant class, and the great organ and his magnificent choir waiting to support him and supplement him, and the great altar to the left of him, and the beautiful new Lady Chapel, done by Roger Fry and Wyndham Lewis and all the latest people in Art, to the right. He thought of the listening multitude, seen through the haze of the thousand electric candles, and how he had planned the paragraphs of his discourse so that the notes of his beautiful voice should float slowly down, like golden leaves in autumn, into the smooth tarn of their silence, word by word, phrase by phrase, until he came to—

'Now to God the Father, God the Son—'

And all the time he knew that Lady Blex would watch his face and Mrs Munbridge, leaning those graceful shoulders of hers a little forward, would watch his face. . . .

Many people would watch his face.

All sorts of people would come to Mr Parchester's services at times. Once it was said Mr Balfour had come. Just to hear him. After his sermons, the strangest people would come and make confessions in the beautifully furnished reception-room beyond the vestry. All sorts of people. Once or twice he had asked people to come and listen to him; and one of them had been a very beautiful woman. And often he had dreamt of the people who might come; prominent people, influential people, remarkable people. But never before had it occurred to Mr Parchester that, a little hidden from the rest of the congregation, behind the thin veil of this material world, there was another auditorium. And that God also, God also, watched his face.

And watched him through and through.

Terror seized upon Mr Parchester.

He stood up, as though Divinity had come into the room before him. He was trembling. He felt smitten and about to be smitten.

He perceived that it was hopeless to try and hide what he had written, what he had thought, the unclean egotism he had become.

'I did not know,' he said at last.

The click of the door behind him warned him that he was not alone. He turned and saw Miss Skelton, his typist, for it was her time to come for his manuscript and copy it out in the specially legible type he used. For a moment he stared at her strangely.

She looked at him with those deep, adoring eyes of hers. 'Am I too soon, sir?' she asked in her slow, unhappy voice, and seemed prepared for a noiseless departure.

He did not answer immediately. Then he said: 'Miss Skelton, the judgement of God is close at hand!'

And seeing she stood perplexed, he said—

'Miss Skelton, how can you expect me to go on acting and mouthing this Tosh when the Sword of Truth hangs over us?'

Something in her face made him ask a question.

'Did *you* see anything?' he asked.

'I thought it was because I was rubbing my eyes.'

'Then indeed there is a God! And he is watching us now. And all this about us, this sinful room, this foolish costume, this preposterous life of blasphemous pretension—!'

He stopped short, with a kind of horror on his face.

With a hopeless gesture he rushed by her. He appeared wild-eyed upon the landing before his manservant, who was carrying a scuttle of coal upstairs.

'Brompton,' he said, 'what are you doing?'

'Coal, sir.'

'Put it down, man!' he said. 'Are you not an immortal soul? God is here! As close as my hand! Repent! Turn to Him! The Kingdom of Heaven is at hand!'

9

Now if you are a policeman perplexed by a sudden and unaccountable collision between a taxicab and an electric standard, complicated by a blinding flash and a sound like an abbreviated trump from an automobile horn, you do not want to be bothered by a hatless clerical gentleman suddenly rushing out of a handsome private house and telling you that 'the Kingdom of Heaven is at hand!' You are respectful to him because it is the duty of a policeman to be respectful to Gentlemen, but you say to him, 'Sorry I can't attend to that now, sir, One thing at a time. I've got this little accident to see to.' And if he persists in dancing round the gathering crowd and coming at you again, you say: 'I'm afraid I must ask you just to get away from here, sir. You aren't being a 'elp, sir.' And if, on the other hand, you are a well-trained clerical gentleman, who knows his way about in the world, you do not go on pestering a policeman on duty after he has said that, even although you think God is looking at you and judgement is close at hand. You turn away and go on, a little damped, looking for some one else more likely to pay attention to your tremendous tidings.

And so it happened to the Reverend Mr Parchester.

He experienced a curious little recession of confidence. He went on past quite a number of people without saying anything further, and the next person he accosted was a flower-woman sitting by her basket at the corner of Chexington Square. She was unable to stop him at once when he began to talk to her because she was tying up a big bundle of white chrysanthemums and had an end of string behind her teeth. And her daughter who stood beside her was the sort of girl who wouldn't say 'Bo!' to a goose.

'Do you know, my good woman,' said Mr Parchester, 'that while we poor creatures of earth go about our poor business here, while we sin and blunder and follow every sort of base end, close to us, above us, around us, watching us, judging us, are God and His holy angels? I have had a vision, and I am not the only one. I have *seen*. We are *in* the Kingdom of Heaven now and here, and judgement is all about us now! Have you seen nothing? No light? No sound? No warning?'

By this time the old flower-seller had finished her bunch of flowers and could speak. 'I saw it,' she said. 'And Mary—she saw it.'

'Well?' said Mr Parchester.

'But, Lord! It don't *mean* nothing!' said the old flower-seller.

10

At that a kind of chill fell upon Mr Parchester. He went on across Chexington Square by his own inertia.

He was still about as sure that he had seen God as he had been in his study, but now he was no longer sure that the world would believe that he had. He felt perhaps that this idea of rushing out to tell people was precipitate and inadvisable. After all, a priest in the Church of England is only one unit in a great machine; and in a world-wide spiritual crisis it should be the task of that great machine to act as one resolute body. This isolated crying aloud in the street was unworthy of a consecrated priest. It was a dissenting kind of thing to do. A vulgar individualistic screaming. He thought suddenly that he would go and tell his Bishop the great Bishop Wampach. He called a taxicab, and within half an hour he was in the presence of his commanding officer. It was an extraordinarily difficult and painful interview. . . .

You see, Mr Parchester believed. The Bishop impressed him as being quite angrily resolved not to believe. And for the first time in his career Mr Parchester realised just how much jealous hostility a beautiful, fluent, and popular preacher may arouse in the minds of the hierarchy. It wasn't, he felt, a conversation. It was like flinging oneself into the paddock of a bull that has long been anxious to gore one.

'Inevitably,' said the Bishop, 'this theatricalism, this star-turn business, with its extreme spiritual excitements, its exaggerated soul crisis and all the rest of it, leads to such a breakdown as afflicts you. Inevitably. You were at least wise to come to me. I can see you are only in the beginning of your trouble, that already in your mind fresh hallucinations are gathering to overwhelm you, voices, special charges and missions, strange revelations. . . . I wish I had the power to suspend you right away, to send you into retreat. . . .'

Mr Parchester made a violent effort to control himself. 'But I tell you,' he said, 'that I saw God!' He added, as if to reassure himself: 'More plainly, more certainly, than I see you.'

'Of course,' said the Bishop, 'this is how strange new sects come into existence; this is how false prophets spring out of the bosom of the Church. Loose-minded, excitable men of your stamp—'

Mr Parchester, to his own astonishment, burst into tears. 'But I tell you,' he wept, 'He is here. I have seen. I know.'

'Don't talk such nonsense!' said the Bishop. 'There is no one here but you and I!'

Mr Parchester expostulated. 'But,' he protested, 'He is omnipresent.'

The Bishop controlled an expression of impatience. 'It is characteristic of your condition,' he said, 'that you are unable to distinguish between a matter of fact and a spiritual truth. . . . Now listen to me. If you value your sanity and public decency and the discipline of the Church, go right home from here and go to bed. Send for Broadhays, who will prescribe a safe sedative. And read something calming and graceful and purifying. For my own part, I should be disposed to recommend the 'Life of Saint Francis of Assisi.'

11

Unhappily Mr Parchester did not go home. He went out from the Bishop's residence stunned and amazed, and suddenly upon his desolation came the thought of Mrs Munbridge. . . .

She would understand . . . .

He was shown up to her own little sitting-room. She had already gone up to her room to dress, but when she heard that he had called, and wanted very greatly to see her, she slipped on a loose, beautiful tea-gown *négligé* thing, and hurried to him. He tried to tell her everything, but she only kept saying 'There! there!' She was sure he wanted a cup of tea, he looked so pale and exhausted. She rang to have the tea equipage brought back; she put the dear saint in an arm-chair by the fire; she put cushions about him, and ministered to him. And when she began partially to comprehend what he had experienced, she suddenly realised that she too had experienced it. That vision had been a brainwave between their two linked and sympathetic brains. And that thought glowed in her as she brewed his tea with her own hands. He had been weeping! How tenderly he felt all these things! He was more sensitive than a woman. What madness to have expected understanding from a Bishop! But that was just like his unworldliness. He was not fit to take care of himself. A wave of tenderness carried her away. 'Here is your tea!' she said, bending over him, and fully conscious of her fragrant warmth and sweetness, and suddenly, she could never afterwards explain why she was so, she was moved to kiss him on his brow. . . .

How indescribable is the comfort of a true-hearted womanly friend! The safety of it! The consolation! . . .

About half-past seven that evening Mr Parchester returned to his own home, and Brompton admitted him. Brompton was relieved to find his employer looking quite restored and ordinary again. 'Brompton,' said Mr Parchester, 'I will not have the usual dinner tonight. Just a single mutton cutlet and one of those quarter-bottles of Perrier Jouet on a tray in my study. I shall have to finish my sermon tonight.'

(And he had promised Mrs Munbridge he would preach that sermon specially for her.)

12

And as it was with Mr Parchester and Brompton and Mrs Munbridge, and the taxi-driver and the policeman and the little old lady and the automobile mechanics and Mr Parchester's secretary and the Bishop, so it was with all the rest of the world. If a thing is sufficiently strange and great no one will perceive it. Men will go on in their own ways though one rose from the dead to tell them that the Kingdom of Heaven was at hand, though the Kingdom itself and all its glory became visible, blinding their eyes. They and their ways are one. Men will go on in their ways as rabbits will go on feeding in their hutches within a hundred yards of a battery of artillery. For rabbits are rabbits, and made to eat and breed, and men are human beings and creatures of habit and custom and prejudice; and what has made them, what will judge them, what will destroy them—they may turn their eyes to it at times as the rabbits will glance at the concussion of the guns, but it will never draw them away from eating their lettuce and sniffing after their does. . . .

THE PEARL OF LOVE

THE pearl is lovelier than the most brilliant of crystalline stones, the moralist declares, because it is made through the suffering of a living creature. About that I can say nothing because I feel none of the fascination of pearls. Their cloudy lustre moves me not at all. Nor can I decide for myself upon that age-long dispute whether The Pearl of Love is the cruellest of stories or only a gracious fable of the immortality of beauty.

Both the story and the controversy will be familiar to students of medieval Persian prose. The story is a short one, though the commentary upon it is a respectable part of the literature of that period. They have treated it as a poetic invention and they have treated it as an allegory meaning this, that, or the other thing. Theologians have had their copious way with it, dealing with it particularly as concerning the restoration of the body after death, and it has been greatly used as a parable by those who write about æsthetics. And many have held it to be the statement of a fact, simply and baldly true.

The story is laid in North India, which is the most fruitful soil for sublime love stories of all the lands in the world. It was in a country of sunshine and lakes and rich forests and hills and fertile valleys; and far away the great mountains hung in the sky, peaks, crests, and ridges of inaccessible and eternal snow. There was a young prince, lord of all the land; and he found a maiden of indescribable beauty and delightfulness and he made her his queen and laid his heart at her feet. Love was theirs, full of joys and sweetness, full of hope, exquisite, brave and marvellous love, beyond anything you have ever dreamt of love. It was theirs for a year and a part of a year; and then suddenly, because of some venomous sting that came to her in a thicket, she died.

She died and for a while the prince was utterly prostrated. He was silent and motionless with grief. They feared he might kill himself, and he had neither sons nor brothers to succeed him. For two days and nights he lay upon his face, fasting, across the foot of the couch which bore her calm and lovely body. Then he arose and ate, and went about very quietly like one who has taken a great resolution. He caused her body to be put in a coffin of lead mixed with silver, and for that he had an outer coffin made of the most precious and scented woods wrought with gold, and about that there was to be a sarcophagus of alabaster, inlaid with precious stones. And while these things were being done he spent his time for the most part by the pools and in the garden-houses and pavilions and groves and in those chambers in the palace where they two had been most together, brooding upon her loveliness. He did not rend his garments nor defile himself with ashes and sackcloth as the custom was, for his love was too great for such extravagances. At last he came forth again among his councillors and before the people, and told them what he had a mind to do.

He said he could never more touch woman, he could never more think of them, and so he would find a seemly youth to adopt for his heir and train him to his task, and that he would do his princely duties as became him; but that for the rest of it, he would give himself with all his power and all his strength and all his wealth, all that he could command, to make a monument worthy of his incomparable, dear, lost mistress. A building it should be of perfect grace and beauty, more marvellous than any other building had ever been or could ever be, so that to the end of time it should be a wonder, and men would treasure it and speak of it and desire to see it and come from all the lands of the earth to visit and recall the name and the memory of his queen. And this building he said was to be called the Pearl of Love.

And this his councillors and people permitted him to do, and so he did.

Year followed year and all the years he devoted himself to building and adorning the Pearl of Love. A great foundation was hewn out of the living rock in a place whence one seemed to be looking at the snowy wilderness of the great mountain across the valley of the world. Villages and hills there were, a winding river, and very far away three great cities. Here they put the sarcophagus of alabaster beneath a pavilion of cunning workmanship; and about it there were set pillars of strange and lovely stone and wrought and fretted walls, and a great casket of masonry bearing a dome and pinnacles and cupolas, as exquisite as a jewel. At first the design of the Pearl of Love was less bold and subtle than it became later. At first it was smaller and more wrought

340

and encrusted; there were many pierced screens and delicate clusters of rosy-hued pillars, and the sarcophagus lay like a child that sleeps among flowers. The first dome was covered with green tiles, framed and held together by silver, but this was taken away again because it seemed close, because it did not soar grandly enough for the broadening imagination of the prince.

For by this time he was no longer the graceful youth who had loved the girl queen. He was now a man, grave and intent, wholly set upon the building of the Pearl of Love. With every year of effort he had learnt new possibilities in arch and wall and buttress; he had acquired greater power over the material he had to use and he had learnt of a hundred stones and hues and effects that he could never have thought of in the beginning: His sense of colour had grown finer and colder; he cared no more for the enamelled gold-lined brightness that had pleased him first, the brightness of an illuminated missal; he sought now for blue colourings like the sky and for the subtle hues of great distances, for recondite shadows and sudden broad floods of purple opalescence and for grandeur and space. He wearied altogether of carvings and pictures and inlaid ornamentation and all the little careful work of men. 'Those were pretty things,' he said of his earlier decorations; and had them put aside into subordinate buildings where they would not hamper his main design. Greater and greater grew his artistry. With awe and amazement people saw the Pearl of Love sweeping up from its first beginnings to a superhuman breadth and height and magnificence. They did not know clearly what they had expected, but never had they expected so sublime a thing as this. 'Wonderful are the miracles,' they whispered, 'that love can do,' and all the women in the world, whatever other loves they had, loved the prince for the splendour of his devotion.

Through the middle of the building ran a great aisle, a vista, that the prince came to care for more and more. From the inner entrance of the building he looked along the length of an immense pillared gallery and across the central area from which the rose-hued columns had long since vanished, over the top of the pavilion under which lay the sarcophagus, through a marvellously designed opening, to the snowy wildernesses of the great mountain, the lord of all mountains, two hundred miles away. The pillars and arches and buttresses and galleries soared and floated on either side, perfect yet unobtrusive, like great archangels waiting in the shadows about the presence of God. When men saw that austere beauty for the first time they were exalted, and then they shivered and their hearts bowed down. Very often would the prince come to stand there and look at that vista, deeply moved and not yet fully satisfied. The Pearl of Love had still something for him to do, he felt, before his task was done. Always he would order some little alteration to be made or some recent alteration to be put back again. And one day he said that the sarcophagus would be clearer and simpler without the pavilion; and after regarding it very steadfastly for a long time, he had the pavilion dismantled and removed.

The next day he came and said nothing, and the next day and the next. Then for two days he stayed away altogether. Then he returned, bringing with him an architect and two master craftsmen and a small retinue.

All looked, standing together silently in a little group, amidst the serene vastness of their achievement. No trace of toil remained in its perfection. It was as if the God of nature's beauty had taken over their offspring to himself.

Only one thing there was to mar the absolute harmony. There was a certain disproportion about the sarcophagus. It had never been enlarged, and indeed how could it have been enlarged since the early days? It challenged the eye; it nicked the streaming lines. In that sarcophagus was the casket of lead and silver, and in the casket of lead and silver was the queen, the dear immortal cause of all this beauty. But now that sarcophagus seemed no more than a little dark oblong that lay incongruously in the great vista of the Pearl of Love. It was as if someone had dropped a small valise upon the crystal sea of heaven.

Long the prince mused, but no one knew the thoughts that passed through his mind.

At last he spoke. He pointed.

'Take that thing away,' he said.

THE QUEER STORY OF
BROWNLOW'S NEWSPAPER

1

I CALL this a Queer Story because it is a story without an explanation. When I first heard it, in scraps, from Brownlow I found it queer and incredible. But—it refuses to remain incredible. After resisting and then questioning and scrutinising and falling back before the evidence, after rejecting all his evidence as an elaborate mystification and refusing to hear any more about it, and then being drawn to reconsider it by an irresistible curiosity and so going through it all again, I have been forced to the conclusion that Brownlow, so far as he can tell the truth, has been telling the truth. But it remains queer truth, queer and exciting to the imagination. The more credible his story becomes the queerer it is. It troubles my mind. I am fevered by it, infected not with germs but with notes of interrogation and unsatisfied curiosity.

Brownlow, is, I admit, a cheerful spirit. I have known him tell lies. But I have never known him do anything so elaborate and sustained as this affair, if it is a mystification, would have to be. He is incapable of anything so elaborate and sustained. He is too lazy and easy-going for anything of the sort. And he would have laughed. At some stage he would have laughed and given the whole thing away. He has nothing to gain by keeping it up. His honour is not in the case either way. And after all there is his bit of newspaper in evidence—and the scrap of an addressed wrapper. . . .

I realise it will damage this story for many readers that it opens with Brownlow in a state very definitely on the gayer side of sobriety. He was not in a mood for cool and calculated observation, much less for accurate record. He was seeing things in an exhilarated manner. He was disposed to see them and greet them cheerfully and let them slip by out of attention. The limitations of time and space lay lightly upon him. It was after midnight. He had been dining with friends.

I have inquired what friends—and satisfied myself upon one or two obvious possibilities of that dinner party. They were, he said to me, 'just friends. They hadn't anything to do with it.' I don't usually push past an assurance of this sort, but I made an exception in this case. I watched my man and took a chance of repeating the question. There was nothing out of the ordinary about that dinner party, unless it was the fact that it was an unusually good dinner party. The host was Redpath Baynes, the solicitor, and the dinner was in his house in St John's Wood. Gifford, of the *Evening Telegraph,* whom I know slightly, was, I found, present, and from him I got all I wanted to know. There was much bright and discursive talk and Brownlow had been inspired to give an imitation of his aunt, Lady Clitherholme, reproving an inconsiderate plumber during some re-building operations at Clitherholme. This early memory had been received with considerable merriment—he was always very good about his aunt, Lady Clitherholme—and Brownlow had departed obviously elated by this little social success and the general geniality of the occasion. Had they talked, I asked, about the Future, or Einstein, or J.W. Dunne, or any such high and serious topic at that party? They had not. Had they discussed the modern newspaper? No. There had been nobody whom one could call a practical joker at this party, and Brownlow had gone off alone in a taxi. That is what I was most desirous of knowing. He had been duly delivered by his taxi at the main entrance to Sussex Court.

Nothing untoward is to be recorded of his journey in the lift to the fifth floor of Sussex Court. The liftman on duty noted nothing exceptional. I asked if Brownlow said, 'Good night.' The liftman does not remember. 'Usually he says Night O,' reflected the liftman—manifestly doing his best and with nothing particular to recall. And there the fruits of my inquiries about the condition of Brownlow on this particular evening conclude. The rest of the story comes directly from him. My investigations arrive only at this: he was certainly not drunk. But he was lifted a little out of our normal harsh and grinding contact with the immediate realities of existence. Life was glowing softly and warmly in him, and the unexpected could happen brightly, easily, and acceptably.

He went down the long passage with its red carpet, its clear light, and its occasional oaken doors, each with its artistic brass number. I have been down that passage with him on several occasions. It was his custom to enliven that corridor by raising his hat gravely as he passed each entrance, saluting his unknown and invisible neighbours, addressing them softly but distinctly by playful if sometimes slightly indecorous names of his own devising, expressing good wishes or paying them little compliments.

He came at last to his own door, number 49, and let himself in without serious difficulty. He switched on his hall light. Scattered on the polished oak floor and invading his Chinese carpet were a number of letters and circulars, the evening's mail. His parlourmaid-house-keeper, who slept in a room in another part of the building, had been taking her evening out, or these letters would have been gathered up and put on the desk in his bureau. As it was, they lay on the floor. He closed his door behind him or it closed of its own accord; he took off his coat and wrap, placed his hat on the head of the Greek charioteer whose bust adorns his hall, and set himself to pick up his letters.

This also he succeeded in doing without misadventure. He was a little annoyed to miss the *Evening Standard*. It is his custom, he says, to subscribe for the afternoon edition of the *Star* to read at tea-time and also for the final edition of the *Evening Standard* to turn over the last thing at night, if only on account of Low's cartoon. He gathered up all these envelopes and packets and took them with him into his little sitting-room. There he turned on the electric heater, mixed himself a weak whisky-and-soda, went to his bedroom to put on soft slippers and replace his smoking jacket by a frogged jacket of llama wool, returned to his sitting-room, lit a cigarette, and sat down in his arm-chair by the reading lamp to examine his correspondence. He recalls all these details very exactly. They were routines he had repeated scores of times.

Brownlow's is not a preoccupied mind; it goes out to things. He is one of those buoyant extroverts who open and read all their letters and circulars whenever they can get hold of them. In the daytime his secretary intercepts and deals with most of them, but at night he escapes from her control and does what he pleases, that is to say, he opens everything.

He ripped up various envelopes. There was a formal acknowl-edgment of a business letter he had dictated the day before, there was a letter from his solicitor asking for some details about a settlement he was making, there was an offer from some unknown gentleman with an aristocratic name to lend him money on his note of hand alone, and there was a notice about a proposed new wing to his club. 'Same old stuff,' he sighed. 'Same old stuff. What bores they all are!' He was always hoping, like every man who is proceeding across the plains of middle-age, that his correspondence would contain agreeable surprises—and it never did. Then, as he put it to me, *inter alia,* he picked up the remarkable newspaper.

2

It was different in appearance from an ordinary newspaper, but not so different as not to be recognisable as a newspaper, and he was surprised, he says, not to have observed it before. It was enclosed in a wrapper of pale green, but it was unstamped; apparently it had been delivered not by the postman, but by some other hand. (This wrapper still exists; I have seen it.) He had already torn it off before he noted that he was not the addressee.

For a moment or so he remained looking at this address, which struck him as just a little odd. It was printed in rather unusual type: 'Evan O'Hara, Mr, Sussex Court 49.'

'Wrong name,' said Mr Brownlow; 'Right address. Rummy. Sussex Court 49. . . . 'Spose he's got my *Evening Standard. . . .* 'Change no robbery.'

He put the torn wrapper with his unanswered letters and opened out the newspaper.

The title of the paper was printed in large slightly ornamental black-green letters that might have come from a kindred fount to that responsible for the address. But, as he read it, it was the *Evening Standard!* Or, at least, it was the 'Even Standrd.' 'Silly,' said Brownlow. 'It's some damn Irish paper. Can't spell—anything—these Irish. . . .'

He had, I think, a passing idea, suggested perhaps by the green wrapper and the green ink, that it was a lottery stunt from Dublin.

Still, if there was anything to read he meant to read it. He surveyed the front page. Across this ran a streamer headline: 'WILTON BORING REACHES SEVEN MILES: SUCCES ASSURED.'

'No,' said Brownlow. 'It must be oil. . . . Illiterate lot these oil chaps—leave out the "s" in "success." '

He held the paper down on his knee for a moment, reinforced himself by a drink, took and lit a second cigarette, and then leant back in his chair to take a dispassionate view of any oil-share pushing that might be afoot.

But it wasn't an affair of oil. It was, it began to dawn upon him, something stranger than oil. He found himself surveying a real evening newspaper, which was dealing, so far as he could see at the first onset, with the affairs of another world.

He had for a moment a feeling as though he and his arm-chair and his little sitting-room were afloat in a vast space and then it all seemed to become firm and solid again.

This thing in his hands was plainly and indisputably a printed newspaper. It was a little odd in its letterpress, and it didn't feel or rustle like ordinary paper, but newspaper it was. It was printed in either three or four columns—for the life of him he cannot remember which—and there were column headlines under the page streamer. It had a sort of art-nouveau affair at the bottom of one column that might be an advertisement (it showed a woman in an impossibly big hat), and in the upper left-hand corner was an unmistakable weather chart of Western Europe, with *coloured* isobars, or isotherms, or whatever they are, and the inscription: 'Tomorrow's Weather.'

And then he remarked the date. The date was November 10th, 1971!

'Steady on,' said Brownlow. 'Damitall! Steady on.'

He held the paper sideways, and then straight again. The date remained November 10th, 1971.

He got up in a state of immense perplexity and put the paper down. For a moment he felt a little afraid of it. He rubbed his forehead. 'Haven't been doing a Rip Van Winkle, by any chance, Brownlow, my boy?' he said. He picked up the paper again, walked out into his hall and looked at himself in the hall mirror. He was reassured to see no signs of advancing age, but the expression of mingled consternation and amazement upon his flushed face struck him suddenly as being undignified and unwarrantable. He laughed at himself, but not uncontrollably. Then he stared blankly at that familiar countenance. 'I must be half-way *tordu*,' he said, that being his habitual facetious translation of 'screwed.' On the console table was a little respectable-looking adjustable calendar bearing witness that the date was November 10th, 1931.

'D'you see?' he said, shaking the queer newspaper at it reproachfully. 'I ought to have spotted you for a hoax ten minutes ago. 'Moosing trick, to say the least of it. I suppose they've made Low editor for a night, and he's had this idea. Eh?'

He felt he had been taken in, but that the joke was a good one. And, with quite unusual anticipations of entertainment, he returned to his arm-chair. A good idea it was, a paper forty years ahead. Good fun if it was well done. For a time nothing but the sounds of a newspaper being turned over and Brownlow's breathing can have broken the silence of the flat.

3

Regarded as an imaginative creation, he found the thing almost too well done. Every time he turned a page he expected the sheet to break out into laughter and give the whole thing away. But it did nothing of the kind. From being a mere quip, it became an immense and amusing, if perhaps a little over-elaborate, lark. And then, as a lark, it passed from stage to stage of incredibility until, as any thing but the thing it professed to be, it was incredible altogether. It must have cost far more than an ordinary number. All sorts of colours were used, and suddenly he came upon illustrations that went beyond amazement; they were in the colours of reality. Never in all his life had he seen such colour printing—and the buildings and scenery and costumes in the pictures were strange. Strange and yet credible. They were colour photographs of actuality forty years from now. He could not believe anything else of them. Doubt could not exist in their presence.

His mind had swung back, away from the stunt-number idea altogether. This paper in his hand would not simply be costly beyond dreaming to produce. At any price it could not be produced. All this present world could not produce such an object as this paper he held in his hand. He was quite capable of realising that.

He sat turning the sheet over and—quite mechanically—drinking whisky. His sceptical faculties were largely in suspense; the barriers of criticism were down. His mind could now accept the idea that he was reading a newspaper of forty years ahead without any further protest.

It had been addressed to Mr Evan O'Hara, and it had come to him. Well and good. This Evan O'Hara evidently knew how to get ahead of things. . . .

I doubt if at that time Brownlow found anything very wonderful in the situation.

Yet it was, it continues to be, a very wonderful situation. The wonder of it mounts to my head as I write. Only gradually have I been able to build up this picture of Brownlow turning over that miraculous sheet, so that I can believe it myself. And you will understand how, as the thing flickered between credibility and incredibility in my mind, I asked him, partly to justify or confute what he told me, and partly to satisfy a vast expanding and, at last, devouring curiosity: 'What was there in it? What did it have to say?' At the same time, I found myself trying to catch him out in his story, and also asking him for every particular he could give me.

What was there in it? In other words, What will the world be doing forty years from now? That was the stupendous scale of the vision, of which Brownlow was afforded a glimpse. The world forty years from now! I lie awake at nights thinking of all that paper might have revealed to us. Much it did reveal, but there is hardly a thing it reveals that does not change at once into a constellation of riddles. When first he told me about the thing I was—it is, I admit, an enormous pity—intensely sceptical. I asked him questions in what people call a 'nasty' manner. I was ready—as my manner made plain to him—to jump down his throat with 'But that's preposterous!' at the very first slip. And I had an engagement that carried me off at the end of half an hour. But the thing had already got hold of my imagination, and I rang up Brownlow before tea-time, and was biting at this 'queer story' of his again. That afternoon he was sulking because of my morning's disbelief, and he told me very little. 'I was drunk and dreaming, I suppose,' he said. 'I'm beginning to doubt it all myself.' In the night it occurred to me for the first time that, if he was not allowed to tell and put on record what he had seen, he might become both confused and sceptical about it himself. Fancies might mix up with it. He might hedge and alter to get it more credible. Next day, therefore, I lunched and spent the afternoon with him, and arranged to go down into Surrey for the week-end. I managed to dispel his huffiness with me. My growing keenness restored his. There we set ourselves in earnest, first of all to recover everything he could remember about his newspaper and then to form some coherent idea of the world about which it was telling.

It is perhaps a little banal to say we were not trained men for the job. For who could be considered trained for such a job as we were attempting? What facts was he to pick out as important and how were they to be arranged? We wanted to know everything we could about 1971; and the little facts and the big facts crowded on one another and offended against each other.

The streamer headline across the page about that seven-mile Wilton boring, is, to my mind, one of the most significant items in the story. About that we are fairly clear. It referred, says Brownlow, to a series of attempts to tap the supply of heat beneath the surface of the earth. I asked various questions: 'It was *explained,* y'know,' said Brownlow, and smiled and held out a hand with twiddling fingers. 'It was explained all right. Old system, they said, was to go down from a few hundred feet to a mile or so and bring up coal and burn it. Go down a bit deeper, and there's no need to bring up and burn anything. Just get heat itself straightaway. Comes up of its own accord—under its own steam. See? Simple.

'They were making a big fuss about it,' he added. 'It wasn't only the streamer headline; there was a leading article in big type. What was it headed? Ah! The Age of Combustion has Ended!'

Now that is plainly a very big event for mankind, caught in mid-happening, November 10th, 1971. And the way in which Brownlow describes it as being handled, shows clearly a world much more preoccupied by economic essentials than the world of today, and dealing with them on a larger scale and in a bolder spirit.

That excitement about tapping the central reservoirs of heat, Brownlow was very definite, was not the only symptom of an increase in practical economic interest and intelligence. There was much more space given to scientific work and to inventions than is given in any contemporary paper. There were diagrams and mathematical symbols, he says, but he did not look into them very closely because he could not get the hang of them. '*Frightfully* highbrow, some of it,' he said.

A more intelligent world for our grandchildren evidently, and also, as the pictures testified, a healthier and happier world.

'The fashions kept you looking,' said Brownlow, going off at a tangent, 'all coloured up as they were.'

'Were they elaborate?' I asked.

'Anything *but*,' he said.

His description of these costumes is vague. The people depicted in the social illustrations and in the advertisements seemed to have reduced body clothing—I mean things like vests, pants, socks and so forth—to a minimum. Breast and chest went bare. There seem to have been tremendously exaggerated wristlets, mostly on the left arm and going as far up as the elbow, provided with gadgets which served the purpose of pockets. Most of these armlets seem to have been very decorative, almost like little shields. And then, usually, there was an immense hat, often rolled up and carried in the hand, and long cloaks of the loveliest colours and evidently also of the most beautiful soft material, which either trailed from a sort of gorget or were gathered up and wrapped about the naked body, or were belted up and thrown over the shoulders.

There were a number of pictures of crowds from various parts of the world. 'The people looked fine,' said Brownlow. 'Prosperous, you know, and upstanding. Some of the women—just lovely.'

My mind went off to India. What was happening in India?

Brownlow could not remember anything very much about India. 'Ankor,' said Brownlow. 'That's not India, is it?' There had been some sort of Carnival going on amidst 'perfectly lovely' buildings in the sunshine of Ankor.

The people there were brownish people but they were dressed very much like the people in other parts of the world.

I found the politician stirring in me. Was there really nothing about India? Was he sure of that? There was certainly nothing that had left any impression in Brownlow's mind. And Soviet Russia? 'Not as Soviet Russia,' said Brownlow. All that trouble had ceased to be a matter of daily interest. 'And how was France getting on with Germany?' Brownlow could not recall a mention of either of these two great powers. Nor of the British Empire as such, nor of the U.S.A. There was no mention of any interchanges, communications, ambassadors, conferences, competitions, comparisons, stresses, in which these governments figured, so far as he could remember. He racked his brains. I thought perhaps all that had been going on so entirely like it goes on today—and has been going on for the last hundred years—that he had run his eyes over the passages in question and that they had left no distinctive impression on his mind. But he is positive that it was not like that. 'All that stuff was washed out,' he said. He is unshaken in his

351

assertion that there were no elections in progress, no notice of Parliament or politicians, no mention of Geneva or anything about armaments or war. All those main interests of a contemporary journal seem to have been among the 'washed out' stuff. It isn't that Brownlow didn't notice them very much; he is positive they were not there.

Now to me this is a very wonderful thing indeed. It means, I take it, that in only forty years from now the great game of sovereign states will be over. It looks also as if the parliamentary game will be over, and as if some quite new method of handling human affairs will have been adopted. Not a word of patriotism or nationalism; not a word of party, not an allusion. But in only forty years! While half the human beings already alive in the world will still be living! You cannot believe it for a moment. Nor could I, if it wasn't for two little torn scraps of paper. These, as I will make clear, leave me in a state of—how can I put it?—incredulous belief.

4

After all, in 1831 very few people thought of railway or steamship travel, and in 1871 you could already go round the world in eighty days by steam, and send a telegram in a few minutes to nearly every part of the earth. Who would have thought of that in 1831? Revolutions in human life, when they begin to come, can come very fast. Our ideas and methods change faster than we know.

But just forty years!

It was not only that there was this absence of national politics from that evening paper, but there was something else still more fundamental. Business, we both think, finance that is, was not in evidence, at least upon anything like contemporary lines. We are not quite sure of that, but that is our impression. There was no list of Stock Exchange prices, for example, no City page, and nothing in its place. I have suggested already that Brownlow just turned that page over, and that it was sufficiently like what it is today that he passed and forgot it. I have put that suggestion to him. But he is quite sure that that was not the case. Like most of us nowadays, he is watching a number of his investments rather nervously, and he is convinced he looked for the City article.

November 10th, 1971, may have been Monday—there seems to have been some readjustment of the months and the days of the week; that is a detail into which I will not enter now—but that will not account for the absence of any City news at all. That also, it seems, will be washed out forty years from now.

Is there some tremendous revolutionary smash-up ahead, then? Which will put an end to investment and speculation? Is the world going Bolshevik? In the paper, anyhow, there was no sign of, or reference to, anything of that kind. Yet against this idea of some stupendous economic revolution we have the fact that here forty years ahead is a familiar London evening paper still tumbling into a private individual's letter-box in the most uninterrupted manner. Not much suggestion of a social smash-up there. Much stronger is the effect of immense changes which have come about bit by bit, day by day, and hour by hour, without any sort of revolutionary jolt, as morning or springtime comes to the world.

These futile speculations are irresistible. The reader must forgive me them. Let me return to our story.

There had been a picture of a landslide near Ventimiglia and one of some new chemical works at Salzburg, and there had been a picture of fighting going on near Irkutsk. (Of that picture, as I will tell presently, a fading scrap survives.) 'Now that was called—' Brownlow made an effort, and snapped his fingers triumphantly. '—"Round-up of Brigands by Federal Police." '

'*What* Federal Police?' I asked.

'There you have me,' said Brownlow. 'The fellows on both sides looked mostly Chinese, but there were one or two taller fellows, who might have been Americans or British or Scandinavians.'

'What filled a lot of the paper,' said Brownlow, suddenly, 'was gorillas. There was no end of a fuss about gorillas. Not so much as about that boring, but still a lot of fuss. Photographs. A map. A special article and some paragraphs.'

The paper, had, in fact, announced the death of the last gorilla. Considerable resentment was displayed at the tragedy that had happened in the African gorilla reserve. The gorilla population of the world had been dwindling for many years. In 1931 it had been estimated at nine hundred. When the Federal Board took over it had shrunken to three hundred.

'*What* Federal Board?' I asked.

Brownlow knew no more than I did. When he read the phrase, it had seemed all right somehow. Apparently this Board had had too much to do all at once, and insufficient resources. I had the impression at first that it must be some sort of conservation board, improvised under panic conditions, to save the rare creatures of the world threatened with extinction. The gorillas had not been sufficiently observed and guarded, and they had been swept out of existence suddenly by a new and malignant form of influenza. The thing had happened practically before it was remarked. The paper was clamouring for inquiry and drastic changes of reorganisation.

This Federal Board, whatever it might be, seemed to be something of very considerable importance in the year 1971. Its name turned up again in an article of afforestation. This interested Brownlow considerably because he has large holdings in lumber companies. This Federal Board was apparently not only responsible for the maladies of wild gorillas but also for the plantation of trees in—just note these names!—Canada, New York State, Siberia, Algiers, and the East Coast of England, and it was arraigned for various negligences in combating insect pests and various fungoid plant diseases. It jumped all our contemporary boundaries in the most astounding way. Its range was world-wide. 'In spite of the recent additional restrictions put upon the use of big timber in building and furnishing, there is a plain possibility of a shortage of shelter timber and of rainfall in nearly all the threatened regions for 1985 onwards. Admittedly the Federal Board has come late to its task, from the beginning its work has been urgency work; but in view of the lucid report prepared by the James Commission, there is little or no excuse for the inaggressiveness and overconfidence it has displayed.'

I am able to quote this particular article because as a matter of fact it lies before me as I write. It is indeed, as I will explain, all that remains of this remarkable newspaper. The rest has been destroyed and all we can ever know of it now is through Brownlow's sound but not absolutely trustworthy memory.

5

My mind, as the days pass, hangs on to that Federal Board. Does that phrase mean, as just possibly it may mean, a world federation, a scientific control of all human life only forty years from now? I find that idea—staggering. I have always believed that the world was destined to unify—'Parliament of Mankind and Confederation of the World,' as Tennyson put it—but I have always supposed that the process would take centuries. But then my time sense is poor. My disposition has always been to under-estimate the pace of change. I wrote in 1900 that there would be aeroplanes 'in fifty years' time.' And the confounded things were buzzing about everywhere and carrying passengers before 1920.

Let me tell very briefly of the rest of that evening paper. There seemed to be a lot of sport and fashion; much about something called 'Spectacle'—with pictures—a lot of illustrated criticism of decorative art and particularly of architecture. The architecture in the pictures he saw was 'towering—kind of magnificent. Great blocks of building. New York, but more so and all run together' . . . Unfortunately he cannot sketch. There were sections devoted to something he couldn't understand, but which he thinks was some sort of 'radio programme stuff.'

All that suggests a sort of advanced human life very much like the life we lead today, possibly rather brighter and better.

But here is something—different.

'The birth-rate,' said Brownlow, searching his mind, 'was seven in the thousand.'

I exclaimed. The lowest birth-rates in Europe now are sixteen or more per thousand. The Russian birth-rate is forty per thousand, and falling slowly.

'It was seven,' said Brownlow. 'Exactly seven. I noticed it. In a paragraph.'

But what birth-rate, I asked. The British? The European?

'It said the birth-rate,' said Brownlow. 'Just that.'

That I think is the most tantalising item in all this strange glimpse of the world of our grandchildren. A birth-rate of seven in the thousand does not mean a fixed world population; it means a population that is being reduced at a very rapid rate—unless the death-rate has gone still lower. Quite possibly people will not be dying so much then, but living very much longer. On that Brownlow could throw no light. The people in the pictures did not look to him an 'old lot.' There were plenty of children and young or young-looking people about.

'But Brownlow,' I said, 'wasn't there any crime?'

'Rather,' said Brownlow. 'They had a big poisoning case on, but it was jolly hard to follow. You know how it is with these crimes. Unless you've read about it from the beginning, it's hard to get the hang of the situation. No newspaper has found out that for every crime it ought to give a summary up-to-date every day—and forty years ahead, they hadn't. Or they aren't going to. Whichever way you like to put it.

'There were several crimes and what newspaper men call stories,' he resumed; 'personal stories. What struck me about it was that they seemed to be more sympathetic than our reporters, more concerned with the motives and less with just finding someone out. What you might call psychological—so to speak.'

'Was there anything much about books?' I asked him.

'I don't remember anything about books,' he said. . . .

And that is all. Except for a few trifling details such as a possible thirteenth month inserted in the year, that is all. It is intolerably tantalising. That is the substance of Brownlow's account of his newspaper. He read it—as one might read any newspaper. He was just in that state of alcoholic comfort when nothing is incredible and so nothing is really wonderful. He knew he was reading an evening newspaper of forty years ahead and he sat in front of his fire, and smoked and sipped his drink and was no more perturbed than he would have been if he had been reading an imaginative book about the future.

Suddenly his little brass clock pinged Two.

He got up and yawned. He put that astounding, that miraculous newspaper down as he was wont to put any old newspaper down; he carried off his correspondence to the desk in his bureau, and with the swift laziness of a very tired man he dropped his clothes about his room anyhow and went to bed.

But somewhen in the night he woke up feeling thirsty and grey-minded. He lay awake and it came to him that something very strange had occurred to him. His mind went back to the idea that he had been taken in by a very ingenious fabrication. He got up for a drink of Vichy water and a liver tabloid, he put his head in cold water and found himself sitting on his bed towelling his hair and doubting whether he had really seen those photographs in the very colours of reality itself, or whether he had imagined them. Also running through his mind was the thought that the approach of a world timber famine for 1985 was something likely to affect his investments and particularly a trust he was setting up on behalf of an infant in whom he was interested. It might be wise, he thought, to put more into timber.

He went back down the corridor to his sitting-room. He sat there in his dressing-gown, turning over the marvellous sheets. There it was in his hands complete in every page, not a corner torn. Some sort of auto-hypnosis, he thought, might be at work, but certainly the pictures seemed as real as looking out of a window. After he had stared at them some time he went back to the timber paragraph. He felt he must keep that. I don't know if you will understand how his mind worked—for my own part I can see at once how perfectly irrational and entirely natural it was—but he took this marvellous paper, creased the page in question, tore off this particular article and left the rest. He returned very drowsily to his bedroom, put the scrap of paper on his dressing-table, got into bed and dropped off to sleep at once.

6

When he awoke it was nine o'clock; his morning tea was untasted by his bedside and the room was full of sunshine. His parlourmaid-housekeeper had just re-entered the room.

'You were sleeping so peacefully,' she said; 'I couldn't bear to wake you. Shall I get you a fresh cup of tea?'

Brownlow did not answer. He was trying to think of something strange that had happened.

She repeated her question.

'No. I'll come and have breakfast in my dressing-gown before my bath,' he said, and she went out of the room.

Then he saw the scrap of paper.

In a moment he was running down the corridor to the sitting-room. 'I left a newspaper,' he said. 'I left a newspaper.'

She came in response to the commotion he made.

'A newspaper?' she said. 'It's been gone this two hours, down the chute, with the dust and things.'

Brownlow had a moment of extreme consternation.

He invoked his God. 'I wanted it *kept*!' he shouted. 'I wanted it *kept.*'

'But how was *I* to know you wanted it kept?'

'But didn't you notice it was a very extraordinary-looking news-paper?'

'I've got none too much time to dust out this flat to be looking at newspapers,' she said. 'I thought I saw some coloured photographs of bathing ladies and chorus girls in it, but that's no concern of mine. It didn't seem a proper newspaper to me. How was I to know you'd be wanting to look at them again this morning?'

'I must get that newspaper back,' said Brownlow. 'It's—it's vitally important . . . If all Sussex Court has to be held up I want that news-paper back.'

'I've never known a thing come up that chute again,' said his housekeeper, 'that's once gone down it. But I'll telephone down, sir, and see what can be done. Most of that stuff goes right into the hot-water furnace, they say. . . .'

It does. The newspaper had gone.

Brownlow came near raving. By a vast effort of self-control he sat down and consumed his cooling breakfast. He kept on saying 'Oh, my God!' as he did so. In the midst of it he got up to recover the scrap of paper from his bedroom, and then found the wrapper addressed to Evan O'Hara among the overnight letters on his bureau. That seemed an almost maddening confirmation. The thing *had* happened.

Presently after he had breakfasted, he rang me up to aid his baffled mind.

I found him at his bureau with the two bits of paper before him. He did not speak. He made a solemn gesture.

'What is it?' I asked, standing before him.

'Tell me,' he said. 'Tell me. What are these objects? It's serious. Either—' He left the sentence unfinished.

I picked up the torn wrapper first and felt its texture. 'Evan O'Hara, Mr,' I read.

'Yes. Sussex Court, 49. Eh?'

'Right,' I agreed and stared at him.

'*That's* not hallucination, eh?'

I shook my head.

'And now this?' His hand trembled as he held out the cutting. I took it.

'Odd,' I said. I stared at the black-green ink, the unfamiliar type, the little novelties in spelling. Then I turned the thing over. On the back was a piece of one of the illustrations; it was, I suppose, about a quarter of the photograph of that 'Round-up of Brigands by Federal Police' I have already mentioned.

When I saw it that morning it had not even begun to fade. It represented a mass of broken masonry in a sandy waste with bare-looking mountains in the distance. The cold, clear atmosphere, the glare of a cloudless afternoon were rendered perfectly. In the fore-ground were four masked men in a brown service uniform intent on working some little machine on wheels with a tube and a nozzle projecting a jet that went out to the left, where the fragment was torn off. I cannot imagine what the jet was doing. Brownlow says he thinks they were gassing some men in a hut. Never have I seen such realistic colour printing.

'What on earth is this?' I asked.

'It's *that*,' said Brownlow. 'I'm not mad, am I? It's really *that*.'

'But what the devil is it?'

'It's a piece of newspaper for November 10th, 1971.'

'You had better explain,' I said, and sat down, with the scrap of paper in my hand, to hear his story. And, with as much elimination of questions and digressions and repetitions as possible, that is the story I have written here.

I said at the beginning that it was a queer story and queer to my mind it remains, fantastically queer. I return to it at intervals, and it refuses to settle down in my mind as anything but an incongruity with all my experience and beliefs. If it were not for the two little bits of paper, one might dispose of it quite easily. One might say that Brownlow had had a vision, a dream of unparalleled vividness and consistency. Or that he had been hoaxed and his head turned by some elaborate mystification. Or, again, one might suppose he had really seen into the future with a sort of exaggeration of those previsions cited by Mr J.W. Dunne in his remarkable 'Experiment with Time.' But nothing Mr Dunne has to advance can account for an actual evening paper being slapped through a letter-slit forty years in advance of its date.

The wrapper has not altered in the least since I first saw it. But the scrap of paper with the article about afforestation is dissolving into a fine powder and the fragment of picture at the back of it is fading out; most of the colour has gone and the outlines have lost their sharpness. Some of the powder I have taken to my friend Ryder at the Royal College, whose work in micro-chemistry is so well known. He says the stuff is not paper at all, properly speaking. It is mostly aluminium fortified by admixture with some artificial resinous substance.

7

Though I offer no explanation whatever of this affair I think I will venture on one little prophesy. I have an obstinate persuasion that on November 10th, 1971, the name of the tenant of 49, Sussex Court, will be Mr Evan O'Hara. (There is no tenant of that name now in Sussex Court and I find no evidence in the Telephone Directory, or the London Directory, that such a person exists anywhere in London.) And on that particular evening forty years ahead, he will not get his usual copy of the *Even Standrd:* instead he will get a copy of the *Evening Standard* of 1931. I have an incurable fancy that this will be so.

There I may be right or wrong, but that Brownlow really got and for two remarkable hours, read, a real newspaper forty years ahead of time I am as convinced as I am convinced that my own name is Hubert G. Wells. Can I say anything stronger than that?

ANSWER TO PRAYER

THE Archbishop was perplexed by his own state of mind. Maybe the shadow of age was falling upon him, he thought, maybe he had been overworking, maybe the situation had been too complex for him and he was feeling the reality of a failure without seeing it plainly as a definable fact. But his nerve, which had never failed him hitherto, was failing him now. In small things as in important matters he no longer showed the quick decisiveness that had hitherto been the envy of his fellow ecclesiastics and the admiration of his friends. He doubted now before he went upstairs or downstairs, with a curious feeling that he might find something unexpected on the landing. He hesitated before he rang a bell, with a vague uncertainty of who or what might appear. Before he took up the letters his secretary had opened for him he had a faint twinge of apprehension.

Had he after all done something wrong or acted in a mistaken spirit?

People who had always been nice to him showed a certain coolness, people from whom he would have least expected it. His secretaries, he knew, were keeping back 'open letters' and grossly abusive comments. The reassurances and encouragements that flowed in to him were anything but reassuring, because their volume and their tone reflected what was hidden from him on the other side. Had he, at the end of his long, tortuous and hitherto quite dignified career, made a howler?

There was no one on earth to whom he could confide his trouble. He had always been a man who kept his own counsel. But now, if only he could find understanding, sympathy, endorsement! If he could really put things as he saw them, if he could simplify the whole confused affair down to essentials and make his stand plain and clear.

Prayer?

If anyone else had come to him in this sort of quandary, he would have told him at once to pray. If it was a woman he would have patted the shoulder gently, as an elderly man may do, and he would have said very softly in that rich kind voice of his, 'Try Prayer, my dear. Try Prayer.'

Physician heal thyself. Why not try prayer?

He stood hesitatingly between his apartments and his little private oratory. He stood in what was his habitual children's-service attitude with his hands together in front of him, his head a little on one side and something faintly bland and whimsical about him. It came to him that he himself had not made a personal and particular appeal to God for many years. It had seemed unnecessary. It had indeed been unnecessary. He had of course said his prayers with the utmost regularity, not only in the presence of others, but, being essentially an honest man, even when he was alone. He had never cheated about prayer. He had felt it was a purifying and beneficial process, no more to be missed than cleaning his teeth, but his sense of a definite hearer, listening at the other end of the telephone, so to speak, behind the veil, had always been a faint one. The reception away there was in the Absolute, in Eternity, beyond the stars. Which indeed left the church conveniently free to take an unembarrassed course of action. . . .

But in this particular tangle, the Archbishop wanted something more definite. If for once, he did not trouble about style and manner.
. . .

If he put the case simply, quite simply, just as he saw it, and remained very still on his knees, wouldn't he presently find this neuralgic fretting of his mind abating, and that assurance, that clear self-assurance that had hitherto been his strength, returning to him? He must not be in the least oily—they had actually been calling him oily—he must be perfectly direct and simple and fearless. He must pray straightforwardly to the silence as one mind to another.

It was a little like the practice of some Dissenters and Quakers, but maybe it would be none the less effective on that account.

Yes, he would pray.

Slowly he sank to his knees and put his hands together. He was touched by a sort of childish trustfulness in his own attitude. 'Oh God,' he began, and paused.

He paused, and a sense of awful imminence, a monstrous awe, gripped him. And then he heard a voice.

It was not a harsh voice, but it was a clear strong voice. There was nothing about it still or small. It was neither friendly nor hostile; it was brisk.

'Yes,' said the voice. '*What is it?*'

They found His Grace in the morning. He had slipped off the steps on which he had been kneeling and lay, sprawling on the crimson carpet. Plainly his death had been instantaneous.

But instead of the serenity, the almost fatuous serenity, that was his habitual expression, his countenance, by some strange freak of nature, displayed an extremity of terror and dismay.

ACKNOWLEDGMENTS

With special thanks to Ray Russell, Tartarus Press, and A P Watt Ltd

All stories copyright © The Estate of H.G. Wells
"Introduction" copyright © Brian Stableford

"The Devotee of Art," *Science Schools Journal*, November/December 1888.
"Walcote," *Science Schools Journal*, December 1898-January 1889.
"The Flowering of the Strange Orchid," *Pall Mall Budget*, August 2, 1984.
"The Lord of the Dynamos," *Pall Mall Budget*, September 6, 1894.
"The Temptation of Harringay," *The Saint James Gazette*, February 9, 1895.
"The Moth," *Pall Mall Budget*, March 28, 1895.
"Pollock and the Porroh Man," *New Budget*, May 23, 1895.
"Under the Knife," *The New Review*, January 1896.
"The Plattner Story," *The New Review*, May 1897.
"The Red Room," *The Idler*, March 1896.
"The Story of the Late Mr Elvesham," *The Idler*, May 1896.
"The Apple," *The Idler*, October 1896.
"The Crystal Egg," *The New Review*, May 1897.
"The Presence by the Fire," *Penny Illustrated Paper*, August 14, 1897.
"The Man Who Could Work Miracles," *The Illustrated London News*, July 1898.
"The Stolen Body," *The Strand*, November 1898.
"A Vision of Judgment," *Butterfly*, September 1899.
"A Dream of Armageddon, *Black and White*, May/June 1901.
"The New Accelerator," *The Strand*, December 1901.
"The Inexperienced Ghost," *The Strand*, March 1902.
"Mr Skelmersdale in Fairyland," *The London Magazine*, February 1903.
"The Truth About Pyecraft," *The Strand*, April 1903.
"The Magic Shop," *The Strand*, June 1903.
"The Country of the Blind," *The Strand*, April 1904.
"The Door in the Wall," *The Daily Chronicle*, July 14, 1906.
"The Beautiful Suit," *Colliers*, April 10, 1909.
"The Wild Asses of the Devil," from *Boon*, 1915.
"The Story of the Last Trump," from *Boon*, 1915.
"The Pearl of Love," *The Strand*, December 1925.
"The Queer Story of Brownlow's Newspaper," *Ladies Home Journal*,
    February 1932.
"Answer to Prayer," *The New Statesman*, April 10, 1937.

HERBERT GEORGE WELLS was born in 1866 into a lower-middle-class family in England. Although apprenticed to a trade as a teenager, his hunger for education led him to secure a grammar school assistant-ship at age sixteen, and two years later a scholarship to the Normal School of Science in London. After leaving school in 1887 Wells taught biology and wrote two textbooks on the subject. Increasingly, his writing inter-ests shifted to journalism and fiction. Wells's first short stories saw print in the late 1880s. His debut novel, *The Time Machine*, was published to critical and popular acclaim in 1895. It was the first of many literary works in which Wells extrapolated the impact of science on human civilization and explored a wide variety of social, philosophical and political ideas through the medium of speculative fiction. *The Island of Dr. Moreau* (1896), *The Invisible Man* (1897), *The War of the Worlds* (1898), *When the Sleep-er Wakes* (1899), *The First Men in the Moon* (1899), *The Food of the Gods* (1904), *In the Days of the Comet* (1906) and the fiction collected in *Thirty Strange Stories* (1897) and *Tales of Space and Time* (1899) are recognized today as seminal works of science fiction. Wells also earned renown as a social satirist with *Love and Mr. Lewisham* (1900), *Kipps* (1905), *Tono-Bungay* (1908), *The History of Mr. Polly* (1910) and other novels. In his time, Wells was respected by distinguished literary colleagues and world leaders alike as a progressive social thinker. He was an outspoken political socialist who ran unsuccessfully for Parliament on the Labor Party ticket in 1922, and a sometimes controversial proponent of sexual liberation. His ambitious non-fiction writing included the best-selling *Outline of History* (1919-1920). He died in 1946.